WELCOME TO COOLSVILLE

Jason Mordaunt was born in Dublin, where he lives and works. *Welcome to Coolsville* is his first book.

Jason Mordaunt

WELCOME TO COOLSVILLE

V

VINTAGE

Published by Vintage 2004

2 4 6 8 10 9 7 5 3 1

Copyright © Jason Mordaunt 2003

First published in Great Britain in 2003 by
Jonathan Cape

Vintage
Random House, 20 Vauxhall Bridge Road,
London SW1V 2SA

Random House Australia (Pty) Limited
20 Alfred Street, Milsons Point, Sydney
New South Wales 2061, Australia

Random House New Zealand Limited
18 Poland Road, Glenfield,
Auckland 10, New Zealand

Random House (Pty) Limited
Endulini, 5A Jubilee Road, Parktown 2193,
South Africa

The Random House Group Limited Reg. No. 954009
www.randomhouse.co.uk/vintage

Lines from 'Coolsville' (Jones) © 1984 are reproduced by
kind permission of Rondor Music (London) Ltd

A CIP catalogue record for this book
is available from the British Library

ISBN 0 099 45026 7

Papers used by Random House are natural, recyclable
products made from wood grown in sustainable forests.
The manufacturing processes conform to the environmental regulations of the country of origin

Printed and bound in Great Britain by
Cox & Wyman Limited, Reading, Berkshire

Decked out like aces
We'd beat anybody's bet
Cuz we was Coolsville

Rickie Lee Jones

Prologue

He might never have 'lifted his leg against the trunk of society', as *Timesene* so elegantly put it, if it hadn't been for the application. The 'mantra device', the media called it.

He was Mantra. He didn't pick the name for himself, but he liked it none the less. It made him sound like the enemy of a superhero. It spoiled it a little for him that everyone thought of him as 'they', but not enough that he wanted to point it out to anybody.

When he first stumbled onto the nefarious device he thought he was experiencing some malfunction of his equipment. He'd been trying to turn a page in the reference section of a web library when his computer froze for a few seconds. There was no hope that he would ever repeat the sequence of commands and keystrokes that eventually loaded the page; he had pressed pretty much everything on his board and uttered all magic known to him in his effort to get the machine going again. When it finally started working it flashed through twenty or thirty links before loading up what looked to be a black screen. It took a little while to become apparent to him that there was anything attached to the site, or page, or whatever it was; let alone a useful application. No one in his right mind would have stopped there longer than it took to issue a quit-back command, but he sat there looking at the blank black screen, exasperated.

After what might have been twenty or thirty seconds, the word READY materialised in neon green in the top left of this sombre picture. Three rows below there appeared a flashing cursor in the same colour. A small red panel lit in his com-stat monitor to indicate that whatever this was, it was primed to accept voice.

'What's this?' he'd said to himself. It had been little more than a whisper; ill-formed sibilance, certainly outside the threshold of acceptability for common voice-ware. Both words, nevertheless, popped onto the screen in front of him in neon red, complete with question mark. Immediately beneath, more words popped up, in the original green, as if in response.

—D.E.M. APPLICATION, VI.

No sound accompanied this development. He eyed the screen suspiciously, before speaking aloud.

'What's D.E.M.?'

—A NAME.

He thought then that he had wandered into some peculiar chat room, into some strange, cult game. In light of his two previous questions he guessed no one was going to mistake him for a regular visitor. He continued with the direct line.

'What does D.E.M. Application do?'

—SERVES THE USER.

'Who's the user?'

—YOU ARE.

For reasons he couldn't explain this had given him the willies. He was positive he had stumbled onto some server reserved for deviants. The address appeared as a long line of symbols and foreign characters. Something prompted him to select and copy it in text before quitting for home, where he erased his web file and, for the first time in years, shut down overnight. It was a week before he went back.

When he did go back, he asked questions of the application on a very disinterested level. He still wasn't sure that it was anything more than a joke. When he asked how it could serve him, he was told it could do so in 'many ways'. It occurred to him after twenty minutes going nowhere in this fashion that the more vague his questions, the more vague were the answers. He began to get more specific.

He visited the site nine times that week, from work and from home, spending more than two hours there each time. Under direct questioning the application claimed to be able to assist him in accessing remote computer systems – hacking, as he knew it. It displayed programs and strategies to him on request and explained their function. By the end of the week he had a firm grounding in something he would previously have regarded as beyond him, and sufficient tools to put his new skills to work.

As intriguing as the scope of the application was to him, he remained suspicious of some hidden agenda; at best an elaborate joke, at worst some terrible entrapment. By the end of his second month visiting the site his suspicions in this respect had abated somewhat, as nothing whatsoever happened to further such an agenda. He was always the active agent. The application never initiated, only ever responded to him. He'd heard rumours before of applications that continued to run after deletion, by fragmenting and settling in various areas of 'lost' memory; a gigabyte here and a gigabyte there, spread across the Big Seven, the monster servers that had been running constantly now for twenty-odd years. The disparate parts of the program were said to operate across the many tenuous links created by the Big Seven in flux. He wasn't technical, and didn't know if it was actually feasible, but he entertained the possibility that he'd discovered some military device, an experiment in artificial intelligence perhaps, that had contrived to exist in this way after deletion, and to which only he had access. He entertained many strange possibilities.

Three months after making his discovery he resolved to set the application a task. With its help he dialled into his bank and planted programs that recorded the computer displays and the keystrokes entered by various of the bank's employees. The programs returned themselves to a location of his choosing after a day. He logged on and studied them until he not only had a number of names and passwords, but understood how to make enquiries, lodgements, withdrawals and transfers. He thought about what he might do for an hour or so, and finally resolved to send another of the application's programs back into the bank's system. The program was primed to move the decimal point on his bank balance two places to the right. He resolved not to change the normal pattern of his spending, just to be sure, but almost a year later no one had picked up the anomaly.

The application had other programs to turn over passwords as you waited, and unscramble encrypted information that would certainly have been regarded as unbreakable; time-consuming processes which he found nerve-racking, like watching a safe-cracker race a long fuse burning down to a stick of dynamite.

He spent whole evenings surfing in the sleeping half of the corporate world, learning his tool. Once he recorded the displays and keystrokes at a nuclear weapons facility. The application had found the dial-in on some government database he had breezed through. He sat for an hour flipping through the displays, scrutinising the stuff of his childhood nightmares, and though he knew he couldn't affect the system, he touched each

6

key on his board apprehensively. He hardly heard himself tell the application to quit and delete, his heart was pounding so loud in his ears.

It was only after his success with the weapons facility that the true value of the application finally came home to him. Encryption, passwords, security appeared all to be useless against it. Any number of agencies would kill him in a second to get access to it. Any number of people would expose him for a price, if they knew. Following this realisation he left it alone for six weeks. When he returned it was as if nothing had changed. It appeared as if he were the only person to know of its existence, and, despite the illogic of the position, that shortly became his belief.

He began to think about a bigger picture, about what he might actually do with his application. Stealing, for which it had already proved to be perfectly constructed, was unworthy and not to his taste. Besides, he was comfortable, and ostentatious displays of riches would only draw attention. He could, in the classical manner, make anonymous donations to charity on behalf of and unbeknownst to the world of high finance. But the charities would probably be too honest. It'd be foolish not to be scrupulously honest. Stealing from a major financial institution was a crime prosecutable under a number of articles in the Universal Offences Against Humanity Act, or the Terror Laws as they were commonly known. The thinking was that if an ordinary criminal could live adequately off the poor, or off those of ordinary means, then only a prospective or active terrorist would need to steal from the rich.

He had a pretty good idea the Terror Laws wouldn't apply to him if he were caught with this application of his. Or if they did it would only be to clarify his conscious relinquishment of 'certain rights normally enjoyed by the law-abiding citizenry' through his contravention of the act. He was sure he'd just disappear. A trial and jail he could deal with – he'd at least get to say his piece – but the idea of disappearing into some underground quasi-military hell frightened him beyond his ability to express.

He remembered a black and white film about a guy who was set up to give the Nazis false information. He was dropped behind enemy lines where he was soon captured. His own side knew he'd get caught, they wanted him to; and they knew that when he did get caught he'd break and spill the phoney beans they'd given him. He had been issued with a cyanide capsule for effect, but the capsule was empty. He tried to use it even before the Nazis started really torturing him. When he realised it wasn't working, his expression was of terror, dumb and absolute. That's what it would be like, he thought, to get caught with this skeleton key; or a mixture of that and the state of mind Ray Milland's character must've experienced at the end of *The Premature Burial*.

It was the cheering that finally pushed his hand – the bloody cheering. He didn't remember this much cheering ever; even when he was a boy and mostly in the company of other small children, where you might expect to hear more cheering than in sober adult society. Worse, the tone of this particular cheer was one of inane conceit; the ugly self-satisfied bellow of over-stuffed herd animals, with overtones of an unmistakable loathing for all that was 'not us'. The nation as a whole was doing well again and everybody was encouraged by the media, the politicians and business to support anyone who was doing so publicly. Supporting, as far as he could see, meant sustaining the cheer. People were given time off work if they used it to cheer. The consensus was that morale was high, whatever that meant. Manic would have been nearer the mark. You had to go far and wide to read a report of deviation from this consensus, and even then the reports he found read more like warnings. One daily told how a man in Cork was hospitalised by twelve good-men-and-true when he'd had the temerity to suggest that the only thing that made the national slugfest team in any real way 'national' was a series of blood transfusions. The tone of the piece left the reader in no doubt but that the fool had been the author, as they say, of his own misfortune.

The economy was on the upturn again thanks to abstinence and diligence generally; and excellent leadership particularly. If excellent leadership had apparently required more sustenance than black bread and sugarless tea, not only was it not denied, but the leaders were enabled to accept their extra rations with good conscience. The sour taste of begrudgery was, happily, a thing of the past.

In the celebrated ranks of the great and good, the fashion designer Triona O'Connell had turned full circle. The *bête noire* of the fashion industry a mere five years before, she had recently become the head of Chanel and was busy dragging it once more into the vanguard of haute couture with her dazzling spring collection. Damian Fitz had been awarded the Turner Prize in London for what a leading critic described as his 'disarmingly conventional revivalist work'. Frank Tierney collected his third consecutive Booker with a heart-warming tale of a drug-addicted actor who drags himself out of the gutter, pockets an Oscar and buys a life-saving operation for his estranged mother. An Irish picture had taken the Palme d'Or at Cannes; two others were selected for honourable mention.

There were a hundred good reasons to cheer, it seemed, but none so worthy as a sporting victory, and there were plenty of those. Both national soccer teams were having a good run of form in a number of competitions, the rugby team looked like they'd make the last four in the Nine Nations, the Grand Prix teams were, if not in the running for the last couple of years, still in the top flight, and we remained world leaders in the more traditional disciplines of snooker, athletics and what was left of showjumping in the aftermath of the affair the press had dubbed 'medium-rare-gate'. In addition, we were embarrassingly well represented in hurling, slugfest and other 'extreme' sports. Soon it was by victories that the populace was measuring the passing of time. Event: Year: Result.

He conceived of his plan in about four minutes one afternoon.

Regardless of the apparent simplicity of the effect, it took two months to put the very first run together. His, or Mantra's, debut was at the Pan-European Slugfest Championships that were held in Dublin late that October. His favourite conglomerate, WentWest, was sponsoring the event, and his favourite captain of industry, J.P. Gillespie, was grinningly at the wheel.

Slugfest was like a tennis tie-breaker played to fifteen points. Since the ball was considerably heavier and travelled a good deal faster than in tennis, the game was played on a longer, narrower court by competitors wearing visor helmets, breastplates and sturdy jockstraps, in the event they should fail to connect with the oncoming missile with racquet or shield. In a long doubles rubber there might be three or four substitutions on account of 'high-velocity impact incidents'. It was fast, exciting and middling dangerous. In the team event the national squad were on a roll. They made the final.

Following the disruption of the final and thinking, as everyone did, that he had been the victim of a subversive group rather than a single individual, J.P. Gillespie used the phrase 'twenty-first-century stormtroopers of cynicism' to a foreign reporter by way of a description of the imagined perpetrators. The subsequent disturbance and delay at the WentWest-sponsored Grand Prix saw the *Chronicle* returning to the stormtrooper motif, only to foist the uninspiring 'J.P.'s S.O.C.s STRIKE AGAIN!' on its sensation-jaded readership.

The disturbance at the *Moose* Cup in November prompted the *Chronicle*'s editor to produce the scraping tool and translate his earlier acronym into 'SAD OLD CILLJOYS'. When he-who-would-be-Mantra interrupted December's rugby international with his antics, Channel Ten News picked up the mantle, their seven o'clock bulletin posing the somewhat tongue-in-cheek: 'STORMTROOPERS OF CYNICISM OR SONS OF ÇATAN?'

It was the redoubtable Noel Fields' fourteen references in the *Indo* the following day to the 'moronic mantra', however, that determined the proper noun that popularly stuck. It helped that he appeared that evening to reinforce this single-mindedness twenty-three more times during an interview with Tom Richard on TuMur TV News (not to be confused with TuMur Radio News (pictures optional), TuMur Web News, TuMur News Europe, TuMur News America, TuMur Foreign News (all formats), TuMur Lite News, etc.).

Mantra always worked its magic on a WentWest-sponsored sporting event and on the broadcast thereof. The sabotage always took the same form. A thin, metallic voice repeatedly issued a twelve-word message from the stadium speakers, and from the speakers on your box at home, if that's where you were watching from. The message was repeated over and over and over. It was extremely loud. Viewers at home did not see pictures from the stadium, only the written message on their screen, and the voice. They flooded their servers with complaints for the duration of the interruptions, which was always exactly one half of an hour.

The first three words of the message would flash three times on the screen, then scroll left out of picture; the next nine would scroll across in groups of three, all in sync with the voice. The voice was of the type that would ask for the salt in the imperative; a cheesy cultural artefact of the 'Take me to your leader!' variety, suggesting a nightmare of enslavement by the relentless, efficient and indifferent alien. It said:

WELCOME TO COOLSVILLE . . . COVER YOUR ASS . . . PASS THE BUCK . . . RESISTANCE IS FUTILE.

Considerable Bad Medicine

PROGRAMME:	Staines at 7.
DATE:	Monday, 16th October.

STEVE:	It's coming up to [time nearest minute] and you're tuned to TuMur Lite.
CUE:	Yawning and stretching FX217. 2"
STEVE:	Monday, Monday, Monday, you heard right. If you're not up yet, brace yourself, it's miserable out – six degrees and drizzling. We're told the roads are very, very greasy and likely to remain that way all day, so, if you're driving [CUE: tyre screeching car crash FX906. 1"] be extra careful.
CUE:	Track 1. 3'15" slow fade up behind Steve
STEVE:	If you happen to be a September baby, you may want to cancel today altogether and stay in bed. Valaria Petrovna in the Chronicle says, 'You are in quicksand today, Virgo, do not struggle. Do not rely on your instincts in this unfamiliar terrain; bide your time, do nothing hasty.' Ominous. Glad I'm a Taurean. [pause]
	Headlines soon. Meanwhile, up for a week of heavy rotation with the eponymous hit from her new movie, it's Rosie Ogawa with 'Build me, Bind me'. Oh yeah.

FULL FADE UP

'Let me through! I'm a doctor!'

Dr Kiely Flanagan removed a small plastic cylindrical phial from a concealed compartment in the back of her desk drawer. She appeared not to have heard the urgent directive, nor to have noticed the wall screen two metres in front of her come to life. She had eyes only for the phial. It was eight centimetres long, on average point five in diameter, opaque white, tapering slightly to a bright red tip. She placed it on the desk and rolled up the sleeve of her rumpled lumberjack shirt slowly and deliberately, her mouth slightly ajar, and her tongue, protruding from the parting, flattened and pressed against her top lip. She took the phial, positioned the bright tip against the now exposed skin of her left biceps and, flexing the muscle, pressed down firmly.

The small *phsst* made by the hypo's gas propellant was lost in the good doctor's sharp intake of breath. For thirty seconds or so she remained perfectly still in her chair, left hand resting at her right shoulder, her right near her left elbow. Then, at first so smoothly as to be almost imperceptible, she began to nod forward. As she moved she straightened her right arm, so that a brief moment later her hand met the corner of the desk, steadying her. The used phial fell from her grip and landed soundlessly on the carpeted living-room floor.

'Jesus!' she said; and after a moment of quiet reflection, 'Jesus Christ!'

It had been some weekend. She reckoned as much anyway, since she'd woken up a short while back feeling like absolute shit. Declan Byrne's going-away party began on the Friday night in Laverne Terrace. Laverne Terrace was relentlessly advertised as one of the Capital's happening spots for over-earners thirty and upward. It may well once have been, but to tell the truth, no one who was anyone much liked the Terrace, except Declan, who, though very nice, was about as hip as a hat.

By the early hours of Saturday morning the party had drifted from the centre of town to the fringes, and had degenerated into a taut, sinewy version of its earlier self. Stripped to the bare essentials, impervious to the attrition of smoke and noise, agile, longevitous and fuelled by meta-phets and real, organic coke (which helped to make it alcohol-dynamic too), it cut the tobacco-smoke fog on a lake of booze through venues numberless, ending finally at the airport bar on Sunday morning, which was yesterday. Kiely, however, did not stop there, but went on and on through the afternoon and well into last night. There were snatches of the whole thing there in her head, like photos flipping over, only with a tunnelled effect because of a blurring around the edges. The image reminded her of the print she framed for her grandmother's birthday years ago, of some boys who had been in a musical group. It had been a good present because Granny Flanagan not only liked the band but was keen on photography too. She explained to Kiely how the photographer achieved the blurred effect at the edges of the picture by shooting through a piece of glass with Vaseline rubbed on it. Kiely's memory of most of the weekend was like that now; a series of stills taken in rapid succession, accompanied by dull clicks and buzzes, like sound waves generated by a huge shutter and motorwind attempting to pass through a viscous medium. Occasionally the frames had a small, clear spot at the centre, for ten, maybe fifteen consecutive shots. Otherwise everything was Vaseline.

There'd been some squabble with the uniforms at the airport – she could remember that – about whether Declan was getting on his plane or not. In her mind's eye she had a shot of him at the boarding gate, barely able to stand, let alone speak up for himself. Valerie, Ian and Roger checking his pockets for contraband, pretending they were looking for a lighter, the four of them sniggering like schoolchildren. Officialdom must've decided Declan would probably sleep through the flight, the state he was in, or at least recognised that he didn't represent a security problem, because the last picture she had in her mind's eye was of Declan waving goodbye with his boarding pass, lipstick all over his face, and Sylvia and Valerie weeping dramatically in the foreground.

They were in two or three other places out near the airport and then it was back to town to the Bronze Eye, where a girl behind the bar insisted on speaking to her very slowly and seriously. What *was* that about? She remembered being at Bar Sinister too. Was that last night? She thought maybe it was. Some bastard poking her in the chest with a fat index finger; a drinks throwing episode with the same guy ending in *her* expulsion. Back here at the apartment a couple of times at least. God knew when. Something about an important message. She couldn't remember. She'd find out later.

Dr Flanagan lifted her head. If anyone had been there to see they would have remarked that she had greatly improved in appearance over the past few minutes. She looked to have put on a couple of pounds somehow, bringing her from cadaverous to willowy. Her colour had returned to such an extent that, together with the fine perspiration on her face, it gave her the appearance of having recently exerted herself; although the exertion might still have been in catching prey and holding it steady while she bit through its jugular. She ran the fingers of both hands back through her hair, collecting the strands that were stuck to her face, tying it up before walking into the kitchen and over to the percolator. As she prepared the coffee and waited, she was aware of a residual nervousness; a shimmering of tissue and spirit, echoes of her physical distress, coupled with a sense of remorse and self-disgust. States of mind and body that were, increasingly, setting the tone for her mornings after. She tried to comfort herself with the thought that the taste she'd taken had all but cured her. She rubbed her arm where she'd administered it.

She filled a mug and went back to the desk in the living room. On the way there an image of her friend Sylvia faded in. An alarmed-looking Sylvia, burned at some stage into the retina of her mind's eye. She couldn't tie her friend's apparent consternation in with any of the weekend's events – those that she could remember – but she noticed that its recollection marked a sudden arrest in the progress of her recovery. So much so, that by the time she sat down again she had decided to take another shot; see if she couldn't get straight for once and for all. It was fine, she thought. She always divided everything into very low doses, so that there was never any danger in treating herself to a little extra; or *much* danger anyway. She popped the compartment in the drawer by punching a code on her keyboard number pad. Simultaneously with the release of the compartment door, a deep, authoritative male voice issued from the speakers in the room, causing her, for the umpteenth time since an old boyfriend had installed the stupid thing three years earlier, to jump.

'Let me through!' the voice said urgently. 'I'm a doctor!'

As her hand went to her heart and her eyes towards heaven, the screen in the far wall, which was on standby, came back to life. She extracted another red-tipped phial and closed the compartment and drawer. Her eye fell on the winking icon in the bottom right of the wall screen display. It told her, for the second time this morning, that she had nine messages. Popular girl, you might think, but four at least would be from her mother, and probably two would be the inevitable person-to-person sales pitches – she paid enough not to get anything pre-recorded. That still left her a pretty popular girl with someone who had to be out of her loop, since she didn't recognise the number the three remaining calls had come from. While Kiely liked surprises, she didn't, for some reason, get much of a 'yes' feeling when she thought about who it could have been; indeed, who it would still be. She reached towards the keyboard and pushed the key to cue the most recent recording. She hoped she'd see her mother's face, its surface stretched, not unattractively, but permanently, into an expression of mild surprise, explaining why she was calling from a friend's house.

Kid C was not nearly as attractive as her mother (he was, in fact, hideous), but she knew of no reason why he should make her overly nervous, which he was now doing. Granted, he was not generally given to calling her at home, being a scumbag drug dealer, but while she freely admitted to owing him a little money for some organic coke (quite a bit actually, but nothing *ridiculous* she was sure), he wasn't the type to get fussed about it. She'd owed him money since time immemorial, he didn't mind, they were friends, sort of. To tell the truth she thought he was an odious little toad, and if she didn't need to restock every now and then, herself and Mr C would never — she could guarantee it — meet.

She looked at his frozen image; his head was like an enormous brown sponge that had been shaped with fine wire and flame by a young and gruesomely Oedipal caricaturist with a particular grudge against men of the Kid's age, which was about forty-five. The artist had grotesquely garnished his creation with yellow dentures and bloodshot sheep's eyes (hidden for the moment by shades). Wire wool had been sparsely arranged high up at the back and sides of the head, a little on the top too, by way of hair.

He was one of those men who wore an abundance of gold jewellery — sleepers, studs, bracelets, watches and rings — and who surrounded himself with what he imagined were 'bee-oo-tee-full wimmin'. It was a phrase he used often when Kiely was at his place. One of many telegraphed indications of his lust for her. She couldn't blame him; obvious tramps seemed to be all he could attract. Kiely's attitude towards the Kid was, consequently, that of a member of royalty to a commoner's mongrel which has locked itself to the royal leg and is alternating the direction of its ill-bred hips at about ten hertz.

It was an attitude that seemed to inflame his desire even more. She kept him sweet by flirting a little with him when she visited, allowing him to believe that there was a faint possibility of their hooking up, if only her schedule weren't always at odds with his. If she was to be perfectly honest she'd have to admit to tormenting him a little too. She couldn't ever remember going out there in a skirt past the knee or a sweater looser than skintight; expensive items, of course, always decent. Obvious stimuli for an obvious animal, and an animal that she felt she had well trained. To a point she was right. Left to his own devices he would have let her away with almost anything. But Kiely hadn't counted on the Kid ever discovering her concealed contempt for him, or rather the ability of Mona, one of the obvious tramps, to point it out to him for her own obscure ends.

The camera which broadcast the Kid's image had been fixed for a medium close-up. Kiely was in prime position then to view not only his ugly, wrinkled and too tanned head, but also his heavily muscled upper body, resplendent in a sleeveless black PVC T-shirt with a diagonal zipper where a breast pocket might have been. The zipper was left open, displaying the Kid's sleepered left nipple. The wraparound shades, she felt, were unnecessary as he was clearly indoors, and, even as her intestines slowly knotted themselves and her sphincter tightened, Kiely scornfully but silently remarked that the white cat he appeared to be stroking on the desk in front of him was an affectation too far. She hit the play button.

'This is my third call since Friday, Dr Flanagan, and I'm surprised, nay disappointed, to note that I have not yet been afforded the courtesy of a reply.'

Kid C's flat Dublin accent was at odds with his often formal turn of phrase. His delivery was slurred, and jerked out of him in fits and starts as if years of abuse had left him punch-drunk. Even more irritating was the unmistakable impression he gave of finding his own long-windedness irresistibly droll.

'This entire debt collection scenario, to be perfectly honest, is a bit old hat. Not the sort of thing I ever expected to have to deal with again. While it does, I'll admit, bring back some old memories, for which I offer my sincere thanks, on the other hand it has seriously upset my accounts staff, who, you'll appreciate, are approaching the year end, or *my* year end at any

21

rate. And since it's extremely difficult to get professional and trustworthy accounting staff to work for a man in my line, you'll understand, Doctor, that I can't afford to piss them off.'

The Kid escorted his white cat gently from the table top and placed his powerful forearms where it had been. His voice dropped to a repulsive parody of intimacy as he leaned in to give weight to his ultimatum.

'As I mentioned in one of my earlier messages, the option to work off your debt is there if you want it. I realise it may seem distasteful to a young woman of your upbringing, but let me assure you, it is infinitely preferable to a number of other options I've been devising against any possibility that this matter isn't treated as seriously as I would like.

'So,' he paused to reveal to her his yellow teeth, 'either you're here, Dr Flanagan, first thing Friday morning with my money, which by then will be eighty large. *Or*, you're here first thing Friday morning, eager to meet some new friends and ready for a career in pictures. I look forward to seeing you.'

Before the machine could play the previous message Kiely told it to stop. She leaned over the edge of the desk and vomited hot coffee into the waste-paper bin on her right, then stood there for a bit, spitting and shivering. The fresh phial was still in her hand and she emptied it into the triceps, flexed as she leaned on the desk, of her left arm. She counted out a minute under her breath, then picked up the bin and walked slowly into the kitchen, turning it upside down in the sink. She opened the fridge door and drank milk straight from the carton, swishing it around her mouth and spitting before drinking properly. She sat at the high counter on the left and made herself eat two plain sweet biscuits with soft cheese and drink three glasses of still spring water.

Kiely leafed through a print of one of last week's dailies.

Coming up to a year of Mantra disturbances, and under pressure from Mantra's sole target, WentWest Inc., the cabinet had voted the group an 'Official Menace', without, she noted, bothering to define the term. In normal circumstances she couldn't have cared less, but she felt it was important not to think about the Kid for a bit.

(ii)

Kiely sat in front of an idle screen drinking coffee and smoking a cigarette. She had viewed Kid C's two earlier messages and had spoken to her friend Sylvia at length. They were agreed that she was now in deep shit. Sylvia didn't think so, but Kiely felt certain that she could have placated the Kid had she got to him after the first message, maybe even the second. By the time he'd left the last one, however, he'd heard that the manager at the Bronze Eye and one of his own men had already spoken to her. Kid C may have been a buffoon, but he knew what his reputation demanded of him, and he was deadly serious. He clearly wasn't making allowances for her condition. He meant that stuff too about the career in pictures, the little creep. A qualified doctor in his debt, and that was how he planned to maximise his profit.

Eighty thousand though! She could hardly believe it. She totted it up roughly with Sylvia's help and it looked near enough right. As a matter of fact the bastard was more than likely being generous. She had stopped at his place, more times than she wanted to know about, for intermediary top-ups. He must have written a whole lot of that into the *toots gratis* column. Sylvia said she'd talk to Ian and Roger and they'd see what they could do; but Kiely told her to forget about it. She was thinking of dropping out for a while, 'getting her head together' as the ever ironical Granny Flanagan might have had it. She told her friend she'd be back in touch as soon as she could.

'See you soon,' said Sylvia.

Kiely winked coolly and hung up.

(iii)

Washed, dressed, combed, made up and perfumed, Kiely was rooting in her dressing table for a small brown address book bound with an elastic band. Years of amphetamine use had left her too paranoid to keep any numbers or addresses other than her mother's on the hard drive, so she depended on her memory, which for the moment was failing her. She duly found the book and brought it into the living room. Held open above her desk it shed thirty or so cards and scraps of paper with numbers printed or written on one or other side, sometimes both. She went through twelve of these meticulously before she found what she was looking for, then swept the remaining cards and paper and the notebook off the side of the desk, swearing when she remembered that the waste-paper bin was in the sink. She punched the number which under duress she had forgotten. She wanted to speak to her good friend John Lyons-Howard, a TV producer and the most promising of her on-again off-again affairs over the last few years. She pressed a key to identify herself in a colourful manner at his end, and hit connect.

John Lyons-Howard's show was *the* big hit at Channel Ten. It was a marvel of investigative journalism called *Expo-Zayet*, anchored by the ravishing Demelza Zayet, about whom the joke went, 'Zayet once, Zayet proud: Loud I am and blonde!'

Demelza's dizziness was legendary, and her uncanny randomising abilities with her lines were sufficient entertainment when the exposé was less than startling, or when the weather demanded she cover up. The 'loud' part of the couplet referred to the fact that when speaking to camera Demelza, where and whenever possible, contrived to stand either beside a huge piece of working machinery or out in a gale, so that she had to utilise her formidable lungs to make her report audible. She was on record as saying that she believed this 'technique' added 'elements of rugged drama' to her work.

Lyons-Howard was aware that his protégée probably wasn't best suited to the career she had chosen and described her, apparently in all seriousness, as a fine example of 'average womanhood' done well for herself. Demelza had an IQ of about sixty, stood that many inches from the ground and possessed roughly the same number of teeth, all of them big and white. She had very, very big natural blonde hair, deep-set liquid blue eyes, and a body which for Channel Ten may have been a miracle of moderation, but once upon a time would have given rise to such adjectives as 'pneumatic' and 'stacked'. She may not have been unique, exactly, but she was about as average as Siamese twins.

Lyons-Howard functioned behind the scenes as canny scandal-vendor and occasional journalist of integrity. Intelligent and capable, he knew that the secret of success in TV was the right blend of reality, celebrity and sensation. His detractors cited his unwillingness to venture into interactive media as a tacit admission of his limitations. They accused him of catering to those intimidated by choice. Those intimidated by choice ran to two million each week, forty weeks a year. At a station where every other offering was made in the fervent hope that extremely lurid programming would one day draw mainstream audience numbers he was top dog, and freer to report what he wanted than he would have been at TuMur or any of the big news outlets. He was a good deal sharper when it came to the assessment of assets than that other animal, the Kid, and probably the only guy in the news media with the balls to go after a big corporate target alone. He would know a good deal when he heard it.

He came on the screen presently, licking his chops like the cat that got the cream.

'Kiely! How delightful!' He made as if he were kissing her on both cheeks.

Kiely had a security program which took care of viruses and pre-recorded 'shitheads' and which screened numbers for her – all the usual stuff. Best of all was the custom encryption so expensive that it appeared as a server on the web and generated an entire network of phoney personalities talking to each other to mask your communications. Naturally it had indicators to tell you if you were being monitored directly, or if a correspondent was surreptitiously attempting to record your conversation. Not that any such recording would be admissible as evidence in court. These days it was all too tweakable; though Lyons-Howard himself still maintained that if you could get it on the box before the inevitable injunction, the layman tended to believe his eyes, regardless of what he was told 'actually' happened later.

The old boyfriend who serviced her computer and systems installed the security program at the same time as that stupid 'Let me through! I'm a doctor!' feature she couldn't find the switch for. Kiely laughed at him when he told her about the big sophisticated illegal security system, never dreaming in a million years it would prove useful.

'Beware the random fucker, babe,' he'd said. 'Always try to legislate against him.'

Kiely's com-stat was going nuts in silence, big red letters flashing an important message and a diagram indicating that she should mute any current communications and take an audio instruction from the computer. She tut-tutted at Lyons–Howard and shook her head playfully.

'You're recording, John. Best turn that off like a good man.'

Lyons–Howard was impressed. 'Expensive equipment, Doctor.'

She nodded back curtly. 'Just until I know where you stand.'

He looked down at his board and hit a key to stop the recording. 'Sounds serious.'

'As cancer,' she said grimly, biting down on the urge to blurt out everything at once and ask him to get her out of all this. 'I'm not going to beat around the bush here, John. I need size-able cash in a hurry and I think you're the man to give it to me.' She watched a twitch in the Lyons–Howard loins echo in the muscle under his left eye.

'I'm intrigued, Kiely. But I can't think what a nice girl like you would have – aside from the pleasure of her company – that I'd be interested in. I think our little show has exhausted the well of medical exposés.' He cocked an eyebrow and sucked in his cheeks, producing a lascivious pout. 'We are talking about the show, aren't we? I mean if you've come to me looking for a dowry I think it's in very bad taste.' Kiely was used to men being keen on her. One of the things she liked about Lyons–Howard was that he had stayed keen, and was never shy about letting her know that he remained that way.

Kiely returned what she hoped was a steady, grave stare. 'What do I do for a living, John?'

He looked at her silently a moment. 'You're a doctor.'

She nodded. 'Where?'

'You've always told me that wasn't important.'

'Do I specialise?' she went on. 'If so, in what field?'

'Alright, alright!' Lyons–Howard held up the palm of his right hand in surrender. 'I know nothing about what you do.'

'Do you know anyone who does?'

Lyons–Howard squinted at her, finally, she thought, dragging his cognitive apparatus out of his trousers. He shook his head. 'No, Kiely, I don't believe I know of anyone.'

'And in all of the time we've known each other, have I ever demonstrated the sort of thoughtlessness or bad taste that would lead you to believe that if I came to you with a story, it would be some run-of-the-mill medical exposé?'

He was smiling broadly now, shaking his head again. 'No, Doctor, I've always believed you to be possessed of finer qualities than that.'

'Thank you, John.' She smiled back at him. 'May I venture just one more question?'

'Of course.'

'Who would you most like to see as the subject of your show?' She raised the index finger of her right hand in warning. 'Think carefully now, and be honest with me.'

Kiely knew that Lyons–Howard believed J.P. Gillespie and everything he touched to be rotten. She also knew that a little more than a year back he had been putting together a piece on brutality by the screws up at WentWest Correctional only for the project to be shelved when the ex-screws making the allegations withdrew their assistance suddenly and without explanation. Years earlier, following Gillespie's opening of

WentWest's food operation in Dublin, and before she had known John, she heard that he had approached every laboratory from Moscow to Seattle in an effort to have the *Moose* soft drink product examined to see if it was as nutritious and beneficial to health as its advertising claimed. He had been rebuffed everywhere.

Lyons-Howard turned his head a little to the left and regarded Kiely from the corners of his eyes. 'Gillespie,' he said to her.

She smiled. 'And how much would you give me for him?'

His expression was a good deal cannier now. 'That, I believe, is one more question than you asked for, Doctor.'

'A rhetorical one,' she said, taking a cigarette from the box beside her and lighting it.

'Oh really!' He sat back in his chair and folded his arms across his chest. 'How much then? Enlighten me.'

She exhaled smoke. 'A bloody fortune, John. A bloody fortune.'

'We can discuss what constitutes a bloody fortune at a later date.' He squinted, indicating the thought process had begun in earnest. 'In the meantime, if your story's worth it, I can get you a generous line of credit and, if necessary, arrange for your safety.'

'No need,' she said. 'I'm arranging that for myself. I'm afraid I won't be around to help you with the production, John. And since I'll want my consideration in cash, you can have J.P. for *half* of a bloody fortune – starting with eighty thousand which I'll require one of your people to take to my apothecary man, as soon as I've satisfied you,' she saw him twitch under the left eye again, 'that this is a runner.'

'The Kid?' He was grimacing – a common enough response.

'The very one.'

'Jesus, Kiely! Still burning it both ends. You didn't hallucinate the Gillespie connection, did you?'

She ignored the question. 'I'll start to script my affidavit and an outline of the set-up as I see it. Get over here as soon as you can, alone. I'm due back at work at two tonight. I'll collect some hard evidence for you then.'

'I'll be there within the hour.' He hung up.

Kiely punched another number into her keypad and the sound of bolts sliding back came from the floor beneath her. She removed a piece of carpet, opened the door of a heavy safe and extracted three passports in the names of Davidia McCall, Roberta Vaughan and Leona Carroll; featuring photographs, respectively, of Kiely as normal, which was strawberry-blonde and blue-eyed; fair-haired and green-eyed; and brunette and brown-eyed. An aunt on her father's side who worked at the Department of Foreign Affairs, up until her death from an abuse-induced heart attack some years back, had arranged for the faultless official IDs in return for recreational chemicals that Kiely had supplied liberally from work and from her account with Kid C. Kiely put Roberta and Leona into a padded envelope addressed to a box number in Athens before booking a flight there in Davidia's name, using her security program to patch the call through a remote location.

(iv)

Kiely's place of work was a secluded research facility twelve kilometres west of Maymon Glades. The main building stood half a kilometre off the road and was shielded from view on all sides by a shallow wooded area of pine trees, shrubbery and bushes. The two hectares of the facility's property bordered land belonging to one of the big food producers whose factory farms took nearly all of the countryside in that area. The next inhabited town along the West Road was nearly fifty kilometres distant.

The facility was conducting trials purporting to investigate the effects of environment and nutrition on the productivity of workers. The three human test subjects had been surgically fitted with sophisticated monitors that fed back information on heart rates and respiration twenty-four hours a day. Exhaustive checks were made every second day on the levels of blood sugar, serotonin, melatonin, endorphins and the rest. The subjects' work areas were bright and as featureless as was practicable to provide the minimum of distraction. They were kept oxygen rich to minimise fatigue. The canteen dispensed food and drink that was heavy on fruit, vegetables, carbohydrate and sugar, and relatively light on fat and protein. When the working day was over the subjects retired to the rest areas, which by contrast with the working areas were low-lit and oxygen deprived. Kiely's job was to monitor the sleep of the subjects, all men in their twenties, and to be there should an emergency arise. Given that her wards were young and healthy and that there were detailed instructions to deal with almost all imaginable contingencies – and a number to call should anything unforeseen occur – she wondered why they needed a doctor at all.

Kiely didn't think she was supposed to know that she worked for J.P. Gillespie; certainly his name had never come up. She had been appointed to her present position by a Frenchwoman, a Dr Bertillion, who had interviewed her, given her the location of the facility and issued her with her instructions. She had never seen the woman again. Her wages were paid by a company calling itself Medicorps. She was paid a substantial salary, Dr Bertillion had explained to her, to perform a simple function without supervision, to refrain from talking to anybody about it, and not to ask any questions. Her employer had been so keen to stress this that she had been woken up in the middle of the night soon after taking up the position, at the apartment of a one-night stand, by two goons with ill-concealed shoulder rigs and a hypo, the contents of which they had used to ensure her young man remained asleep.

'Your new employer asked us to drop by and reiterate the seriousness of the secrecy clause as outlined in the verbal contract,' one of them said; then they drove her home.

It had been an accident – mostly – that left Kiely with information that connected J.P. Gillespie and WentWest Correctional to drug tests that she was sure *had* to be illegal, unless things had gone totally out of control these past couple of years and she'd been too out of it to notice.

One day in a café in town she'd met a driver in Kid C's employ called Cookie. Cookie was a small mousy guy, nervous and shy, but trustworthy and brilliant with vehicles. His best attribute, as far as Kiely was concerned, was that he was indiscreet around her, always ready with titbits of information for the beautiful doctor. She had entreated him to join her and they were eating lunch and chatting at the back of the room when Kiely's attention was drawn to a big man, about six feet two or three and built with it, wearing a dark suit and standing at the service counter waiting on a take-out. She'd seen him a good few times at her place of work, coming out of a small office to the right of the coffee mess, on his way home she'd assumed. She'd only ever seen him when she had the eight to two shift.

'You know McCann?' Cookie had whispered to her.

'Who?'

'The big guy.' He'd been careful to gesture with his eyes only. 'Freeway McCann. He's J.P. Gillespie's enforcer.'

'J.P. Gillespie has an enforcer?'

The driver had nodded, pulling his eyebrows up around his hairline.

'No,' said Kiely, 'never seen him before.'

Cookie went on to tell her about the time that Freeway McCann arrived at the Kid's place, on the matter of an inmate at WentWest Correctional who had been attempting to 'organise' some of the workforce for the Kid's benefit – Cookie hadn't known the exact details. McCann had come to explain that there wasn't any great interest in the Kid's initiative, and to demonstrate the extent of this non-interest he had brought along the inmate's head, in a sturdy plastic bag, which he threw into the Kid's lap. One of the other boys had pulled out a pistol and aimed it at McCann's head, but McCann just walked up to him and stared him down – *stared him down!* The Kid must have been suitably impressed, as Cookie had begged Kiely not to relate it to anyone, lest it might get back. Cookie explained that it was less a taboo subject as far as the Kid was concerned, than it was an event that had never happened.

When Kiely got back on the late shift towards the end of that week she checked with Mark, the guy she was relieving, whether the big guy down the hall had been in. Mark, aware that he wasn't meant to be discussing his work and yet loath to refuse her, nervously told her he'd seen him leave about nine. Kiely made a beeline for the coffee mess when Mark left, to case McCann's office. She discovered there the truth of something a teacher had once told her; that power begets arrogance, and arrogance eventually begets sloppiness. McCann hadn't bothered to lock his door. The building was more than seventy years old, little more than a cave by modern standards. Apparently it had never been seriously updated, and it wasn't equipped with anything in the way of security.

It seemed ridiculous considering the warning she'd received, but she had triple-checked. She was free to walk into the office and turn on the terminal, which she noted was stand-alone. Access to Mr McCann's system, of course, required a password, and since she knew nothing about the man other than he'd once cut someone's head off, she only had one idea and wasn't even sure of the spelling. Her only hope now was that he would be as lazy with his password as he had been with the door. Her old computer boyfriend had told her that most terminals came out of the factory with one of a number of default passwords, mostly physical constants so eggheads wouldn't forget them. He'd given her a list. Ever mindful of the impending rainy day, Kiely had memorised it.

She got access to McCann's system with the speed of light, so to speak: two, nine, nine, eight. There was very little on the machine, and she didn't want to spend too much time in there, so she dumped everything from the hard disk into her cell. As she was leaving the office, Kiely noticed a small refrigerator behind the door; she had a quick look in and saw dozens of small bottles with labels that read 'Boxer' on the front. She closed the door and returned to her office.

(v)

Lyons-Howard arrived within the promised hour, toting a bottle of Chablis, a bunch of grapes and an expensive-smelling blue cheese. Kiely began to bristle a little at his cavalier attitude. She reminded herself that he wasn't aware her life was in danger, only that it might be sometime in the near future.

'Is work always so tough, John?' she asked.

'Eat, drink and be merry, girl, for tomorrow . . .' he left it unfinished and smiled sheepishly. 'What time do you leave for work?'

'Half past midnight.'

'It's just gone four now, you can afford a couple of glasses, and you look like you could use a little nourishment.' He marched off into the kitchen. 'Got any crackers?'

She looked at his back in disbelief. 'Yellow tin, in front of you . . . up.'

He came back shortly with three plates, two knives, the cheese, the washed grapes, assorted crackers, some butter, two glasses and the open bottle. They took seats on opposite sides of her desk and Lyons-Howard half filled the two glasses and started chopping cheese.

'So, Kiely, tell me how you got in with J.P. Gillespie, what you have on the old bastard, and why you're coming to me with it.'

'As I explained,' she said, 'I want money.'

'No thought for my quest to do battle with malfeasance wherever I may find it?'

'Don't make me smile, John, my lips are chapped.' She took her glass and settled back in her chair. 'The fact that we are — acquainted, let's say — obviously featured large in my decision.'

'But you know Charlie Murray over at VGN as well, don't

35

you? Murray has a lot more money to throw around than me.'
Lyons–Howard was arranging his initial efforts on the largest
of the three plates. He put his thumb sideways in his mouth,
ostensibly to ingest a minuscule piece of cheese, and looked
at her from under his eyelashes in a way he had come to equate
with the effusion of sincerity.

'Yeah,' said Kiely, 'but I always got the feeling that Murray,
despite protestations, held a certain admiration for J.P.'

'Not as impossible a position as you make it sound.' He
sipped his wine, then looked at the glass approvingly. 'He's a
smooth, shrewd operator, J.P. Not what you'd call likeable,
but successful. Enough of the right people seem happy to
inhabit his pockets for that reason alone.'

'Well yes, but I think Gillespie may have lost the plot here.
No one minds a guy like that bending the rules a little, but
you could dress up what I've got as offences against humanity.'

'I'm no saint, John, and I make no apology for being desirous
of money. Neither do I think that contributing to the coffers
of Channel Ten is a particularly moral act. It just happens to
be less immoral than contributing to the coffers of VGN,
who, if they used this at all . . .' She trailed off, as if control-
ling her emotion had caused her to lose her point.

'You must be in it deep, Doctor; very little oxygen is getting
to your brain if you think I'm going to fall for "Conscience
Kiely and the Lesser of Two Evils". I happen to know that in
addition to being a closet J.P.-ist, which may or may not matter,
Charlie Murray is president of the underground lavender club,
and maintains an outrageously reactionary position towards the
chemical entertainments; factors which render him impervious
to *both* of your considerable charms.' Lyons–Howard wiggled
his eyebrows.

'Yeah, okay,' she put up her hands. 'What do I care what

you think I think?' She was beginning to remember why she put up with this guy. 'For what it's worth, I know that you've had a couple of cracks at J.P. already. I thought you might be better motivated than anyone else.'

'Indirect cracks,' he smiled. 'And you think I've got something as unprofessional as a *vendetta* going, is that it?'

Kiely cocked an eyebrow. 'You can't turn this down, you have to go for it.'

Lyons-Howard shrugged. 'Maybe, maybe not. We're not doing too badly, and this might all seem like too much hassle, but I'll listen to what you've got.'

He was shitting her and they both knew it. If she had information that said Gillespie only changed his underwear twice a week he'd have bought it from her.

She went on to explain as much as she was supposed, officially, to know about her job. She told him also about her chat with Cookie and her removal of information from Freeway McCann's terminal at the research facility.

'Okay,' Lyons-Howard said when she'd finished, 'J.P. is making no secret of the fact that he's financing research in this area. The dirt must be in the files you stole.'

'All of the files except McCann's own notes are protected with *very* heavy-duty encryption, so I have little enough to go on. He's obviously making the notes so he can report back to J.P., and from reading them I think it's safe to assume that neither of them has a background in any of the sciences.'

'Gillespie's a bizz-grad, and he's since received – read "bought" – some honorary doctorates and whatnot from various institutions. McCann has a Master's in mayhem and grievous bodily harm,' Lyons-Howard said and laughed.

'As far as I can see,' Kiely continued, 'the environment and nutrition are just a front. What's really going on is that the subjects are surreptitiously being given a drug that renders them more controllable and more productive. In other words they do exactly as they're told and they work faster for longer. The test substance is referred to in the files as 'Boxer'; no explanation for that.'

Lyons–Howard smiled grimly. 'A workhorse.'

'McCann's notes are patchy on chemical detail. He describes Boxer as, and I quote: "a synthesis of a henbane derivative and recent developments in meta–phets . . . designed to mimic specific neurotransmitters associated with conformity and obedience . . . facilitating the release of the neuropeptide, beta-endorphin, in conjunction with conformist or obedient behaviour".'

'Does that sound plausible to you?'

'Plausible maybe. The only henbane derivative I've ever heard of is scopolamine, which used to be employed as a truth serum. You're talking about the same type of effect; manipulating your subject, making him more co-operative. The meta–phet, I imagine, is just to keep him awake and sharp. More than that I can't tell you. You'll have to isolate and open those encrypted files and get somebody qualified on it.'

'What if we can't open the files?'

'If you can't open the files you'll still have McCann's notes, my affidavit and a sample of the substance.'

'You have a sample?'

'I'll get it tonight. McCann has a fridge full of it in his office.'

'Why does he have it? Why not the doctors?'

'I think the drug is manufactured in another part of the facility. McCann takes a supply away with him periodically and has it mixed with *Moose*; that's how it's given to the subjects.'

Lyons–Howard looked ill. He enjoyed the popular soft drink,

and, because it was produced by Gillespie's company, he considered it his tragic flaw. 'What do you think Gillespie is planning to do with this exactly?'

Kiely rolled her eyes to heaven. 'Relax, I doubt he'll attempt to use it on the public en masse. The three test subjects are convicted felons seconded from WentWest Correctional. The inmates there do a lot of the usual prison work: travel bookings, telemarketing, sales, whatnot. They can't, however, use the guys with tattooed faces and diction like flushing toilets for anything other than donkey work, which not even the blow-ins will do any more, and which is as a consequence commanding better and better money. WentWest, as you know, have recently completed a new wing and have very kindly offered to take many more such hard cases from the state than they used to.' She blinked twice silently, as if allowing him to come to the conclusion by himself. 'I think they want to corner the market in grunt work, and Boxer will enable them to outbid the laugh academies for it.'

She produced a disk from her drawer and pushed it across the desk. 'My affidavit and the files from McCann's terminal,' she said.

Lyons–Howard picked up the disk and turned it over in his hands. 'There's little security where you work; am I right?'

'Far as I've seen, non-existent, virtually.' She didn't like the look on his face. 'Why?'

'I'd like to get your three subjects on camera. Open the show with excerpts from our interviews with them. No intro. They tell us a little about their lives, they explain what they've been doing day-to-day, et cetera. Parallel to that we run a similar profile of J.P. maybe, or the company, or something; combine the two gradually. You know the sort of thing.'

'Forget about it.'

'C'mon, Kiely! From what you tell me, all you have to do is tell them to hop in the car and shut up, and they're fulfilled.'

'I said forget it. Anyway I drive a two-seater.'

'I'll lend you a car.'

'No!'

Lyons-Howard pulled out his palm unit and touched the console, fitting an earpiece as he waited for a pick-up. A second or two later his connection was made.

'Martin, John here, listen up. I want you to organise one point one million in cash before close today.' He listened for a moment himself. 'Exactly. Give it to Rose to put safe. And stay around, we'll be working late.' He turned to Kiely. 'I'll keep eighty grand of that for the Kid; you can have the million upon delivery of the three boys to our production lot.' He handed her a card with the address. 'I'll be there all night making preparations.' He was all matter-of-fact, like it was a done deal. 'Furthermore, as soon as J.P. is out of the way you'll be entitled to another half million, which I'll wire to you wherever you are. Okay? Do you want me to organise a car for you?'

'No,' calmly; a tantalising pause. 'There's a station wagon ambulance at the clinic; drives the same as a car. I'll use that.'

Lyons-Howard relaxed into his chair. He picked up the wine bottle, offered a refill to Kiely which she declined, then poured his own. 'Can I ask you a personal question, Kiely?'

She shrugged. 'Don't see why not.'

'All this,' he waved the back of his hand over the desk, 'for an eighty-grand debt. I can't believe you'd have difficulty raising that amount, yet you want me to believe you're hocking the crown jewels to cover it. What's up?'

Kiely sighed heavily. 'Like the old song goes, I'm sick and tired of feeling sick and tired. I'm sick of living in this sewer, and I'm tired of my life, which only seems to be a social life. The only reason I took this job in the first place was to finance the spiralling cost of that social life, without having to do any actual work. I went thirty-three last month, John. I should want to do something other than guzzle booze and pop amphetamines. Fucksake, I need a shot just to get myself straight in the morning.'

Lyons-Howard nodded. 'There's got to be more to life than this.' He was silent for a moment. 'Where will you go?'

She shook her head. 'Forget it.'

'I might want to visit. Check you're okay.'

'I might want you to visit, John, but I'll call and invite you.'

He smiled. 'I gotta move.'

(vi)

As angelic as they may have looked in their respective slumbers, it would never be said of David Hayden, Thomas Donnelly or James Clarke that they slept the sleep of the innocent. Although not one of them had yet reached his twenty-first birthday, they had between them managed to extinguish three hundred and forty-three years of human existence. Hayden and Donnelly it might have been possible to muster some sympathy for, inasmuch as the PCP they had taken had rendered them temporarily psychotic, precipitating an uncharacteristic, but nevertheless savage, stabbing incident outside a city-centre restaurant that left three middle-aged businessmen sharing approximately two hundred and seventy knife wounds and an appointment in oblivion. Hayden's defence had made much of the fact that he had been born addicted to the shit that passed for heroin in the run-down apartment complex where his drug-whore mother lived and plied her trade. It was further pointed out that he had been beaten and buggered senseless by a succession of remorseless animals who had moved in to live off his mother's paltry earnings.

Thomas Donnelly had grown up three doors down from Hayden and hadn't fared much better. His mother was one of fourteen who died as a result of some dealer being overly generous with the scouring powder when cutting his gear. Tommy had been eight years old. His drunken father's appearances at the family home became less and less frequent, until by the time Tommy was twelve the old man wasn't showing up at all. His friendship with Hayden led to his being raped on a number of occasions by two of Hayden's stepfathers. He decided to turn this experience into an earner and was soon trading his favours for cash or for any substance that would render him insensible.

During the relation of these sad beginnings the jury had seemed sympathetic, but all sympathy evaporated in the righteous heat of their victims' shining careers; both were found guilty. The judge had clearly seen it all before. Wearily he told them that they were inhuman scum who had, in his personal opinion, no right to their lives. He sentenced them to life without the possibility of parole.

James Clarke was a less likeable fellow altogether. He had, one November evening, robbed two elderly sisters of their cash and jewellery to finance a drugs party for himself and his friends. He had extracted the whereabouts and combination of the sisters' small safe by tying them up, dousing them in lighter fuel and threatening to set them alight. As he left the house with his swag he flicked his cigarette end at one of the women, who immediately burst into flames. Her sister died of a terror-induced coronary watching.

Later that same month, made paranoid to the point of explosion by his relentless drug abuse, he had killed a family of three while on his way to another heist. He emptied an automatic pistol into their vehicle through the front windscreen when he perceived the driver to be attempting to hurry him off a pedestrian crossing by revving the engine in an irritable manner. Clarke's defence couldn't cite his upbringing as a mitigating factor. He had been well provided for. If his parents were to blame, it was because they trusted the boy, believed him to be responsible. They were both forced to work to make ends meet, leaving James mostly unsupervised. Mr and Mrs Clarke were, to say the least, surprised to find that James hadn't been at home doing his homework.

The three boys were sleeping the sleep of the exhausted then, having spent their day moving small ball-bearings from one Petri dish to another with tweezers. They had been engrossed in their task for a record fourteen hours, plus three twenty-minute breaks during which they stuffed themselves with carbohydrates and soft drinks. Dave, Jimmy and Tommy had loved every moment of their industry; pleasing the doctors felt so good to them. They had become extremely adept at their task, averaging between them seventy-two ball-bearings per minute. Inevitably there were a number of short breaks for the toilet, which meant that momentum had to be built up all over again, but a couple of laboratory technicians were said to be working on a solution to that particular problem. Overall the doctors had been very pleased.

Two doors up the corridor Dr Mark Leonard sat in a control booth, ostensibly monitoring the sleep of his three youthful wards. He was, in fact, monitoring his wristwatch and awaiting the arrival of Dr Flanagan, who was to relieve him. Dr Leonard didn't like staying late here. He didn't like this work full stop, but it was all he could get to keep him in the style to which he was accustomed until his appeal finally went through. He'd been struck off the register while working as an abortionist. Nice easy work that. If you were running smoothly six or seven a day wouldn't take more than four hours; and, not counting what Sergei would kick back for the foetuses, it had been enough to keep him fine. He'd had a respectable level of stress inasmuch as he had heard that Sergei sold the discarded tissue on to some very dodgy clinics, which was something you wouldn't want to be associated with; but at least the Commissioners hadn't picked up on it as a source of revenue.

The Revenue was the reason he'd been reduced to working these unsocial hours. He was unfortunate enough to have been the subject of a sting operation run by a couple of ambitious girls who worked at the Commissioners' office. They had come to him pregnant and a little short of the normal fee, but with cash. He wasn't aware where they worked, obviously, and he decided to take the chance. Who wouldn't have, for Christ's sake? When the items failed to show in his returns the following April he very shortly found himself without a licence to practise and answering to charges from the Inspector of Taxes, whose star witnesses happened to be the two recently promoted tarts he'd done the scrape on in the first place.

His solicitor and counsel were looking into many old entrapment cases for very few clues and sucking up a shit-load of his money in the process. It was necessary, therefore, for him to sit here half the night monitoring the sleep of real criminals.

Dr Flanagan arrived a little late, and, being a tad distracted, seemed oblivious of the fact that she had kept him waiting. Leonard despised this unapproachable self-consumption of hers, while at the same time lusting after her. Ever anxious to appear the cool observer, hopeful of some opportunity to impress her, he said nothing, but nodded at her absently.

'I'm sorry I'm late, Mark,' she said eventually, bending to his will. 'I should really have called to let you know I was on my way. I had to get a taxi.'

Well, well, he thought, she wasn't usually so talkative. He looked at her with his mouth hanging open and his eyes lidded, as if a great believer in carbon monoxide as a nasal decongestant. The expression was supposed to say: *Late?*

'No worries, Kiely.' He wanted very much to communicate this sense of indifference. It wouldn't be the routine she usually got from guys and this should confuse her; give him more time to manoeuvre. 'Don't tell me you crashed the Nyson?'

'No, it's in for service,' she said. She was peering at the readout on a small portable terminal. He gazed absorbedly into his own screen, looking down at the keyboard every few seconds and hitting a key or two, then looking ahead again and nodding to himself.

'Anything strange?' she asked.

'Nothing.' Leonard picked up a clipboard, examined it briefly and replaced it, then sighed deeply.

'Mark?'

'Yeah?'

'I know we haven't talked much, but –' She broke off abruptly as if worried beyond endurance, but coping well.

He looked at her with what he hoped would register as mature concern. 'What is it?'

She marshalled her strength and carried on. 'I'd like to discuss something with you. Are you in a hurry anywhere right at the moment?' She blinked twice and lowered her head a little, looking at him from under her lashes.

'No, no. All the time in the world.' Leonard's indifference

was out the window, and he was dusting down his very best bedside manner.

'Thanks, Mark. Let me get some coffee first. Can I get you some?'

'Sure. That'd be great.'

She moved behind his chair as she went out into the corridor, placing her left hand on his shoulder and giving it an affectionate squeeze. Outside at the coffee mess she filled the machine and started it brewing. She walked over to Freeway McCann's office where she found the door again unlocked. She went to the refrigerator in the corner and pocketed a number of fifty-mil phials marked 'Boxer', then produced a hypo and half filled it from one of them before returning to the coffee mess to wait for the percolator to finish its work. She placed two mugs on a tray with spoons, milk and sugar and emptied the hypo into one of the mugs before pouring the coffee in on top. She estimated a guy as slightly built as Leonard would probably be under the influence in around fifteen minutes. Her only problem was what to talk to him about for that time.

(vii)

Dr Leonard walked out into the foyer of the building where Bobby, the security guy, made sure everyone signed in and out. Bobby pushed the book towards Leonard as he approached.

'Out a little later than usual tonight, Dr Leonard,' he said, looking back to where Leonard had come from. 'Mind you, with a colleague like that Dr Flanagan, I'm surprised you ever leave.' He looked at Leonard, hoping, as they had done many times previously, to share a ribald laugh at Dr Flanagan's expense. He found himself instead staring into the business end of one of those electric stun guns. It occurred to him to wonder where the doctor had found it, but before he could make an enquiry more eloquent than a puzzled look, Leonard jammed the device into the left side of his neck and discharged it, leaving the old man twitching ever so slightly in his chair. Leonard went behind the desk and removed the keys for the ambulance, then dialled an extension on Bobby's terminal. Kiely's face popped up.

'Everything set?' she asked.

'Yep,' he said, 'Bobby's out – or whatever – and I've got the keys.'

Kiely stared at him in disbelief. 'What the fuck do you mean "whatever"? Check!'

Leonard found himself suddenly and profoundly distressed at Kiely's dissatisfaction. He quickly felt for a pulse in Bobby's wrist while holding his ear close to Bobby's mouth. His hand was shaking and his heart thumping loud in his ears, but after a couple of seconds he was able to tell her that the doorman was unconscious, not dead.

Kiely sighed and closed her eyes for a moment. 'Good. Bring the ambulance around to the side entrance.'

With Kiely's enunciation of the word 'good' Leonard felt a fresh wave of well-being wash over him. He patted the twitching body of the security guard on the shoulder and headed out to collect the ambulance.

(viii)

Dave, Jimmy and Tommy were standing inside the side entrance with their arms folded, shifting from foot to foot. They had been told not to speak and were enjoying their compliance with this instruction. They glanced from one to the other, smiling quizzically. This wasn't part of the usual routine, but they'd been promised a review of their parole positions if they took part in this and did exactly as the doctors said. Besides, doing as they were told felt *so good*. These doctors really had rehabilitated them. The beautiful doctor came back and held the door open in front of them. The fact she was a honey made doing as you were told that little bit more pleasant.

'Okay, get into the back of the ambulance, sit down, fasten your seatbelts and remain silent.' The boys complied. Kiely hopped into the passenger seat. 'Let's go, Mark, nice and steady. We don't want to attract any attention.'

Leonard pulled out smoothly and headed for the main gate. He stopped at the gate, checked the road on either side, then turned left and headed towards town. He was mulling over what they'd been talking about earlier, still wondering how he'd been willingly complicit in the terrible experiments being perpetrated on these poor boys. It was all very strange to him now; he'd known most of the facts that Kiely had explained to him, and guessed those he didn't know, but it all seemed somewhat clearer since they'd spoken. It made him feel a lot better to have been in part responsible for this rescue. It might even help him get his licence back.

'I don't know what I was thinking taking a job like this, Kiely, I really don't. I'm glad you put me straight on it. What time are we going to the studio to meet your friend?'

Kiely was looking out the window, only half listening to him. 'We're going there directly.'

'Jesus, those guys work late. When I was doing terminations I tried never to work after three in the afternoon.' He glanced in his rear-view and once at Kiely, who looked more beautiful than he had ever seen her. Come to think of it he was feeling better than he had in a long time; still, something was nagging at him. 'Kiely?'

'Yeah?'

'D'you think Bobby'll be alright?'

'I hope so.'

He shuffled in his seat a bit and squinted as if trying to focus on something that refused to comply. 'We're in deep shit, aren't we?'

'My friends will get you protection.'

'I saw this show once where a Mafia informer –'

'Mark?'

'Yeah?'

'No more talking.' She passed her right hand over the console on her side until she found some music she liked.

(ix)

Gillespie, in common with many eminent businessmen, was extravagant in some areas and positively mean in others. Himself and Freeway McCann had organised the security arrangements for the precious research facility on a budget that didn't quite match what between them they spent on suits in a year. About a third of this sum went on the three geriatrics who manned the lobby of the facility in eight-hour shifts. All three had forfeited their state pensions as a result of being convicted of one petty offence or another and were therefore grateful for the buttons J.P. threw their way. J.P. and Freeway figured there wasn't much danger of a leak from inside the facility, since anyone with concrete information about what actually went on in there was not economised on, and in any case had been effectively warned about the importance of silence. The fact that the facility was in the middle of nowhere and employed a 'Private Property – Keep Out' sign ruled out casual enquiries or visitors, obviously. In addition, after years of watching people bow and scrape it had become difficult for either J.P. or Freeway to imagine that anyone would do anything to contravene their wishes, especially after a warning. As far as they were concerned, people like Kiely Flanagan didn't exist, or if they did it was because they were deranged and impossible to legislate against.

The rest of the facility's security budget was expended upon the persons of Mick and Frank Cooper; no relation. Mick and Frank were incontrovertible proof that if you shelled out peanuts you got monkeys. They were employed as a mobile unit responsible for the night-time security of the research facility. Basically they had nothing to do other than be available should something go wrong. They were supposed to take a call every hour from whichever of the old boys was manning the lobby to ensure all was well, and keep themselves sharp, their vehicle fuelled and their weapons loaded should the worst ever come to the worst, which nobody realistically expected it ever would.

Mick and Frank got this cushy number because they were business associates of Freeway McCann, assisting him with the distribution of the small arms and munitions he imported. His blind eye at customs was organised by J.P., who took a percentage. Off their own bat, Mick and Frank had acquired interests in a number of ventures in the field of entertainment, the most recent being an establishment which the manager referred to as a 'gentleman's club', about six kilometres south-east of the research facility, in one of the less fashionable suburbs. This was where they could generally be found when they were supposed to be on security duty for Freeway – in the office overlooking the main room of the club, watching the girls go up and down the runway entertaining the gentlemen.

When they weren't at the club they'd usually take beers and a couple of spliffs out to the lake in People's Park, at the edge of Maymon Glades, and veg out watching *Pitch Above*, 'the show for today's Renaissance man', on the IB Channel; from the ImprovB Media Organisation – 'dedicated to the further evolution of humankind'. They'd spend entire evenings there in the car, stoned and half drunk, saying 'wow' at the screen every time a photogenic science graduate used a number with more than six digits.

'Nembutal?' Frank said, not taking his eyes from the credits, which rolled too fast to read. He was sporting a jowly expression of puzzled mistrust. 'You're going to call the place "Nembutal"?'

'Well I don't want to call it *Shangri-La*, but I want to go for the same basic idea. *Nembutal*,' Mick exhaled the word as gently as thirty-a-day allowed. 'It's a nice relaxing sound,' he reflected wheezily.

'It ought to be. Do you know what it means?'

'It's Muslim heaven or something, isn't it? Remember we saw the show where the guy was talking about algebra in Africa way back when – in that.'

'Nah, that's something else. I think it's drugs.'

51

Mick had a sudden intuition his friend might have been right. 'Drugs, like dope? Or *drugs* drugs?'

'*Drugs* drugs.'

'Ballocks!'

Another of Mick's business interests was a site on the outskirts of the city, which he could never afford to build on. Even if he'd had the money to, by now he had scornfully refused to sell the patch to almost every developer and builder in town, and it was unlikely that anyone would undertake a project for him at this stage, no matter how much was offered. Most consistently he'd refused the plot to Hither Twice Toys, who'd been back and forth over years with offers well in excess of the property's value, and who were having problems keeping middle management because of the fact that, while they could provide company cars, they couldn't provide parking at head office, and they certainly couldn't support the parking and recovery fines they'd accumulate. They wanted Mick's plot and couldn't understand why on God's green earth he wouldn't sell. Five times the value they'd offered him! The board was not happy. A number of them were in favour of taking out a contract, but their MD, Steven Fox, argued strongly against it, on the grounds that being semi-underworld himself (as Fox's researches had revealed) Cooper could easily get tipped off, 'and then it's turds in the air-conditioning'. Fox opted for a wait-and-see. The cost of the limo fleet was bearable, and sooner or later something had to give.

Mick Cooper's father was much to blame for the discontentment of the Hither Twice board, inasmuch as he had drilled it into Mick that if he ever got his hands on property, or, God forbid, land, he was never to sell it; that there were always ways to earn from such an asset without having to relinquish ownership of it. Ownership being the thing as far as Mick's old man was concerned. He warned him that people would arrive with fabulous offers, would resort to threats even, but that he was not to sell, under any circumstance. The property, it seemed, was somehow worth more than the money offered for it. Mick wasn't sure how exactly that came to be, but trusted his old man. Against all other advice he remained steadfast in not parting with his asset.

Instead he decided to engage in a modest development of his own. He stacked old ship's containers on it and rented them out to interested parties. If the board at Hither Twice were disgruntled at Mick's refusal to sell, they were livid at what his development had placed in their backyard. Mick got a hundred ship's containers from a guy he knew, ninety-six of which (four rows stacked three high) he rented to whoever wanted them and whatever they wanted them for, as long as they could afford it. The last four he had converted into eight bathroom units, on the remote possibility that any of his clientele might decide to spend the night in their containers. He had electricity sorted by means of second-hand emergency generators which his clients were responsible for filling with diesel. He had been introduced to some big shot at the waterworks who had released the water supply in return for being introduced to the manager back at the strip club, who could help satisfy the big shot's appetite for jailbait, in the very strictest confidence. The crux of Mick's present difficulty – the 'Nembutal' question – arose from the fact that on one of his and Frank's occasional sojourns around the city dump he had sourced a huge piece of solid oak. He wanted someone to carve a name into it, so he could hang it over the entrance to his Utopia. This evening he had set himself the task of deciding on a name.

'"Nagana"! Isn't that Muslim heaven?' Frank had been racking it for the past few minutes.

'Yeah, that's it! Nagana.' Mick took his beer from between his knees and popped his seat back into its upright position. 'Nagana,' he tried it again. 'Very relaxing.'

'It has that effect,' agreed Frank, 'like one of them chants.' Frank began repeating the word under his breath over and over. 'Nah-gah-nah-nah-gah-nah . . .'

The two boys were addicted to the IB Channel. It ran documentaries twenty-four hours a day on popular science, nature, wildlife, foreign cultures, you name it. Frank and Mick honestly believed they were 'evolving' by watching the box, and while it's true some of what they allowed to wash over them actually stuck, it never did so in any useful fashion.

Mick tired quickly of listening to Frank's repetition and broke in, 'Will it suit, d'you think?'

'No reason why not.' Frank didn't appreciate the gruff interruption.

Something occurred to Mick. 'What time is it? Have we heard from Bobby?' He eyed the unit built into the dashboard suspiciously. 'Have we had trouble with this before?'

'Can't remember.' Frank started banging the dashboard to encourage the unit's correct operation. Nothing happened. 'Shit! Get your cell and call him.'

Mick pulled a palm unit from his jacket on the back seat and punched the connection. They waited a minute for Bobby to pick up. When he didn't, Frank began to look worried and started the engine.

'Hang on,' Mick was getting out his side of the car, 'I have to piss.'

'Hurry.'

As Mick stood facing out into the lake pissing, the occupants of one of a number of other vehicles parked there, all containing teenage couples, noticed him and drew the attention of everyone else by flashing their headlights and sounding the horn. It caught on quickly and soon seven other vehicles were doing likewise. Without any discernible halt in his progress, and without so much as looking up, Mick recovered his pistol from its holster under his left arm and discharged it twice above his head. The weapon was of the type known as a 'hand-cannon' and the noise was sufficient to momentarily drown out the collected car horns; the muzzle-flash, if you were lucky enough to get to dwell upon it, was also impressive. He was allowed to finish in silence.

'That's class, Mick,' said Frank as his companion regained the car, 'real class.'

'Thanks, Frank.' The sarcasm was lost on him. He looked back over his shoulder and pointed through the rear windshield. 'Let's move.'

About six or seven kilometres outside Maymon Glades a red and white station wagon ambulance passed them in the opposite direction at a sedate pace. Mick finally raised Bobby, the doorman, back at the clinic, and he rather groggily made the connection for them. Frank screeched to a halt and swung the car around. When they had the ambulance in sight again, less than three minutes later, and were bearing down on it, its siren started up and the red lights on the roof began flashing; there was a notable increase in its speed, indicating that the occupants were a little quicker on the uptake than Mick and Frank.

'Fuckers're on to us!' One thing at least hadn't escaped Mick.

'Tyres!' Frank roared, and Mick rolled down his window and started taking pot shots with the hand-cannon. The ambulance began swerving from side to side. Frank got up close and tried to ram it. Mick continued shooting into the tarmac rapidly unfurling beneath him until his ammunition was spent. He loaded a fresh clip and was steadying himself for the next volley when the ambulance slid into the downhill left-hander just outside the Glades. Two shots issued in rapid succession from his weapon just as the ambulance went sideways and flipped into the air.

'Got it!'

It was, to say the least, a fanciful claim. The ambulance rolled seven or eight times, then slid on its roof into the barrier on the right side of the road before rebounding into the grass verge opposite. Frank brought the car to a halt. As he killed the engine they could hear the car's terminal ringing above the screaming of the ambulance engine. Mick and Frank looked at each other. Freeway McCann's ID flashed in the top left corner of the screen. Frank picked up. He had to raise his voice a good bit to make himself heard.

'Freeway, there's been a heist, or something, at the clinic, but we got the fuckers responsible.'

'I know,' McCann was deadly cool, 'Bobby called me.' He paused for a moment, blinked, and ran his tongue across the uppermost part of his lower lip, as if taking account of their situation remotely, via the taste buds. 'Please tell me that when you say "got" you mean "detained".' Mick and Frank swallowed in dry throats. McCann remained eerily impassive for a number of seconds, his screen image the essence of deadly patience, until Frank – as McCann knew one of them would – came clean.

When Frank had finished his quick summation, Freeway sighed heavily to let them in on his disappointment.

'That's too exposed an area to risk a proper clean-up job. I want total destruction of the evidence. Remember you don't have much time. The boss is not going to take any risks with the likes of you, so if you're caught you're dead men. The best

I'd be able to do for you under those circumstances would be to make it quick. *Comprende?*' The boys nodded silently.

When Freeway disconnected they walked around to the back of their vehicle and opened the boot. Frank reached in and took out a small sledgehammer and a device that resembled a harpoon. Mick unzipped a canvas bag full of long tubular objects.

'Who's gonna do this?' Mick wanted to know.

Frank looked pale and weak. 'We'll flip for it.'

'Okay,' said Mick, 'but the best of three.'

'Fuck that, Mick. We don't have time.'

(x)

It was dark when Papa Charlie woke. The clock on the bedside table said three fifteen. He shook his head, and covered then uncovered his ears a couple of times, to establish that he was no longer dreaming the horrible noise that had leaked into and eventually woken him from his nightmare. It was a screaming, hissing sound, much fainter than he imagined could have woken him. He sat on the edge of the bed blinking back tears; he wasn't the better of the dream. It was a recurring one, had been since he was a boy. His father is standing in an urban wasteland, like a bombed-out city, wearing the green T-shirt he used to do the gardening in. It gives him a mouldy, flea-bitten appearance. Papa Charlie's father is surrounded by a throng of angry, belligerent people. He is frightened. After a short while in which he looks from one to the other of them, wide-eyed and uncomprehending, the throng advances with stones which they throw at him, then they walk away, leaving him standing, but cut and bruised and scared and angry.

This time the dream had been different. After the stoning there had been a loud whoosh and a flash of light in the sky, and the crowd had been called away by a siren or klaxon. It was this sound that had become, as he gradually woke, the sound he was now listening to. It appeared to be coming from out on the road.

Without forming any actual words he made audible complaints as he struggled out of his bed, then went to his bedroom window and parted the blinds with his fingers. There was a flickering light some way up the road to his left. The terrible sound persisted faintly. It had a thin, metallic quality, but an insistence that put him in mind of petulance and anger. In his mind's eye he saw a huge metal insect on its back fighting to get right side up, and making that noise in protest.

He couldn't make out much more than flickering light through the window. There were no houses up there; he was pretty much on his own this far out. Maybe no one else knew. He went to his bedside table and retrieved a pair of spectacles. He pulled on trousers, shoes and a sweater and took his cell out to the front door.

His eyes were still glazed over from sleep and the spectacles were filthy. He removed them and rubbed at the lenses with the front of his sweater. He could see fire, certainly, but there was a blinking red source also, too regular for fire. Could be the cops were there already. Could be the cops themselves had crashed. Wouldn't be the first time someone had come off the road trying to negotiate that bend too quickly.

He dialled the number of the emergency services as he walked out of his garden and towards the scene of the apparent conflagration. He was in pretty good shape for a man in his mid sixties and had covered maybe a quarter of the distance by the time his call was picked up at the other end.

After he'd given the services what information he could he was halfway there. A gentle breeze was blowing in his direction and he thought he could discern a spitting sound beneath the screaming that he now recognised as the vehicle's engine. A quick analysis of the olfactory information carried on the breeze suggested a hideous notion – something was cooking.

Welcome to Coolsville

PROGRAMME: Staines at 7.

DATE: Tuesday, 17th October.

STEVE: It's [time nearest minute] – Tuesday
the seventeenth. You're tuned to
T.L.R.N.

CUE: Fanfare 61. 3"

STEVE: It's overcast and still cold, [cue:
wind 8 FX357. 1"] eight degrees, [micro
laugh] getting up to ten in some places.
Expect rain later. [short pause]
If you're feeling out of sorts this
morning and you don't exactly know
why, you'd do well to look at the
MICA poll released today. It seems
that over seventy per cent of people
consider Tuesday the lousiest day of
the week. What happens is we expect
Monday to be lousy, so we go easy on
ourselves, and we're lulled into a
false sense of security once it's all
out of the way. Then Tuesday morning
rolls around and we suddenly realise
that not only is it four full days
to the weekend, but we still have to
do everything we didn't do yesterday!
[cue: alarm bell FX458. 2"] Yikes.

CUE: Track 1. 3'15" quick fade up behind
Steve

STEVE: I'll open with this again. Terrific.

FULL FADE UP

Marshall McLemon sat deep in the bowels of the WentWest
Archive searching for a batch of A5 paper invoices, the very
existence of which, in the opinion of his friend and colleague
Papa Charlie McCormack, was problematical. WentWest's
Archive & Record Management section itself resided deep in
the bowels of WentWest's Life & Pensions building, stretching
down three floors beneath the underground car park. That was
where Marshall McLemon sat searching, in the gargantuan
storeroom right in the bottom.

WentWest's Life & Pensions building adorned the centre of
Maymon Glades, a subopolis thirty or so kilometres due west
of the Liffey mouth, popularly known as Coolsville. In the last
five years, on the back of the economic upturn, efforts had
been underway in the media to have the 'Coolsville' moniker
applied to the entirety of the Dublin Megalopolis, on the
grounds that the influx of money made it an attractive, or
'cool', place to live. As far as the upstanding denizens of
Maymon Glades were concerned the name had only ever been
a pejorative one, and any move to extend its use was a trav-
esty of taste. The name had been coined by cons and ex-cons
who had served time at WentWest Correctional, whose twin
blocks squatted a kilometre north of the Glades and were

clearly visible from any first-floor window there. The explanation of the name most palatable to Glades' residents was that Maymon Glades was where the WentWest Correctional Institute, or the 'cooler', was located, hence 'Coolsville'. It was probably truer that the name described the reception the parolee received when he arrived in Maymon Glades. It was well understood that the only thing for sale in the Glades to a released man was a ticket out of there. Since the town was on the only route anywhere from the prison, everyone who spent any time there, including visitors and prison workers, all had to arrive and depart through Maymon Glades, and they all knew about the 'Coolsville shoulder'.

Marshall McLemon was Glades through and through; second generation. He'd never have to worry about the 'Coolsville shoulder' – they knew their own in the Glades. Nevertheless, Marshall wasn't enjoying his day; the absence of enjoyment precipitating solely and directly from the task in which he was now engaged. Normally he came to his work with the pleasant anticipation with which one would visit an old friend. Normally he would putter about amid the myriad of text documents, sound recordings, video and motion-picture footage, as happy as any man can be at his work. Normally the future was an open-ended invitation to discovery, not the eternity preceding the location of a possibly non-existent file. Normally he wouldn't be found dead in an area designated 'Accounts'.

He fastened the cover on another batch of invoices, having checked that the reference numbers on the outside accurately described the contents, and replaced them on the shelf. He pulled down another batch, opened it and began leafing through, flipping back to the front cover every few seconds to check the list. There had been a craze for deep and historical audits in the last eighteen months, the like of which he had never seen in his time with WentWest, and he worried that more and more this sort of thankless and tedious task would eat into work which he considered infinitely more important. Papa Charlie said that the audits were so that the people who had all the money could continue to keep it. Papa Charlie, Marshall knew after five years of working with him, was down on 'the rich'. Marshall had once opined that if the rich didn't invest their money, then no one would have a job, and there would ensue terrible social unrest. Papa Charlie had laughed at him. 'God bless them,' he'd said. 'God bless them one and all!'

It had been said to McLemon, in other circles, that it was this cynicism which saw Papa Charlie relegated to the Archive, but Marshall didn't think that Papa Charlie considered his position as one of relegation, and *he* certainly didn't think of his own position as such. He had, in fact, asked for it. That he got the job he always ascribed to the fact that he was fast friends with Coleman Gillespie, J.P. Gillespie's son; had been since college. Others would give you the impression that anyone could have walked in off the street and taken the job, such was the prestige it commanded among those of a more ambitious bent. The Archive was seen, incorrectly it has to be said, as all the stuff everybody was finished with, but which for legal reasons couldn't yet be discarded. There was more to it than that.

WentWest had absorbed many and varied companies and businesses in its seventy-five-year history. All, or nearly all, of the attendant records came to the WentWest Archive eventually. WentWest may have been seventy-five, and some of its acquisitions older, but they had only thought to build an archive twenty years ago. Back then there'd been a staff of thirty working shifts to get everything catalogued and filed. Nowadays it was just Papa Charlie and Marshall. As records arrived from fresh acquisitions their downloads were monitored and problems referred to Systems. Once downloaded, a series of tests was run and the item was then filed away. There were tonnes of records, paper, microfiche and disk, going back fifty or more years, still to be C&C'd. Papa Charlie said that if WentWest were really interested in having this backlog dealt with, they would have employed the requisite number of staff to do it – it wasn't like they didn't have the money. As things stood, the old man figured they could afford to take their sweet time about it, and so they devoted three half days a week each to the backlog. The day-to-day arrivals from existing WentWest companies required little or no work, other than a quarterly check of the various databases.

Their only other task was to respond to enquiries seeking historical information. Enquiries of this type were generally thin on the ground, and the enquirers usually of such low standing that they were easily fobbed off, or happy to wait, if it transpired that the item hadn't yet been catalogued and wasn't readily available. But occasionally, like this morning, some big shot that you couldn't say no to got on and you got stuck with a time-thieving bastard.

Among its acquisitions over the years WentWest had absorbed production companies, television stations, radio stations, newspapers and magazines, and had thus collected movies, sound recordings, TV shows and manuscripts by the truckload. Papa Charlie had been cataloguing and organising the collection for ten years before Marshall arrived. When Marshall had first encountered it he hadn't believed it possible that so much material could exist without his ever having heard of it. Papa Charlie told him that much of the material had been deliberately taken out of circulation. Somebody somewhere decided that people wanted new stories, that they were sick of reruns and adaptations and stuff inspired by other stuff; it was a new millennium after all. The face of entertainment had changed. Quality was replaced with the sensational and the cheaply produced. Self-contained narratives with beginnings, middles and ends were abandoned for never-ending daily dramas that limped along from one unlikely premise to the next, year in, year out for decades. Worse than that were the shows that the punters made themselves – compulsively mundane yet irresistibly cheap. Most horrible of all in Papa Charlie's view was the absolute abandonment of any narrative for the simple, immediate drama of sport. It was, he said, a tragedy that to most people Casablanca represented nothing more than a Moroccan football team.

Marshall shared many of the old man's prejudices. Because of a reluctance to interact socially, the result of a few difficult years in primary school, much of Marshall's life had been taken up in the solitary consumption of popular culture, late twentieth century mostly, though he was no slouch on the earlier part. It was an interest he picked up from his father, who for many years as a single working parent had been too tired to watch television as it happened and had opted instead to use his recorder. He found one day, when his son was about thirteen, that he had succeeded in recording almost four thousand hours of movies, dramas and reviews. Since there was little being broadcast at that time that he would have enjoyed exposing young Marshall to, they began to watch the recordings together. Before he entered college at fifteen, Marshall had already placed his own catalogued and cross-referenced archive of the core of his father's recordings on the web. To be appointed, therefore, one of the curators of *the* mother lode of such material seemed to him less a relegation than a dream come true.

He had to admit, though, that it was a dream come true only inasmuch as all this stuff was there and available to them. It was proving difficult to share with others. The attitude of their boss, J.P. Gillespie, towards this hoard of narrative had for them a depressing history. They had been submitting proposals for a web exhibit – *the* Exhibit, as they called it – directly to J.P. Gillespie for the past three years without success. 'What jewels?' he had wanted to know when Marshall described the Exhibit to him. He had been greatly disappointed to discover Marshall had been speaking figuratively.

Initially their plan had been for a permanent web installation, a vast museum of entertainment, with customised virtual constructs that would give a visceral experience of how people used to consume these entertainment artefacts. They had planned to assemble exhaustive biographies of the protagonists; histories and overviews of movements and genres; definitions of terms lay, technical and obsolete; lists of seminal works and performances, all divided and subdivided and cross-referenced to afford maximum friendliness to a potential user. With each of J.P.'s rejections they had dropped their sights a little, until their most recent submission, a response to which they presently awaited, was a temporary installation which eclipsed Marshall's adolescent solo effort only in terms of scope.

Marshall filed another batch of invoices at the end of the row he'd been working on and marked his place. It was time for his break. He dusted down the legs of his trousers and strolled the one hundred metres to the basement room's main entrance, browsing the markers on the shelves on the off chance he'd see something of interest. He pushed through the swinging doors, took a last look behind him and elbowed the button for the lift.

Up a floor and left out of the lift, Marshall walked down

the corridor twenty paces and through a set of swinging double doors into his and Papa Charlie's spacious and therefore hard-to-heat office. They were two floors below ground so their window was a large screen, a 'three hundred', nearly two and a half metres across the top, which would display any number of views taken by cameras in the centre of Dublin. Papa Charlie was at the drinks dispenser to the right of the big screen, hovering in front of the Ha'penny Bridge and the few cold characters crossing it, waiting on the caffeine-free coffee-style drinks to accompany doughnuts and Danish.

'Any luck?' the old man wanted to know.

'Not yet.'

'Don't worry, I'll find it later. J.P.'s secretary was on ten or so minutes back, said J.P. wants to see you immediately.'

'Jesus,' said Marshall, 'he usually memos the rejection. Maybe it's good news.'

'Don't get your hopes up. He might want to tell you to stop bothering him face to face.'

Marshall pulled his chair over in front of Papa Charlie's desk and sat down. Charlie had made a cryptic reference to 'foul play' in relation to his adventure the previous night and Marshall wanted to get back there. He mulled over the choice of confectionery in front of him before picking up a big sticky Danish. 'So did you make the dailies this morning?'

Charlie pushed a steaming mug in front of Marshall and sat down. 'Just about. Page five, two paragraphs, "local man raised the alarm", that sort of thing.'

Marshall nodded towards the screen on the old man's desk. 'Let's see.'

Papa Charlie tapped a couple of keys and turned the screen so Marshall could see page five of the *Chronicle*.

'COOLSVILLE CONFLAGRATION FLAMBÉS FIVE.'

Marshall read quickly through the story in silence, munching determinedly at the Danish. He summed up briefly when he had finished. 'Victims as yet unidentified, no witnesses, local man raises alarm. I hate to tell you, Charlie, but for a claim to fame it's not much of a story.'

Papa Charlie liked about Marshall that he had found many ways to ask what the big deal was. He started to say something, then stopped.

'What is it?' Marshall asked.

'Last night as I woke I thought a car passed the house in the direction of town. It would have to've passed the crash. Why didn't it stop?'

Marshall shrugged. 'Maybe the car passed earlier and woke you for a moment. The crash woke you later and you connected the two – not unusual.'

'I don't think the crash woke me, Marshall, I think the car passing the house did.'

'Did you mention it to the cops?'

Papa Charlie shook his head.

'How serious can you be about it, then? You've been thinking about it all night and all morning, so it seems important. It's probably nothing.'

'Probably.' Papa Charlie looked anything but convinced.

Marshall stood up and walked behind his friend to the coat rack. He placed a reassuring hand on Charlie's shoulder. 'I'm going to see what J.P. wants. Keep your fingers crossed it's good news.'

(ii)

A train arrived as McLemon hit the platform, and he climbed on. His father, Jack, loved the monorail, often walking seven or eight stops for no better reason than to take the train back. Jack said that, futuristically speaking, it was the real thing, and only criticised it to the extent that its design didn't allow for fins. He sold his car the day it went into service, vowing that the next one he bought would be capable of flight, and enquiring of a four-year-old Marshall when he thought they'd be issued with their rayguns.

The train was as fast as it was futuristic and McLemon was walking through the heavy glass doors of WentWest Head Office an hour after his summons was received at the Archive. Being personally acquainted with J.P. he was known by all the doormen and had only to make a cursory show of identifying himself as he made his way to the elevators. He took one to the penthouse and stepped out into the outer office where Josephine, J.P.'s far too beautiful secretary, fielded calls for her boss.

'Morning, Josephine.'

She looked up from the magazine in front of her. 'Hi, Marshall, go ahead in, he's waiting for you.'

'Any idea what's going on?' It was a pointless question and he knew it.

She shook her head. 'I know I have to get him to the Green Room so he can run through his speech before the ceremony and press conference. That's in a half an hour so don't keep him.' J.P. was opening a new wing at WentWest Correctional.

Marshall proceeded without pause to the dark heavy door on his left and hit it twice with his fist. A muffled noise from

71

within gave him to understand that he'd been admitted. He turned the handle and pushed the door in.

J.P. Gillespie wasn't a particularly short man, but his rotundity gave that impression. Marshall had his right profile in view as he stood and looked out of his office window into the bay. His short-cropped red hair clashed with his ruddy, hypertensive complexion, and the excess flesh on his face seemed in danger of obscuring his vision utterly, the way it gathered around the eyes. Marshall knew that he would have had to fork out a month's salary for a suit like J.P.'s, but regardless of the expense he went to, J.P. never looked like anything but a dandified thug. The voice didn't help. J.P. was born into an Irish neighbourhood in New York where he lived until his parents decided to repatriate to Dublin when he was ten years old. His first meaningful interaction with Dublin, as he told it, arrived in the form of a smack in the back of the head from a fruit vendor, upon his voicing the question, 'Hey, Maw, what language is dem broads speakin'?' While it was probably apocryphal the tale was at least original. Marshall was one of the few people who recognised the majority of J.P.'s New York anecdotes as inelegant variations on material stolen from old recordings of George Carlin and Woody Allen, the latter's canon trimmed for tell-tale Jewry and excess of art. J.P. was fiercely proud of his New York origins, imagining for some reason that his American heritage gave him an edge in business. He figured early that it was a good idea to guard the accent jealously, and he fought against the encroachment of Dublin phrasing by keeping a firm idea in his mind of what he thought a New York accent was, and occasionally refreshing this idea from old movies and television. So successful was he that when he emerged from college, aged twenty-two, he was left with an accent that would easily have been at home in a Damon

Runyon yarn. Either way, the effect was less 'Captain of Industry' than 'Bowery Bum'.

'Come in Marshall, sit down.' It came out *Moyshull* and *siddown*, but there was no mistaking the edge of irritation in the man's voice.

'Thanks, J.P.' McLemon was respectfully hesitant. 'What's going on?'

J.P. turned and regarded Marshall silently for a second or two. 'I don't know, Marshall, I was hoping you could tell me.'

McLemon was, to say the least, perplexed. 'Come again, J.P.?'

Gillespie didn't say anything for another few seconds, but sat down slowly and deliberately in his chair and interlaced his fingers on the desk in front of him.

'What do you know about Henri McCambridge-LeMans, Marshall?'

'Virtually nothing, other than he's the Chairman and Chief Exec of WentWest Europe, and he's French.' Marshall wasn't being fully honest. He'd heard talk around the company that McCambridge-LeMans was vanity personified and had a machine for tanning between his toes.

'You didn't know he was arriving in Dublin today?'

'No, J.P.' Again Marshall was being economic. It was widely known throughout the group that the Chairman was bringing over a team of electronic-countermeasures experts to try and foil any attempt the Mantra organisation might make to sabotage the European Cup match later that week. The move was seen as an indication that J.P. had failed in this area, so Marshall didn't think it diplomatic to admit knowledge of it.

'And you have no idea why he might have asked for you to pick him up from the airport?'

'Me, J.P.?'

'Yes, you.'

'Has he mistaken me for one of the chauffeurs?'

'No, McLemon, he knows you work in Record Management. You haven't contacted anyone in the Paris office about . . .' J.P. seemed lost for words for a second, 'about anything?'

McLemon decided enough was enough and showed J.P. the palms of both his hands, 'Look, I don't know what's going on, J.P. I don't know anything about the man other than what I've already told you, and I certainly didn't contact him, or attempt to make contact with him. You know me, J.P., better than you know a lot of the people who work here, and you know I'm not the sneaky type.'

J.P. looked at him intently. 'I know *you're* not, Marshall, but can you speak for that colleague of yours?'

Marshall looked at J.P. as if this wasn't worthy of him, when in fact it was. J.P. was only ever cognisant of Papa Charlie's existence when he met with Marshall, but when he was aware of Papa Charlie he didn't much like it, inasmuch as it reminded him of how wilfully unimpressed Charlie had always seemed in the face of wealth and power, especially J.P.'s.

'Okay, okay,' J.P. finally gave in under Marshall's disapproving gaze. 'I've been under a bit of pressure recently and I'm seeing assassins in every corner. I'm sorry.' He was silent for a few seconds, apparently thinking. 'Look, Marshall, I know why McCambridge-LeMans is here. The quarter-finals of the European Cup are coming up this week. Since WentWest are the main sponsor, he's bringing in some people to try and prevent another Mantra outrage, and make me look like even more of an idiot into the bargain. What I don't know is why he wants to see you. It may turn out to be nothing, a mistake as you say, but as it stands it's exactly the type of loose end I don't like. Now,' Gillespie leaned forward in his chair and was careful not to blink, 'if you can take it that I will arrange funds to put in place a temporary installation of your little project, as per your last submission, can I in return have an assurance that you will report to me anything you think might be relevant in respect of your meeting with McCambridge-LeMans?'

McLemon took a deep breath as quietly and evenly as he could through his nose and crossed the fingers of his left hand at the side of his chair. 'Deal,' he said.

Gillespie stuck out his flabby hand, smiling, 'Always knew you were a team player, Marshall. Thanks a lot.' This wasn't strictly true on J.P.'s part. The fact of the matter was that despite Marshall's friendship with his son Coleman, J.P. thought of him as an untrustworthy potential anarchist, especially in light of the fact that he spent so much time with that other deviant, Papa Charlie McCormack. 'We'd better get you something to pick the Chairman up in.'

'When's he arriving?'

Gillespie looked at his watch. 'His plane's due to land in two hours. You'd better get moving.' He pointed Marshall towards the door and pushed a button on a panel on his desk. 'Josephine, release a car for Marshall to collect the Chairman in.'

'*The* Chairman, J.P.?'

'Yes, Josephine. *The* Chairman.'

'Hadn't we better send a chauffeur?'

'For reasons best known to himself, the Chairman wants McLemon.' And today of all days, J.P. thought, I'm not about to argue with the guy.

(iii)

While stopped in traffic on the way, Marshall searched the car's onboard for images of McCambridge-LeMans so he could recognise him at the airport. The man was quite tall, that or he made it a policy only to be photographed with shorter people; it wasn't unheard of. Looking at the pictures Marshall thought that the Frenchman might have had something to be vain about. He looked to be in his late fifties or early sixties, though Marshall knew he was nearer his mid seventies and that WentWest had blossomed under his chairmanship for over thirty years. His slightly wavy, thick white hair was longer than was generally accepted for business, and the Frenchman brushed it back off his thin, regally creased face, letting it curl just above his shirt collar. In all of the pictures that Marshall found, McCambridge-LeMans wore rectangular gold-rimmed dark glasses.

McLemon pulled into one of the WentWest reserved parking spaces at the airport and went into the first-class arrivals hall. The traffic had been a bitch and McCambridge-LeMans' plane had already landed. The Frenchman, however, was nowhere in sight. McLemon approached the enquiries desk and was directed to the first-class lounge. His quarry was at the bar with a small short-haired woman in a pilot's uniform. McCambridge-LeMans seemed to sense his approach and turned to face him before he was within five metres. Even in the dimly lit lounge the Frenchman wore the shades, and as Marshall got up close, reaching for the Chairman's extended hand, he could see they were as impenetrable as welding goggles.

'Mr McLemon,' the Chairman smiled broadly, 'it is a great pleasure.' McCambridge-LeMans' voice was an even tone of perfect enunciation in a rich French sauce, and his greeting the very soul of sincerity. He was indeed tall, six four or better, and his hand engulfed Marshall's. The Frenchman placed his left hand over their clasped rights and squeezed gently. Marshall couldn't help but like him right off.

'Hello, sir,' Marshall said. They released their respective grips and McLemon, taking a quarter-step back, was surprised to find himself performing a minuscule bow. 'I'm sorry I'm late.'

'Not at all,' the Frenchman waved his hand in dismissal, 'we are early; it is the fault of Sylvie.'

The woman in the uniform turned to Marshall, and gave him a curt nod. She picked up the glass in front of her, drank off its green contents and stepped down from her stool. She looked at McCambridge-LeMans. 'You'll call?' He nodded his assent. She turned to Marshall once more. '*Au revoir, Monsieur* McLemon, *bonne chance*.' A smile touched her lips and she left.

'Please take a seat,' said the Chairman, 'and tell me what can I get you.' He held up a finger and the barman approached, raising his eyebrows in enquiry.

McLemon did as he was bid, and addressed himself directly to the barman as he climbed into the stool opposite the Frenchman. 'Mineral water, thank you.'

'Nonsense!' McCambridge-LeMans shook his head with good-humoured irritation. 'You must have a *drink*!'

'But, sir, I'm driving.' Marshall found himself blinking like a startled animal.

'Sylvie was *flying*, Marshall, but she knows that there is no drinking after death,' he paused conspiratorially, 'and that tomorrow we die.' McCambridge-LeMans patted Marshall on the knee, laughing gently. 'Besides, there are, I am sure, alternatives to your driving.' He held up two fingers to the barman who made his way back to his cocktail shaker.

Marshall smiled at his host. 'What is it we're drinking, sir?'

'Whiskey sours,' said the Frenchman, taking a box of cheroots from his pocket, 'and my name is Henri.'

Marshall nodded. 'Henri,' he repeated. He waved away the offer of a cigar. The two sat in silence as the barman finished his preparations and brought them two more greenish drinks. McCambridge–LeMans made a brief salute with his, which Marshall emulated before sipping attentively. The bitterness took him by surprise, but he was relieved not to taste the whiskey.

'You are no doubt wondering why I have asked you here today, Marshall.'

'Mmm,' Marshall, blinking against the tartness, nodded before swallowing. 'Everyone seemed to think it unusual that you didn't use a chauffeur.'

The expression on the Frenchman's face hardened and Marshall could have sworn that the temperature dropped. 'J.P. was perplexed, no doubt.'

Marshall had to stop himself shrinking away from the look on the Frenchman's face. 'Well,' he said, 'intrigued at least.'

The Chairman laughed. 'Well held, McLemon, well held!'

The validation made him bolder. 'So, Henri, why did you ask me here?'

'Your father is Jacques McLemon?'

Marshall nodded. 'We say "Jack".'

'I was at a genealogical site when I came across his name,' said the Chairman. 'He appeared to be looking into areas I myself was interested in. I mentioned the name in front of someone from Personnel who told me we had a McLemon in Dublin, so I asked you here today, to see if you knew Jacques, which you do.'

Marshall smiled. 'I see.'

'Is your father a genealogist?'

Marshall had an idea the Frenchman already knew. 'Amateur,'

he said. 'He's been tracing the line on his father's side for years now. He seems to think it's something of an enigma. There're a few interesting characters, I'll give him that.' Marshall turned to place his empty glass on the bar. From the edge of his vision he could see McCambridge-LeMans remove his shades and rub at both his eyes, one after the other, with the back of his right hand. When the Chairman turned back to face his companion Marshall's heart missed a beat. Free of the shades he could see the irises of McCambridge-LeMans' eyes, and what he saw stopped his heart in his chest. The Frenchman's irises were of a highly unusual luminescent silver blue. That wasn't in itself what had shocked Marshall. He'd seen it before. In fact, only for a genetic readjustment, they'd have been his eyes too.

'I'd be very interested in meeting your father,' the Chairman was saying. 'You see, I have good reason to believe that we may be related.'

(iv)

It was typical, as far as Officer Tony Eustace was concerned, that he be assigned to the scene of some excitement long after the show was over. It had been the story so far with his career in law enforcement. Another day he might have been more philosophical and reasoned that he was paying his dues, but the extent of his instructions last night really took the biscuit: no one's to touch anything, they told him.

There wasn't anything left around here that anyone would want to touch. The two young forensics guys, who'd been left behind after all the senior people had gone, had taken an early lunch about an hour back. They'd been charged with figuring out how many bodies had been in the vehicle. They'd done a lot of smoking and yawning and looking off into the distance. It was a thing with plain-clothes officers that Eustace had noted in the past, this tendency in the face of gruesome death towards terse indifference. They had been busily practising a sort of Trappist, crime-scene weariness, as though they were approaching their laconism finals. To be fair to them, Eustace fancied they could have eaten doughnuts at an autopsy, as far as keeping a blank expression in the face of horror went; but, as he soon found out, they wanted to tell you all about it just as much as the next guy. Their main problem in establishing the number of occupants was the absolute devastation of the victims. Fragments of bone had been all that was left, and it was going to be a job finding the choicer morsels in the mess the fire brigade had left. For reasons the fire brigade were being a bit tight-lipped about, they had succeeded in employing a water-delivery system of truly awesome power, which had blasted most of the evidence out of the wreckage of the vehicle, off the road and into the bushes alongside it. In the end the forensics officers felt the best way to tell how many people were in the vehicle was to wait until someone reported it missing and work from there. No one in reality gave a shit, this was just another boring traffic accident. All anybody wanted to know was how many bodies and who they were so they could close the file; good police work, no mystery. Police work, they had been told, wasn't like the box, it was like the bank. There was more scope, obviously, to exercise the Will to Power, but this was not something that had been explicitly stated.

Officer Eustace decided to have a cigarette and get a squint at the dailies. He turned the squad car to face the cordoned-off area and sat in the passenger seat (to monitor the possible approach of senior officers) and began scrolling through the *Chronicle* on the vehicle's onboard.

After a few minutes of relative leisure a brisk rapping at the driver's window nearly had Eustace out of his skin. He jerked towards the sound, dropping the smouldering butt of his cigarette at his feet. He was forced to grind it into the carpet so as not to look even more foolish to the young Oriental woman in black who had opened the driver's door and was leaning in and smiling.

'I'm sorry if I startled you,' she said, and he was convinced at that moment that to startle him was precisely what she had meant to do; although even Officer Eustace would have agreed that it was necessary for him to gauge all such impressions in full acknowledgement of his having a *very* suspicious nature.

'I came out to look at the crash site,' the young woman said cheerily. 'I wondered if I might talk to you for a moment.' She was holding out a card which he took. There was a photo of her in the top left-hand corner, black bob, almond brown eyes, cute as a button. *Cute* cute too, he was sure. The card read:

SR. JASMINE YLANG–YLANG

THE VERVAIN SOCIETY

NEW YORK • PARIS • TOKYO

There was fine print a little further down, addresses which he didn't bother with, because he got another start when he found her sitting in the driver's seat with the door closed behind her, waving smoke away from her face, and himself wondering how she got from standing to sitting, from outside to inside, without his noticing. He looked at the card again.

'My mother is an aromatherapist,' he said, holding the card

up to her face and indicating what he regarded as her dubious name with his index finger. She plucked the card from his hand and put it in the small pouch in her sweater, producing in the one fluid movement what he recognised as a passport. She held it open in front of his face just long enough for him to see it was the same girl and the same name; he did not note the country of issue.

'You'll need to know, in that case,' she said, replacing the passport, 'that I do not pronounce the "Y".' She looked at him squarely and blinked once. Her accent was for the most part neutral, redolent of the East but no more. She was darker than Eustace thought Japanese people were, but that might have been because all the Japanese people he ever saw lived in Ireland. She was tall too, one seventy, thereabouts. She blinked once more, calmly.

'I don't think I've ever heard of the Vervain Society,' he said.

'We're a society of educators, mostly. We teach in disadvantaged countries, but we do other things.'

'Such as?'

'The Society is gathering statistics on devastating traffic accidents worldwide, preparing a report on the levels of death and destruction people are willing to accept in order to get from place to place in a hurry. I'm here on other business, but I took the opportunity to visit the scene of something,' she paused, as if unsure of the next word, 'fresh.'

'I can't see, Ms Ylang-Ylang, that visiting the scene of a tragedy like this would be of any greater benefit to a layperson than reading the police report, in terms of gleaning statistics.'

'Perhaps,' she shrugged, ignoring what she felt was an invitation to assert her qualifications. 'Certainly there wasn't much to look at. The fire service seems to have been somewhat heavy-handed.'

Eustace found himself excited all of a sudden. 'Were you inside the cordon?' he demanded.

She cocked her left brow. 'My official answer would have to be, no.'

'You're not allowed –'

'Nothing has been disturbed.' She raised a hand to calm him and looked out the front of the car to the crash scene, drawing his attention there. He felt a bit foolish, getting worked up about it. The yellow and white police tape contained an area of wet black ash and some small debris from the ambulance, which the fire brigade had not bothered to take with them. Forensics' white box van was securely locked. What could she have done?

'Have they identified the dead, or the owner of the vehicle yet?' she asked.

'I'm not sure, I haven't been updated since last night. They don't consult me about much.'

'So you don't have information on the accident circumstances.'

'I don't think anyone does. There were no witnesses.'

'The news said a local man reported the incident. Can you tell me who he was?'

Eustace stiffened a little. 'Mr McCormack has given a full statement, and you're asking, Ms Ylang-Ylang, for more than statistics!' He winced visibly when he realised he'd used the witness's name. It was the only thing they'd given him to do that was of any importance, and the old man had asked him specially to keep his name out of it as far as he could. When he looked at Ms Ylang-Ylang again she had a hand in front of her mouth, and he could see by her eyes she was laughing.

'He doesn't want to be disturbed!' He couldn't help smiling a little himself.

'I'm not the news service, Officer, I'll be discreet. May I have his full name and address?' She was holding a cell ready.

'You didn't hear this from me.'

She input the information he gave her and clipped the cell back onto her belt. The witness, Mr McCormack, lived in the first house along the road behind them and worked in the WentWest building, further back in Maymon Glades proper.

'Would I be correct in assuming that this hasn't been a particularly thorough investigation?'

'What's to investigate? The vehicle crashed, caught fire and people died.'

'When people consider a thing to be routine, they see considerably less than they often should. A lesser-ranked officer would have a better chance of discovering something important under such circumstances. This would be in his interests, no?'

'This is grisly, certainly, but it's still just a car crash. Precious little glory to be had here.'

Sister Jasmine pressed her lips together and made a *hmmm* sound. She produced from her pouch what appeared to be a circular plastic cap or lid, about four centimetres in diameter, of no colour, cloudy. The word 'LEYNER' stood in relief on top and small numbers were cut into the side. 'I found it further up the road,' she nodded ahead, 'about two hundred metres.'

'What is it?' he asked.

'Come now, Officer . . . ?'

'Eustace. Tony Eustace.' He held out his hand, which she ignored.

'Officer Eustace, I expect you to earn *some* of your accolades.'

'You don't actually know that it's anything?'

'Well, maybe,' she was less unsure than she was making out. 'When many of the people you've associated with have worked in disadvantaged countries, you quickly become accustomed to hearing the names of American arms manufacturers.' She was only short of spelling the last three words, so slowly and deliberately did she enunciate them. She opened the car door behind her and climbed out. 'I'll call you in a day or so to see what you've found.' She headed back towards Maymon Glades on foot. He watched her in the rear-view until she disappeared.

(v)

McCambridge-LeMans sat at the bar awaiting the return of his young companion, who had taken a short walk to clear his head and find his brand of cigarettes. He was reading the dailies on a small screen provided by the barman and keeping an eye out for the start of the news so he could see the coverage of J.P.'s press conference on TuMur. All things considered he was pleased with the way his afternoon was going. He had a good reason to give Gillespie a tongue-lashing when he saw him later, and depending on what he saw on the news, he might have something to torment him with too; in addition to which he had managed to locate two distant cousins. The second was bliss to Henri. Marshall's flash of recognition when he'd taken off the sunglasses had been precious. He'd seen instantly the fact of their kinship.

Henri hoped desperately that Marshall would prove to be Dr Julie Bertillion's 'close genetic match', the most recent short-term grail in his quest for immortality, or the closest available life-span. It was a quest Henri and Julie shared. Once they had been lovers, but it hadn't worked out on account of a rather harmless (but to him irritating) power fetish she harboured. They eventually came to an arrangement whereby she was content to serve, and he was content to find her invaluable. That had been more than forty years ago. Julie's medical team, working on the immortality problem, had ordered up the closest blood relation that Henri could find; they specified he should be as young as possible too. Julie told him to think of it as a copy and paste exercise. From the graft they took from his kinsman they were going to regrow him, gradually and slightly differently.

Whatever it was they were going to do, here he was, less than a year later, having cocktails with the prospective donor. That was why, aged seventy-five, he was still the Chairman and CEO of WentWest Europe. He still had more potency than any thirty-five- or forty-year-old MBA anyone cared to stand in his path. Julie of course had helped, had kept him vital all these years. She had great faith in her gift to succeed in this endeavour. She took every treatment he took. At seventy-two she looked a healthy fifty-five. She had had her grandniece in place as her close genetic match since the team formed the idea. Appropriate samples of the girl's genes were already in storage. Julie talked to Henri, with a tantalising frankness, about seeing the start of the next century. He dearly hoped that, in due time, Marshall would consent to the donation. In the meantime Henri was prepared to give the boy anything he wanted, allow him to sample the benefits of a rich and powerful friend.

The trouble with finding the blood relative for Henri was that he had been the only child of two only children, and was orphaned very young. He didn't know if he had any blood relatives alive, and, if so, how distant they'd be. The problems of availability and what Julie's team called 'genetic dilution' had at first seemed insurmountable. Soon after that, he discovered by accident a little trick of his ancestors, how they had trans-mogrified their identities by slightly changing their surnames. He had better luck then. That was the way of it always; things just fell into place for Henri McCambridge-LeMans. When he finally found Marshall, Julie had been ecstatic, imagining they could move ahead with the original plan. When his contin-uing enquiries indicated who Marshall actually was, she was completely dumbstruck.

Marshall McLemon was the first and, so far as anyone knew, only human ever brought to term in an artificial womb. Julie had known one of the doctors responsible. She had a name for him: Spooky. Spooky and the rest of the team responsible for this miraculous feat had vanished less than a year after the successful birth. Interest in the field followed with indecent haste. Julie maintained it was a certainty that Marshall had been 'augmented'. Spooky had been part of a godmaker cult; some referred to them as 'medical deists'. All he ever used to talk about was 'augmentation', '*after* Homo Sapiens' and 'building humanity for the future'. Longevity, she explained, was a clear priority with them and would certainly have been introduced, with other advantages, at a very early stage in the gestation. This was a great find. Whatever Henri lost because of genetic dilution he would more than make up for in engineering. While it remained unspoken and to his mind unfounded, he could sense the expectation from Julie that a detailed investi-gation of young Mr McLemon might yet yield something unforeseen but extraordinary.

The young man himself was endearingly gauche, all thumbs socially, heart-achingly pretentious, far too serious. For all that, he communicated something – innocence, openness – that made you feel safe with him and, at the same time, protective of him. A sense that he trusted everything you told him to be true, and which invited you in turn to be candid with him; a sense that he'd never sit in judgement. Henri would have to be wary of that, he couldn't yet afford to be too honest with the boy. Nevertheless, he looked forward to drawing him out, indulging him; to teaching him to value his instincts, and to helping boost his confidence. He liked to think they'd be together long into the future.

Henri coughed to draw the barman. As he approached there appeared on the small screen in front of Henri the man TuMur had begun calling 'the news anchor to end all news anchors'. Henri ordered a coffee and a sandwich.

Tom Richard looked congenially, but seriously, towards the viewer out of centre screen. 'Good afternoon and welcome to TuMur TV News. I'm Tom Richard.

'Mr J.P. Gillespie today hosted a ceremony at WentWest Correctional Institute to mark the opening of a new maximum-security wing. With Mr Gillespie were The Chief, Dr Jack O'Mahony, and Justice Department supremo David Cahill.

'Following a brief ceremony, Mr Gillespie retired with an entourage of celebrity well-wishers and members of the press to the WentWest Green Room for an informal press conference.'

Tom Richard looked at the screen in his desk as they went to the report. The scene was a wide shot of the Green Room at WentWest Head Office. Reporters and celebrity well-wishers sat in rows of chairs in front of the podium. One of them was half standing, half crouching, with a limp hand in the air to attract attention to himself.

'Mr Gillespie!' he called. 'Ethan Collins from the *Chronicle*.'

'Ethan, please!' J.P. Gillespie, five feet ten, corpulent, red-faced and glowing, leaned too far into the microphone when addressing the reporter, producing a sound full of pops and wheezes which had required considerable softening prior to broadcast. 'You've been barracking me, Ethan, for twenty years now,' Gillespie said. 'I think at this stage you might at least call me J.P.' J.P. looked around him, face set in a wide grin, making sure everyone was enjoying his magnanimity as much as he was. They all appeared to be smiling at least. He looked back to the reporter in the gallery and waved a finger at him. 'And you can take down that arm now, Collins. You're beginning to remind me of my old hometown.' Gillespie looked grinningly about him again, seemingly oblivious to the fact that his Statue of Liberty joke went right over the head of its butt, as it were, not to mention the rest of the assembled audience. The only chuckles came from those sycophants who could recognise when Gillespie was again trying his hand at humour, and were determined to continue in their encouragement of his endeavours. Among these enthusiasts was the producer of the broadcast, who had clearly augmented the disappointing wave of tittering on the soundtrack with several hundred hearty guffaws from a can.

The broadcast action switched back to the studio just in time to catch Tom Richard still looking at the screen in his desk. For a period of three heartbeats a wry smile played on the split lozenge of his lips, set as they were within his granite jaw. It was his demonstration of his own appreciation of Gillespie's élan. The anchorman turned back to the camera, a wrinkle above his sculpted left eyebrow expertly conveying a modicum of gravity, and producing sighs in an unfairly good percentage of his female audience aged twenty-five to fifty.

'While it was generally a celebratory affair,' Tom Richard told his audience in tones of firm admonition, 'Mr Gillespie *was* called upon to answer some tough questions.' The paragon looked briefly to his left, as if ensuring something or someone was secure and in position. 'Anyone wishing to see more of that press conference can access it now using options, or later at our archive.' He paused briefly to introduce a widening of the eyes and a positive wrinkling of the lips. 'I'd advise catching it later, though, and staying with us as we go over to Art Reilly who has some interesting news about the big soccer match on Friday. Art?'

It would have come as no surprise to someone working in demographics that the small number who opted, at that point, to watch the rest of TuMur's coverage of the press conference consisted mostly of professionals and senior management types. Not perhaps all of the stature of Henri McCambridge-LeMans, but similar nevertheless. Men and women who were confident in the never-expressed idea that it was their duty to society to monitor the goings-on in the political, business and wider worlds. That they never found fault with any of it was modestly held by them to be an illustration of the fine job they were all doing. And, since vigilance was ever required in the maintenance of tight ships, these civic spirits often found it necessary that the soccer wait.

'Well, J.P.,' Ethan Collins of the *Chronicle,* still half standing, managed to cough between the two words, 'there's been talk that maybe you're going too far out on a limb with this latest project. Okay, the state is footing half the building costs, but WentWest will have spent twice that in two years if you figure in the maintenance of one hundred and fifty maximum-security prisoners. How are you going to show a profit to a board of directors that you're already rumoured to have frosty relations with, when most experts in the field agree that it's nigh on impossible to get hard cases to work? Short, that is, of employing foul means, which most would assume are not an option in light of last year's allegations of brutality among your prison officers.'

J.P. glowered momentarily at his press secretary before smiling back at Mr Collins from the *Chronicle*. 'Thanks for bringing that up, Ethan, I've been waiting for an opportunity to put that one to bed.

'We had a firm of independent investigators look into that situation and they could not find one piece of supporting evidence to prop up that slander – unless you want to call the testimony of convicted felons *evidence*.' Laughter rippled through the audience. 'As with many of these personal attacks, this one, as we all know, originated in the offices of Channel Ten News, who, despite residing on the lunatic fringe of news reporting, weren't mad enough to actually run a feature. Because you can be assured that if there'd been one iota of twisted truth in the story they'd've had a field day making a two-hour special out of it!' Murmurs of agreement filled the room. J.P. took the opportunity to take a sip from his glass of water.

'As to the rest of it, my relationship with the WentWest board is the same as it's been since day one; that's to say challenging. If challenge begets friction,' J.P. shrugged his shoulders, 'I dunno, sue me – but get used to it.'

J.P. paused. 'I think it's a mistake –' He stopped himself short and with an apologetic wave of his hand asked the audience to disregard the phrase. 'I *know* it's a mistake to view us as a purely profit-driven organisation. Our involvement in this project stems from an honest desire to improve quality of life for these tortured unfortunates. You can't, of course, expect perfection, otherwise we wouldn't need incarceration; but there's always room for improvement. WentWest's investment began three years ago. It's already considerable. We put a team

91

together to look into precisely the problems posed by maximum-security prisoners, and how best to diffuse these problems while channelling the enormous energies of the subjects into a concerted effort to promote internally a greater sense of self-worth and well-being.'

J.P. began counting off on his fingers. 'We've had clinical psychiatrists, motivational psychologists, anthropological behaviour analysts, nutritionists, homeopaths and hypnotists all thinking outside of the box about how to improve things inside.' The beginnings of laughter in the audience were stifled when it became clear that J.P. hadn't intended any humour. 'Now, it wasn't always easy to get these people to agree – I won't lie to you – but the one thing that there was consensus on most readily was the importance of work in the formation of any balanced personality. Their first order of business, therefore, was to develop a system to encourage our prospective clients to explore what we've come to call *el-pee-dubyah*: the Liberating Power of Work.' J.P. leaned on the podium and looked out at the audience, allowing them to soak it all in. 'And,' he waved his right hand dismissively, 'as far as we're concerned, it's onward and upward from there.'

'Can you tell us anything about this system, J.P.?' someone shouted from the back.

'Sorry, boys,' J.P. threw out his arms like Al Jolson, 'the patent hasn't come through yet.'

Ethan Collins thanked J.P. and was about to sit down when he remembered something. He stuck his arm in the air again as he spoke. 'Eh, J.P. It seems to me you could have saved money on the nutritionists by providing *Moose* rations for your, eh, guests.' Laughter again from the audience.

Back in the studio Tom Richard licked his lips unconsciously. Everyone was aware that he endorsed the product, but they would have been surprised to discover that he actually used it. *Moose* – 'juice with a moo' – the hugely popular beverage produced by WentWest Foods, was a milk-based cold drink in various flavours, also available with croutons of a cereal-like substance floating in it which apparently never went soggy. It claimed to be fortified with vitamins and trace elements, and was advertised as being not only tasty and refreshing, but healthy too, and, with the croutons, a worthy surrogate for a missed meal. Tom Richard lived on the stuff.

J.P. Gillespie had brought forty per cent of *Moose* production to Dublin a decade back and was now producing over fifty million units a day for export alone. That crack from the reporter had been a set piece, the price of Ethan Collins' unvetted question. J.P.'s tendency to contrive always to mention how his success with *Moose* had benefited so many had become a bit of a joke, but J.P. in this respect was not proud. The product got a regular mention and the fact that he could be light-heartedly pilloried gave him a more human public image, which, if he was to be honest, he could use.

'That's not a bad idea, Ethan,' J.P. said to the man from the *Chronicle*, and a devilish glint escaped from under his fat eyelids. 'Tell you what, on Monday I'll draft a proposition that says, when this wing's fully operational, every WentWest inmate will get two bottles a day, on me.' The audience cheered and followed with prolonged applause.

Henri McCambridge-LeMans closed the screen and pushed the unit away from him. Free *Moose* for the prisoners had been decided on months back. All they had had to do was come up with a good reason for giving it away, since no one was going to believe in unprovoked goodwill on their part. Henri was chagrined to discover that J.P. had just solved the problem with an ostensibly extravagant gesture, and had done no harm to himself publicly into the bargain. Not for the last time would McCambridge–LeMans remind himself to maintain a high level of respect for Gillespie as an adversary, even if he appeared to be a besuited baboon.

(vi)

It was half past three in the afternoon. Marshall McLemon had four whiskey sours inside him and couldn't have cared less. He sat in the passenger seat of the vehicle he had arrived in. McCambridge–LeMans drove in his shades, though the autumn sun was hidden behind a low and livid canopy and it was fast getting towards dark. He steered with his right hand only. With his left he smoked and gesticulated. For some time now, though, he had been forced into silence, as Marshall, fuelled by the booze, had been putting forth on the construction of his and, the boy kept reminding Henri, Papa Charlie's Exhibit.

For his own part, McLemon kept telling himself that it was okay to discuss the Exhibit with the Chairman. Since J.P. had already okay'd the temporary installation there was nothing underhand in it. He wasn't *trying* to achieve anything, he was just talking about work. But the truth of it was that in the back of Marshall's mind he knew that he didn't place much value on the word of J.P. Gillespie.

'We've been cataloguing, cross-referencing and rating this stuff for five years now, Charlie for ten years before that. There's music, film, scripts and books, television, radio, you name it. A lot of it is really very good. It goes beyond mere entertainment, says something about the way people lived, and still has resonances in how life is today. It's only been separated from us in time, not in meaning. People think that years ago life was different, that you can't appreciate what people in the past liked without studying in detail how it was they lived. I think that's some crap someone thought up to sell people a bunch of shiny new shit, to throw them off, to keep them away from the vast reservoir of meaningful narrative that was becoming available to them during the web's infancy.

'Anyway, I got to thinking about my own part in this relationship, or mine and Charlie's, and I figured that what we are is a biological "link". We can connect people to these narratives, and we can do it efficiently because we know the good from the bad. We've spent the time watching and listening to lots of tripe so that we could discover a few gems. Eventually a few became a few more and the discoveries snowballed.

'When I took the position and met Papa Charlie, he used to groan about the fact that no one seemed to have any appreciation for the older entertainments. They didn't have the appreciation because they didn't know they were there. That was when I started thinking about the Exhibit. I keep calling it that, but in my mind it seems more like a vast museum, bubbling away somewhere on the web.

'And it's not just the work I'm interested in, but the history, the people, the times, technologies, prejudices, the whole shooting match. Take popular music at the turn of the century. The politics and the personalities are a whole lot more interesting than the actual music. The recording industry was grinding to a halt because its target market was comprised almost entirely of children, and the kids' attention had been grabbed by other things, which wasn't surprising since nobody was putting much effort into the music. Record execs and artists alike were running about like headless chickens trying to save their careers in the light of ever-decreasing sales, and were providing better entertainment shafting each other and stabbing each other in the back than the music ever could have. Eventually anyone who was actually interested in buying real music discovered they could get it down the line, direct from the artist. And they didn't have to buy a certain size product, they could select what they liked and skip what they didn't like. Live music came back in a big way: not like the nineteen forties exactly, but it started providing a living again for people who'd gone to the trouble of learning an instrument. As a matter of fact, I'm conducting a series of interviews with a guy who lived through the whole thing, who was responsible in part for the way things are now. He's the leader of the outfit my friend Bluey plays in; a real character. I'm recording all the anecdotes and gossip he can remember for the Exhibit. There'll be selected sounds and songs to ground the Exhibit chronologically, but I'm hoping his stories about the behind-the-scenes shenanigans will be one of the most popular features.'

Marshall stopped and McCambridge-LeMans took as long a look at him as driving would allow. 'I can't see your passion impressing J.P. very much. He was never particularly given to artistic pursuits, and I know first hand that he regards that part of the Archive as a complete waste of space. He took it under duress and stuck it in the deepest hole he could find. He would much rather have had something he could turn a profit on. I'm very surprised to hear he's backing this.'

Marshall looked at McCambridge-LeMans, who appeared to be concentrating on the road. He didn't want to be seen to be shafting J.P., but at the same time he wanted someone in a prominent position to know about the promise J.P. had made. J.P. was notoriously fickle, would make light of reversing or forgetting a given decision. Marshall was afraid something similar might happen. Unless, of course, J.P. knew that McCambridge-LeMans had heard about his undertaking. It was too big a deal, Marshall decided, to be allowed to rest on a whim of J.P.'s. And anyway, he smiled to himself, wasn't blood thicker than water?

'J.P. said that I could have a temporary installation, if I divulged to him everything of interest that transpired between us today.'

The Chairman nodded thoughtfully. 'Up until which point he had been less than interested in your work, yes?'

Marshall shrugged. 'Pretty much.'

'And are you as wary as I, Marshall, of someone who wants to do you a favour only when he needs one in return?'

'I suppose.'

'Nothing has transpired between us that could prove of any conceivable interest to J.P., and nothing is likely to do so in the future; you can be honest on that point. I'll see that you get everything you need to progress what appears to be very worthwhile work, and exhibit it in a permanent form. I think it has fabulous PR potential. And I expect nothing more from you in return, other than for you and your father to join me for dinner some night this week.'

The rest of the drive was conducted in silence. Marshall was fighting a grin that kept threatening to spread across his face. He could hardly believe it. The project would finally go ahead *in permanent form*! He hadn't allowed himself hope under J.P.'s patronage, but now, with the support of the Chairman of WentWest Europe, there was no stopping it. He couldn't wait to see Papa Charlie to tell him.

(vii)

J.P. Gillespie's office door crashed open at the same moment as Josephine buzzed him.

'J.P., the Chairman's here!' Her voice was hurried, agitated, as if McCambridge-LeMans had caught her by surprise, which he had. By the time her finger lifted from the talk-switch the Frenchman was halfway across the room, bearing down on J.P. J.P. jumped to his feet and extended his right hand.

'*Bonjour*, Henri, *mon ami! Comment allez-vous?* Ha hah!' J.P.'s accent rendered his attempts at French odious to the native speaker.

McCambridge-LeMans threw himself into the chair facing J.P.'s desk, then tossed his dark glasses onto the desk, exposing J.P. to his remarkable eyes, revealing the super-cooled rage boiling off the surface of the cold fusion, mercury blue irises.

'There was a time, Gillespie, when I would have been justified in having you executed. I want you to believe me when I say that if execution were an option, it is a task I would undertake personally.' McCambridge-LeMans lit a cheroot, then studied for a prolonged moment the sleeve of his perfectly cut, very dark, grey suit jacket. J.P. knew better than to say anything. Instead he waited, glad of the few moments' silence. He closed the document he'd been scrolling through for inspiration: a list of 'quotes' purporting to originate in Sun Tzu's *The Art of War*. J.P. had scarcely ever read an entire book from cover to cover, including *The Art of War*. But one night, when he was still at college, he had scanned through a translation of the treatise for quotable quotes, adapting them where they didn't quite suit his purposes and compiling from them a list of bastardised aphorisms from which he shamelessly began to spout, attributing all such wisdom to 'the Master'. The only items of solace he'd found before the Frenchman interrupted him were 'Sieges exhaust the strength', and 'He who would win must know when to fight and when not to fight'.

McCambridge-LeMans' impressive physicality and healthy complexion he owed to years of idling on tennis courts and in the man's presence J.P. was conscious of his own corpulence. It was easy to imagine McCambridge-LeMans, even now at his age, sliding into sliced backhands. The bastard must still keep his hand in, as he always looked fit; fit and smug. J.P.'s own wife had noted it, to the extent that she almost climbed into his fancy French lap at last year's Paris dinner; telling him that he had 'an attractive air of cool composure', and picking lint off his lintless dinner jacket. At one point J.P. thought that he was going to have to douse the old cow with the water from the champagne bucket.

'I am at a loss to know how you let this happen, J.P.' The Frenchman turned those points of light his direction again, regarding him with predatory disdain. 'May I assume that necessary steps have been taken to distance us from this embarrassment?'

'Yes, Henri.'

'Tell me what happened.'

'We're still not a hundred per cent sure. It appears that one of our night monitors, Mark Leonard, stunned the doorman and took the ambulance, three of our subjects and his colleague who had been in to relieve him. Why, we don't know. The doorman alerted one of our mobile security units who gave chase, during which the ambulance crashed. Due to the proximity to Maymon Glades they had to assume someone had heard the collision or seen something, and called the emergency services. They were forced to incinerate the bodies in case of autopsy.'

'Everyone in the ambulance died in the crash?'

J.P. squirmed in his chair. 'That hasn't been confirmed as yet.'

McCambridge-LeMans smiled at him without humour. 'I'll be interested to see how you manage to confirm it now.' The Frenchman looked away again, as if to bring his revulsion under control. 'Tell me,' he said, 'just how many mobile security units are you operating?'

Josephine buzzed through at that point from the outside office. 'Mr McCann is on the line, J.P. Shall I put him through?'

J.P. looked at McCambridge-LeMans, who answered her, 'Yes, Josephine, put him through, and then go on home.'

Freeway McCann's image popped up on J.P.'s wall screen.

'Hello, Freeway,' McCambridge-LeMans again took the initiative from J.P. 'What have you to report?'

Freeway had been warned by J.P. of the Chairman's impending arrival and didn't betray any surprise at seeing him. 'I was talking to Mick and Frank, the security unit on duty last night,' he said. 'Something interesting came up. They're partial to various recreational substances which they score from a guy known as the Kid. It seems our Dr Flanagan was into considerable debt with this dealer, who was keen, for reasons not entirely economic, to get her involved in his porno business. He was putting the screws on her pretty hard by their account. She may have been the motivator here, rather than Leonard. The lock to my office has been jimmied,' he lied, 'and three phials of Boxer are missing. I think she may have used some of it to co-opt Leonard.'

'Any ideas where she was going?' McCambridge-LeMans asked.

'Someone in the media. They pay out big and quick, and a smart girl like that could have made this look like a very promising package, even if she didn't know J.P. was involved.'

'You think she did?'

'Yeah. I went over to her apartment and gave it a going-over. Bitch had illegal encryption on her system. I had to rent a military code-breaker to access her files.' Freeway was silent a moment; the expression on his face said he was pleased with himself. 'I turned up two media names; Charlie Murray from VGN, and John Lyons-Howard from Channel Ten.' McCann had picked the addresses up off the floor of the woman's apartment, but he never missed an opportunity to allow his expenditure to show results.

J.P. perked up at the mention of these names. 'Charlie's mine. If she'd contacted Charlie we'd have known about it. It has to have been that fucker Lyons-Howard.'

Freeway nodded on screen. 'Yeah, pretty much as I figured. He's really developed a thing for J.P.'

'Pick up Lyons-Howard and this "Kid".' McCambridge-LeMans pronounced the name as if it were something unclean. 'I'd like to have a word with both of them.' The Chairman was about to terminate their exchange when something else occurred to him. 'And, Freeway, bring along your security unit.' McCann and Gillespie blanched. 'They may yet be in a position to redeem themselves.' He cut the connection.

'Seems to be panning out nicely, all things considered.' J.P. rubbed his sweaty palms together nervously. McCambridge-LeMans closed his eyes and took three deliberately deep breaths by way of telling Gillespie to keep his stupid mouth shut.

'You've been skimping on the security budget, J.P. Your greed is insatiable. It has certainly been your downfall in this matter. How much time have we lost? How much has been exposed here? You must understand that this is a long-term investment; you cannot turn a profit on it overnight. We are attempting to make useful the useless, to help them contribute in some way, and it is a procedure that requires patience, a virtue I advise you to acquire, J.P., and soon.' The Chairman took a long pull at his cheroot, then sighed fumes. 'You have repeatedly failed to put a stop to Mantra's sabotage, making us look like fools, and now this! The board is extremely disappointed.' McCambridge-LeMans threw his hands up. 'And then, at the very depths of my disappointment I chance upon one tiny item of redemption in your character.'

J.P., who had been staring at his shoes, looked up and eyed the Chairman suspiciously.

'I was astounded, J.P.,' McCambridge-LeMans continued, 'to hear that you have become the patron of a noble, yet in all probability a loss-making, enterprise. This . . .' McCambridge-LeMans clicked his fingers as if lost for the *mot juste*, ' "project" of McLemon's, J.P.; I would hardly have credited you with such foresight.'

J.P., in fairness, was not quite the dullard that the Frenchman would have painted him, and sensed something fishy in this. He walked warily around the prize that the Chairman held out to him.

'To be honest, Henri, I haven't paid much attention to his plan, but he's done a lot of work on his own time so I diverted some small funds his direction. Since it appears to be something you approve of, I'll look into it further.'

'I was doing some research into my family history when I stumbled across his father's name. I wanted to set up a meeting with him. It appears we may be related, distantly. Has the boy been with the company long?' McCambridge-LeMans had turned into the soul of affability.

'Four or five years,' Gillespie told him. 'He's a friend of my son. He asked me for the job in Record Management when he left college. I gave it to him 'cause I thought we were going to need someone down there when McCormack, his colleague, retired, but the old boy seems determined to hang on till the bitter end.'

'He also has done a lot of work on the project. I imagine he would like to see it finished,' Henri said thoughtfully. 'It could be excellent PR for us to have something like that in place on the web, but it would have to be very well done.'

J.P. knew what that meant: that meant money.

(viii)

'Jesus!' Papa Charlie McCormack stared in open wonderment at the card in his hand and then back at the young Asian woman who had handed it to him. 'A real live Vervain Mystery Girl!'

Sister Jasmine grimaced. 'We prefer "Sisters of the Vervain Society".'

'I beg your pardon, Sister,' Papa Charlie handed back the card and motioned Sister Jasmine towards the chair McLemon had earlier left in front of his desk. 'I didn't mean to cause offence.'

The term 'Vervain Mystery Girls' had been coined by a US senator twenty years previously, when attempting to implicate the headmistress of a Vervain school for orphans in Gaza in the alleged murder of an Israeli fat cat. The fat cat, who had been disputing ownership of the quarter-acre the Society's ramshackle schoolhouse was built on, had been found dead in a laneway known to be popular with prostitutes, their pimps and their clients. The absence of anything to indicate a cause of death prompted the senator to comment that the sixty-eight-year-old headmistress had undoubtedly lured the man into the lane by means of her womanly wiles, before striking him dead with 'one of those touch-of-death deals' that he felt were an integral part of the Vervain curriculum. The coroner's report stated heart failure to be the cause of death, and added that there was no reason to suspect foul play, a fact upon which the senator did not feel inclined to comment.

The Vervain Society had been founded by a rogue Jesuit, Father Gabriel Vervain. Though few would have believed it, Papa Charlie had, in his early days, considered opting for Jesuitical study. Not that he ever had anything resembling a vocation – a confused socialism, perhaps; vague good intentions, certainly – but the learning and discipline seemed to set them attractively *above* everyone else; like they'd already got a look ahead up the road. It was the idea of being *apart*, more so than *above*, that had eventually scared him off. At the time he was a little ashamed of what he felt was a weakness for society, but in later years he was glad of it, and was happy also that his desire for indoctrination hadn't developed into much. There was the celibacy question back then too; it had begun to fall into disuse, but not as much as he would have needed for his comfort. Not that, in the absence of vows, he'd become Valentino exactly.

In addition to being educators like the Jesuits, the Vervain Society maintained a similar reputation for intellectual superiority. This, and the fact that there was a good deal of secrecy surrounding them, made them immediately and continuingly interesting to Papa Charlie.

'To what do we owe the honour, Sister?' he asked. 'It's rare we get anyone interested in the material we keep here.'

'Actually, Mr McCormack, I had hoped to speak to you about the accident which you reported to the police last night.'

'I see the federalés have been as discreet as ever.'

'In fairness to Officer Eustace, it was more a slip than a deliberate disclosure. In any case I have ordered a copy of the police report, so it would only have been a matter of time.'

Papa Charlie turned to his keyboard and hit a couple of keys. 'I have a copy of my statement here,' he said. 'I'm not sure I can add anything further. What's your interest in this?' Following his discussion with Marshall earlier, Charlie had put his idea about another vehicle being at the scene on a mental back burner. He was excited now at the prospect that this young woman had heard something along similar lines.

'It is not this incident particularly that we are interested in. We are gathering statistics on many fatal motor accidents around the world for a report we are producing entitled *Acceptable Losses*.'

'Oh,' said Papa Charlie.

Sister Jasmine sensed in his body language some disappointment. She put her elbow on the desk. 'Did you feel last night that there was anything,' she paused for a second, '*unusual* seems hardly the right word under the circumstances, but I think you know what I mean.' An almost imperceptible tightening in the muscles around the old man's eyes told Sister Jasmine that he did.

'I think a car going by the house woke me. Regardless of its direction it would have passed the accident. Why didn't it stop? Was it an accident at all?'

Sister Jasmine was recalling the accident scene and the location of Papa Charlie's house. West of Papa Charlie's it was almost eight kilometres before the first turn off that road; east, back into the city, the first turn was about a kilometre.

'You did not mention this to the police?' she asked.

McCormack shook his head. 'I probably should have said that I *believe* I heard a car. I wasn't that lucid and I wouldn't like to burden the cops with my beliefs. Even if I were sure of it, I couldn't identify the vehicle. At the expense of sounding paranoid, I would also prefer not to be foremost in the attention of the authorities for any extended period. I've done my duty. I now wish to fade back into obscurity.

'The elderly, Sister Jasmine, are not much valued in our "strong democracy", and if old is coupled with anything resembling even mild eccentricity, which in this society can often be very innocuous stuff, then the amalgam can interfere, quite frankly, with one's liberty.' Papa Charlie smiled at her. 'And I'm just too old for that shit.'

The Sister looked at him without, she believed, betraying any pity. She had visited places during her training where people had been struggling against something; slavery and co-ercion, usually, of one sort or another. All of the communities she had worked with had been much poorer than any Western democracy, yet they seemed more alive than here, where so many people had given up struggling for *anything*, either out of ignorance or out of fear. In many ways the poor were better off. At least they knew they had a fight on their hands.

Papa Charlie recalled for her his statement to the police. It was terse and factual. He had woken at three fifteen according to his bedside clock. He was aware of a noise out on the road. It was quiet where he lived, at the very edge of Maymon Glades, and a light breeze was blowing eastward. He saw a flickering through the window which alerted him to the possibility of fire. He ventured out to take a closer look, and called the fire brigade and police when he was sure something was burning. They arrived minutes later and he was taken to Maymon Glades Station, where his statement was taken by Officer Eustace, then he was dropped home. Reminded at that point of the somewhat bovine countenance Eustace had presented to her, Sister Jasmine despaired momentarily that he would succeed in turning up anything using the evidence she had given him. She attempted to dispel this dread by telling herself that it would be wrong to judge the man by his unfortunate expression.

'I think you are right, Mr McCormack. I think there was another vehicle which would have passed your house going back towards the city, in order to quickly avoid any connection with the accident.'

Papa Charlie's eyes widened. 'Do you think the police know?'

'No,' she said, 'and there is not much to spark their imaginations. I believe I may have found something worth looking into which I have given them. Perhaps I can talk to you again soon?'

'Of course. Don't get me wrong, Sister,' he said. 'If someone has to answer for this I'll help. I just don't want to be exposed to,' he hooked a thumb over his shoulder, 'that machinery, without good reason.'

Sister Jasmine nodded. 'I understand. I am waiting to speak to Officer Eustace. I will contact you again.' She smiled at him. 'In the meantime I have other work to attend to.'

'May I ask what interests the Vervain Society here?'

'Mantra interests us,' she said.

Papa Charlie seemed surprised. 'The code breakers?'

'Certainly many of us would be interested in how they unravel encryption and cover their tracks so well; but on the whole we are more interested in civil disobedience in general, and we consider this group to be part of that tradition. I've been here more than a month and I've all but finished. However, I'll stay to see if Cypol turn up anything on Friday.'

'Perhaps I can be of more help to you than you think.' Papa Charlie started banging at his keyboard. 'I'm not only a professional archivist, but a compulsive one. I've kept every clipping related to Mantra's activities. They might prove of some interest to you. Do you have your cell?'

Sister Jasmine was touched by the man's thoughtfulness. She handed over her palm unit and walked around Charlie's side of the desk to see his screen.

'Giving away company secrets, P.C.?' A dark-haired young man entered the office, somewhat unsteadily to Sister Jasmine's eye, and looked at her in a way that confirmed the old man's assertion that they did not often receive visitors. Sensitive to many subtle moods, Sister Jasmine recognised that an altruistic response appeared to have been triggered in her upon the appearance of the young man. His features had a high degree of symmetry, his eyes, a doleful grey, were ever so slightly bigger than they ought to have been, and his mouth just a little swollen. He looked younger than he probably was, which helped the trick; the childlike eyes drew sympathy, like the boy in a story she'd read once, whom everyone loved on sight. It was precisely understated. He would never suffer that lack of basic trust the very beautiful fall prey to. Sister Jasmine found the spell falling away as soon as she identified it.

'This is Sister Jasmine Ylang-Ylang, Marshall, of the Vervain Society. She's researching Mantra and I'm contributing my clippings.' Papa Charlie nodded towards Marshall, smiling. 'This is my youthful ward, Sister, Marshall McLemon.' The two shook hands.

'They say this town is full of spies and agents eager for Mantra's expertise; that, or information about their software supplier. I doubt many of them are as open as you, Sister, in their search.' His voice, Sister Jasmine noted, had a pleasingly manly pitch, yet was not at odds with his youthful look. He seemed confident in company without being overeager.

'As I was explaining to Mr McCormack,' she smiled, 'we are more interested in the phenomenon as part of a trend in civil disobedience.' Sister Jasmine took her cell back from Papa Charlie and thanked him, promised to call him the day after and bid them both goodbye.

'Nice-looking,' said McLemon when she'd left. 'You believe that stuff about trends in civil disobedience?'

McCormack looked hard at Marshall. 'I doubt the Sister lies, except in extraordinary circumstances. Have you been drinking?'

'Had a few with Henri McCambridge-LeMans at the airport.'

Papa Charlie whistled. 'Big cheese, McLemon, *big* fucking cheese!'

'Well, P.C., I don't know about anyone else in this town, but you and I, workwise at any rate, are about to move into Coolsville proper!'

(ix)

McCambridge-LeMans stood at the window of his hotel suite looking out over the lights of an apparently silent city. It was the type of view he normally enjoyed, but he found he couldn't get into it this evening. A faint hum in the background, air-conditioning probably, destroyed the absolute nature of the silence, and the room was too warm for him to forget that he was indoors. He closed his eyes and smiled regretfully. Tearing strips off J.P. Gillespie usually left him feeling better. Gillespie's preliminary report, however, had been waiting for him when he arrived at the hotel, and it had taken the edge off his enjoyment. While its bulk was certainly attributable to padded employment records and official documents of questionable relevance, it was nevertheless a thorough and intelligent assessment. He was convinced, moreover, that it represented J.P.'s most concentrated personal output in years. Gillespie was that type of 'leader' whose ongoing success peers and minions alike often wondered at. It was explained by saying he was a great motivator, which, Henri felt, said more about the injudicious rapacity of the waged than it did about any charisma Gillespie might have laid claim to. What the report told Henri, with surprising directness, was that even an apparent baboon like Gillespie needed certain qualities before he could operate successfully, qualities that would allow him to locate and deal with the pressing, prominent issues of the moment. The nose and opposable thumb of middle management. Gillespie had both, with application and nerve thrown in for good measure. It was as well, Henri thought, that he remember some of J.P.'s finer qualities.

The leak at the research facility had so nearly been calamitous. J.P. had included in his report some good background on the producer John Lyons-Howard, and it was with some reluctance that Henri allowed himself to consider what the man might have done with the material at his disposal had he completed his exposé. The background on him said he was very much the maestro when it came to jerking reaction. It was easy for Henri, having studied some short analyses of the man's work, to imagine how the female doctor would have looked: her charm and intelligence beautifully offset by the hint of dissolution, and balanced to rights finally by the promise of essential integrity in her blonde hair and the sprinkling of freckles under her eyes. The male doctor would have served as a mere 'back-up brain', so it didn't matter overly that he looked like a weasel. The WentWest inmates, the savages they had managed to control and utilise, would have been painted as pitiful orphans; the viciousness of their crimes muted; every morsel of deprivation seized upon and highlighted. All the while a grave and frowning reporter would have declaimed nebulous rhetoric allegedly concerning society's responsibility to these poor unfortunates. Images of J.P. Gillespie would have been rendered black and white, almost all of it replayed in painful slow motion, because Lyons–Howard would have known it to be the only way possible, on the one hand, to make J.P. Gillespie seem classy, and, on the other, graceful. There are no two things that indicate evil incarnate better than class and grace, and J.P. Gillespie at normal speed and in living colour was woefully short on both counts.

Whatever way Lyons–Howard went with the finer points, it would have been necessary to programme heavily against it. Current wisdom said that nearly seventy per cent of people expected a little skulduggery in business, so a special sports feature, some big crowd-puller, would draw an audience away from an exposé of corporate corruption. The prison angle was a problem though, since prison and criminality (and especially prison) continued by reason of their lurid nature to be popular topics through all social strata. Even if the media could be encouraged to play it down by concentrating on the legalese surrounding the inmates' implied consent, and WentWest could recover any intellectual property lost to them before their codes were cracked, enough foetid air would have been thrown up to bring a few canny vultures to the same way of thinking. Once someone else was working on a similar project the value halved for sale to the military. While that wouldn't be a disaster, far from it, it would be a lot less satisfying, considering the low overheads and the absence of other research in the field.

Henri walked down into the room's lower level and over to a leather armchair. His cell sat on the low table next to it. He sat in the chair and manually dialled a long number from memory. A hugely overweight man with an enormous grey moustache and a green military jacket appeared on the screen.

'Keane!' The Frenchman greeted his respondent with obvious delight.

'Henri!' General Keane Somerville, as was his manner, looked flabbergasted when he need only have been surprised.

The two men exchanged pleasantries. Henri lamented that the pressures of work kept him so often from his friend's company. General Somerville was deeply touched. In reality it wasn't easy for Henri to see his old friend any more. Somerville had always been eccentric, it had been part of his considerable charm, but in the last decade or more a mental deterioration had set upon him in earnest. They had been quite friendly once, not real close, but genuine. It seemed to Henri that the more time went by the more significance the relationship attained for him.

General Keane Somerville wasn't a real general. He hadn't ever been in any officially recognised army, though he had always been a great enthusiast for military culture. His father was an extremely wealthy and successful politician and had thrust upon Keane at the age of thirty-five an enormous inheritance of land and money. Military-mad Keane immediately launched into the building of a barracks and training ground for a private mercenary force.

In the following fifteen years 'General' Somerville rented his services to shady individuals and corporations alike, and led his men on numerous lucrative 'security operations' from Bogotá to Tianjin.

On his fiftieth birthday Somerville and what was left of his team retired from the field. Back home, he concocted the idea of the Transient Shelter Project. Camps, like his original military training camp, only more comfortable, where people without work or a place to live could be put up, fed and detained until they could be offered the opportunity to interface with prospective employers. This was back when there were many such cases. The lure was the address. If you had the address you could claim the welfare. Only the way Keane saw it was that since it was his address, he'd best decide how to squander the income.

Somerville's father saw to it that the state was happy to foot the bill. He even had the shelters made a legal requirement for those who, for *any* period, were without both work and a domicile. The TSP aggressively pursued their profits. Soon there were one hundred and seventy-five thousand 'clients' to be processed and over one hundred and fifty million a month in welfare payouts to do it with. It wasn't hard making the economies of scale work. Those successes securing a job through the Shelter Project were immediately housed by their employers, but for the first six months they were paid not in hard currency but in vouchers for a certain selection of retail outlets chosen by those employers. For that reason a goodly percentage of TSP 'clients' found it difficult to get out of the system, revisiting their shelter facilities on a twice-yearly basis, each time their six months was up on a job. The employers were lavishly thankful to the Project and the 'clients' in question were just thankful; there were those who never left the shelters at all.

The General had planned the Project so well that in two

years it was running itself, thirty facilities operating like clock-work. He got itchy to do something else and decided to build another military training camp; this time absolutely cutting edge and state-of-the-art. A place where the überkiller could go for a little polish. As lucrative as the TSP was, most of Somerville's battle-weary comrades were soon eager to get out of what they called the 'babysitting mission', and many of them threw them-selves into the training camp with great enthusiasm. As a result the camp expanded to four camps in two years, with a collec-tive reputation for producing and operating the most effective security and military operatives, cradle to grave. The camps were goldmines to boot. As Somerville's eccentricities began to fall outside the boundaries of good taste (for instance when he tried to order a couple of people shot), his colleagues, painfully aware of his high connections but wishing to distance them-selves from a possible scandal, effectively pushed him out of the training camps and back to the TSP. They ceded to him their shares in the Shelter Project, and left him titular head of the training camp so he would accept the 'deal', but Henri could see at the time his friend had been deeply hurt. It seemed also to accelerate his mental decline. Not that the old man had gone completely gaga; he still deserved peers' respect, and every now and then Henri liked to remind him he was part of the gang.

'I wanted to ask a favour of you, Keane.'

'Of course, anything.'

'I have a security detail – two men – that isn't terribly secure. They need a crash course in all the basics, and a fuller under-standing of the term "loyalty". Do you think you could fix something up for me?'

'Starting when?' the General wanted to know.

'As soon as possible. I'd like to start them working off their debt.'

'Are they well motivated?'

'Will compliant do?'

'It's a beautiful quality in a student. If there are only two I'd suggest an initial week or so with one of the instructors for a level-two programming and basic training. Maybe back to half duty then for a fortnight, still bunking at the camp, and training and participating in seminars the rest of the time, then another week living there but doing full duty, and then we'll see.'

'Sounds perfect.' Henri paused. 'I need you to see that the men get a certain refreshment twice a day. Do you know our product *Moose*?'

The General nodded. He knew it but he didn't think much of it, which was strange since you could swallow it.

Henri smiled grimly. 'This is a custom version. I'm supplying it directly. I wouldn't advise anyone else to touch it. More than that I cannot say.' He shrugged. 'Try to think of it as a flourish of black irony, which the fools themselves are doomed to miss.'

General Keane Somerville chuckled. Conspirators together. He loved it.

'Is J.P. still maintaining his usual level of custom to the Project, Keane?' Henri asked.

Somerville nodded vigorously. 'He's always got something. Buys me lunch every now and then. Likes to work with my man McGrory.'

'You may hear from him before the week's out. That TSP brand of persuasion may yet prove useful.'

They said goodbye with Henri making vague promises about dropping in before he returned to Paris.

A little later the lobby buzzed his room to tell him Dr Bertillion was on her way up. He was sharing the suite with Julie, but she lived in fear of interrupting one of his meetings. He moved to a sideboard on his right and put ice in two glasses.

115

He came forward with two whiskeys as the door opened. Dr Bertillion was a tall, slender woman with short, sandy hair, striking in a delicate, fine-featured way. She dropped her bag beside the coat stand inside the door and, unbuttoning her close-fitting jacket, walked to an armchair and fell into it before kicking off her shoes. Henri handed her a drink.

'Thank you,' she said. 'Are there cigarettes?'

McCambridge-LeMans pushed an ornate wooden box towards her. 'How was your trip?' he asked.

She blew out a match and turned her palms up, pulling her shoulders forward as if in pain. 'We were diverted to some tiny airfield north of Dublin because of congestion. If the plane hadn't been so small and almost out of fuel we'd still be airborne, I'm sure. The best they could find to take me into the city was a vehicle somewhat less comfortable than a metal rick-shaw on cobblestones. I'm crippled.' She took a mouthful of the drink and winced swallowing it, then pulled greedily on the cigarette. 'You saw Gillespie, I take it. How bad is it?'

'Three subjects dead. I would say we've lost four months, maybe half a year. The doctors, as you know, weren't key figures. Otherwise it looks okay; we should have everything contained tonight. I'll need you with me. I want two big men as far under as is legal.'

'Fine,' she nodded. 'You met young McLemon also. How did it go? Is he the one?'

Henri smiled. 'Yes, I believe he is. We liked each other, which is nice. He looks encouragingly young for his age. I'll meet the father later in the week. How long will you need the boy when it comes to it?'

'I don't want to tie myself to a time frame, Henri. I have many tests I wish to perform; some may run him down a little. I'd like a month with him at the very least.'

Henri rubbed his chin. 'A month.'

'This isn't going to happen today or tomorrow, Henri. First you need time to gain his trust. He won't be jumping onto the examination table for us this weekend.'

Henri accepted her reprimand.

'You'll also need as much information as the father can recall about the original procedure,' she continued. 'Anything the doctors said. We can't hope for notes or charts, I suppose.'

'I doubt it.'

'Have you had dinner? I'm starved.' Julie picked up her drink and her cigarette and moved towards one of the bedrooms.

'No,' said Henri, 'I'll wait for you.'

(x)

Burnam Lane was well off the main thoroughfare in Maymon Glades, a fact that mattered little to its residents as most of their businesses were in wholesale. For that reason the outlets there tended to forgo window displays, and with a few large stores and a cineplex backing onto it, the Lane featured vast areas of blank concrete, the only relief from which was reinforced frosted glass and functional delivery points. If it was uninteresting by day and unlikely to attract much attention, by night, with all of the shutters rolled down, it was a forbidding place with only two faint points of light: the Nose Bag, a restaurant of the cheap and cheerful variety, and the Blind Pig.

Had it been nearer the heart of Maymon Glades, the Blind Pig would still not have been the place to draw the thirsty shopper or the lunchtime suit. Even the intrepid tourist who had wandered away from the Mall and its tributaries, and was in search of refreshment and a place to find his bearings, would only as a last resort have been tempted down its dank staircase. Clancy, the fat, pink, cane-wielding pig over the door of the club (and therefore at street level), in the horn-rimmed cheaters and pork-pie hat, had certainly attracted considerable attention of a photographic nature from this element, but the establishment itself never took much business as a result. The occasional backpacker, fresh from some Eastern trail and fearless, might brave the seedy stairwell and wander in looking to mix with the 'real town', but he'd be disappointed. A cloud of moral grime would follow him from the door, setting him ill at ease. As he came out of the narrow hallway and into the main room, its atmosphere warm, damp and heavy with tobacco, coffee and hashish, he'd be assailed by one of the many strange sounds the regulars liked to listen to. A snare might shuffle like boots on frost behind a spare bass only there to remind him he had bones, before a trumpet or soprano saxophone, at strange and irregular intervals, would spew out a staccato cluster of honks and squeaks that tore through the smoke and the heat like tiny, sharp, frozen stars. He'd wind up drinking a beer, maybe going solo at one of the pool tables, then he'd leave. Late on a Saturday afternoon he might do better for himself; get to chew the rag with the newer element among regular gig-goers who'd stop in for a drink on their way to feed. Marshall was pretty sure, though, that no one, fresh off any street in any town, would have got much out of an effort to engage any of the Pig's hardcore regulars in conversation. They were off-putting without being threatening in any physical way, being comprised mostly of the musicians who played there and certain of their entourage. A type generally at home in the shade, who tended, even when they had length of bone, towards the weedy. It was a mode of expression they had more than anything that led to the feeling of intimidation. Marshall never saw one of them with his head straight on his shoulders, and recalled how unsettling it had been on first meeting and speaking with them. A constant bobbing accompanied the patient progress of their sparse, drawling conversation. They'd listen with their heads tipped back and eyes lidded, as if everything that came to their ears that wasn't music was in some way suspect; nodding forward they'd be ultra-distant, concentrating on some gothic, polytonal mantra; inclined either side might indicate profound interest or lust. It could move a roomful of assassins to distinct unease, or out-cool a spy convention.

When he'd first been introduced to the Blind Pig by Bluey, Marshall had actually been drawn to this stand-offishness on the part of the regulars. He'd known instinctively that the slightest display of extroversion on his part would only have alienated him further. Being associated with the bandleader, Slide Benson, had been a boon to his easy acceptance, yet even when he'd been introduced to everyone he'd been cautious. If asked for an opinion during a discussion of the merits of a particular set, for instance, he'd say 'I liked', or hedge with 'I preferred', rather than specify something as 'good' or, God forbid, otherwise. He was always careful to point up his dearth of musical ability, quietly indicating that while he'd had some instruction on the keyboard as a boy – knew the clefs, the names of the notes, rudimentary time and a little harmony – his achievements had been marked by mechanical dexterity rather than any real warmth of interpretation. If pressed further he would explain how he had never been able to view the instrument as an extension of himself. The lines of separation between the information on the page and the sound from the instrument were numerous and clearly defined for him: the page to his eyes, his eyes to his brain, his brain to his hands, his hands to the keys. The problems associated with public performance of the simplest tune, he was sure, would have defeated him.

His modesty was appreciated by the musicians. They came to see him as a fellow traveller, a creator, just with a different set of instruments; or that's what they told him.

As Marshall got to know the various musicians better he came to realise that they were ordinary people, as concerned with money and food and a place to live as the next guy. The players' cool he came to see as a product of drug use and the semi-conscious fabrication of a façade, through language and attitude, designed to perpetuate a certain mystique, to keep a barrier between performers and audience even when they weren't on stage. Papa Charlie had laughed when Marshall gave voice to this; he didn't seem to think it was a new thing. Eventually Marshall wrote it up into an entry for the Exhibit, with Papa Charlie helping by giving it some historical context and naming it *Hep Cats' Corner*.

Marshall, still a little woozy from the drinks he'd taken earlier that day, hopped out of a taxi in front of the Pig, paid the driver and ran down the stairwell through the low doorway and out of the rain. Lucy Grant, co-owner of the Blind Pig with Slide Benson, and, for her sins, his girlfriend, was a petite redhead of indeterminate age. She was standing by the ticket kiosk as Marshall entered, and she reached out a hand to him in greeting.

'How are you, Lucy?' said Marshall; they touched cheeks briefly.

'Grand, son. They're just finishing their set. Go on down, I'll see you a little later.'

'Thanks.' Marshall walked on past her, down a narrow corridor on the left, into the main body of the establishment. The room sat a hundred and fifty comfortably, with standing room for about half that again in the bar area. There were considerably fewer present as Marshall arrived. On the stage at the top of the room were the eight musicians comprising Plastic Alto. Coleman 'Bluey' Gillespie was out front, five foot six or seven out of his shoes and as scrawny as his old man, J.P., was fat. Tightly curled, wiry red hair left his scalp in all directions, giving a halo effect under the flashing red and green lights and framing his bright blue eyes, perversely large nose and thin mouth, which looked to be of the type most at home in a sneer. Clarinet in said mouth, Bluey was taking the lead in his own setting of a 'Moonglow'/'Moon River'/'Fly Me to the Moon'/'Blue Moon' medley, which he had entitled *Jupiter Suite*. Slide Benson, the band's founder and leader, was wont to describe the arrangement in his introductory preamble as 'haunting', and sure enough it was funereal in tempo, desolate in timbre, and discordantly eerie in its harmony. The bass was felt more than heard, brought in with slow attack by means of a volume pedal, and much work was called upon from Jean-Paul, the percussionist, in the area of woodblocks, vibra-slap (which Slide called the 'viper-slap' on account of the fact it sounded to him like a 'rattler') and slightly flat bells. It really did feel like it was from another planet. Bluey Gillespie was basically an adequate musician with the sort of good taste that came with a half-decent ear and an awareness of his technical limitations. Bluey had a reputation among the musicians and some of the regulars for excessive cleaning of his instrument, which gave rise to questions regarding his competence. And while Marshall had to admit that Bluey was a little lazy, he always referred the questioner to *Jupiter Suite* on the matter of his friend's ability.

Marshall ordered a beer from an idle waiter and walked to a table at the left of the stage. He sat and checked the display on his cell to ensure his recording equipment – a mini-cam over his left ear and a tiny microphone on his lapel – was all in order, then reattached the unit to his belt. Marshall's drink arrived as Gillespie reeled out a couple of bluesy runs by way of a finishing flourish, took the brief and scattered applause, and stepped off the stage to join him. Bluey flopped into a chair, stretched his legs out under the table and looked around the sparsely populated venue.

'Should be more in for the next set,' he said, and tapped the wood simulation in front of him twice. 'Slide, get me a beer, will you?' he called to a skeletal figure gliding his way from the stage to the bar, before turning back to Marshall with a smirk dimpling his cheek. 'Dad tells me you've been hobnobbing with some of the rich and powerful on the WentWest board of directors.'

'I believe they're *all* rich and powerful on the WentWest board; but,' Marshall went for the full Gallic gargle with the pronunciation, 'I picked up Mizyeu Mackembrazh(uh)-LuMoh(n) from the airport, if that's what you mean. Says he's interested in discussing some point of genealogy with my old man, so the three of us are going to dinner some time this week.'

'Nothing in it for you job-wise then.' Bluey was still smirking.

'Dunno,' Marshall swallowed with a little difficulty, 'see what happens.'

Slide Benson walked from the bar to their table with two beers in his left hand and one to his head. It must have been thirsty work on stage, Marshall figured, as he watched him guzzle the entire bottle without recourse to air. Benson sat down and took a joint from the supply in his breast pocket, which was rumoured to be never-ending. He lit it, inhaled deeply and held the smoke in his lungs, eyes closed, for a full minute, while Marshall and Bluey looked on in amused silence. When the minute was up he tipped his head back and released the smoke into the air directly above him.

'How's it goin', Marshall?' he said, before taking another huge drag, then three short ones, sucking the whole lot down and handing the spliff to Bluey while looking to Marshall for a response.

'Fine, Slide, fine. Yourself?'

Slide, exhaling very slowly, made the so-so sign by rocking his open hand in the air. '"Tired-a livin', scared-a dyin'",' he said finally, looking around him again briefly. 'Y'know the scene.'

Bluey, holding his own lungful of smoke, passed the joint to Marshall with his right hand while lightly slapping Benson on the shoulder with the back of his left to catch his attention, as it had now drifted to the backside of his girlfriend, Lucy. Bluey waited a few seconds before exhaling and speaking.

'Marshall here has come to the notice of the chairman of the board over at WentWest. He may soon be moved up the corporate ladder, maybe even onto the stairs. These interviews you're doing could rise out of obscurity and into the spotlight; could mean great things for the band.'

Marshall took a drag, looked at Slide and shook his head silently to say this was all so much bullshit, but Slide figured he already knew that.

'You wouldn't like it, Bluey,' said Slide. 'People would say the only reason WentWest were giving us a profile was because your name is Gillespie, not because Marshall has friends in high places; and everyone's suspicion would be confirmed that music only provides you with pin money, and that industrial espionage is your main source of income.' Slide laughed.

Bluey laughed after a second, but he squirmed a little too. 'What do you mean?' Marshall wanted to know.

Slide clapped Bluey on the back. 'Last Saturday this genius exposed Jimmy Mead, owner of the Westward Ho! Club, as the scum-sucking thief I always knew him to be.' Slide leaned in, elbows on the table. 'Y'know we're out at Westward Ho! every Saturday as of six months ago. Rather than a fee, we signed a percentage deal with Mead, only to find out he's been holding back on us, door and bar, every week for the entire time . . .' Slide paused and shrugged, 'in all probability.' He tipped his head Bluey's direction. 'I had an idea he'd been leaving us short, but Bluey got the proof. The Saturday before last he leaves his palm unit in Mead's office, "by accident". He rings Mead the next day, says, "I left my cell in your office, but don't worry, I have a spare. I'll shut the one in your office down from here and pick it up next week, if that's okay, your worship." Mead is happy to oblige. What he doesn't know is the "cell" Bluey left behind is a disguised surveillance device which is activated when the unit apparently powers down, and which silently records, in full stereo and glorious technicolor, everything that happens in the office for the next two days; which I'm glad to say included the counting of the receipts from the Saturday night. The entire matter is now in the hands of my bona fide blood-drinking solicitor.'

Marshall looked at Bluey, smiling coolly. 'So the old Bluey G. surveillance fetish has found itself an almost decent use. Gretta Donald will be pleased.'

Slide took his beer bottle from his lips. 'Who's Gretta Donald?'

Marshall smiled sardonically. 'I'll let himself tell you.'

124

The bandleader cocked an eyebrow at Bluey, who shrugged. 'I was young, Slide, I needed the money. I'll tell you about it another time.'

Bluey got up from his seat smiling bitterly at Marshall. 'Oh, and fuck you very much,' he said, and stalked off to the bar to order more beer. Slide and Marshall laughed quietly.

Up at the bar, Bluey was less happy with that last exchange than Slide or Marshall might have imagined. Okay, he'd have preferred that Slide didn't bring up the Jimmy Mead thing in front of Marshall, but he'd meant well. However, Marshall had no business bringing up Gretta Donald; it was so long ago, and it had all very nearly been a complete accident.

Bluey found he'd been touchy around Marshall for some months now. Maybe he was seeing a little more of him than he needed. If he thought about it things had been going slowly downhill ever since he had introduced Marshall to the Pig and he'd started sucking up to Slide and massaging his ego, so as he'd agree to be the subject of the longest series of interviews ever recorded in the history of tedium. Lately this whole business had gone beyond the beyond. The non-stop affirmation of the talent and perfectly correct opinions of Slide Benson had reached sick-making proportions. The worst of it was that flattery was completely unnecessary; it wasn't like Slide was ever going to turn down an opportunity to talk about himself for hours, upon hours, upon hours, on end. Once upon a time Bluey wouldn't have minded, but the old fool was beginning to believe his own self-serving 'hysterical ficts' and to afford himself grotesque airs to boot. Thankfully the whole business was winding down, as Slide was off on three weeks' holiday in the Mediterranean next week, and Marshall's recordings of him were culminating with the taping of Plastic Alto's gig that coming Friday.

When Bluey got back from the bar he couldn't put the beer on the table because the two gobshites were poring over it trying to find a piece of flint that had popped out of Slide's Zippo. After a few more seconds Slide found the flint, fumbled it into his lighter and screwed in the spring. Bluey got the beers down and noticed Lucy making a beeline in their direction, as Slide was preparing to light up a fresh joint with his refurbished lighter.

'You're aware you're back on in twenty minutes?' Lucy said, taking in Slide's lidded eyes and unsteady-even-though-seated posture.

'Oh right!' Slide said, wilfully missing her point. 'We better get some cheese sandwiches and assorted deep-fried snack foods.' Lucy looked at Slide steadily for a second then walked off shaking her head.

'I haven't forgotten about Gretta whatsername,' Benson said to Bluey, lighting the spliff. 'Mead though, that was class. Fucking suits'll get you every time. I seen more than one of them pigs in action, and their favourite place to work, as they say, was in the pit of corruption. Some of these bastards . . .' Slide shook his head as if lost for words. This generally signalled the onset of a yarn. He reclined in his chair and Marshall put a hand discreetly under his jacket and activated his recorder.

'Back when you lads were just twinkles in your mothers' eyes,' Slide said, 'I was starting out with a combo called The Kaffir Kats. There was still a recording industry then – worth billions worldwide – and we got a one-album deal with a label called Bag O'Nails, a subsidiary of one of the three major distributors at the time. The A&R exec assigned to us was a guy over from London, name of Damian Cheesewring.

'Now I'm no altar boy, never was, but Cheesewring had

scum for marrow. He went around the place bullshittin' out of him, constantly wired, or drunk, or both, without so much as one wrong note in his head and all the business acumen of an Arctic trout. Got the job, I figure, 'cause his old man was well to do,' Slide gave an apologetic look in Bluey's direction, 'and because he had something going with a bigwig in the mother company. Both public school boys I believe. He claimed bisexuality, Damian, but he was less an all-rounder than he was "not fussy", if you take my meaning.' Slide looked as if he still couldn't fathom the depths of depravity. 'You wouldn't've left this cat alone with your *dog*.

'We were in the green room at the Boom Club, entertaining some friends after a gig one night – all of us out of our gourds. I went back to the dressing room to try and find my hand-carved ivory hash pipe, so I could impress the pants off a Dutch young-one who'd joined us after the show. I caught Damian in the dressing room with a plastic bag over his head, a cord around his neck and a snootful of Bolivian marching powder, trying to slip it to Mikey, our bass player, who was incapacitated 'cause Damian had spiked him with Rohypnol.

'Anyway, I chased the fucker out of there, and what does he do, only shows up at rehearsals two days later like nothin' happened. Mikey knocked him on his arse for his trouble and Cheesewring reported back to the company, whereupon Mikey was promptly terminated, because assaulting an employee of the company constituted a breach of contract. Interestingly that clause did not work in reverse, so Mikey tried to have criminal charges brought against Damian to see if he could bargain his way back. Damian talks the fucking company into buying off the federalés, who give Mikey the choice, pretty much, of emigrating with a clean record or staying and facing assault charges of his own.

'The rest of us were gonna call it a day, but the company insisted on getting their album before we went. God knows why, wasn't like that many people had ever heard of us. We ended up cutting seventy minutes of deliberately abstruse, mostly atonal, freeform fusion for them. Three pieces in all, collectively entitled *Discombobulation*.

'Best part, though, was that we got Mikey to play the bass on everything, and not by remote either; barely such a thing at the time. We put in a phoney budget request – apparently signed by Cheesewring and dated prior to Mikey's termination – which we fully expected to be shredded, but which some gobshite authorised. We wound up recording the album in a studio in Berlin, where Mikey was living. The hotel bills alone came to twenty-five grand for the month; studio and tape costs were about twice that; and we got rid of almost ten grand on incidentals like limos, drugs, entertainment, what have you.' Slide laughed. 'All old money too. The "album", such as it was, never got a release, and I lost the only copy of the recording I ever had years ago. Cheesewring, who had been so out of his mind for so long that he couldn't say for sure whether or not he had signed and submitted the budget request, had a complete nervous breakdown and got thrown out when they discovered he'd been doing deals with his artists' agents: agreeing with the agent to tell the artist that they got, say, a fifty-grand advance, when it might be sixty or seventy, and Cheesewring and the agent would split the surplus. He was in and out of court for a couple of years after, until the mother company finally went under.'

'I know Bag O'Nails,' said Marshall. 'I logged their catalogue into the WentWest Archive a few years back. We must have collected the salvage when the holding company went bust. I could probably get you a copy of the recording.'

'A few years ago, McLemon? How the fuck do you remember stuff like that?' said Benson, who was nevertheless interested in hearing his fledgling efforts again.

'People might well wonder how you remember yer fuckin' *name*, loverboy, the things you do to your head.' It was Lucy with beer and food. 'These are your last before the next set boys, 'cept for you, chicken,' she ran a finger through Marshall's hair, 'and you're finished with this shit too, Benson, for the time being.' She took the joint, which had gone out during his monologue, from the ashtray in front of Slide and lit it for herself. 'Talk to you later.' Benson watched her strumpet's gait as far as the bar, then turned back to the food and grunted appreciatively.

'Oh yeah.' Something had occurred to Slide; he looked directly at Marshall. 'See if you can get me that, eh . . .' he described circles in the air with his index finger, rewinding to the *Discombobulation* masters, 'other thing.'

Marshall nodded. He rescued a foil bag of MSG Surprise from the tray just before Slide and Bluey descended on it, and pushed his chair back from the table so that he could stretch out his legs. The two boys stared straight ahead and munched silently.

Slide, Marshall thought, was long overdue his holiday. He looked as if he hadn't seen the light of day since the turn of the century. With his scrawny neck disappearing into his faded black T-shirt and his bony arms holding the sandwich in front of his face, he looked like a distant relation of the undead; a beer/cheese/flavour enhancer E621 vampire, staving off the maddening prospect of immortality with soft drugs and music. He didn't look his age either, despite everything. His full head of unkempt, grizzled hair, his extraordinary thinness, and the years of regular if unspectacularly moderate abuse, left him looking misused and dried out, but still in his late thirties. In fact he had been known on the music scene in Dublin, London and Berlin for nearly thirty years now, the earliest part of his career having coincided with the decline and eventual collapse of what had been the recording industry.

Robert Benson III was, like Bluey, the product of a privileged upbringing; his father, Bobby Junior, having inherited the lucrative True Grit Bathsalts empire from his father before him. Young Robert was enrolled at the Midvale School for Gifted Children following his primary education (although even Slide would agree that his gifted status was perpetuated by his father's contributions to the school), where he took, in addition to the normal curriculum, courses in 'Rock: The Serial Abuse of Rhythm and Blues'; 'Mavericks of Contemporary Popular Music'; and 'Advanced Blasphemy with the Electric Guitar'. Following graduation at the age of eighteen, and to his family's horror, he met and married the glamour model and actress, Francesca Fumer, a woman some years his senior and many IQ points his better. The marriage was short-lived and, for Benson, a painful affair. As soon as he reached his majority, and with it full access to the trust fund set up for him years before, Francesca filed for divorce. She took half of the trust fund and hightailed it for foreign climes, leaving behind a somewhat embittered Benson. 'It was fun while it lasted/I'm a cold embittered bastard/And I'm gonna drink that bitch out of my mind', was his country-flavoured commemoration of the affair, and the song remained in his set to this very day. Back in the past, Benson sensibly threw himself into his work, and less sensibly into low-grade abuse of alcohol and drugs. It was about this time he got involved with The Kaffir Kats and Damian Cheesewring.

He had more success a couple of years later with The Jackson

Whites, a mainstream outfit which did good business out of a short resurgence in public interest for well-crafted, catchy pop tunes. The Whites released three records in just over a year, which was considered a colossal work rate at the time and brought no small amount of critical suspicion as to their 'credibility'. The recordings sold well enough (particularly *Reflections on the Coca-Colonization*, which did over a million worldwide) that Benson more than recouped whatever he had lost at the hands of Ms Fumer – financially speaking anyway. He farmed much of his earnings into a small studio with a big live room, and did well by anticipating the defection from mainstream record companies of serious music enthusiasts, who favoured recordings of live music performed by flesh and blood musicians, which Benson distributed down the line on the fledgling web. With a good financial base he was enabled to put together his own outfit at last, and exploit the old standards which were kept from an entire generation by format FM radio and music television; and a few of which, tantalisingly, had entered the public domain, leaving no royalties payable. (Whatever Benson may have been, he remained the product of a wealthy background.) This outfit, called, somewhat pretentiously, Perpetual Pentecost, lasted for seven years, commanding a good deal of respect from its audience and peers alike, although gleaning only modest returns for its efforts. As the band members headed into their mid thirties and began to think about settling down, many of them opted for more lucrative career choices and Slide had to start from scratch with a different generation of musicians. So began Plastic Alto, which had been a going concern ever since and had survived many personnel changes. Bluey Gillespie had come on board three years previously, and Marshall began attending their gigs regularly, especially at the Pig, round about then.

Slide's voice brought Marshall out of his reverie, and he was glad to find he'd left the recorder running, as he appeared to have missed something. As he focused though, he recognised this as an old theme of Slide's which he'd heard a number of times, and was sure he had a version or two of on disk.

'It seemed ridiculous to me at the time,' Slide was saying to a bored-looking Bluey, 'to assign labels of distinction, or to apply such grave terms as "discipline", or "art", to composition that anyone with half a mind to do *could* do – anyone with a few hours to spare and the unmitigated gall to refer to the resultant conglomeration of digitised noise as *music*. Work that represents, in the final analysis, the efforts of hobbyists.' He shrugged as if in wounded disbelief. 'Yet that's exactly what happened. A generation of kids woke up one morning and asked themselves why they should pay separately for something which already existed as jingles and as the soundtracks to games, TV and movies, and in the blurred areas of "development" between these bright bands on the entertainment spectrum; something any click-and-drag artist could do if he bought the software and the samples. The kids started taking what music they wanted off the web instead, for free. Only corporate entities, if they wanted it, had to pay for the stuff. And every kid who wanted to had his electronic étude posted there. It became impossible to predict or control what would be popular next. In addition, the composers seemed disinclined to approach the limelight, especially when the number of stalkings and assassinations began to get seriously worrisome. They just took the money. The absence of an attendant personality left the work in the embarrassing position of having to sustain its own reputation as "great", which in the majority of cases it wasn't able to do for very long. Seekers after celebrity eventually lost interest, and the musicians – who'd never gone away – were left: the good, the talented and the virtuosi; slaves, slackers and savants; drunk, stoned and sober – pretty much like the civil service.

'If the musicians did nothing else at least they spared us those extravaganzas where a bunch of technicians gave each other prizes for work which, side by side with the real thing, was of about as much consequence as a fart in a force-ten gale.' Slide put up the palms of his hands and shook his head as if someone had complained. 'That's what used to happen; with support from critics who, if they knew anything, should've known better. And of course by the TV people, who to my mind never knew shit from Shinola anyway. I'm not saying that in the long run techs didn't contribute something musical, of course they did – but mostly by accident. Techs support the body of talent in a given field, or they should. Most would agree that it would be unrealistic to expect them to support the discipline artistically over a protracted period, but that's what went on, for decades!'

Slide sank back into his chair, out of breath and anything further to say. He looked at McLemon as if to ask, 'How was that?' and Marshall returned a look he hoped was affirmative. Seemingly satisfied, Slide cast a glance in the direction of the stage, where the other musicians were drifting back to check instruments and readouts.

'Suppose we better get back to it,' he said to Bluey.

Gillespie turned to Marshall. 'You hanging around?'

'I've got a closed session with Slide next break,' he said, 'then I have to split; early start tomorrow.'

'Right,' Bluey said, a suggestion of dejection apparent. 'I'll prob'ly talk to you. Take it easy.'

'If I get it easy, Coleman,' Marshall smiled and tried unsuccessfully to meet his friend's eye, 'I might go the double.'

(xi)

Freeway McCann finally caught up with John Lyons-Howard at the airport; walked up to him in the departure lounge, cool as you like. Lyons-Howard knew that there was no sense in making a scene. If McCann was approaching him in this easy fashion, he had to assume that whatever this was it was a done deal. Best to play along and not force any issues. McCann, as respectful as he was relaxed, made a polite request for Lyons-Howard to accompany him to a meeting with Mr J.P. Gillespie. The way he put it Lyons-Howard almost felt as if he had a choice. They went through a door marked for security personnel only, out onto what appeared to be part of a runway. A limo glided up beside them and McCann opened the back door for him and climbed in behind.

'Sorry to have disturbed your plans,' he said. 'We're not keeping you from anything urgent, are we?'

Lyons-Howard was still stumped by the sarcasm-free delivery. 'A couple of small things needed looking into in London,' he finally managed. 'The trip was predominantly personal.'

McCann gave him to think that he understood by pressing his lips together tightly and nodding. 'We'll have you back on track very shortly.'

Lyons-Howard, beneath his calm exterior, had been trying to get himself used to the idea that, in all likelihood, he was as good as dead. McCann's last utterance, however – his entire demeanour in fact – seemed to indicate possibilities he had not thought to entertain.

'Do you have anything to drink here?' he asked, feeling he had very little to lose by it.

'Certainly.' The mini-bar was in the floor between them;

McCann opened it. 'What do you want?' Lyons-Howard was thinking that if McCann wasn't so big he'd make great cabin crew.

'Vodka and tonic.' He watched as the big man poured and served his drink, imagining him in a deflated life-jacket, indicating the positions of the emergency exits prior to the long haul somewhere safe and far away. He had to extinguish the image. He didn't want to get too cocky. Instead he cursed himself for not moving faster earlier in the day. One hour, even half an hour, would have done it. He'd been too much consumed with the idea of not *looking* like he was bolting. He'd played it too cool. Half an hour earlier and he'd have been collecting his baggage in London now. He took a long pull from his glass and settled into the seat, feeling the drink's initial cold turn quickly alcohol-warm in his gut. McCann hadn't been stingy with the vodka, which, he supposed, could mean a number of things.

'Smoke?' McCann held out a pack.

Lyons-Howard hadn't ever tried smoking. He reached over. 'Why not?'

They arrived at their destination some twenty minutes later. The place looked to Lyons-Howard like an industrial estate, which didn't surprise him much. His spirits had sunk again by the time the vehicle stopped and they were called upon to get out in front of one of the many identical red brick units. McCann walked to a door on the right-hand side of the low building and held it open for him. He stepped into a makeshift hallway constructed of pressboard hoarding and lit with fluorescents. A narrow corridor ran off to his right and ended in another door. An authoritative foreign voice assailed him from that direction; French.

'We are in here, Mr Lyons-Howard, please join us.'

McCann had left him with the cigarettes. He lit one and

walked to the door, opened it and stepped through. His knees gave a little when he saw the bodies in two of the chairs in front of him, but he got it together quickly and he didn't think anyone had noticed. He took a drag at the cigarette to calm himself, but the blasted thing had turned on him and was making him dizzy. He squinted through the smoke he was making at the two bodies. They were thrown backward in their chairs and each appeared to have been shot through the forehead; their hands were cuffed behind their backs. There was a third chair containing a little ugly guy who looked as if he'd been dragged backward through a hedge. He was cuffed and gagged and had all the appearance of a man with a lot on his mind. Lyons-Howard decided it must be Kiely's dealer, Kid C. He was glad they didn't know each other. The fat redhead over to the right, out of the light and almost in the middle of the floor, that was Gillespie. He was talking to someone quietly on a cell, apparently oblivious to Lyons-Howard's arrival. Out of the centre-left of his field a big tanned white-haired man in shades approached, his hand out. Lyons-Howard clumsily moved his cigarette from his right to his left hand so as he could shake. If Lyons-Howard had been in a boardroom he would have described the way the Frenchman took his hand as warm and sincere.

'I am Henri McCambridge-LeMans, Mr Lyons-Howard.' The Frenchman looked at the cigarette in Lyons-Howard's hand, then at Gillespie. 'Bring an ashtray, J.P., would you?' He turned and stood beside Lyons-Howard to regard the three people in front of them, silently. J.P. arrived with a floor-standing ashtray which he placed between the two of them before taking a position on McCambridge-LeMans' left. The Frenchman produced and lit a cheroot, then drew Lyons-Howard's attention to the two dead bodies with its smoking tip.

'These are the men responsible for the crash last night. Their duty was clear, to detain our runaways in order that J.P. could attend to their grievances. Instead five valuable people are dead, and our position in this matter is in danger of exposure. All placing in jeopardy a considerable investment.' McCambridge-LeMans turned to face Lyons-Howard, his arms crossed across his chest. 'Exposure is your stock-in-trade, Mr Lyons-Howard, is it not?'

Lyons-Howard nodded.

'Don't get me wrong, I understand your position. Business is, after all, business. But surely you can appreciate that at this delicate juncture I require certain assurances from you with regard to any further exposure of what you know about our work at the clinic.'

Lyons-Howard swallowed hard. 'What sort of assurances?' he asked, and while there was the slightest tremor in his voice, he thought he sounded more confident than his gagged compatriot looked. The Kid was endeavouring to move away from them by pushing his chair backward. He was alternately shaking his head, and trying to bury it in his chest; saying, with the limited facilities available to him, that he did not need to hear anything that transpired between them. While this happened Gillespie spoke softly but quickly to McCambridge-LeMans. Lyons-Howard was left to watch the Kid try to writhe pathetically towards the back of the room. After Gillespie had finished his report, McCambridge-LeMans put his right arm across Lyons-Howard's shoulders and motioned him towards the door he had come in through a few minutes back.

'I'd like to get you onside, John – do you mind if I call you John?' The Frenchman did not wait for an answer. 'You have valuable experience in the communications business that would be of great benefit to us at WentWest. As a matter of fact there's a young man in our Archive who is undertaking a very interesting project which I am sure would benefit from your expertise. It's a labour of love which will undoubtedly win us some very good PR. However, if there's the possibility of turning a harder profit on it, tastefully, I'd like to see it developed . . .

'Take a few days to arrange your affairs with Channel Ten. We'll contact them to tell them you're coming across, so you won't encounter any contractual problems.' Henri handed him a card. 'Freeway is outside, he has a car for you, and he has booked you a flight to London together with a suite. Take a few days for yourself also. You'll quickly learn to appreciate the good things you have, and can continue to have, long into the future.' It was as if he were speaking to some recalcitrant schoolboy. Lyons–Howard found the tone strangely comforting. The Frenchman didn't have any faith in him as an adversary, he felt sure of that, surer than he was about *being* an adversary. He was a bit confused on that score. It didn't seem as though Gillespie was directly responsible for Kiely's death, as he had assumed initially when his runner had returned with news of the crash. The men who were responsible had paid, it seemed, and dearly.

McCambridge–LeMans was staring at him benevolently, nodding and making a compressed smile of understanding. 'I'll call you in a day or so,' he said. He turned and walked back through the door, leaving Lyons–Howard alone in the corridor again.

(xii)

McCambridge-LeMans walked back into the main room. He would have liked to have been surer about Lyons-Howard. If J.P. had had his way the producer would be dead already. For J.P., 'it's a jungle out there' had ceased to be a metaphor years ago. The Frenchman hoped that Lyons-Howard knew the worst rumours about J.P. were true, and would therefore be thankful for his life and decent enough to play along. Besides, having opposed J.P. on the debriefing and assassination initiative, it would be tiresome to have to think of an alternative should Lyons-Howard not wish to contribute.

The Kid appeared to Henri to have reached his peak of excitement. His piggy eyes were on stalks and he was rigid in his chair. McCambridge-LeMans took a chair from against the wall, placed it in front of the Kid and straddled it. He produced a pair of scissors and pushed one of its blades up between the Kid's face and the gag, pulling it away from the Kid with a smooth sawing motion. J.P. put a bucket at the Kid's feet into which he spat the gag. He attempted to speak, but McCambridge-LeMans raised a finger to silence him. J.P. released the Kid's cuffs and arrived at his side a few moments later with a glass of water.

'Rinse,' McCambridge-LeMans instructed him, 'spit, and drink if you need.' The Kid did so, thinking it was very nice of them to consider it. He'd nearly shit himself when he'd seen the scissors, but he was a good deal calmer now. For a gangster, the Kid was actually a piss-poor performer when it came to violence; he really didn't like it much. Naturally he felt that, as a gangster, it had been in his interest to conceal this sensitive edge. That's not to say that he didn't feel the mettle of the hardest gangster might be tested by being flanked for an hour by two corpses, but just at the moment the Kid would gladly have put his name to a self-help programme entitled 'How to be Chicken *and* Succeed in the Criminal Underworld', if only he were allowed to go home.

'People don't understand sometimes,' the Frenchman said to him, 'when they talk about Hobson's choice, and they say it is "no choice at all". It is not so. There is clearly a choice: a choice between *that which is offered* and nothing.'

The Kid didn't quite know what he was talking about but was prepared, for the time being, to listen to anything.

'It is perhaps best to remember,' McCambridge-LeMans continued, 'as our friends here readily testify,' he gestured with open hands toward the corpses on either side of him; the Kid was reminded of a priest, 'that the *nothing* on offer today is spelled with a capital "n".' J.P. arrived at his side with a brief-case. 'How much did the woman owe you?'

'It doesn't matter,' said the Kid.

McCambridge-LeMans insisted, 'How much?'

'Eighty grand.'

The Frenchman took the briefcase, opened it and extracted four bundles of cash which he threw in the Kid's lap. 'Regard it as a retainer. I suspect you have your uses, Mr Kid, is it not so?'

'Absolutely!' the Kid agreed.

'Excellent. We can always use a good man.' The Frenchman got up from his chair and handed J.P. the scissors. 'If you go with Mr Gillespie he will brief you.'

When Gillespie and the Kid had left, Julie Bertillion approached the Chairman from the darkness in the far left of the room. She was dressed in a white doctor's coat and was brandishing a hypo.

McCambridge-LeMans pointed at Mick and Frank in the chairs. 'How long before they can walk out to the car?'

The shrug which accompanied Dr Bertillion's warning was redolent of insolence. 'Henri, I can have them jogging for you in five minutes' time, if that is your wish, but they will pay. For all such treatment, eventually, they will pay.'

McCambridge-LeMans' nose wrinkled as he peeled away the bogus wound from Mick's forehead. 'A stately pace will be fine for the moment, Julie. From now on treat them as you would any of my investments. Mr McCann will come for them in fifteen minutes.' He walked out into the corridor and towards the front door, buttoning his jacket and burying his left hand deep in his trouser pocket against the cold.

Freeway was waiting outside the door. He'd been wanting to ask the Chairman about Mick and Frank. He didn't feel it was an unreasonable request, yet found himself nervous about making it.

'What . . . sir,' he finally managed, 'is going to happen to Mick and Frank?'

'Mick and Frank, Freeway, remain in my debt,' said McCambridge-LeMans. 'I want you to collect them from Dr Bertillion in fifteen minutes, bring them to the office, take full inventory of their holdings and everything accruing to them in the foreseeable future, and have them sign a couple of contracts that say I own both of their worthless hides. Don't take too long about it, I'll want to speak to them tomorrow.'

Son of Lemon

TuMur Lite Radio News

PROGRAMME: Staines at 7.
DATE: Wednesday, 18th October.

STEVE: It's [time nearest minute], Wednesday.
               You're tuned to TuMur.

CUE: Oh what a beautiful morning FX311.
               2"

STEVE: Dry today, clearing a little in the
               east, but temperatures not getting
               above nine or ten. It's winter folks,
               in all but name, get used to it.

CUE: Don't think I can take much more of
               this FX339. 2"

STEVE: Three-time Booker winner, Frank
               Tierney, spoke to reporters last night
               from Hollywood, where a number of the
               major studios are courting him for
               the rights to his latest blockbuster.
               In addition to talking ritz and glitz,
               Frank tells how he never actually
               wanted to write, it was something his
               wife pushed him into. Are we meant
               to feel sorry for this guy?

CUE: Track 1. 3'15"

FULL FADE UP

(i)

J.P. Gillespie sat in his office awaiting the arrival of his son Coleman. He had summoned the boy more than two hours previously and the wait had left him tetchy and irritable. McCambridge-LeMans' close proximity wasn't helping either. The Chairman's adversity had always been a given, but J.P. liked it better when he could deal with it at a distance. Having the son of a bitch standing over his shoulder, operating in the unhealthy field of those terrible eyes, was a royal pain in the ass.

He browsed the surface of his desk, looking for something to do while he waited. Between yesterday and today he'd been as busy as he'd been in years. He'd almost forgotten how good was the sense of accomplishment. A fresh batch of recruits was being organised from the new wing at WentWest Correctional so that they could restart the Boxer trials. Upon his arrival this morning he discovered that Henri had foisted new security measures on him. They cost five times what he'd been spending previously, but J.P. had implemented them without question to avoid locking antlers with the Frenchman again. McCambridge-LeMans also had him use his influence with the police to ensure that no investigation or coroner's inquest followed the crash. He hadn't liked exposing himself in that way, but it had turned out okay. He'd hastily arranged a meeting with Twomey Fitzstrickland, the chief of police, that morning, with an apparently distraught Dr Julie Bertillion in tow. Dr Bertillion, in addition to feigning upset, pretended to be less than fluent in English, in order to justify J.P.'s presence. J.P. explained to Fitzstrickland that Julie was heading up an 'environment and nutrition' project on WentWest's behalf and that the ambulance had belonged to her clinic. In accents that would have embarrassed a vaudevillian, Dr Bertillion suggested that some emergency must have arisen 'durink ze nayt', but that they 'deed not naow ze natoore off eet', going on to suggest that at this stage they weren't ever likely to find out. She tearfully bemoaned the loss of her talented medical staff and her faithful subjects. It was some performance. J.P. figured a half-litre in snot and salt water went into three of his heavy cotton handkerchiefs.

Fitzstrickland, expertly filleted of all inquisitiveness, knelt before the distressed doctor, patting her gloved hands and her silk-stockinged knees, assuring her that everything would be okay. Dr Bertillion wondered aloud how she could face the bereaved at the inquest. Fitzstrickland wondered what purpose an inquest would serve at this juncture. J.P. took Fitzstrickland aside and warned him that he shouldn't make promises he wouldn't be able to keep. Fitzstrickland said not to worry and to leave it to him. It occurred to Fitzstrickland to ask if WentWest were sponsoring the soccer next season. J.P. said he had pan-European season tickets available with flights, room and board included; first-class all the way. Fitzstrickland said they sounded fabulous but he couldn't afford a bargain even. J.P. assured him that he could.

All in all it was a small victory in an episode that had undoubtedly done him a great deal of damage with the WentWest board and pushed his dreams of chairmanship back years. In addition he'd given the Frenchman a chance to beat his chest and tear up the underbrush, which left the old codger looking as vigorous as ever.

Rather disquietingly, Henri hadn't once brought up this scheme of his to rumble Mantra before the big game this week. The Frenchman seemed more interested in playing buddy-buddy with the McLemon kid while proposing to siphon off even more of J.P.'s budget to fund that ridiculous Exhibit. What the fuck could McCambridge-LeMans want with the boy? He'd listened to that codswallop about them being distantly related, and while there may well have been truth in it, he was sure there had to be more; and none of it, he was certain, favourable to his position.

On the upside, he had to admit that the adversity had him feeling sharper than he had for a long time. Routine had left him mentally flabby. Things had been coming too easily and complacency had brought near disaster. If he was going to get out of this he would have to be alert, cagey and, when the time came, ruthless.

He was about to ask Josephine if there'd been any news of his son, when she buzzed him from the outside office to tell him that the Chairman was on the line. J.P. sighed; this wasn't going to improve his mood, but Josephine patched him through nevertheless.

'Good morning, J.P.,' McCambridge-LeMans groaned. The Frenchman appeared at a peculiar angle on the screen and for a moment J.P. was puzzled. He looked to be prone on a bench, his shoulders bare and a strange expression that might have been pain washing across his face.

J.P. found himself excited for a moment at the idea that McCambridge-LeMans had injured himself in some way. An injury might take him back to Paris, or at least leave him laid up here in town, and out of J.P.'s way. His excitement, however, was short-lived. Two delicate hands rounded the Frenchman's shoulders and proceeded to knead the trapezius muscles, eliciting another groan from McCambridge-LeMans and very nearly drawing one from J.P.

'Morning, Henri,' he said, in his most urbane tone. 'Availing ourselves of a little shiatsu, are we?'

A sardonic smile wrinkled McCambridge-LeMans' mouth. 'Yes, J.P.,' he replied wearily. 'Ingrid here has a degree in it from the Karolinska Institute,' the Frenchman paused, 'in Tokyo.'

J.P. heard giggling in the background, then a fair-skinned, blonde-haired, blue-eyed Swedish beauty stuck her head into the frame from over the Frenchman's right shoulder.

'Conichiwa, Gillespie-san,' she said, laughing.

McCambridge-LeMans laughed too and J.P. tried to stretch his dry lips across his drier teeth.

'I'm expecting a visitor, Henri,' he said tetchily. 'Was there something in particular you wanted?'

McCambridge-LeMans gave J.P. an icy stare, then turned to Ingrid and asked her if she would excuse them for a few minutes. He sat up on his bench and placed his unit on another platform level with his head, looking beyond it briefly to see that the girl had moved out of earshot. 'I am interested in how your damage limitations are progressing.' The Frenchman paused and smiled cruelly. 'Well, I trust.'

'Yes, very well,' said J.P., so smugly that as soon as the words left his mouth he was embarrassed for himself.

McCambridge-LeMans watched with great satisfaction as J.P.'s neck and face achieved new levels of rosiness. 'Julie told me your meeting with the police chief was successful. What about the rest of it?'

J.P. loosened his tie and cleared his throat. 'The parents of the two doctors seem satisfied with the idea that their offspring perished on a mission of mercy. Mrs Flanagan in particular appeared relieved. Seems the daughter was something of a tramp. Leonard's parents were pretty much the same; didn't seem to think him a great loss. They've been given the handsome insurance pay-off and nobody even mentioned a coroner's inquest.'

'Okay,' said McCambridge-LeMans, a hint of disapproval in his tone. 'What about our three inmates?'

'Two of them, David Hayden and Thomas Donnelly, we don't have to worry about: scum-o-rama. They hadn't had sight nor sound of their drug-addicted families in years – out of the system and likely to stay that way if they can help it. I got the Kid to make discreet enquiries with his contacts at the Institute and it seems the two boys were friends who kept to themselves. Hardly anyone even remembers their names.' J.P. coughed quietly into his hand. 'James Clarke's people may present us with a problem. Mr James Clarke senior is said to have a Master's in his statutory rights. I'm given to believe he's the type who'll want to see the accident report, the police report and the coroner's report before he personally interviews everyone involved.'

McCambridge-LeMans yawned. 'What are our options?'

'We've had some luck there. I found something in the inventories you sent me earlier of Mick and Frank Cooper's worldly goods. Mick appears to own a piece of land in town.'

'Yes.' The expression on McCambridge-LeMans' face changed to something approaching interest.

'It's a vacant lot behind the Hither Twice Toys building. Hither Twice have offered Mick a few kings' ransoms on a number of occasions for the property. They're desperate to build a car park. So far Mick has, for reasons best known to himself, refused to sell.'

McCambridge-LeMans was becoming bored again. 'Your point being?'

'Mr James Clarke senior, potentially the second biggest pain in our mutual asses this year, works for Hither Twice.'

The Frenchman cocked an eyebrow. 'I see.'

'I know Steven Fox at Hither Twice quite well. In exchange for our selling him Mick Cooper's property, I think he'll be happy to have Mr Clarke sacked and evicted. As soon as he is without a job and a domicile Clarke will officially be designated transient. He can be kept under wraps and incommunicado at a shelter for, I figure, a year. When he gets out his son's demise will be old news and we'll see to it the trail is ice cold.'

'Your friend at the Shelter Project is agreeable?'

'Trent McGrory's his name, one of the Project administrators. I haven't spoken to him but he will be. I'll give Fox his number and let him make his own arrangements. McGrory will see to it that Clarke is picked up quickly after his sacking, that his file is buried under a pile of other new admissions, that no questions are asked and that Clarke is kept quiet. He'll do pretty much anything for a supplemental. One of his kids has some tough-ass cancer and needs constant medical care.'

McCambridge-LeMans nodded. 'Excellent. What about the Kid; anything?'

'The Kid's scared shitless and eager to please, but I'm not convinced he's much of an asset. Outside of the small service he did us at the Institute, he's attempting to source exotic, high-grade stimulants and analgesics for Dr Bertillion's medicine cabinet. He says he can get excellent prices, though the doctor may have to refine the goods.'

The Chairman shrugged.

J.P. looked at his shoes under the desk and then back into

his screen. 'Freeway is anxious about Mick and Frank. How are they?'

'I know he is, and they're fine,' said McCambridge-LeMans, looking at the ceiling and rubbing his right shoulder. 'I am determined to recoup what they lost us through their stupidity, so I am having them trained in correct security procedure. Freeway will see them soon enough.'

'Freeway also asked about the club they own . . . owned. Would you be prepared to sell it over to him?'

'No. Frankly, Freeway doesn't have the taste to turn a decent profit on it. I'm giving it to a friend of mine who'll at least make something classy out of it.'

J.P. nodded grimly, then leaned closer to his screen as if his proximity to it might augment secrecy. 'Are you sure about bringing Lyons-Howard on board? That bastard's trouble.'

'Yes, J.P., I'm sure,' the Chairman said evenly.

J.P. persisted. 'I don't trust him. I'd be happier if he disappeared. Like the Master says, we shouldn't miss an opportunity to overcome the enemy.'

'Your misreading of Sun Tzu was never endearing, J.P. "Overcome" does not mean "slaughter". You have forgotten that "captured soldiers should be well treated and kept", and "A kingdom destroyed will never again come into being; nor will the dead be brought back to life." As long as you are associated with me you will play it my way: friends close, enemies closer.'

'No good will come of this.'

'It might help, J.P., if you attempted to think positively.' The Chairman disconnected.

After a protracted bout of sighing and grinding his teeth J.P. walked to the cabinet on his right, lit a cigar and poured himself a drink. He sat back behind the desk and aggressively fingered a small panel on his console.

'Josephine, has there been any word from that little shit yet?'

'Coleman, sir?'

'Yes, Coleman.'

'No, sir . . . oh, hold on, the elevator's on its way up.'

'Send him straight through.' He ended the exchange without allowing her to affirm his instruction and, cigar clenched in teeth, grappled with his chair in a bid to get it closer to his desk.

When Bluey breezed through the door he found his father attempting to brush cigar ash from his right trouser leg and smacking the back of his hand against the front of the desk in the effort. A short and ill-formed string of obscenities issued from J.P. and Bluey, noting his father's temper, forwent the wisecrack that had leapt to the tip of his tongue upon noticing the two fingers of whiskey in the glass on J.P.'s desk. He took the chair in front of the desk and waited in silence for his father to finish his ablutions.

J.P. regarded the young man sternly from under his brow. 'Do you enjoy keeping me waiting, Coleman?'

'No, J.P.' Bluey was wide-eyed with amazement, as if the very suggestion that he might deliberately vex J.P. had him insulted. 'It's just that –'

J.P. cut him off with a wave of his hand. 'Don't bother,' he said. 'I don't know why I ask any more.' He put the glass to his head and emptied it without recourse to the act of swallowing. 'Pour me another and get one yourself,' he pointed to the cabinet and smiled, 'we'll be toasting a new arrangement.'

Bluey put ice in a glass for himself and came back to the desk with the decanter. 'Arrangement, J.P.?'

'Yes, Coleman,' he said, fingering the rim of his glass, 'I feel it is incumbent upon me as a responsible parent to discon-

tinue my unquestioning subsidy of your . . . chosen career.'
The last two words were pronounced with a palpable sneer.

Bluey half smiled. 'You're putting me on.'

J.P. shook his head.

'Jesus, J.P. This is serious. You've got to know that I can't
live on what I earn with the band. And it's not as if you need
a tenth of what you've got.'

J.P. shrugged and affected an air of resignation. 'I may be in
dire need of it, Coleman, sooner than you think.'

Bluey's eyes narrowed to slits and he took a quick, nervous
nip from his glass. 'What are you getting at?' he asked.

'There are things afoot, son, which could see a drastic curtail-
ment of my expenditure. Things which might possibly be avoid-
able were I not short-handed in certain sensitive areas.' J.P.
reached into the ashtray and relit his cigar. A thick cloud of
smoke hung over the desk between them.

'What things?' Bluey was getting a tad suspicious. 'What areas?'

'The business world isn't always a matter of contract and
agreement. People must implement these things, and where
people meet there will invariably be interpersonal difficulties.'

'If you're talking about the Frenchman, J.P., that's never been
a secret exactly. And you seem to have managed him so far.'

'Yes, but he appears to have established some sort of a rapport
with young McLemon.'

'So,' it was Bluey's turn to shrug, 'hasn't he got some business with Marshall's old man?'

'Do you believe that?'

'Marshall told me so to my face, J.P., and he's not much of
a liar. I'm not saying he wouldn't play an angle to get more
money for his precious Exhibit, but I hear you've given him
that.'

'Not by choice, I can assure you. And it occurs to me that

one day he'll be finished with the goddamn thing. That day is a good deal closer now he's got these added resources. What will he want then?'

An exclamation of absolute and utter disbelief escaped Bluey. 'You're not seriously suggesting that Marshall could *do* your job, let alone want it?'

J.P. pulled pensively at his cigar and inhaled deeply. 'The toughest thing about this job, Coleman, was getting it. All I have to do is throw my weight around, keep people thinking I know what they're up to, and delegate. The Frenchman objects to my cutting corners and skimming off the top, but the board won't let him replace me as long as things are running fairly smoothly. Things have gotten a bit fucked up around here recently. The Chairman has me taking the rap for it and as a result I'm out of favour with the board. Not enough to lose me the position yet, but if McCambridge-LeMans has a viable replacement somewhere down the line, he might convince them to opt for it rather than run the risk of me screwing up again.' He paused to pull at the cigar and regard it appreciatively. 'As for whether McLemon would want the job,' he said, 'I've got a feeling that the Chairman has plans to give the boy a taste for the finer things in life. Mark my words, it'll only be a matter of time.'

'Okay, fair enough, say it were true, and the Frenchman did manage to pull it off and,' Bluey clapped a hand to his forehead in disbelief, 'Marshall usurped you as the head of WentWest operations in Ireland, you'd still be disgustingly rich by anyone's standards. I don't see that you've got that much to worry about.'

J.P. laughed softly. 'My business dealings haven't always been what you'd call squeaky clean.' Bluey made a *quelle surprise* face which J.P. chose to ignore. 'They've become even less so in the last few years. Out of the WentWest fold, clear of their influence and protection, I'd be a target for every high-achieving jackal, vulture and shark in the media, in politics and in lawyering who wanted to make themselves a name. Not to mention every son of a bitch I stood on on my way up here who figures on having an axe to grind. My money wouldn't hold those bastards off for long.'

'So you're cutting me off to save for an inevitable rainy day, and a battle you know you can't win,' said Bluey dejectedly, feeling a little sorry for the old boy, but mostly wondering how much he ran up every month on the card J.P. had given him. The cash he got from Slide was probably an average wage, but he spent most of it every week on entertainment.

J.P. smiled, clearly revelling in his son's discomfiture. 'Don't panic just yet,' he said. 'I like to think that there are always alternatives.'

Bluey was relieved to think that maybe J.P. was stringing him along, that maybe things weren't as bleak as they had been painted. 'What did you have in mind?' he asked.

'What I had in mind was to put myself back in the board's good books.'

'How?'

'I don't know yet, but that's only half of it. I also want to remove any possible pretenders to my position.'

'Meaning Marshall.'

J.P. looked at his son squarely and nodded. 'That's where you'll come in.'

Bluey moved back in his chair. 'Forget about it. You can't ask me to fuck over friends.'

'Drop the pretence, son, and mind your language,' J.P. smiled, 'this is your father you're talking to. You grew up in my house, remember? Your so-called friends were only ever interested in you because of the extent to which you were indulged. You knew it too, and you never had any qualms about discarding them as soon as you were bored with them. So don't tell me about how much you value friendship.'

Bluey closed his eyes a moment and uttered a barely audible obscenity. J.P. flinched inwardly at the hurt he had inflicted, but steeled himself to press on. It was, after all, necessary.

'McLemon was more of a curiosity, because of his peculiar birth and the fact that he didn't appear to envy your privilege. Marshall's an okay guy, I'm not saying otherwise, but don't tell me that you don't pick up an occasional bit of flak from him about being the little rich kid. Sure, he probably dresses it up as a good-natured ribbing, but ask yourself where that comes from. Good old-fashioned covetousness, that's where.'

Bluey got up and went to the cabinet to put more ice in his glass. J.P. had the decanter ready to pour when he got back to the desk. 'Look, Coleman, I'm not asking you to off the fucker. Just find out as much as you can about what goes on between him and the Frenchman. We need a couple of small things that will rule Marshall out as my possible successor. He does a great job down at the Archive and that's where he should stay. Nothing worse than that. The Frenchman's the real adversary here; Marshall's his pawn. We just have to take him out of the game. He never even has to know.'

Bluey looked sullenly from under his eyelids at his father. 'Christ Jesus, J.P.'

J.P. leaned forward and put his elbows on the desk, holding his glass up at eye level. 'Get real, boy,' he said, softer now but deadly serious. 'That place you live in is nearly three grand a month without bills. You've spent almost twice that in the last eighteen months in shoe stores alone. There has to *be* a payroll for you to remain on it. You have to understand that you're only protecting your own hide here.' J.P. looked at the desk in front of him, then back at his son, forlornly, he hoped. 'And helping save mine, if that means anything.' He paused meaningfully. 'Coleman, I need you on board here. I can't manage without you.'

Bluey looked up at the glass J.P. held suspended over the centre of the desk. His own rose from his lap towards it, exceedingly slowly, but eventually they clinked.

(ii)

It bothered Jack McLemon that what he regarded as the core of his life's work looked so meagre. He scrolled forward through the pages and back again, hoping to shake something loose, correct some technical glitch in his machine that would cause the document suddenly to expand to twice its present size. He zoomed out to view it at a distance. Tapping his pen against the screen and speaking the numbers in a whisper through his teeth, he counted the pages again. The count held steady at a disappointing twenty. More than thirty years' work for twenty pages. Meagre didn't accurately describe the achievement.

Jack walked out of the study and into the kitchen, hoping a change of scenery might help him look at it in a different light. He put water in the kettle to make tea and leaned on the counter as he waited for it to boil. They were closely typed pages, he told himself; and anyway, it wasn't thirty years' work, it was work that had happened over thirty or more years, during which he'd had a whole other career and had raised a son. He took a deep breath, a mug from the cupboard and milk from the fridge. If he increased the spacing between the lines it would read easier and he might get as much as thirty pages out of it. The graphic of the family tree was a bit cramped too, perhaps it didn't all have to be on one page. If he spread it out century by century he'd get three pages out of it. The eighteenth and nineteenth could fit on one page and the twentieth on its own. The last page would be a bit sparse, but no matter. He made and poured his tea and sat at the kitchen table alternately blowing and sipping at it and staring into space.

The arrival of this distant cousin, Henri McCambridge-LeMans, had forced his very first attempt to organise his genealogical discoveries into a chronological sequence of events that resembled something he could call a history. As a consequence he had to recognise the fact that the decades of research he had done amounted to little more than a scattered non-arrangement of names, dates and sketchy biographies. Before it had always seemed an achievement just to turn up a single verifiable fact every now and then; who could be bothered hanging it on a tree? Always there had been the shadow of a construction in his head that kept him moving in the right direction, but he had never felt it necessary to get it all down before. There simply hadn't been anyone to tell it to.

Information about his forebears had been very difficult to come by because of a phenomenon – a mutability of name – that Jack would eventually refer to as 'the Shifting'. The Shifting, he would discover, was a phenomenon that stretched back over two hundred years, but the greatest single manifestation of the effect occurred in his father's immediate family, all of his father's brothers contriving, for one reason or another, to introduce changes, or shifts, into their surname.

Phineas McLemon and Mary McLemon (née Curtis), Jack's grandparents, brought four sons into the world; Big Jack – Jack's father – Luke, Mark and (Matt)Hew.

Phineas McLemon had not known his own parents, and was brought up in an orphanage run by the Daughters of Destitution. Phineas was a man cursed with the strong impression that he existed for greater things, and he moved bitterly through life feeling that somewhere along the line a terrible mistake had been made. Nevertheless he attended to his marital and parental duties conscientiously, if sternly, alternately falling into imaginings of his reward in the next life, then berating himself with his next thought for what he felt was his avarice and pride.

Devoutly Catholic in the old-fashioned way, Phineas forced pre-school morning mass and interminable evening rosaries daily upon his reluctant offspring. 'Who made the world?' he would often ask following another mind-numbing rosary. 'God made the world,' they would intone in unison, as though drugged. In an effort to snap them out of this catalepsy he would sometimes spring on them the question, 'And *when* did he make it?'; the only correct answer as far as Phineas was concerned being in accordance with Bishop Ussher's calculations.

Phineas's second son Luke was a precocious boy with a good head for figures and an indecent ambition for financial security. By his early twenties Luke was firmly positioned on the up-flight of the hierarchical escalator in one of the big commercial banks. His promising career, however, was cut short in his twenty-fifth year when he felt it incumbent upon himself to flee the country amid what were thought to be justifiable accusations of embezzlement. He wrote a disgusted Phineas a month or so later that he was in London and well; and while his father did not divulge the return address to the authorities, who would certainly have expedited prosecution, he did not reply either. Phineas unceremoniously threw all further correspondence bearing a London postmark into the fire unopened, and for about two years, after which his correspondence dried up, Luke opted to write to his mother at the address of a friend. It was on finding these letters, following his grandmother's death, that Jack's interest in the family history was kindled.

Jack discovered in the letters that his uncle had managed to obtain a National Insurance number under the name Luke Lemoine, which Jack was later to learn had been an earlier form of the family name, although Luke was undoubtedly ignorant of the fact. Jack doggedly followed the few sparse clues in the letters until they finally led him to his uncle's booze-soaked and embittered widow, Rita. She had cackled her disbelief at him down the telephone line, like some withered Dickensian crone.

'You come and visit yer auntie Rita,' she'd advised him. 'Bring a jeffrey to cover medicinals and I'll tell you all you'll ever want to know about the fabulous Luke Lemoine.' A 'jeffrey' was explained to him in terms of its being 'two thousand nicker'. A short period of haggling resulted in Jack recording their telephone conversation for less than half a 'monkey'.

Luke, it transpired, had invested the bulk of his ill-gotten gains into a holiday company and an oil company. One dull August evening a few months after he had arrived in London it was confirmed that his investment in the holiday company was lost. At the beginning of the following year his shares in the oil company slid to rock bottom; the price at which, in despair, he finally sold. He was now dependent on his badly paid but cushy job monitoring community radio for breaches of the broadcasting code, a job he had taken for pin money and to keep him out of the bookies' and the pub during the day. He still managed, according to Rita, to spend an inordinate amount of time in both, and it was while Rita was working behind the counter of a bookie's office that they met.

A note of unvarnished aching crept into Rita's voice as she recalled Luke's having considerable money that year on Anatoly Karpov, L'Escargot, Arthur Ashe, Tom Watson, the West Indies and John Walker. She had had to give up the job as they had made their friendship obvious, and coupled with Luke's extreme good fortune it had aroused suspicion with her employer.

They married on the crest of this good fortune and then their winning streak ran out. Luke still had his job and Rita picked up bits and pieces of casual work where she could. She was unwilling, for reasons she would never tell, to take a full-time position with anybody, and the sporadic nature of her earnings became a source of tension between them, Luke being a man, he often explained to her, who liked to know where he stood. They continued to gamble moderately and drink heavily. Late in the evenings they fought often and the following morning they could never recall why, but the feeling of animosity carried into their short-lived sobriety. Years of the same-old same-old passed. Some of her friends began having children whose names she never remembered, and whom she couldn't tell apart one from the other, tending rather to regard them as impediments to further excess; they were always demanding something or needing attention. Rita had long since decided not to fall into what she regarded as 'that trap'. She joined Luke in the bar one evening after work, where he was sitting with some of the regulars, their friends. He caught the barman's eye, then nodded in her direction by way of drawing his attention to her approach and requesting her usual. For the first time she noticed in his expression a suggestion that this was a disagreeable chore he was performing. As the year passed she noticed this attitude towards her more and more. Another night he had addressed Ray Winkle across a full table: 'How long is it, Ray, since you broke up with Lisa?'

'Eight months,' said Ray.

'What age are you now?'

'Twenty-six.'

'Don't leave it too long, son,' said Luke, casting a sideways glance at Rita. 'Sort it out before they all turn into cold, hard bitches on you.'

In the uncomfortable silence that followed, Rita found herself wishing him dead. Two weeks later she had her wish. Luke's wiry, lifeless body was carried out of a downtown massage parlour, much to the distress of his nineteen-year-old Romanian masseuse.

In terms of detail Jack had less luck with his other two uncles, but nevertheless managed to identify the Shifting in both cases. His father had told him that his uncle Mark had, at an early age, opted to join the merchant navy to escape Phineas's bitter reign. On request Jack was given leave to peruse the records of the shipping line his uncle had worked for and discovered on the crew manifest of the good ship *Maidez* one Mark *McLernon*, Seaman First-Class. Jack's father had always maintained that his brother Mark was an unlikely candidate for a sailor, being a shy, uncommunicative and unassuming man. Jack surmised that the name McLernon had been a typographical error which his shy uncle had opted to use rather than cause a fuss. He traced Mark to an address in Leeds during the mid nineteen seventies and discovered that he had eventually changed his name by deed poll to McLernon prior to marrying, but the trail ended with the marriage certificate.

Hew McLemon's name suffered less from a shifting than it did from a forcing. Of all the brothers, he had inherited the lion's share of Phineas's bitterness. He was a mean-spirited young man who fancied himself as something of an icono-clast. He constantly goaded his devoutly Catholic father. Mostly they argued about Darwin, Hew reserving the bulk of his vitriol for his father's Creationism, and what he, Hew, felt to be a starkly untenable position, that of the entire human race originating with one couple who had been dropped intact on the brand new planet in late October of 4004 BC.

At the culmination of the screaming match that saw relations break down utterly and irreparably, Hew swore that his children would only ever be ashamed of one of their ancestors – meaning Phineas himself – and resolved, in a fit of direst pique, to change his name to Hew McLemur; a fact which Jack later verified.

(iii)

'Officer Eustace.'

'Ms Ylang-Ylang, aren't you the early bird.' Officer Eustace's sour attempt at a smile communicated many things to Sister Jasmine's fine sense; good-natured *bonhomie* was not among them. Never at her most diplomatic in the early part of the day, Sister Jasmine was in no mood for him.

'An ill-advised analogy, Officer Eustace, which doesn't paint you in a very good light.'

'What?' he said.

'Inasmuch as I've caught you.'

Officer Eustace blinked twice, then jerked his head, as if to clear it of some tangible detritus. 'I'm very busy, Ms Ylang-Ylang, what can I do for you?'

Whatever was wrong with him, she thought, left him unsteady on his cognitive feet. She hadn't responded well to his somewhat obvious display of irritation either. She felt if she were to get any good out of him she'd better throw him something he could work with and let him get rid of her quickly. 'I wanted to know if you turned up anything interesting on the item I entrusted to you, the plastic cap.'

'I didn't, I'm afraid,' he said blankly. 'I've since been assigned elsewhere.' He paused then for a matter of seconds, staring back at her out of the screen. When it was clear she wasn't going to go away that easily, he continued uninterestedly. 'I checked the serial number on the lid, or whatever it was, with Leyner Defense, as you helpfully suggested –'

'I didn't mean you to contact the company directly. I had hoped you might have other resources.'

'Nevertheless,' Eustace shrugged, 'they don't have a product which corresponds. Must be another company or, as I now suspect, something entirely unconnected. Either way I think you're barking up the wrong tree, and, as I initially suspected, there's nothing to investigate here. There certainly aren't any fucking brownie points to be had.' The delivery of an obscenity without particular emphasis had always seemed to Officer Eustace to be an effective means of communicating valediction. He was dismayed to find that Ms Ylang-Ylang took no such cue.

'The response from Leyner Defense is hardly surprising,' she said evenly. 'Have you identified the bodies? The owner of the vehicle?'

'No. As I explained, I'm working elsewhere.'

'Would it be possible for you to send me a copy of the report?'

'No, I think it's better if I avoid talking to you at all.'

'Officer Eus–'

'Ms Ylang-Ylang, since my initial contact with you my career seems to have gone from static into full reverse. I'm here drafting reports from the incoherent ramblings of officers I previously considered my juniors; being punished, in other words, for pricking about with your force-fed initiative when I should have been doing what I was told to do, which was to keep people like you away from the crime scene! Now, before I'm ejected from the force altogether, goodbye!'

Sister Jasmine's screen went blank and she pushed it back away from her face. She turned her attention to the cold breakfast which Room Service had deposited at her door earlier. She hadn't expected much from the police, but perhaps just a little more from Eustace himself. He had undoubtedly been clumsy with his enquiries and premature in bringing the matter to the attention of his superiors; not to mention inelegant in owning up to it. She had chosen badly. Perhaps one of the young forensics officers would have been better after all.

As she finished her cereal Sister Jasmine's screen beeped to signal an incoming call from Maymon Glades Police Station. She had to swallow quickly before answering. A uniformed senior officer appeared at the other end, smiling like a PR man.

'Good morning, Ms Ylang-Ylang. Superintendent Riley here at Maymon Glades. I understand that you made a request for a police report. May I ask what it's in connection with?'

'I'm drafting my own report for the Vervain Society on the recent road accident outside Maymon Glades. I felt the police report was essential. Surely Officer Useless has explained to you.' She smiled demurely and, after the briefest fluttering of the lids, cast her eyes floorward.

'Officer . . . Eustace?'

'Yes, just so.'

Superintendent Riley was unsure as to whether he had heard an actual insult or some peculiarity of speech. When he thought about pointing out to her what she had in fact said, his 'discrimination' indicator went to DefCon Two. He eyed her suspiciously and coughed before returning to the script. 'I can arrange to have a copy of our report sent to you as soon as it's completed.'

'Thank you, do you know when that will be?'

'As soon as we've contacted the next of kin in each case. A few of the families involved appear to be transients and they're proving difficult to locate. I can't, therefore, be specific as to the time frame. Either way, Ms Ylang-Ylang, I feel I must make it clear to you that we are not pursuing any other inquiries in relation to this incident. It appears to have been a simple case of reckless driving.' The Superintendent sat smiling at her in silence for a few seconds. Clearly the briefing was over.

'Thank you, Superintendent,' Sister Jasmine said at last. 'I look forward to hearing from you.' She hung up, not anticipating her copy of the report any time soon and certain that she would have to make considerable noise before she heard from the Superintendent again. The police could plausibly spin out that excuse about the transient families for a long time to come. It could even be true.

She looked at the two other plastic caps she had retrieved from the accident scene, then traced her finger across the name on each. Maybe there *was* another company called Leyner, or maybe Leyner was itself a product name. It was possible that Mr McCormack was mistaken in thinking a vehicle passed the accident without stopping. Perhaps there would be no risk after all in connecting to the Vervain database to confirm that these caps were not, in fact, from the casing of some offensive weapon. She began to suspect herself of concocting a suspicious scenario in an effort to give greater import to her maiden assignment, as if being here was not honour enough.

'Those who do not know you by work or by reputation,' Sister Superior Suki de Chardin had said before her departure, 'will now sit up and pay attention. It is a simple task I ask of you. The only significant fact is that you will journey alone and unsupervised. It is a way I have developed over the years of identifying those I consider particularly able among us. Beware, however, of falling into complacency, Jasmine – be ever vigilant. Among the crème de la crème it is more difficult to excel, and often it seems easier to draw attention to your laurels than it does to continually affirm your reputation.'

Sister Jasmine was satisfied that she was not depending on past glories here. She would review her work on Mantra in a day or so, but she felt confident that it was good. It was hard for it not to be, since she was in virgin territory. Mantra exhibited profoundly different characteristics from those of the common cyber-terrorist. Viruses had been the bane of big business for decades. They had increased steadily from humble beginnings, in their frequency, in their novelty, and in the destructiveness of their payloads. They were the prime motivator in the rapid development of advanced countermeasures programs and the illegal status of heavy-duty encryption, now reserved for the military and other government agencies, and, of course, the rich. Here in the Western world lengthy prison sentences were meted out to those found responsible for the creation or deliberate transmission of a destructive virus. In Saudi fifteen years before, all twelve members of a group calling itself *Libre* were publicly executed for having succeeded by means of a virus in putting a halt to oil production for two days. The Indian Children's Union downed tools for two days in protest. The world's media covered both events solemnly, and confidently predicted that, sad though it was, one day those kids would have a better understanding of how the world worked.

Mantra's strategy, though, was an unusual one. Rather than attacking the WentWest network, costing them countless millions in software, hardware, labour and new security, Mantra seemed hell-bent on *irritating* WentWest's markets, through the disruption of WentWest-sponsored sporting events. After a year the Mantra disruptions hadn't seriously affected stadium attendances, but bodies were nevertheless threatening to pull out of contracts left, right and centre because of the sense of the ridiculous which the disruption gave to the whole event. A sense which the games themselves could live with but which the advertising couldn't. It was possible for the viewer at home to avoid Mantra if he wanted. All he had to do was start his viewing a half-hour after kick-off and he could miss Mantra's contribution via an edited stream. This method, however, wasn't all that popular, as the idea of watching something as it happened captured the public imagination a lot better than watching something half an hour after it had happened. The difference to the viewer was something Sister Jasmine didn't quite understand, but the upshot was that nearly everybody suffered the disruption nearly every time, and a sales-against-time chart showed that the products advertised at disrupted games had taken a noticeable downturn over the last year.

Regarding responsibility for this 'terrorism', she had discovered that 'opinion' held that the originators of these events must hail either from some bunch of militant feminists, since women never liked sport, period; or from the physically challenged community, because who else would have the time on their hands, and from where else could such rancour for the beauty and athleticism of sport emerge. A number of disabled organisations were reporting an increase in incidents of crutch-kicking and wheelchair-shoving by youths sporting sweaters emblazoned with the legend 'Back Home Bitch', but the media seemed oblivious to its value as a news item. It was an ugly outgrowth of an otherwise intriguing phenomenon which the representatives of women and the physically challenged rained righteous scorn upon and which Mantra, along with the rest of the abuse aimed at them, seemed happy enough to ignore.

The really intriguing aspect, to her mind, was that Mantra had at their disposal such an obviously powerful tool, potentially more destructive than any virus, and yet they seemed content to trot out the same three tired phrases in the same archaic format *every time*! 'Cover your ass ... Pass the buck ... Resistance is futile' scrolled across millions of screens like an old screen saver. The voice which accompanied the printed word seemed like an afterthought. Despite the cheesy look of the stunt, the apparently untraceable nature of what some referred to as the 'stealth program' was, she was advised, 'breathtaking'. WentWest weren't advertising what measures they'd taken to counteract the problem, but for it to perpetuate for almost a year without detection was unthinkable. The subtext of the exercise seemed to her to say: Look what we've got. What do you think we'll do with it next? The suspense in the boardrooms must have been awe-inspiring.

(iv)

Jack McLemon's initial success in the genealogical field drove him further back in time and his researches led him to discover that the name-changing phenomenon observed in his uncles went right back to his great-great-great-great-great-grand-father, Guy LeMoineau. If this weren't exciting enough, Guy's son, Lucien, proved to be the sort of character serious genealogists dream about.

In his *Memoirs* Lucien LeMoine, by then calling himself Lucien Lehmann, describes his father, Guy, deserting from the army at Toulon in 1793, very soon after greeting the arrival of the new artillery commander with the words, 'Half a man is better than none.' It must be stressed, however, that the few recognised authorities who have actually read the *Memoirs* view the vast majority of the work as apocryphal. Jack wouldn't have minded the lies if only he could have located a copy of the memoir, but it had ever eluded him. What is certain is that Guy travelled to Louisiana in the United States, identifying himself there as Charles LeMoine, eventually obtaining some small amount of celebrity as a gambler, bon vivant and charmer of women.

The author of the *Memoirs*, Lucien, grew up something of a talent with that dark aspect of charm: cuckoldry. At the age of twenty-three he was caught ministering to the needs of the 'pleasantly upholstered (but sadly neglected), flame-haired, full-mouthed young wife of a prominent citizen of Louisiana'. His unique recollection of the event is recorded thus, in the one scrap of the infamous *Memoirs* that Jack managed to locate:

When the bedroom door burst open I leapt from the young woman's embrace. Standing naked with my back to the room's small window, I faced the wronged husband across the bed. The man had his sword drawn and was moving the point from side to side very slowly, an icy expression clear in his small brown eyes.

'You'll forgive me, sir,' he hissed, 'if you found me unavailable and ill-prepared for guests. I trust you've managed in my absence. I fear I may have naught to offer you now . . . but cold cuts.'

I was ever regarded as a steady, practical young man, and would certainly not have been considered of the kind given to idle boasting; so while good common sense dictated that I draw my weapon against the necessity of defending myself, mature recollection shows my sincere wish to diffuse the situation without violence was embarked upon with ill-chosen words.

'I warn you,' said I, 'I am an adept swordsman.'

As the offending word fell from my dust-filled mouth my adversary turned deathly pale. No fear this, for he was a gentleman of calibre. Upon the realisation of his rational mind that there was no way now to stand down, the life-blood, quite sensibly, retreated into his body, further from the imminent battle. His advance was as dignified as it was inexorable. He anounced it memorably.

'I heard, sir,' said he, 'as I ascended the stair, glowing reviews of your prowess from the mouth of my own wife. Since I've had no reason to doubt her judgement in the past, it would seem that in the matter of ability you may well be without equal. I feel justified, however, in taking issue with you on the question of licence; for even when age and common decency demand my cutlass remain inactive much of the time, you'll appreciate that pride insists I walk the plank sooner than swab a wet deck!'

Sadly, he was not so elegant with the blade.

Lucien was forced to flee to Europe. He travelled widely throughout the continent in the years following, under a variety of names. He continued to slake his lust variously and frequently, and recorded all such encounters in lurid detail for later inclusion in the scandalous *Memoirs*. He eventually settled in Berlin, where he inveigled his way into the household of a wealthy but credulous mineralogist by passing himself off as a talented herbalist. Lucien and Johann, the mineralogist, together concocted a restorative cordial which proved very popular, being very scientifically described on the label, which was all the rage at the time. The drink was composed of calcium carbonate, mint, cinnamon, cloves and alcohol. On the reverse label you were urged to shake vigorously; the exercise, according to the begrudgers, being the sole source of benefit. The two sold product and franchises to big, healthy, blond young couples travelling from Germany to the American north-east. For an added fee the prospective émigrés were instructed in technical terminology and sales technique, and issued certificates attesting to their graduation from the *Berlin Academy of Specifickal Nutrition.*

Soon merchants began arriving with orders to take back to the New World and Lucien and Johann concocted new products with ever more startling effects on the physiology of the consumer. The business boomed and Johann and Lucien became fast friends. Johann often spoke of Lucien as the son he never had, and Lucien returned the compliment by taking Johann's family name upon the occasion of his marriage to the mineralogist's eldest. All in good time and with consummate grace, Lucien Lehmann became head of the household, and by means of his now steady and sober influence it prospered for a century.

(v)

It was a little after ten when the lobby buzzed Sister Jasmine to tell her that Mr McCormack was in to see her. It was their third meeting in two days. The previous evening he had brought her cross-references from the WentWest Archive concerning Mantra's chosen phrases, and he'd already vetted the hits he'd got so as she wouldn't have to waste her time, as he put it, 'wading through crap'. She thought it endearing the way he mumbled an apology after employing a crudity, like he wished to make amends for getting carried away with himself, but did not want to draw too much attention to something he wasn't sure she'd noticed in the first place. He told her that many of the references he found were linked only tenuously with the three phrases, but were nevertheless entertaining. He timidly suggested that correctly placed one or two of them might 'moisten and add colour' to an otherwise dry analysis. If she was a little miffed at the suggestion of dryness in anything she might produce, she forgot it in warm contemplation of his thoughtfulness. She was unsure how he had located her so quickly in a city of some seven millions, but she wasn't particularly worried, as his intentions appeared benign. Indeed, the way he looked at her sometimes she suspected they might be positively honourable.

Following the relative ugliness of her encounters with Eustace and the Superintendent, she found her spirits lifted by the prospect of Mr McCormack's company. She opened the door to his knock and he shuffled sideways and silently into the room, smiling shyly. If he'd had a hat, she thought, he would have been holding it gingerly above his knees by the brim, rotating it nervously between the tips of his fingers.

'The cops cleared the last of their stuff from the accident scene yesterday evening,' he told her. 'I could see them from the attic, packing everything into that white van, sweeping debris off the road into the undergrowth at the side.'

'Yes,' Sister Jasmine nodded resignedly, 'I spoke to a Superintendent Riley a little while back. He informed me in no uncertain terms that their investigations were concluded, then explained that it might be some time before delivery of the report.'

'Oh.' Papa Charlie looked from side to side comically, as if wary of some unseen scrutineer, before extracting a sheaf of papers from inside his jacket and handing them to her. 'Sorry about the hard copy, it's an old habit.'

Sister Jasmine looked from the police report back to Papa Charlie. 'Where did you get this?'

Papa Charlie waved her enquiry away. 'Ask me no questions,' he said.

Sister Jasmine nodded her understanding and pointed Papa Charlie to the couch. She stood at the window quickly reading through the report. When she'd finished she took a seat in the chair across from him and threw the report on the coffee table. 'That's appalling work. They haven't even included your statement.'

'I'd say it's due for burial, not public consumption. I made a couple of discreet enquiries and no one's ever heard of the company who're supposed to have employed those two doctors.'

Sister Jasmine leaned forward to look at the report again, lifting the first two pages. 'Medicorps?'

'Yeah.' He was quiet for a second, thinking. 'I wonder if anyone's processed an insurance claim for the vehicle. We might find something that way.'

She went back to the report. 'It says the insurance information is unavailable.'

'I don't know,' he shrugged, 'there might be a way around that. I'll look into it.'

Sister Jasmine sighed. 'Before you arrived I was trying to convince myself that I was inventing all of this apparent intrigue.'

'I was thinking the same until I walked out past the bend in the road.' He reached into his hip pocket. 'About three or four hundred metres past the bend I picked the first of these up, the other about five hundred more beyond,' he threw two spent shells on top of the police report. 'They're forty-fives, the name inscribed on the end there is —'

'Leyner,' she said, getting up and walking to the high table to the right of the window.

'Yeah,' said Papa Charlie, following her with his head, 'how did you know?'

She picked one of the plastic caps from the table top and threw it into his lap. She gave him a couple of seconds to read the name before telling him about her conversations with Officer Eustace and the Superintendent. 'I think your find clearly indicates foul play,' she told him, 'but I'd like to run this serial number through the Sisterhood's database to be sure. My worry is that if the people who did this feel they have sufficient reason, there's a chance they'll be scanning the web for related enquiries.'

'Jesus,' said Charlie, 'that's paranoid. There might be a way to limit our exposure depending on where we run the search from, but I can't make enquiries until later. Can I talk to you in the meantime about something I believe the Vervains have done some useful work on? It's a wacky idea about the Mantra phenomenon I'd like to run past you.' He paused for a moment before gesturing vaguely over his shoulder. 'I've got to check in at the Archive briefly; do you want to make the trip with me, then go get a cup of coffee and talk?'

'Certainly,' she said, displaying a brightness that was out of place with the major theme of their exchange. She couldn't help it. First he had been thoughtful, now he was being interesting.

It was a fifteen-minute walk from Sister Jasmine's hotel to the Archive, and traffic being what it was there was no quicker way of getting there. Jasmine took the lead and Papa Charlie followed in her wake as she deftly steered her way through their fellow pedestrians, most of whom seemed to be coming towards them. Papa Charlie noticed that at no point in her progress was there any suggestion of hesitation; people just seemed to get out of her way. He imagined her directing the oncoming drones with flicks of her eyes and movements of her head so subtle that they would not be aware that they had in any way been manipulated. Charlie revelled in being seen with such an impressive creature. She was attired in her customary black; at least he assumed it was customary as she had been so dressed on the three occasions they'd met. She put him in mind of a priest, but yesterday she had dismissed the idea that the Vervain Society was a religious order.

'People who know something of us often make that mistake,' she'd said, 'probably on account of the fact that our founder was once a Jesuit. It's true I suppose that the history, psychology and philosophy of religion is a popular topic with the Sisterhood. I mean, if you're going to try to educate people, you may as well do it with reference to their belief systems. But the Society's teaching to its initiates is that God, if it exists, is unknowable, so why waste your time? Although it's not put in those terms exactly.'

There was a confident, almost cocky roll to her shoulders in what was an otherwise disciplined gait, and when things thinned out enough that he could get abreast of her, he found himself unwilling to encroach too closely upon her personal space. They made the rest of the journey in silence.

When they reached the Archive Marshall wasn't in evidence. McCambridge-LeMans' intervention in the funding of the

Exhibit had given the boy a new-found appetite for work. He was probably in the basement digging. Papa Charlie checked his messages and left a note for Marshall to the effect that he'd be back later, together with a disk with the specifications for one of the constructs. He made his way back towards the door where Sister Jasmine was waiting.

'This Archive, what's kept in it?' she asked him.

'Lots of things.' Papa Charlie looked back into the office behind him, as if the two desk terminals, the screen, the drinks dispenser and the junk that had gathered on and against the walls could in some way illuminate his answer. 'Financial documents, employee records, minutes of meetings, stuff like that, from companies long since absorbed and forgotten by WentWest. That's not the material, mind you, that Marshall and I are primarily interested in, it's just the shit end – excuse me – of what we do. Marshall and I have been devoting quite a bit of time to putting together an Exhibit which we hope to have constructed on the web, drawing attention to the choicer morsels among the entertainment features. Those,' he pointed to the disk he had put on Marshall's desk, 'are the numbers for a virtual construct of a cinema in nineteen forties London. The viewer goes through the lobby, where he can see soldiers among the people on the street outside, and far in the distance he can hear an air raid siren. He continues into the packed theatre then and gets to see *Casablanca*. A cultural public service sort of thing was the original idea. I don't know how long that'll last now that McCambridge-LeMans appears to be getting behind the project. No doubt he'll contrive to turn a profit on it, despite the allegedly "demanding" nature of much of the work to be displayed.'

'Who is McCambridge-LeMans?'

'The Chairman of WentWest Europe. Seems him and my

young colleague are cousins to some degree. I don't care what happens, as long as I continue to get to do what I'm doing.'

She asked some vague question about research, just to keep him talking. She was fascinated by a sense, an image, she had of him as someone who could lose himself completely in these diversions. Of course, she felt she had a basic understanding of their attractions for him, having adequately familiarised herself with – and learned appreciation for – many thought-provoking and worthwhile items in the fields of film, music, art and literature; but she favoured the direct muscularity of solid fact over the fanciful wanderings of the imagination, and viewed with a degree of suspicion any artifice which would seek to draw so much of her concern, as these things invariably did. She wondered about the effect these mirages would have on someone who gave himself up to them so readily and so often. She could recall Sister Candice Maligña lecturing on the subject, reading with her patented dour expression the trite lyric of some popular song, or the dialogue from some cheap drama. Looking at him and listening to him Sister Jasmine couldn't believe that Papa Charlie's whole life had been mapped out in advance by the mores of pop songs, movies, books, advertisements, all the sounds and images which, over the years, had been unloaded on his particular demographic. Sister Candice had often dryly observed that those conditioned by the Western democratic tradition were known to consult, in brief, their agendas for the coming week in the less than subtle directions of their horoscopes: *This week you will resolve to work harder, and you will find happiness in new love*. As exaggerated as Sister Candice got on the subject of indoctrination in the West, Jasmine had always expected that she would readily detect signs of such indoctrination; indeed, in a good proportion of the population she believed that she had. She was pleased not to have detected even the subtlest of them in Charlie. Despite his willing immersion in these trivialities, he maintained a welcome and impressive independence of thought and expression.

'So,' he was saying, 'I suppose that's just a long-winded way of saying that it depends on how comprehensive you want to be.' She hadn't heard much of what he'd said in response.

'Coffee?' he suggested, and ushered her with an arm extended towards the exit. She walked ahead of him, listening to him breathe all the way as if he were smelling flowers.

(vi)

Jack McLemon once flew to Birmingham to bid in an auction. He had cursed the organisers at the time for being sticklers for tradition and not doing the thing online. Figuring in the air fare, it had cost him four times what he'd intended spending, but years afterward he talked of being glad of the experience. His dogged persistence in the acquisition of a diary at that auction eventually revealed to him that the current form of his family name, McLemon, owed itself to the impatience and arrogance of the author of the diary, a midwife at a lying-in hospital in Birmingham who had officiated at the birth of Jack's grandfather, Phineas McLemon. The diary proved a far richer source than he could ever have hoped, as the author told in detail the small amount of information she managed to find out about Phineas's parents during the guilt-ridden winter of her existence. The few facts she had, and her frequent surmises, made possible many confirmations and links for Jack among and between his other small sources.

Günter Lehmann, the expectant father, and grandson of Lucien, was a dashing if somewhat indecisive German of independent means. A travelling collector of international folklore and music, he found himself on the west coast of the old sod a few years before what he would later refer to as the 'Kaiser's War'. There he encountered one Pegeen-Sue Tom Ben Gilhawley, or Pegeen Susie-Tom, as she was known for short. Pegeen was a cool, confident young woman, unwilling to regard her plain looks and limp constitution as barriers to a better life, and too downright curious to allow a specimen like Günter go by without a thorough inspection.

The daughter of a *Seanchaí* – though many argued otherwise in light of his pedestrian style – Pegeen quickly realised her value to the scholarly German and was soon to be seen walking about the village with him, copying the authentic Irish spellings of noteworthy names in local lore into his scholastic ledger.

Benedict Gilhawley was not, as has been said, an outstanding *Seanchaí,* but he was the only one in the area willing to do it for a long time. His skill with letters, the ability to record, was his primary asset as a storyteller and was responsible for keeping intact many scenarios, names and places which would otherwise have been forgotten. Benedict's work with – and his daughter's marriage a few months later to – a man such as Herr Lehmann acquired him great esteem among his community. So much so that he graciously allowed himself to be eased into the role of curator of the form in that locale, while steering two mere curates (whom he had ever regarded as arrogant young Turks) into Herr Lehmann's path as better examples of 'style in performance'.

For their own part Pegeen Susie-Tom and Günter were well suited and happy. They were both practical people, if lacking a little in passion, who succeeded in catering for each other in respect of companionship and the affections to a pleasant and mutually satisfactory degree. They were a long time married with no show from Pegeen, but Günter didn't seem to mind and she wasn't sure she did herself, as work was going well and she was enjoying the new experience of travel. By the time the war broke out, childlessness seemed like a blessing.

Günter emerged from the war the very model of physical perfection, but with a marked predisposition for staring into the middle distance and saying very little. He had been quite normal when first he returned, until an uncle had made reference to his 'bravery in service' at a gathering of the extended family. Günter had spoken to Pegeen on a number of occasions over the following few days about reconciling the term *bravery* with the act of walking deliberately and directly into machine-gun fire. It was a concept which appeared to perplex him greatly. He had then lapsed into a general silence, speaking rarely, and even then only in a mumble, as if his attention were elsewhere. Over the next year or so Frau Lehmann convinced herself that he must still be thinking, and fully expected to be apprised of his conclusions at some undetermined point in the future. News from home of her father's loss at sea brought her close to a breakdown. When she fell pregnant she was brought back to herself a little, but never fully.

Günter's mumblings in English were a singular aural experience and only intelligible to his wife. Sister Ramsbottom, the midwife in question, had a gift for languages in keeping with the rest of her countrymen at that time, together with a keen determination to complete the papers appropriate to the birth of this couple's son before the close of her shift. Frau Lehmann, had she known of any confusion, would certainly have put things to rights, being careful in such matters. But the myopic weakling had been through what the doctors all agreed would have been an ordeal for the strongest of women; and while they were very quick to reassure a bewildered Günter that she was not in Death's district, let alone his driveway, it was clear that she was in no condition to attend to any clerical work.

Ramsbottom knew the woman was Irish, having met her upon her rushed admittance, and had wondered at the time where these Sinn Feiners got the gall to flaunt their ill-gotten gains here, in the very heart of the realm. Had she known from whence Günter issued she would surely have refused them further service in person; but as it was she was not au fait with this Johnny Foreigner malarkey. So much so that it was her solemn conviction that Günter was speaking Gaelic when she enquired of him what his newborn son's name was to be. Günter's mumblings confounded her, and her fear that he might have been labouring under the effects of alcohol did not prompt her to double-check with him. His mangled enunciation, therefore, of *Fintan Patrick Lehmann* registered in her auditory system, and subsequently on the birth certificate (following its necessary translation into the King's own English) as *Phineas McLemon*.

A fire that same night in the hospital took the lives of twenty-three people, including Frau and Herr Lehmann. The aftermath was an orgy of confusion and many records were destroyed. Günter's grief-stricken family made persistent enquiries by letter and telegraph regarding the status of young Fintan Patrick, but no such child was to be found. Ramsbottom, as she later confessed, realised her mistake at the time, but on account of some perverse strain of pride in her otherwise unblemished administrative record, she saw to it that 'Phineas McLemon' was given to a representative of the Daughters of Destitution and taken back to Ireland as an orphan.

In the last few years Jack had often taken to wondering if something along the lines of fate had turned the eye of Marshall's biological mother, Marsha Ní Brádaigh, in his direction in order to perpetuate that quirky element in the development of the McLemon clan. They had been in the same company on campus on one or two occasions and had attended many of the same lectures, but Jack had known nothing about her until such time as he took possession of the letter which accompanied her unusual bequest. Marsha had been terminally ill for a long time. She hadn't ever expected to finish her degree, but as it turned out was making progress on her Ph.D. when she finally succumbed. Her greatest concern was that in dying young she would miss what she referred to as her 'right to replacement'; that being her opportunity to put some part of her genetics into the next generation through procreation. In light of her terminal status she didn't feel it fair to involve anyone in a relationship; besides, her doctors advised that in all probability she wouldn't be able to carry to term. She told Jack in her letter that she had long admired him because of his openness, honesty and environmental zeal, and that if circumstances had been different she would certainly have pursued the question of a relationship. Her solution in the long run was to bequeath him a batch of her frozen ova, with a request that should the technology to gestate a foetus in an artificial womb be developed in time, and should he be agreeable, he fertilise one or more of them to produce a child. His other option, which Marsha professed to be less optimistic about, was that Jack's chosen partner might consent to carry one of the fertilised ova. All questions of how the child was to be brought up and by whom she was happy to leave to

Jack. Jack graciously accepted his legacy, on the one hand because it appeared to please the bereaved parents greatly and on the other, if he were to be honest, because he didn't ever think the technology would be developed. He certainly couldn't conceive of any prospective partner consenting to carry a dead woman's child.

A student working for one of the university papers came to interview him a week or so after the reading of the will. He kept his answers suitably glib and non-committal. A decade later he was to receive a much more interesting visit.

Dr James Lilly approached Jack at the offices of the Environmental Council, carrying a copy of the student paper from ten years before. Dr Lilly was possessed of an extremely personable manner and proved an expert communicator. He displayed an impressive knowledge of Jack's area of expertise and, by and by, openly confessed a great interest in his strange inheritance. Dr Lilly told Jack that he represented a group of scientists who believed themselves to have perfected an artificial womb suitable for bringing a human foetus to term. He wanted Jack to consider making available to them the twenty-five ova left to him together with sufficient sperm for fertilisation of the eggs. Lilly's idea was that if they could get a foetus out of their contraption alive, they'd get phenomenal publicity if the achievement was tied to the story of the dying girl. Naturally enough he didn't express it in that way exactly, but as Jack remembered it, that was pretty much the gist. Jack had always been honest about the fact that the money figured large in his initial acceptance, but slowly he got to thinking about what he was doing and about the responsibility he was under-taking. As the time got close the doctors pressed him pretty hard on the question of genetic modifications, but by then Jack wasn't interested in anything but a normal, healthy kid. He didn't care if it was blond or brunette, short or tall, male or female, he only had one request on the genetic front.

'Don't do anything,' he said to them, 'only spare it the eyes.'

(vii)

'The thing I wanted to ask about –' said Papa Charlie, framed in the window of Mitzi's, a coffee room around the corner from the Archive. 'I was wondering if there was any truth to the rumour that a body of work has recently been completed by the Society regarding human interaction,' he paused to clear his throat, 'with what I can only think to call *alien intelligences*.'

This was going to prove a lot less interesting than Sister Jasmine had hoped. She looked at him blankly for a prolonged moment before speaking. 'It's a fact, Charlie; and it so happens that I worked on that very project during my secondary phase with the Society. Although,' the corners of her mouth curled in a smile suggestive of nostalgic comprehension, 'it is my own belief that I was assigned to that project as a punishment. It would not have been my choice, you understand. The first part, as I recall, was less trying than the second. We covered the experiences of the ancient prophets and ran up to Joseph Smith, Bernadette Soubirous and the events at Fatima.'

'By that scale mine would be a modern times enquiry.'

'Which began,' Sister Jasmine grimaced, 'in the Californian desert with Mr Adamski and his Venusian Space Brothers.'

'Aha,' said Papa Charlie, 'you mean this man is alleged to have actually *met* alien creatures?'

'I believe "beings" is the polite term, but yes; why, what was it you had in mind?'

'A more remote mode of contact.'

Ever so slightly the Sister's eyes rolled heavenwards. 'There are many examples,' she sighed. 'A Dr Vinod in India was said to have been a conduit for messages from an entity referring to itself as the Nine. He was "possessed", as it were, by this alien intelligence. As far as I could gather this meant that the doctor used a different voice when conveying the alien's message than he did in his normal life, and gave all the appearance of being in a trance during its transmission. Vinod was acquainted for a time with a Dr Puharich, who was associated with the young Uri Geller, whose unofficial Church, you'll no doubt be aware, has enjoyed great popularity ever since his alleged assumption into the bowels of a flying saucer – although given the Church's dove-ish take on the Palestinian question the Israeli authorities have been working on different theories regarding his disappearance. Puharich and Geller were said also to have received instruction from an alien overlord, the messages appearing, I think, on magnetic tape. I seem to remember that in Spain a Señor Sesma received telephone calls from a planet he maintained was in orbit about the star astronomers have designated Wolf 424, and a Mrs Swan, from I know not where, apparently took dictation for the Universal Association of Planets; the phenomenon was referred to in the literature as "automatic writing".'

'The information or messages these people received, or claimed to have received,' Papa Charlie asked, smiling, 'was there anything of value there, or can I assume from your tone that the experiences were deemed worthless?'

Sister Jasmine refused to be enamoured of the topic. 'Those interested in this area as a legitimate discipline, who do not

186

accept the physical and psychic components of these phenomena to be, in any sense we understand, "real", will of course argue that there is considerable significance in the fact that humankind generates these myths at all.'

'Not you though.'

'I have little tolerance with the yearning expressed for external assistance with putting humankind's house in order – be the assistance quasi-divine, ultra-technological or both.' She looked out of the window onto the narrow street, a hard mask descending upon her otherwise soft features. 'People should take responsibility for themselves and the world they live in. Instead, especially here in the First World where these phenomena are most common, they have allowed themselves to be moulded into societies of spoiled and grasping infants, without the inclination towards any degree of self-denial, without the long-term vision to see that their environment is not infinitely renewable, without the courage to object to the blatant immoralities of corporations and states, perhaps even the ability to recognise them; without . . . without humanity.' She stopped a moment before tossing her head towards the ceiling. 'And they look to the heavens for deliverance, to the traditional repositories of all that is supposed to be good, believing for some reason that they deserve it.'

'I know,' said Papa Charlie, a grim admiration in his expression, 'they sicken me too.'

She turned back to him then suddenly, alarmed; shocked at her own arrogance and vitriol, and yet, down in some deep and secret place that rarely benefited from expression within the Sisterhood, pleased that he appeared to agree. Mostly, though, she wanted to back away from the statement, to assert her belief in the essential goodness and morality of mankind, a morality so basic that even children had an intrinsic understanding of it, a morality only eroded by the rigours of institutionalism.

Papa Charlie saw her surprise and alarm and shrugged. 'It's okay,' he said. 'It's hard *not* to feel that way sometimes.' He sipped his coffee, peering at her from over the rim of the cup, revealing a shy, apologetic smile when he put it down again.

'Why are you interested in these stories of revelation?' she asked. 'Earlier you mentioned Mantra.'

He coughed into his hand softly. 'I was reading some stuff I'd dug up at work along the same lines, and got to thinking about these things in terms of the Mantra phenomenon.'

She squinted at him. 'You believe Mantra to be an alien agency dedicated to the disruption of sporting events?'

'No,' he laughed, 'but perhaps a human conduit obtained an alien program, downloaded it somehow, and became gradually aware of a staggering potential. The "events" staged may be a test of the untraceability of the mischief. Maybe there's more to come.'

'Certainly, what's to follow has always been the greatest worry for the authorities. With that probability Mantra have succeeded in producing edginess in high places, tantalisingly prolonged by the apparent want of novelty in their work. The authorities can estimate how much information has been tracelessly introduced into and extracted from their systems with each run, but Mantra's identical and repeated attacks on predictable targets is suggestive of a great confidence in the sophistication of their program, so the authorities' estimates may only be indicative of a pulled punch.'

Papa Charlie nodded. 'They know Mantra's holding jacks, but it could be a lot better.'

'Exactly. For the moment they seem reluctant to reveal more of their hand or to name stakes, and so everyone must wait and wonder; and while I'll admit this powerlessness is perplexing, it's hardly grounds from which to extrapolate alien intervention. Progress is a series of sharp inclines and expansive plateaux; there's nothing to indicate yet that this technology is anything more than one such developmental leap.

'Besides,' she swirled coffee grounds in the bottom of her cup, 'the technology seems far too useful. Most of the information gleaned from alleged contact with aliens has invariably been dross, or requests for proofs of faith from the contactees. I've never heard of anyone receiving anything as ordered as a program.'

Papa Charlie, unsure now of what one night last week had seemed a plausible theory, continued nevertheless with his train of thought. 'I just thought that since the authorities haven't turned up a single clue to the identities of these people, maybe it wasn't *people*, maybe it was just one person. To be frank, I love a lone gunman. If you think about it, it'd be a lot easier to keep secret, which might go some way towards explaining the absence of so much as a good rumour.'

Sister Jasmine shook her head as she considered it. 'Too much work for one person.'

Papa Charlie nodded. 'That was where the aliens came in.'

She rolled her eyes ceilingwards and did a parody of Oriental speech. 'G.I. Joe see too many movie.'

He laughed. 'I get carried away.'

Sister Jasmine smiled at him. 'I think that despite the time frame and the parochial radius, this could well be something like a marketing campaign aimed at the international military. Cover your ass, get protected; pass the buck, pay up; resistance is futile, you can't afford not to buy. Maybe the bidding will begin after this coming showdown with the heavyweight intrusions team. If Mantra succeeds in beating them.'

She suggested more coffee and got up from her seat to order. Papa Charlie opted for milk this time. He was silent when she returned to the table, staring out the window, more relaxed than he'd seemed earlier. She let him be and watched the activity behind the counter. She wondered what had led him to his strange idea about Mantra's technology.

Charlie drank from his glass and rolled a serviette across his top lip to erase any tide mark. 'How did you get involved in the Society?' he asked her, staring at the open napkin.

'The Vervain Mystery Girls?' she laughed, and watched Papa Charlie's shoulders rise and fall like a bubble in hot mud.

'Cool name,' he said after a moment, then tipped his head back slightly as if beckoning to her. 'Tell me.'

'My parents met a Sister Suki in Guatemala, before I was born. They were helping to organise popular agitation. Sister Suki is one of those we call the First Chosen – she was directly recruited by Father Gabriel. The three became friends and worked together often. Two years later, when I was eight months old, soldiers came and arrested my parents. I was left with Sister Suki. People who were associated with my parents began to disappear soon after, and Suki spirited me out of the country to Vervain Prime. She returned to Guatemala to hear that my parents had been released without charge, but they were never heard from again. It was unsafe for Suki to stay in Guatemala. She realised then that work had taken up so much of her association with my parents that she knew very little about them, other than my father was Malaysian and my mother of Japanese and Nigerian blood. They never spoke to her of their families, only of the future. She made what enquiries she could to trace my extended family, but there was nowhere else for me in the end.' She paused for a moment. 'It's an unremarkable story,' she told him when he appeared disinclined to speak. 'There are many like it among the Sisterhood.'

'Wasn't that how it all began? Homes for orphans.'

'There are many tales of the beginning. Most of the First Chosen have written about it in some form or other, but there is no official history.'

He winked at her. 'Just do your best.'

(viii)

It remains unclear as to why after thirty-three years Father Gabriel Vervain SJ broke with his Jesuit brothers. It is known that he had remained boundlessly idealistic, resourceful and energetic beyond the reasonable age for such virtues, and it is thought that the price for these gifts may have been a certain impulsiveness.

'There's the distinct possibility too,' wrote Sister Candice Maligña, in the slim but celebrated *Memories of Gabby*, 'that all of that education probably made the little bastard headstrong and uppity.' This was something of a joke, inasmuch as it was well known that one of Father Gabriel's pet hates was the waste involved in overeducating people with skills and information of questionable practicality; an accusation he was to level from time to time, not only at himself, but at all of the First Chosen. As Sister Suki de Chardin told it, 'This particular aversion seems to have stemmed from the neglect the Father felt his gastronomic centre suffered during a spell in a menial clerical position with the Society of Jesus, the neglect being brought about, in his opinion, as a result of his "having constantly to come up with sufficiently stimulating conversation for a bunch of overeager, overeducated filing clerks – over lunch!"'

Since the mid to late nineteen sixties the concept had been forming in Father Gabriel's mind of a community of decently educated, many-faceted and reasonable individuals, dedicated to the improvement of mankind's lot globally, and not requiring licence or strength from a common pool of dogma. The spirit of those times, the tide of social upheaval, not only left him with the sense that his idea could work, but with a powerful desire to change the world in an alarmingly short period of time. To do this, ironically, he was going to need reasonable, altruistic companionship of the most overeducated variety imaginable, and he was to find it in what, for him, were the uncharted waters of womanhood.

If he had looked ridiculous to his Jesuit brethren while throwing himself into the pond of activism, he at least proved to be a strong swimmer, and the fresh waters of need soon cooled his idealistic ardour and focused his abilities. He begged and borrowed and sold up what possessions he had in order to finance a trip around the world. For two years he travelled, receiving food and shelter from friends and friends of friends, speaking at dinner parties and informal gatherings of his hopes for the future and of his desire to further these hopes through activism. As a result he collected appreciable funds for his cause, but more importantly, he began to assemble a network of correspondents with similar ideals. From among these he would eventually select the First Chosen.

His most significant acquisition came while touring the Middle East. Following a spirited argument in favour of a two-state settlement of Palestinian grievances based on the 1967 borders, Father Gabriel was invited to enjoy the hospitality of an unnamed billionaire oil sheikh. The Sheikh was a hard-nosed businessman whose take-no-prisoners tendencies had been tempered by the birth of his son, whose emotional distance and taciturnity were eventually ascribed to autism. No expense was spared in treatment for the youngster, but in his now softer heart of hearts, the Sheikh would have gladly given his billions just to know the boy was reasonably contented, let alone have him communicate this fact directly.

The arrival of Father Gabriel at the Sheikh's household saw a small but encouraging improvement in the boy's condition, manifesting itself, occasionally, as something approaching playfulness. The Sheikh was convinced that Father Gabriel was in possession of a healing gift and pressured him for suggestions as to how else he might draw the boy out. Father Gabriel did not respond at once, but ruminated on the problem for over a week. He finally presented himself to the Sheikh in his library one evening.

'Porpoises,' he said.

'I beg your pardon?' said the Sheikh in his most polite Oxbridge tones, not sure if this strange but endearing little man was indicating that the boy should have some greater *purpose* to his life, or if he was indeed hearing him correctly.

'Introduce the boy to some porpoises,' said Father Gabriel, quietly but emphatically, making a little swimming mime with his right hand.

The Sheikh was beginning to think at this stage that Father Gabriel's oud was short a string, but was aware also of the notion that madness is often present in those exhibiting great intuition. He nodded solemnly, thanked his guest, and set about the task of bringing dolphins to the desert.

It was a year before he heard from the Sheikh again. Father Gabriel was in New York, planning to amass considerable funds through the execution of some dubious deals, with the help of a couple of disillusioned stock exchange insiders later to become Sisters Hillary and Philomena. The dolphins, it transpired, had been a resounding success, and the Sheikh's son was much improved. The Sheikh, overcome with gratitude, wanted to know how he could contribute to Father Gabriel's noble efforts, specifying that no expense would be too great.

'I need a property from which to work,' said Vervain. 'It must be isolated, above all, and, if possible, somewhere with nice weather.'

'I think,' said the Sheikh, 'I may have just the thing.'

Father Gabriel got himself a nice little island about five miles by five in the South China Sea which the Sheikh's father had picked up for a song during Diem's sponsored terror campaign in Vietnam in 1954. It was an idyllic spot, with a couple of beautiful beaches and about a million palm trees. The Sheikh took it upon himself to provide living quarters and two schoolhouses, and utilised the island's powerful waterfall to run a customised hydroelectric generator, thus effecting an impressive degree of indigenous self-sufficiency.

There were twelve First Chosen. Father Gabriel had settled on the number for old times' sake. He chose from among his many contacts the most dedicated, most radical, most able and, ironically, most educated. Every continent was represented twice at least, and the girls' talents ranged from computers to kung fu. In addition to their native tongues, English, Spanish and French were the languages common to all twelve women, and Father Gabriel found it incumbent upon himself, after a lengthy hiatus, to jump back into the dreaded books. 'Olé!' they'd shout when the *Padre*'s grammatical constructions left something to be desired. He would inform them, in tones of good-natured crustiness, that unless they were prepared to make 'that curséd noise' for the rest of his life, they'd better stop now. Drawing attention to his advanced age, he explained that his brain had become inflexible, and a foreign language learned with an inflexible brain was going to be left with a certain character, like it or not.

Much speculation surrounds the fledgling Society's acquisition of funds, and present-day questions addressed to any of the surviving First Chosen concerning such matters are wont to produce the ejaculation of a few cryptic non-sequiturs. What is clear is that the funds were acquired in record time by means of severely sharp practices. The monies were then turned into legitimate stockholdings under a variety of different names so as not to draw attention to the Society itself. Progress was as swift as the acquisition of wealth and Father Gabriel was, for the most part, a very happy man, although he was sometimes unnerved to find himself involved with what he referred to as 'a crowd of giggling women'. It often seemed to him that they were not taking matters as seriously as they might, and that during discussions of policy and planning they often sounded more like a hundred women than twelve. They would excitedly discuss the possibilities available to them in terms that owed too much to levity, in the Father's considered opinion. More disorienting, and eerily sinister, was the sudden appearance during these levitous discussions of an alarming screech which seemed to emanate randomly from each of the women in turn, like a disembodied spirit trying to find a home, entering a particular individual then leaving in a split second, and causing a single paroxysm of shrieking delight in each of its brief hosts. The banter, the laughter and the shrieking would swirl and settle naturally, and within it all there would have been a communication which Father Gabriel generally missed.

Over the months, the meetings became more formal, the

women falling into three groups of four which he insisted on moving between, believing that they had equally divided linear problems. He would have done better to stick with one group and listen. As it was he began to feel, with a slowly burgeoning sense of relief and gratitude, that the control of, and responsibility for, his hazy conglomeration of ideas was gently being wrested from him.

The women took stock of the fortune and began to flesh out the Father's framework. He ran around from place to place wondering what was going on, only occasionally recognising the fact that the women never let him go anywhere empty-handed. When someone in officialdom needed talking up to, the Father was given a brief rundown of the situation and marched in to do the talking up. Sooner than he would have ever imagined possible, work began in earnest for the formation of his Society.

(ix)

Marshall sat at his desk in the office staring bleary-eyed at the screen of his terminal. He replayed the segment he was editing again and again but it still wasn't right. A simple problem normally sorted in a matter of minutes had him frustrated this last half-hour. Incidental music, supposed to rise and fall between two sections of a Slide Benson monologue, was fading too soon behind the voice. He kept missing his place, going too far back, looking at values and then forgetting them the moment they left the screen, making a note and then forgetting where he'd put it. He didn't trust his ears or brain any more.

'Save and shut down,' he instructed, pushing the screen away and rubbing at his eyes. His gut rumbled; it was after nine o'clock.

Marshall heard the door of the office swing shut behind him and turned to find Henri McCambridge-LeMans leaning against the bookcase, a black jacket slung over one shoulder. His black polo neck, narrow and sharply creased black trousers and dark glasses left him resembling a ripe beatnik. 'I ran into the same brick wall myself a little while back and decided enough was enough. Have you eaten?'

Marshall shook his head. 'I was being reminded of the fact as you came in.' He patted his stomach, then looked quizzically at the Chairman. 'How *did* you get in?'

McCambridge-LeMans held up a small, flat, rectangular piece of black plastic. 'I'm the boss, Marshall, remember?' McLemon looked abashed and the Chairman continued, 'I stopped by to let you know that in my capacity as boss it has been possible for me to arrange with J.P. to provide you with a little help on the work front. You can start moving some of the paper records upstairs for collection. You'll be left to deal with enquiries in your specialised field, but the rest we'll have dealt with elsewhere.'

McCambridge-LeMans stepped further into the room and readjusted his glasses on the bridge of his nose, drawing Marshall's attention to the fact he was being regarded intently. 'I have also taken the liberty,' he continued, introducing a slight hesitancy into his delivery, 'of arranging for a media professional to aid you with the construction of your Exhibit.'

'Great,' said McLemon, a little hesitant himself. 'Thanks.'

'Don't worry, it's still your project,' said the Chairman. 'If anyone ever disagrees with you on that point you just talk to me. Now, how about that bite to eat?'

McCambridge-LeMans had a car waiting to take them to a club he retained membership of on the Green. The drive took a little less than an hour and the Chairman apologised for the necessity of making a few calls on the way, all of which he conducted in French. Marshall picked up only a few words clearly: *prisonniers*, *projet* and, inevitably, *Mantra*. He found himself relieved that the Chairman was discussing other WentWest business.

Marshall was uncomfortable with Henri's suggestion that a 'media professional' help them with their work. He and Papa Charlie had an understanding about what constituted material worthy of the Exhibit. Their partnership had been five years in the making and they were of one mind regarding development of the work. They'd had five years of discovery, discussion and argument that would be impenetrable to an outsider. Marshall sat quietly in the car and attempted to dissociate himself from his possessiveness and his paranoia. He told himself that there was a bond here, at least as far as the Frenchman seemed to think, that ran deeper than any employer–employee relationship, that was more durable than any contract, that could well aid in the triumph of his modest will. All it required was a degree of compromise, and there was no disgrace in compromise. Even Papa Charlie grudgingly admitted its occasional necessity.

The car swung around the Green and came to a halt at the kerbside. A man approached from a doorway in what appeared to Marshall to be hotel livery and opened the door for them. They walked up the steps and into the musty hallway of the club, where another deferential soul took their coats. There was a large room on their left with a bar, red leather chairs and dark wood panelling; the air was heavy with cigar smoke and the smell of liquor.

'I thought we might take something in the bar, rather than a full dinner,' said McCambridge-LeMans, and someone appeared to lead the way to a table by a window overlooking the Green. As they seated themselves another member of staff arrived with menus. The Chairman took a brief look at his before ordering an egg salad sandwich and something called *Filou*.

'"Filou"?' Marshall whispered.

'It's a strong beer,' the Chairman explained, 'brewed by French monks. It's very good. It is also exclusive to the club.' Under the circumstances Marshall decided that he'd better have the same. They sat in silence awaiting their orders. Marshall looked around and took in his surroundings in more detail. There were about twenty people in the bar, dotted about the place in little groups, talking quietly, reading from small screens or books. The occasional clink of glassware, the unobtrusive, light orchestral music and the murmur of conversation were blunted and softened by the smoke and the leather and the low lighting. The depth and richness of the atmosphere put Marshall more at ease than he'd felt in a long time. The food arrived and they ate in silence.

The men and women here were undoubtedly the movers and shakers and captains of industry that Charlie would rain scorn upon from time to time. The responsibility of maintaining the great unwashed didn't seem to have taken too much out of them. For the most part they were tall, well-fed types, dressed in expensive fabrics and displaying a small fortune in well-executed cosmetic surgery. Despite the surgery and the absence of one grey hair between the lot of them, Marshall knew them to be of Charlie's or his father's generation and their vanity seemed to him a ridiculous and sad thing. Charlie would consider this venue a prime target for the old anarchist's black fuse bomb. He flicked a glance sideways at the Chairman, and fancied he could see his antipathy mirrored. If McCambridge-LeMans didn't look his age it was probably because he had never worried about it.

Henri put his cutlery on his plate and wiped his mouth. 'Do you have an estimate as to when your Exhibit might be in place and running?' he asked.

'Papa Charlie thinks as much as two years for everything, but it should go into effect in three or more self-contained stages.'

McCambridge-LeMans considered this momentarily. 'I would like to see you do well with this, Marshall. You'll have to reallocate a lot of work starting next week. That should be no problem. John Lyons-Howard, the gentleman I spoke of, will be with you in a few days. I will tell you more about him when I have had a chance to meet him properly, but I hope that he will be instrumental in helping you get this thing in place a lot sooner than your present estimate indicates. We simply can't wait years for this.' Henri pointed at the plate in front of Marshall before drawing himself up to his full sitting height and peering towards what looked to be the top of a spiral staircase at the far end of the bar.

'Finish up,' he said, 'and we will see what excitement we can find in the Oubliette.'

(x)

John Lyons-Howard nervously drummed his fingers on the arm of his aisle seat, drawing a brief sideways glance from the woman at the window to his right. He turned towards her and stared into the side of her head until she dropped her gaze further into the book on her lap. What he really wanted to do was punch her on her tiny nose, or knock a few crinkles into her flawless plastic complexion. He looked away again and took a deep breath. The rollercoaster ride of speed and booze over the last twenty-four hours had left him dangerously unreasonable. He had to get a grip on himself. The acceleration at take-off had driven him into a head spin and he was eager for the steward to arrive with the drinks trolley. He wanted to take the edge off the blast he'd taken earlier in order to get his ass back in gear, pack his bag and get to the airport in time for his flight. He'd made it alright, but without time to stop at the bar for something to cool him out. The overnighter had been an imitative tribute to Kiely; up and down on speed and booze. He'd thought he'd finished with hard living years ago, but recently time to think was the last thing he felt he wanted, and he'd got out of it the best and only way he knew how. Realistically, thinking was probably what he should have been doing, and across a web of neurons safely tucked into some bottom drawer, he knew it.

The steward finally arrived and Lyons-Howard waited for his companion to decide whether she wanted tea or coffee, a decision which, it seemed to him, took an inordinate amount of time. He chewed at the inside of his mouth with his back teeth, and just as he feared he might draw blood she settled for a cola.

'Something for yourself, sir?' the steward asked him.

'Yeah, two large vodkas and tonic.' He could see to the right, out of the corner of his eye, his companion begin to look round again, then stop herself. The steward had no compunction, however, about cocking an eyebrow.

201

'Nervous flyer, sir?' This guy was all questions, and Lyons-Howard had to bite down on the urge to bark 'No! I'm a fucking alcoholic!' at him. Instead he held out his hand so the steward could see it shake.

'Lost my old man in a plane crash – 'aught one,' he told him. 'I'll calm down once I've taken the edge off and started concentrating on some work.' He flipped open the cell on the tray table in front of him and smiled maniacally at the steward. The steward smiled back and put the drinks on his tray table before moving on. Always travel first-class, Lyons-Howard thought to himself, they'd have restrained you for the rest of the flight had you done that in steerage.

With the drinks in front of him Lyons-Howard began at once to feel more at ease. He powered up the cell before pouring, then disengaged the machine's audio output and watched the text of Kiely's affidavit scroll up the screen in front of him, under Kiely's beautiful talking head.

My name is Kiely Elizabeth Flanagan. Up until three years ago I was a registered medical doctor, number 10542699. I make no secret of the fact that I was delisted on account of my drug use, but this has no bearing on the revelations you are about to hear. For the past thirteen months I have been employed by a company calling itself Medicorps, monitoring the sleep of subjects in a prolonged drug trial that purports to be a study of diet and environment in terms of efficiency . . .

He could nearly recite it by heart now, and had to check himself that his lips weren't moving lest he further alarm his companion in the seat beside him. When Kiely's affidavit ended he punched up the encrypted files Kiely had taken from McCann's terminal at the research facility. No one he'd asked online had wanted to touch them; such it seemed was the nature of the encryption that they'd all disconnected immediately and he'd been left none the wiser as to the contents. He had nothing that could hurt Gillespie or McCann or their boss. All he would manage to do by releasing what he had would be to get hurt himself, killed most likely, like those two poor bastards at the warehouse, shot like dogs. He kept going back to his trip in the limo with McCann; how he'd been better than half convinced he was a dead man; how he'd calmly accepted the inevitability of it and refused to fight. In a way, he supposed, he had been dead ever since he consented to take that ride. He certainly hadn't felt alive in his London hotel room, just a shell of bitterness and muted grief. And despite the semblance of life he'd exhibited when out on the town drunk and stoned, he'd known for years that that wasn't living. Kiely had known it too, and the first thing she'd done to extricate herself from that nether world of depravity and the half-life of intoxication had put her over the edge for good. It had been a foolish risk maybe, and in his own thirst for scandal he had egged her on to it. But it hadn't been her fault and it needn't have ended the way it did. It was difficult for him to ascribe the blame to the two corpses he had seen, they'd been so pathetic. What made it more difficult was that the Frenchman and Gillespie wanted him to blame the poor bastards. They'd have been infinitely more detestable alive, he was sure. Gillespie and the Frenchman had made a mistake in killing them. They'd hoped to appeal to his sense of justice and had instead drawn on his sympathy.

He checked the time and shut down the unit. They'd be landing in about thirty minutes, he figured. McCambridge-LeMans wanted to see him at WentWest Head Office on Friday to give him a rundown on the installation he was supposed to be working on. He drained his glass and his stomach tightened painfully around the cold liquid. He poured his second in on top of the half-melted ice, watched its effervescence leap from the surface of the liquid, and thought about how he'd need a little of that vigour to get himself up for this meeting. He'd lost count of the amount of times he'd been up, then down, in the last twenty-four hours. Not that he cared; he was dead already.

<h3 style="text-align:center">(xi)</h3>

The Oubliette, as one might expect, was in the basement of Henri's club, and was accessed by the single spiral staircase Marshall had seen in the bar above. The bar of the Oubliette, to their left as they hit the end of the narrow twist of black metal, was an art deco wonder built of wood, leather and marble, illuminated by warm globes and elongated lozenges of yellow light. The tiling in the floor around the bar extended three metres. Marshall was glad to get to it and off the carpet which had more give in it than he found was comfortable for walking. A man came out from behind the bar when he saw them, and did that French thing, putting his head either side of McCambridge-LeMans' for a moment while holding his upper arms near the shoulders. Henri introduced him as 'Marbles' Moloney, the Oubliette's manager. The Frenchman had the emphasis on the second syllable, Mar*bells*. Moloney ordered drinks for them and entreated Marshall to take a table. Henri said he would follow with the drinks.

Marshall walked to the edge of the lush carpet and looked ahead, waiting for his eyes to get used to the darkness. Moloney and Henri spoke quietly to each other behind him. There were tables sparsely arranged on the floor with large comfortable chairs around them and booths against the wall. There were enough people in the place to make it seem lively, but even with all of the tables and booths full it would never seem crowded. Waiting staff patrolled the floor in crisp white shirts and black bow ties; the girls all in short tight black skirts and fishnets, the boys all in indecently tight black trousers. They were all perfectly proportioned and flawlessly featured as far as Marshall could see. He caught Henri's attention and indicated a booth in the corner to his right before moving towards it. It was the best free vantage point, with a view of the bar and of the small stage and dance floor. He walked over, removed his jacket and sat down. He was lighting a cigarette when a petite but perfectly formed waitress arrived at his table with an ashtray and serviettes.

'May I get you something to drink?' she asked. She had an attractive smoky quality to her voice. Marshall's pulse raced for a second when he looked at her; she was exquisite. She had short, shaggy dark hair, a sallow complexion, big deep-blue eyes and a provocative crimson swelling beneath her barely extant nose. Marshall figured she was about five or six years older than he was.

'No thank you,' he was disappointed to hear himself say, 'it's on its way.' He pointed back towards the bar and she followed with a turn of her beautiful head.

'Henri!' she exclaimed softly, smiling. 'I didn't realise he was here.' Marshall saw a look of disappointment in her right profile before she turned back to him. 'I'm Mandy,' she said, jabbing a thumb into her chest. 'I don't want to disturb Henri while he's talking to the boss, and I'm off backstage and won't be out for a bit yet. Would you give him something for me?'

'Sure.'

It would not have occurred to the average male to do

anything that would increase the physical distance between himself and Mandy. No rational process would have been required to illustrate the essential foolishness of such an act. It would have been a given. As it was, she had already succeeded in suppressing that reflex in Marshall McLemon that made him blink every fifteen or twenty seconds, and the tears welling in his eyes made her, as far as he was concerned, gleam all the more. When her head descended towards his he made no movement, and when she pressed her lips against his own he only closed his eyes, squeezing out the accumulated water, which ran in two thin lines down either cheek. Her mouth engulfed his and her tongue probed between his lips and ran across his teeth. Her lipstick had a distinctive flavour that reminded him of a brand of chewing gum. When she disengaged, his head remained tipped back and from somewhere he heard her say, 'Thanks.' By the time he opened his eyes again she was gone. Her sudden absence brought him back to his surroundings and, though no one gave any sign of having noticed the kiss, he blushed deeply. The last of the blush had not subsided when Henri arrived at the table with their drinks. He placed a tall red cocktail in front of Marshall and took a seat opposite him. Marshall, trying to appear nonchalant, dabbed at his mouth with one of the serviettes before picking up the unfamiliar concoction and taking a long draught. It tasted exactly like Mandy. He looked up in surprise only to find McCambridge-LeMans had been waiting for this very reaction.

'Did you enjoy meeting Mandy?' he said.

'Yeah,' said McLemon, looking from the drink back to the Chairman. 'She asked me to convey her warmest regards.'

'We'll see her again in due course,' said the Frenchman. 'Drink up.'

Marbles Moloney arrived at the table a few moments later

with a waiter who resembled an overdressed Greek statue, carrying another tray of drinks.

'You gentlemen mind if I join you?'

The question appeared to warrant no further response than McCambridge–LeMans shifting around in the booth. Moloney sat opposite Marshall, completing a triangle of which the Chairman was the apex. The waiter placed the drinks on the table and left. The Frenchman drew a box of cheroots from the jacket beside him and offered them around.

'How did you like Mandy?' Moloney grinningly asked Marshall.

Marshall shrugged. 'I liked her.'

Moloney nodded his approval and laughed. 'I think you'll enjoy your visit with us, young man.' He picked up his glass and held it over the centre of the table for a toast. 'Cheers!' he said and they all touched glasses. He drank off half the contents of his own and put the glass on the table in front of him. He clapped his hands together and rubbed them as if he were cold. 'Anyone got any money on the final tonight?' he wanted to know. He was referring to the slugfest match in Budapest between the erratic Irish genius, Troy Fitzgerald, and the Argentinian Iceman, Juan Borges. Fitzgerald had dropped out of the slugfest circuit for more than a year following his marriage and the birth of his son. At twenty-six he still had a few years in him and had begun training in earnest again in January, although, save his share in the team victory that April in London, he was without a major title well into the second half of the season. Borges had remained in the top ten for five years, reaching the number one spot on three occasions, and was the clear favourite for the match.

'Call it a hunch,' said the Chairman, 'but I quite like Fitzgerald for this and I have a small wager on him.'

'That's where the smart money is – most bookies have him at seven to four, but I can actually get twos.' Moloney looked at Marshall and Henri as if this last lot were giving away money. 'What people are forgetting,' he continued, 'is that Fitzgerald was always a slow starter. Sure, his serve percentage has dropped into the seventies, but even when he was top five his serve percentages never went to more than eighty-one in the first two quarters of any season. And need I remind you what stage we're at now.' He looked from Marshall to Henri, his eyes wide. 'A study of the stats will show you his serve percentage climbing rapidly and steadily in the second half of every season he's ever played. On the other hand Borges drops off towards the middle of the season, loses concentration and can't be depended on for the big occasion – never won the Moore Cup, for instance – *plus* he's had a lot of matchplay so far this year. If you want to look at Fitzgerald's return figures, they *never* drop from twenty, *and* he tends to group them into consecutive twos and threes; Borges could never do that, gets more breaks from faults than anything else, depends on solid play and single breaks at crucial points, and in that respect, as I've said, he should be coming into his suspect phase about now.' Moloney sat back and folded his arms. It was clear he felt Fitzgerald's victory was assured in light of this incontrovertible evidence.

'Do you have a bet on the match?' McCambridge-LeMans asked Marshall.

'No, I –'

'Put five hundred on Fitzgerald for Marshall,' the Frenchman instructed Moloney, who drew a cell from his pocket and tapped in the details before Marshall could raise a protest.

'Excellent,' said Moloney, 'we can settle up after the game.' Marshall was dumbfounded. He quietly drained his drink and moved his second into place in front of him. What was Henri thinking off? Was the five hundred a gift, or was Marshall expected to ante-up out of his own pocket should Moloney's predictions prove unfounded? Marshall had never bet on anything in his life, and he wasn't sure he wanted to start now. At the same time he felt too embarrassed to attempt to withdraw the bet. Five hundred was nearly a quarter of his monthly salary after deductions, but it was probably peanuts to this pair. He had enough in the bank to cover the bet, but it would be a lean end to the month should the erratic Irish genius lose. The dubious thrill said to be inherent in such activities had manifested itself as a faint queasiness – five hundred bananas!

The money was gone, he decided. There was nothing he could do about it now except tighten his belt for the rest of the month. It'd give him a chance to concentrate on the extra work he had ahead of him.

As Marshall started into his second Mandy-flavoured cocktail and another waiter arrived at their table with three more, a deep metallic drone started in a speaker somewhere. It registered in the floor as a dull vibration, the effect of which was strongest around the sinuses; the ghost of some dentist's drill almost. It was joined then by other synthetic, nearly-pure tones, and stage lights came up in front and to Marshall's right. The small stage was now inhabited by a bald man of sixty-five or more, in a light grey Nehru jacket and black trousers, operating banks of ancient silver and black machinery studded with little red and green lights. In the two square metres available to him he managed to do a lot of moving about; side to side, upstage and down, he went from component to component, turning knobs, sliding faders, opening and closing filters and envelopes and tapping up increments. It appeared to Marshall that he was going to some effort to produce a sound that was decidedly ugly.

'The floor show,' Moloney announced proudly, as a stiff insistent bass line jumped from the speakers and figures rushed from each side of the stage to mount eight pentagonal perspex platforms that had risen out of the small dance floor in front. Beams of shifting coloured light shot from the ceiling to illuminate the figures, who had begun dancing to a percussive slapping sound which accompanied the bass. The figures were those of four men and four women who appeared to Marshall to be naked; although they moved so fast, in a flurry of arms and legs, with violent waves and shudders running through them, that even without the flashing lights he couldn't have been sure of it. As he turned in his seat to watch them, he saw from the corner of his eye that some of the crowd had begun to shuffle forward from the dark end of the room behind him and take empty tables nearer the dance floor, the better to see. The strobe-like effect of the lights rendered the spectators expressionless, and their progress towards the stage fitful and alarming. Marshall found he couldn't get comfortable again until they were all seated.

After a couple of minutes one of the dancers broke from the others and came towards Marshall and his party, vaulting onto their table and continuing to dance. Marshall kept his eyes front and down. He could tell from the size of the feet that it was a girl. He flicked a glance at Marbles and Henri, who appeared to be enjoying the performance, the butt of a cheroot smouldering between Henri's fingers, Marbles alternately sipping at his drink and licking his lips.

'Hey!' A voice above him brought his head up. He hadn't expected to be addressed by the performer and was caught unawares. He looked up to see Mandy, naked as a jaybird but for a thong, and smiling at him about it. This woman seemed hell-bent on embarrassing him. Unsure what to do he tried a very unconvincing smile and gave her a little wave before returning his gaze to the drink in front of him. She leaned over and put her index finger under his chin to lift his head. That was decided then, he supposed, and tried smiling again. It occurred to him that he seemed to have very little control over what happened to him this evening, the kiss, the bet, this. The idea calmed him a little, and he took another gulp of his drink without taking his eyes from Mandy. She was very beautiful. The music dropped then suddenly, both in tempo and in volume. The dancers leapt from their supports, and Mandy from the table, and disappeared at either side of the stage again.

Marbles leaned towards him. 'The composer and performer is Claude Haquen, the Belgian maestro, quite famous twenty-five or thirty years ago.'

Marshall was nodding, glad no one was making reference to the appalling scene that had just occurred. 'The *enfant terrible* of a type of minimal electronic composition,' he expanded on Marbles' intro, 'vilified by those subscribing to the prevailing ethos at the time as a charlatan, but he retained some kudos among a small group of serious composers and critics.'

'There's very little you can tell Marshall about such things,' the Chairman said to Marbles. 'He's one of the curators at our Archive.'

Moloney couldn't quite keep a certain oh-I-see out of his expression.

'No one's heard anything from this guy in years,' Marshall continued. 'I assumed he was dead or something.'

'Or something?' said Moloney, wryly.

'As I understand, a lot of people who were into the electronic

211

music scene used an array of neuro-toxins for their psychedelic effects. As this generation moved into their mid forties,
a couple of hundred thousand of them lapsed into comas as a
result of the action of the toxins, which, it turns out, had
continued long after the psychedelic effect had subsided. Far's
I know a lot of them are still there.'

'Well,' Marbles shrugged, 'old Claude survived. He flies over
here three times a month; we're his only gig because he owes
me a small fortune on a couple of ill-advised wagers, and we
like exclusivity here at the club. Doesn't talk to me any more
though, 'cause I added the dancers to his show – didn't like
that much. He just takes what I pay him and goes back home.
Doesn't do an awful lot for his money, to be honest, except
run around between those machines shading the tones. He's
got a stochastic program on one of those things that composes
for him. He says he just interprets the machine's improvisation
in terms of timbre, or something. I don't know much about
any of it. I just think he's cute in an old-fashioned sort of way,
and there's always a great reception for the show.'

Marshall stifled a snort of derision. Papa Charlie wouldn't
have listened to this for long. The term 'shit artist' would have
been aired by now. It was Papa Charlie's conviction that people
like Claude Haquen put working musicians out of jobs.

'Did it ever occur to you, Marbles, that your customers may
only endure Monsieur Haquen because of the dancers?'
McCambridge-LeMans asked.

Moloney affected an ironical pout. 'That's a point,' he said,
'but equally, the dancers' performance may only be as enthralling
as it is on account of their enjoyment of Claude's "thing".'

This was too much for Marshall and the derisive snort finally
escaped him. Moloney looked at him in surprise, as if this pale
librarian might actually be in possession of teeth.

'We'll ask Mandy what they think of it when she comes out so,' said Marbles with a decisive nod of his head.

Marshall reddened from his neck up to his forehead and drank off a good portion of his cocktail in an effort to cover his discomfiture. He was looking at his glass and thinking that he was feeling a bit light-headed, when Marbles caught the attention of one of his waiters and ordered another round with a circular motion of his index finger. The thought of trying to keep up with this pair all night made Marshall feel all the woozier, and he decided it was time to splash a little cold water on his face against the onslaught ahead.

'Where, eh, is the –' he began, before Moloney guessed.

'Behind where you came in, go left past the stairs and you'll see it to the right. Oh, and by the way,' Marbles added, winking, 'you're an incubus.'

'Right,' said Marshall cautiously. He got out of the booth and headed back towards the spiral staircase on the thick carpet, which, if anything, had increased in its elasticity since he last crossed it. Maybe it wasn't the carpet, he thought. Maybe it was him. Between the beer brewed by mad French monks and the Mandy-flavoured cocktails he didn't know how much he'd actually had to drink. Four or five beers down at the Pig, maybe a spliff, he could handle. Equally, he knew where he stood drinking wine, but spirits were a new thing to him. As he passed the bar he felt he drew the attention of a bunch of suits to his right, who had returned to the shadows from the tables up front following the floor show. Their murmuring dropped a little and was replaced by a hissing, clicking noise he imagined a hive of insects might make after lights out.

He made it to two doors marked 'Incubi' and 'Succubi' and Marbles' cryptic parting shot made sense. Recalling his designation he pushed through the correct door to find himself in a dimly lit room in which every surface was painted black.

Having groped around and found the basins, Marshall washed his face and allowed the cold water to drip off for a minute before drying. He emerged from the bathroom feeling a deal fresher. The carpet didn't seem to roll against him so much on his way out and the suited men and women in the shadows seemed less threatening. Claude Haquen was back on stage, adjusting the tones of a slow, quiet piece created by his compositional program, while a lone female dancer undulated atop a perspex platform. As the booth came into view Marshall could see that a waiter was serving yet more drinks and that the company had expanded. He knew Mandy would be part of this expansion and felt his faculties sharpen all the more at the prospect of looking at her again. When he got to the table she was sitting on McCambridge-LeMans' right just inside of his space. A blonde girl sat between McCambridge-LeMans and Moloney. She was introduced as Ingrid. Mandy turned when he arrived and gave him a look of good-natured indignation.

'Marbles tells us, Mr McLemon, that you don't care for Claude's stylings very much. I can only hope you had a better opinion of our performance.'

Marshall cleared his throat as he took his seat beside her. 'I know something of music,' he explained apologetically, 'but nothing, I'm afraid, about dance.' He was amazed that in the short time she had been away he had actually forgotten just how beautiful she was. He was aware of wanting to impress her, or, more accurately, of not wanting to displease her.

'Well,' she said, 'I'm sure we can get around to familiarising you with a few steps before the night's out.'

Oncle Henri

PROGRAMME: Staines at 7.

DATE: Thursday, 19th October.

STEVE: It's just gone [time nearest minute], Thursday the nineteenth, and you're tuned to TuMur.

CUE: Fanfare 647. 1½"

STEVE: It's still cold, [CUE: wind 3 FX152. 2"] back down to seven or eight degrees, [CUE: groan FX894. 1"] but the good news is the rain's back. [CUE: thunderbolt 7 FX747. ½"] Whoopee. [pause]

    I see May Watson [CUE: wolf whistle FX369. ½"] in an article in this month's Style Monitor tells us that women in the twenty to thirty age bracket have lost interest in boys and want men again.

CUE: Primal grunt 4 FX123. 1"

CUE: Track 1. 3'15" slow fade up behind Steve & FX

STEVE: 'The last few years' flirtation with boyish androgyny,' she says, 'will be superseded by a desire for the meatier relationship which only the more mature man can provide.' Lock up your daughters, I'm off the diet!

CUE: Saucy devil FX996. ½"

STEVE: It's Rosie . . .

FULL FADE UP

(i)

Marshall was aware of a profound sickness, possessing a single white-hot point of focus, which quantumesquely contrived to occur behind each of his closed eyes simultaneously. He had every expectation of looking in the mirror, at some point in the near next-couple-of-hours, to find someone had driven a long nail into his forehead. There was insult to this injury which, through its insistence rather than his effort, he eventually recognised as the voice of a woman, cajoling him in tones far too perky to do that which he was least inclined to do, which was wake up.

'Come on, Big Spender, it's your boss.'

'Jesus!' The lids of what were undoubtedly his bloodshot eyes cleaved to the orbs themselves and the contents of his skull reeled with his attempt to sit up. The brain-reeling made his stomach contract three times, just hard enough to bring tears to his appreciative eyes. He was forced to inhale and exhale slowly and deliberately to avoid vomiting. 'What time is it?' he croaked at no one in particular.

'Time you were up, my extravagant friend,' McCambridge-LeMans answered from the cell Mandy shoved into the hand Marshall had been attempting to put to his head. 'I was speaking with the chef of Le Manducat at my hotel this morning. I was very impressed with him; French, of course. He has what sounds to be an intriguing red wine sauce, which he serves with fillet of pork, fried rice and steamed vegetables. I'm dying to try it. I may go with prawns to begin, or mackerel. If their cellar is half as good as he says we will have to try three bottles at least; anything less would be a sin. Why don't I meet you and your father there tonight at eight?'

'Sure,' said Marshall, blinded momentarily by another shooting pain in his head. A pain which at least had the decency to cut through the fresh wave of nausea brought on by Henri's culinary musings. 'But don't line up anything like last night,' he gargled at the Frenchman, 'you'll kill both of us.'

Henri smiled. 'Excellent. Now get yourself straightened out and get to the office. It is important to make the effort every day. I want to study your grand design before I meet with Mr Lyons-Howard, so polish it up and bring it tonight. I will call you later.'

In addition to being sick, Marshall was now incredulous to boot. 'You mean the *whole* thing?'

'Well, of course I mean the whole thing. What have you been doing up until now?'

'We have some expanded features, but mostly we've been concentrating on individual, personal essays.'

Henri was very curious; this he demonstrated by speaking quite slowly. 'But what format is the *big* picture in? The plan!'

'It's not in any format, it's just out there – when we talk and that,' Marshall trailed off, his incredulity ousted by the sense of himself as rank amateur. The sickness remained as vigorous as ever.

'You can't expect to operate without a plan, Marshall. Give me detail where you have it by all means, but I want to see that vast expansive thing I've heard you speak of. And I want it tonight. You have to prove yourself less and less the longer you're on the top flight, but to get here you *do* have to prove yourself.' McCambridge-LeMans smiled and looked to the edge of the screen, raising his voice a little. 'Mandy, see to it he gets out in good shape.' He hung up.

Marshall dropped the portable onto the bed, sat up straight and finally got a hand to his head. Out of the corner of his watery eye the blurred, naked figure of Mandy made its way through the living room and into the kitchen.

'Not a bad place,' he heard her shout to him over the opening of the fridge and the activating of the water dispenser. 'But you should really get a decorator in. It's dull.'

Marshall laughed, then groaned with pain. 'That's a little out of my league,' he said.

'Nah,' she said, 'it's a small place. You've got more than enough money left to do a nice job with it. Nothing too fancy.'

Enough money? Marshall had to think hard before the previous evening started coming back to him and he knew what in hell she was talking about.

When the Argentinian Iceman went up three sets in just under thirty minutes' game time, Marbles Moloney started going on and on and on about how there was no way back for his opponent, Fitzgerald. Marshall, sick and tired at that stage with listening to Moloney on any topic, but mostly irritated that he was about to go down five hundred clams on the bastard's recommendation, decided, for pig iron, to disagree with their host. They continued to disagree through a lengthy medical time out, in which Fitzgerald received treatment for an alleged groin strain. There had been a good amount of drink taken when the match resumed and Marshall had by that time convinced himself that the erratic Irish genius could actually do it. Moloney stood to lose two grand should the Argentinian win. Marshall, in what could only be described as a fit of pique, rashly staked that amount against Moloney's winnings should Fitzgerald prevail in the following four sets. The bet was accepted and the Irish genius shifted erratically between a solid, average game and, when it really counted, a great game, taking the last four sets by the narrowest of margins. The Chairman had laughed uproariously at Moloney's expression when Fitzgerald put his Championship point return past the rapidly melting man of ice, whom fatigue had left irrigating the barren soil of no man's land. Moloney coughed up with good grace; said he wouldn't have believed it only he'd seen it; best fuckin' slugfest match ever. At the end of the night Marshall liked him a lot better, and was relieved to find out from Henri that Moloney could well afford to lose his two grand, let alone forfeit his winnings. The Chairman also let it be known that Marshall's bet was his gift, or would have been had Fitzgerald failed. Marshall had spent like a maniac then, refusing to let anyone pay for anything for the rest of the night. But despite his generosity he was sure he had better than four and a half grand left.

Mandy returned to the room with a bowl of breakfast cereal and a glass of water. 'I could fix you up with a guy I know if you like.'

'Sorry?' Although Mandy had provided him with something of an education when they got home last night, he felt now that she was making some wild assumptions regarding his sexual appetites.

'Wouldn't cost even two thousand,' she said.

He looked at her blankly.

'A decorator,' she explained.

'Oh,' he said, hoping she was going to drop that subject soon. 'We'll see.'

Mandy shrugged and pushed the bowl of cereal at him. 'Here, eat.' She rested the glass of water on the bedside table and rummaged through her handbag, withdrawing a small bottle of pills. Marshall looked at the contents of the bowl without relish.

'Eat,' said Mandy, noting his hesitancy. 'I can't give you this without something in your stomach.'

'I'm not taking that.' He regarded the pill she was holding with suspicion.

'You are if you want to get a day's work done.'

'What is it?' He put his head in his hands.

'A mild amphetamine, nothing serious.'

Marshall massaged his temples.

'Don't worry,' she said, patting his forearm and kissing the top of his head. 'Believe it or not, I'm a registered nurse. And I used to work for a guy who was . . . well, a type of chemist; so I had to get my diploma in pharmacology too.'

He looked up. 'This, presumably, was after you won that cup you told me about in Paris, for cookery.'

'Yes,' she said happily. 'I was still in college then. I think that was the same year I made the gymnastics team.'

(ii)

A grey drizzle blew up the street from behind Papa Charlie as he headed out towards Mitzi's for lunch. He got a seat at the counter and ordered a sandwich, before clipping on his earpiece to get the audio from the screen in front of him.

'You want a drink with that?' the waitress asked.

'Yeah, milk.'

'Milk drinker? We have a special on the new flavour *Moose* if you like. Grape and original malt.'

'Milk'll be fine, thanks.'

She put up his drink and went to serve another customer. Papa Charlie flicked idly through the channels on the screen. It was five past the hour and the news channels were all out with their sports reports. The majority featured lengthy speculation as to whether a Mantra disturbance could be expected during the coming Friday's European Cup quarter-final. Especially in light of the fact that McCambridge-LeMans had commissioned Cypol's best men to foil Mantra's high jinks. Papa Charlie thought it highly likely the normal disturbance would follow regardless. Brent Sturmer and Wayne Grant, Channel Ten's guest sports pundits, were of the same opinion.

'It's got the high profile they like,' Brent was saying. 'They've never hit, for instance, a tractor pull or a drag race.'

'And long may that remain so,' said Richie Dickerson, the anchorman, who was obviously a fan.

'Do WentWest sponsor stuff like that?' Wayne asked the air in front of him.

'This is a WentWest-sponsored event, which as we know is the main thing,' Brent went on, wrestling a cue out of Wayne's question and ignoring the anchorman. 'And it's telling that the Chairman of WentWest is in town this week with the same Cypol team of Latvian countermeasures experts who foiled the intrusion into the Wells Bank system last year. I've heard people saying that because of this Mantra won't show, but I feel that they're such a bunch of twisted freaks that the opportunity to *reach* . . .' he emphasised the word grotesquely, shoving his upper body forward and bobbing his head from side to side like an insolent teenager, 'an audience of these dimensions will draw them in regardless of the dangers. Even in a best-case scenario the hard-working public will to some extent be held to ransom, because Mantra'll have to run their gimmick before the Cypol boys can locate them. I personally wish they'd just go away.'

'And so say all of us, Brent, and so say all of us.'

Papa Charlie flicked over to TuMur where they had a guest 'medical expert' talking about ear plugs.

'I think that for the people in the auditorium at the time of a disturbance they are essential. The decibel levels are certainly in a range that, in some cases, can produce permanent damage to the hearing. And it's clear from this, and from the fact that eight-hundred-odd people have admitted themselves to hospital because of these pranks, that Mantra, whoever they are, have as little regard for people's health as they do for their right to enjoy this type of entertainment.'

'Thanks, Bob,' said Tom Richard, the TuMur TV News anchorman. 'Of course, Bob, on TuMur we like to talk about sport as a *core of grittiness*, or a *crucial decision*, sometimes *a way of life*, but never *this type of entertainment*!'

Bob laughed. 'Sorry, Tom. I know what you mean. I'm a golf nut, it's an obsession.'

'That's the stuff!' Tom laughed along. 'And I know you wanted to mention that your agency is providing a government–approved plug for everyone attending Friday's extravaganza.'

'Two plugs, Tom. Two each.' Bob was on a roll with the gags.

'Catch you at the game, Bob.' Tom had had enough of that. 'Next we're going to Niles Riordan with a story that has Troy Fitzgerald caught *in flagrante de trio*, during the celebrations following his epic win last night . . .'

Papa Charlie flipped the unit into standby and finished his sandwich staring blankly at the saver. He wanted to call Sister Jasmine. He didn't have much (anything, if he was honest) to tell her, but found he wanted to call her anyway. Running level with this desire was the fear that she might be fed up looking at him. It'd be something like four times in three days, after all. If he thought about it one way it seemed perfectly reasonable that he should get together with her to discuss an item of mutual interest. In other ways he found himself suspicious of his own motives. How much did he care about this alleged crime? How much would he have cared if it hadn't happened on his front door? A thousand fatal car accidents a year, and a thousand more unsolved or unexplained deaths; why should he give a shit about this one? Was it the accident at all? If Jasmine wasn't involved how interested would he now be? For that matter, how interested could she be in a man his age?

He mulled it over staring into the mirror on the far side of the counter. The man looking back was unkempt and sloppy. He wore a week's beard and hadn't had a haircut in nearly two years. His clothes were warm and baggy and his shoes soft and brown. Papa Charlie could remember a time he wouldn't even have considered brown shoes.

He decided in the end to opt for the cooler approach with Sister Jasmine and he dropped her a short note rather than call her again:

MADE INSURANCE ENQUIRY. NO DICE. WE CAN DO SERIAL NUMBER ENQ. LATE TOMORROW EVENING. SEE ME 20:00 HRS AT THE BLIND PIG. THE ONLY PLACE WE CAN AVOID SOCCER. MAP ATTACHED. MAIL ME IF THERE'S A PROBLEM.

P.C.

Papa Charlie was used to Marshall being slow and deliberate at his work and it perplexed him, therefore, upon his return from lunch, to see the boy run about in so frantic a manner. He'd blurted out something about preparing a sketch of the proposed structure of the entire Exhibit so Henri McCambridge-LeMans could show it to 'John Lyons-fucking-Howard'. He had then demanded of Papa Charlie, virtually ordered him, to dredge up some old ideas and models for inclusion in said sketch. Papa Charlie had been patient, he'd remained silent, sitting with his arms folded against his chest. After a number of seconds Marshall realised he'd been out of line. Charlie sat him down and in doing so saw his pupils were the size of pinheads. Marshall saw the look and took a couple of deep breaths. He recounted the events of the previous evening, or most of them. Reading between the lines Charlie was pretty sure the boy had been in the saddle last night, maybe for the first time; and with as artful a guinea-hen, by the smirk on his face, as ever shook a tail feather. The woman had obviously been laid on by the Frenchman, though to what end Charlie didn't know. Perhaps it was McCambridge-LeMans' belief that such an experience might imbue the boy with more confidence, or perhaps he had seen Marshall's dissatisfaction with the suggestion of John Lyons-Howard coming on board and hoped to bring him to heel with such confectioneries.

There was about a minute's silence, during which Papa Charlie fancied the boy calmed a little more. 'Looks to me like you're trying to cram a whole lot of new stuff into a perfectly modest outline,' he said, looking at the disks and tapes piled on Marshall's desk.

'Yeah,' said Marshall, looking at the eight-track cartridge in his hand. 'He said he wants expansive and I hoped to maximise the level of any backing we get.'

'Permanent installation is pretty maximum, Marshall.'

'Yeah but, in for a penny, y'know.'

'At the features end focus on the stuff we know best,' Papa Charlie advised. 'Skim over the sketches of ideas, making it clear research is required, which is dependent on the level of funding, blah blah. When you get to "level of funding", move onto some of the techie stuff, the types of platform you see us using, production issues. He doesn't appear to want to wait two years to see this finished, so he's not expecting us to do it alone. You've only got to assure him of our ability to direct the project. He's been smart enough already to provide us with Lyons–Howard; to help, I imagine, with publicising and day-to-day management, which we've no experience in.'

'What do you make of that?'

Papa Charlie shrugged. 'Seems sensible.'

'But a guy who's had a couple of pops at J.P. already? And who's got to be hugely expensive into the bargain?'

'Maybe the Chairman just likes pissing J.P. off.'

'That's clear enough. He doesn't need us for that. Maybe he really sees the potential here.' Marshall seemed to relax a little more. He threw the cartridge in his hand onto one of the piles on his desk. 'Still a shit-load of work, even if I ignore all of this.'

'Here,' said Papa Charlie, tapping at his board. 'I've spruced up the features on Belmondo, Bogart and Brando and added what I think to be the definitive list of their signature pictures – you can see what you think yourself. I've also fattened up the catalogues in the Vaudeville, Ragtime and Swing features and drafted copy for the voiceover in each case. They're all eminently presentable.'

'Thanks,' Marshall smiled. 'Y'know, I've got a feeling this is going to be big.'

'It was always going to be big,' said Charlie.

Marshall shook his head. 'Bigger,' he said.

'Virtual auditoriums, cinemas, theatres,' Papa Charlie tittered, carried away for a moment with the excitement of it.

'Auditoria,' Marshall corrected.

'Either's acceptable.'

Marshall wiggled his eyebrows and threw his arms out expansively. 'Virtual drive-ins!'

'Jesus,' said Charlie, 'that *would* be great.'

'We could have all-nighters once a month, showing all five "Apes" movies back to back.'

Papa Charlie grimaced. 'That'd be popular.'

'We could construct a virtual Vampira to do the intros at the Theatre of Horror!'

'Yeah,' Charlie laughed, 'we could have her spouting Coyne Fariss's *Essays On the Preternatural Imagination.*'

'Excellent,' said Marshall, smiling and staring into the middle distance.

Papa Charlie hoped he was right. Curator of a digital museum might not have been everyone's idea of a dream job, but it came close enough to theirs.

'Don't count your chickens, buddy boy.' Papa Charlie poked a rigid forefinger twice into the air directly in front of him, the line it described transfixing Marshall's breastbone.

Marshall blushed. 'I know.'

(iii)

Slide Benson was sitting on the living-room floor of his apartment, the inevitable joint burning in an ashtray beside him,

watching an old recording of himself with an early collabora-
tion called The Welfare Chisellers at the Millennium celebrations in the Boom Club. His intention had been to find and
copy his solo performance that long evening of 'Save The Last
Dance For Me' for McLemon's biography of him, but he'd
become so interested at the beginning of the tape in counting
those performers and friends now dead that he'd ended up
watching for more than two hours.

His bit finally rolled around and Benson was distraught to
see himself fairly stagger towards the front of the stage in a
manner the very antithesis of everything he now considered
professional. His recorded self was armed with drink, cigarette
and ukulele. He remembered messing about with the instrument in the week before the gig, after Francesca, his bride of
six months, had presented him with it for Christmas. His choice
of this sole and inexpertly fingered accompaniment was a
measure of his maudlin attitude towards that particular new
year. He felt at the time, being the wrong side of eighteen and
already sliding towards the indignities of decrepitude, that his
personal celebration of something much bigger and much newer
than himself ought to be dolorous and melancholy in the
extreme. What he achieved was plaintive and sour, and more
affecting than he could have perceived at the time because of
a faint edge of unconscious hysteria brought about by a sustained
interest in some of the more powerful psychoactive substances
available to him. His shaky too-slow calypso rhythm faltered
every time he went for B flat major, and his voice cracked and
squeaked on the highest note, the word *home*. The impression
his performance left was not one of a man's confidence in the
fidelity of his child-woman, as with the other renditions he had
heard, so much as the sickly sweet imaginings of some deranged
stalker of an unsuspecting and tragically popular female. He

watched it through twice with great satisfaction, before dumping a copy to disk for McLemon.

On the floor beside Slide was a large chest from which he had taken the tape in the first place. He replaced the tape, dragged out a bunch of old photographs and, relighting his joint, began flicking through them. There were a lot of old promo shots of him with The Kaffir Kats; candid shots taken in the studio and around the Bag O'Nails building, Damian Cheesewring appearing more often than he liked. Looking at Mikey, the bass, and Keith, Rob and Martin, drums, keyboard and second guitar respectively, he could nearly taste the hunger they'd had at the time for what they'd liked to call 'a piece of the action'. He recalled how they'd been willing to compromise every decent musical sense they'd had in order to make it, on the under-standing that when they were big, they'd be free to do, musically and otherwise, whatever they wanted. Their naïveté was an embar-rassment to him even now, and he reflected that in the end things had worked out better. After the dissolution of the Kats and of the industry he had played pretty much what he wanted to, and had gleaned a decent if unspectacular living from it. There were shots of The Jackson Whites and the various incarnations of Perpetual Pentecost, the best of which he put aside for scanning and onward transmission to McLemon for the biography.

His door buzzed and he accessed the hall monitor from the screen in front of him to see Bluey Gillespie's red Afro bobbing outside his door. A few seconds later Bluey walked in and, snatching the joint from the ashtray, threw himself in the armchair next to the window.

'Whatcha doin'?' he wanted to know.

'Just organising some stuff for McLemon's, eh . . .' Slide didn't want to use the word 'biography' in front of Bluey, 'whatcha-macallit.'

'Exhibit,' Bluey offered.

'Right.'

'You know where Marshall is? I called the Archive a couple of times but I'm not getting an answer.'

'Haven't seen him. But just because you don't get an answer doesn't mean they're not there; y'know what that pair are like. He'll be at the Pig on Friday though.'

'That's tomorrow.'

'For real?' said Slide.

'I was hoping to catch up with him before then.' Bluey sighed, then without invitation leaned over and started rummaging through the chest. While Slide continued sorting photos Bluey took a handful of old manuscript books and proceeded, to Slide's slight irritation, to try and sing the tunes off the page. His success with this venture could at best have been described as moderate.

'Steely Dan,' said Bluey, whose attention had drifted from an uninspiring melody line to a dense clump of five notes on the stave below it, which he figured might be a B seventh with additions. 'That a *him* or a *they*?'

'They,' said Slide.

'Any good?'

'Musically slick, lyrically incomprehensible. Long gone, in any meaningful way, by the time I discovered them.'

'Don't suppose anyone knows where their daddy lives now,' said Bluey, dropping the book and picking up another. 'Didn't know you were into trad, Slide.'

Slide laughed without looking up. 'The Dan weren't trad, man. Jazz-influenced certainly, but a pop band. If you wanna talk about trad in terms of jazz you gotta go back to King Oliver's Creole —'

'Not *jazz*,' said Bluey, shaking the book in his hands, 'this!'

Slide looked up. 'What's that?'

Bluey read from the cover. '*Collected Airs and Lyrics from the West of Ireland.*'

Slide peered at the book in Bluey's lap and shrugged. 'Picked it up in a second-hand shop, I'd say; never looked at it again. Must be a hundred years old.'

Bluey continued to stare at the cover, perplexed. 'I've heard this name before,' he said.

'Who, the author?'

'Editor, compiler,' said Bluey, shrugging and squinting at the printed name, 'whatever.'

Slide took the book from him and looked inside. 'Well, I can guarantee you never met him,' he said, looking at the date of publication.

Bluey nodded vaguely but without actually hearing. He'd drifted back years before, to the morning after some wild party when Marshall had still been living with his father and the two of them had fallen asleep in the living room upon their arrival home in the early hours.

The party was one of those things thrown by a positively geometric chick at college who, in a desperate effort to achieve some semblance of cool, had invited every leather-clad arts undergraduate and wannabe musician (often the same people) who had ever so much as looked sideways at her. Bluey remembered they had drunk the place dry, walked most of the food into the carpets, turned the girl's father's study into a dope smoking den, emptied the family's medicine cabinet, pissed on the curtains and attempted to make jelly in one of the downstairs toilets. He smiled to himself, remembering Marshall trying somewhat ironically to console their tearful hostess while guzzling one of her old man's expensive Bordeaux by the neck, before the whole thing came to an abrupt and hysterical end when Willie Sheridan suggested to her that maybe a ride would make her feel better, and they'd all been thrown out on the street for the long walk back to the Glades.

The following morning Jack McLemon had been good enough to keep the noise to a minimum in an effort to let them sleep it off. But something had happened about noon of that day that made him forget their delicate constitutions and come bursting into the room shouting, 'The *shift*, Marshall! I've found the fucking shift!' It wasn't something you were going to forget in a hurry. Jack was repeatedly slapping the palm of his right hand against the cover of a big book he held in his left, and looking at his dehydrated and nauseous son with those silver eyes burning like acetylene torches. 'My great-grandfather – your great-great-grandfather – wasn't a Lemon or a *Mc*Lemon, he was German! Some silly cow screwed up the name on his son's birth cert! It should have been *Lehmann*! The name was Günter Lehmann!'

Marshall had said, 'That's great, Dad,' before staggering out to the downstairs toilet to be noisily ill. Jack had been too pleased with himself to be really disgusted.

'Jesus,' said Slide when Bluey told him. He fingered the decaying gold embossment on the cover of the slim volume. 'Weird.'

Bluey held the butt of the joint up in front of his face and scrutinised it carefully. 'Jack'd probably give you good money for it,' he said.

Slide's smile was deeply sardonic. 'You're a chip off the old block for sure, Gillespie, y'know that?'

Bluey crushed the butt into the ashtray. 'Fuck you.'

(iv)

Jack McLemon was well used to getting double takes from people on account of the colour of his eyes, but he hadn't ever experienced quite the look he got from the maître d' of Le Manducat as he came through the door. The head waiter, dismayed to find his easygoing sang-froid had momentarily deserted him, recovered quickly and moved forward to greet this second ocular wonder.

'Monsieur McCambridge-LeMans is at the bar, sir,' he said knowingly. 'May I take your coat?'

Jack divested himself of the coat, which the maître d' handed off to some lesser mortal, and allowed himself to be ushered down towards the bar.

Sitting side-on between two small groups of people and being afforded a generous amount of elbow room was a tall, elegant gentleman, dressed in a dark casual suit and pullover, with longish white hair brushed straight back off his face. The man was free of the shades Marshall had mentioned, and Jack noted the argentine gleam in his eye, which might well have appeared a trick of the light to the casual observer. The waiter drew away with a bow and Jack watched his quarry pull luxuriously on a long thin cigar, then blow a fine plume of smoke at the spotlights over the bar. He walked towards him, coughing softly into his hand, and the tall man turned to him, smiling, then eased himself off his stool and took two steps forward, both arms extended in welcome, both silver irises shining with pleasure. He took Jack's right hand in his own, and cupped his left under Jack's elbow. Still smiling, he stared deeply and silently into Jack's eyes.

'I had a strong sense of connection when I first met Marshall,'

he said after a moment. 'But it is only now that my suppositions
– my *hopes* – have an incontrovertible affirmation.' He paused
impressively. 'I am Henri McCambridge-LeMans.'

Jack found himself battling with an uncharacteristically broad
smile in an effort to enunciate clearly. 'Jack McLemon,' he said,
nodding briskly. McCambridge-LeMans led him by the elbow
to the stool across from his own.

'Tell me what you would like,' said the Frenchman, looking
towards the barman, who was wondering if this eye thing was
disease or fashion.

'Johnnie Walker Black,' said Jack, squinting at a row of bottles
behind the bar, 'with ice.'

McCambridge-LeMans looked at Jack in amused astonish-
ment. 'Is this more than a coincidence?' he said, holding up
his own glass.

Jack laughed heartily, explaining that it was the only thing
he saw on the shelf that he recognised. Nevertheless he was
glad of the opportunity to release through laughter the build-
up of tension that had overwhelmed him on first looking into
the eyes of his long-lost cousin. It was a sense that told him
his great labour was not just some dusty historical tract, but
the genesis of an ongoing, living epic that might yet stretch
far, and gloriously, into the future.

The barman put a folded napkin on the bar in front of
Jack and set his drink upon it. The two men sat across from
one another for a minute in silence and sipped at their
whiskeys.

'Tell me, what is it you do, Jacques?' McCambridge-LeMans
asked.

Jack was grateful for the conventional opening. 'I'm retired
now.'

McCambridge-LeMans feigned surprise. 'So young?'

Jack smiled. 'Well, I'm sixty-two now, but I did retire young – at fifty. I worked for the Environmental Council for twenty-five years. I got disillusioned pretty quickly – ran into more politics than conservation – so I squirrelled away some modest funds, and made one good "investment" – for want of a better word – and got out as soon as I was eligible for my pension. We were a pretty ineffectual bunch at the Council, got rode over, or bought off, by every developmental shark that ever surfaced in this town. J.P. Gillespie being a prime example.'

'You don't like J.P.?'

'Never met him, but don't imagine I would. With a lot of other people, I don't much care for the effects of his "influence" around here.'

'Yes.' McCambridge-LeMans made a face of regretful resignation. 'The city has certainly changed. I still like it, but the memories of my earliest visits are of a different place almost.'

'Yeah,' Jack agreed, remembering suddenly a vitriolic argument he'd had in a bar thirty years before. 'There used to be some character about the place, before the likes of Gillespie came crawling out of the sewers, dragging with them the creed of the sixty-hour week and seeing to it that everything without a redeemable cash value got slung in the gutter. Next thing you know people are walking around with fucking murder in their eyes, ready to bludgeon anything and anybody that gets in the way of their next worthless acquisition.'

McCambridge-LeMans smiled. 'I can see where Marshall gets his passion.'

Jack shrugged. 'I saw my chance to change things bought and sold, Henri, the fervour's probably just bitterness. As for Marshall –' he trailed off.

Henri leaned forward earnestly. 'Tell me.'

'I suppose he's like a lot of kids – so much seems to wash

over him. He's got passion for his work, which is fair enough, but it's not the same as *com*passion, or passion for liberty and equality and all that good stuff people used to think was important.'

'Maybe he thinks it futile to try and change anything until sufficient people are aware that there are alternatives to the lifestyles they choose and to the environments that spring from them.'

'Maybe,' Jack relented. 'I see him so into the nitty-gritty of his material that I wonder if he's forgotten how we used to value the bigger picture. One afternoon, in more imperious tones than you'd expect from a ten-year-old, he informed me that Eisenstein said that there was the material and there was what you did with it, and what you did with it was always the most important thing. He had a thing for the humanity in those old narratives; or the pure abstract joy taken in an old trumpet solo or a piece of chamber music. Maybe the important thing is that he wants other people to know about it. If I've achieved anything it's because I'm responsible for some of that.'

'How so?'

'When there was still money in nostalgia – before the cycles got so short that people finally recognised they were being ripped off, but before the prevailing obsession became to value absolutely nothing but the new – you used to get a lot of reruns and black and whites on the tube, which I liked. The problem was, I never seemed to have time to watch them when he was young. So, I kept recording and recording everything I didn't have time for, until I had an entire bookcase full of disks. Then when he was old enough to sit up with me nights, we'd watch them together. TV had gone right down the toilet by then. There was no attention span any more and nothing that wasn't amateur video would play, unless it had an explosion, a beating, a murder or an act of sexual congress every ten minutes.' Jack laughed. 'I suppose I was a snob about it. I didn't want my kid to grow into one of those culturally starved automatons who didn't have enough imagination to do anything else once they clocked out except sit in the line of fire of the tube and *absorb*. I tried to encourage Marshall into stuff I thought was worthwhile. It wasn't all highbrow – don't get me wrong – we enjoyed escapism as much as the next guy. But I tried to stress the importance of having to think about what it was you were consuming, to sift the good from the bad, and, occasionally, to postpone your gratification. Compared to where he and Papa Charlie are at now, though, I was very much the dilettante.'

'Well,' McCambridge-LeMans relit his cheroot and blew the smoke above Jack's head, 'your efforts appear to have taken him to the brink of something I think will be quite remarkable.'

'You're getting behind the project, I hear,' said Jack. 'I have to say I was surprised. Not to be offensive, but one might be forgiven for thinking that everything with WentWest was profit without limit.'

'It has been for a long time,' McCambridge-LeMans agreed. 'But I've long argued that we should give something back, in the way of some cultural monument. In the past such projects were generally undertaken by individuals of great personal wealth. With a room full of board members answering to a plethora of grasping shareholders it is more difficult. Marshall's Exhibit could work as a useful example. The overheads are low, since we own all of the material for display, and it is only a matter of assigning web space and footing the bill for the construction. Once in place there's an outside chance it will pay for itself, but more importantly I hope it will gain the company kudos as a philanthropic undertaking, and smooth the way for other such ventures in the future.'

Jack nodded. 'For Marshall's sake I'm glad you're taking that view. I don't think he was getting very far with J.P.'

'J.P. doesn't have as much influence with the board as I do, but the hardline profiteers do listen to him, and they would support his contention that the Exhibit is a frivolous expense, regardless of the low overheads. He took the Archive only at the board's insistence, as part of the deal to get the prison, but he never wanted it. He was happy enough to let Marshall and his colleague plod along on the project in their own time, as long as the day-to-day work was moving along and they didn't make demands on the budget. I have been successful, however, in convincing him to support me in my patronage of the Exhibit for the time being. Although I must confess to having not wholly philanthropic reasons for seeing it completed and seeing that it succeeds.'

Jack smiled like he'd been waiting for something like this, and McCambridge-LeMans made apologetic acknowledgement.

'I'm seventy-five years of age, Jacques, and the topic of retirement has been introduced within my earshot on more occasions recently than average would allow. I have no family – orphaned as a child in arms, parents each only children, grandparents dead. The pressures of my work over the years have proved inimical to the establishment of steady relationships. This disconnectedness has affected me; not radically, but deeply. It is not terrible by any means, but now I wish it were otherwise. Who knows, soon I may have a lot of time on my hands.'

McCambridge-LeMans laughed quietly then fell silent. After a moment an expression of puzzlement clouded his features. 'I had papers for my grandparents – they were the starting point in my search for family. Someone to share my experience of experience with, if you understand me. Confidants, companions, heirs even.'

238

Jack nodded. 'Family covers it.'

'At first it looked like I was to be stymied at the outset,' the Frenchman continued. 'My searches for the children of my grandparents' siblings kept constantly running into dead ends. For sure they were born; I found the birth certificates. They possessed, some of them, school, college and work records, but after a time the trail would just disappear. As if they had fallen off the face of the Earth.'

Jack had been twitching in his chair like a maniac since the Frenchman's pause and could no longer contain himself. 'The Shifting!' he said in an excited stage whisper. 'A propensity for the family name to undergo radical corruption as members fall into difficulties and require new identities.'

McCambridge-LeMans sat up straight in his stool and pointed his index finger at Jack's chest. 'Yes! I found this. A name that was too close to its original. Then I went to a site where I could test variants of my own name and discovered a number of articles about Lucien LeMoine who had a number of such name changes, and there I discovered your name also.'

'The Fait Accompli site on La Rochelle.'

'Indeed. The articles were all by dead men and you left a note requesting assistance from anyone who visited who might have anything. Unfortunately you were many streets ahead of me and I had nothing to offer you, but I took the liberty of checking you out. I was very excited by the possibility I had a living relative, albeit distant.' McCambridge-LeMans took a drag from his cigar and briefly held up his glass of whiskey for Jack to see. 'When I discovered that Marshall worked for WentWest I began to feel there was more at work than mere coincidence. The comfort this knowledge brought me was enough then. I did nothing about it for over a year. Work commitments kept me busy, and then suddenly they demanded my presence here. I felt it was time to act, so I called Marshall to meet me at the airport. He impressed me greatly.

'Anyway, the point is that some of my directors feel that J.P. Gillespie is too self-motivated, too greedy to properly represent our interests here. Eventually, in a few years, mind you, it is acknowledged that his replacement will prove necessary. Marshall's insouciance with this sizeable project is a real eye-opener, and if – *when* – he succeeds with it, I would like to offer him the opportunity, in time, of a greater challenge.'

Jack sat back in his stool. He was impressed but sceptical. 'Marshall's hardly trained for the job, is he? Even if he were, do you really think he'd be interested?'

The Frenchman conceded the point with upturned palms and a pout. 'I'd like to try to get him interested early enough that he could embark on some retraining, but the job is not beyond him by any means. It is mostly delegation. There is a highly organised support structure in place as it is. There's little enough to do except understand what goes on in order that you can report back to Head Office and fight your own corner. There would be enough free time for him to indulge his true interests to the full. Call it a privilege of leadership.' McCambridge-LeMans put his hand up as if to draw a halt to the proceedings. 'But we're getting ahead of ourselves. I only wished to get your blessing, as it were. I would rather you did not say anything to Marshall for the time being. I want him in the position where the Exhibit is well under way and he is feeling good about it before I put the proposition to him properly.'

'Certainly,' Jack agreed. 'The more secure his position, the happier I'll be.'

The Frenchman waved away the suggestion of any insecurity on Marshall's part. 'Even if he rejects the idea out of hand, he'll remain the well-paid curator of the Exhibit for as long as he pleases.'

'Can I have two more of these?' Jack said to the barman as he passed them.

'I believe your table is ready now,' the barman replied, noting the advance of the maître d'. 'I'll have them brought down.'

The head waiter arrived and stood beside them, smiling, with an arm extended towards the restaurant floor. 'This way please, gentlemen.'

They took their seats and McCambridge-LeMans informed the waiter they were expecting one more and would wait to order.

'I wonder where he's got to?'

'I charged him with bringing me a synopsis of his project. I expect he'll be a little late.' The Frenchman smiled mischievously.

Jack slouched back in his chair, stretching out his arm to make sure his whiskey was within reach. 'Can I get one of those cigars?' he asked Henri.

'I remember your story,' said the Frenchman, handing Jack a cheroot. 'I read it at the time in the newspaper, but I didn't make the connection until I looked into who you were last year. The dying girl leaves her eggs to her lover so he can have their child; very moving.'

'Well, sort of,' said Jack. 'When it got down to it there was a significant down payment by the doctors for the use of the ova.'

'Why did they not go into production afterwards?' Henri asked.

Jack was silent a moment. 'I don't know,' he said. 'Marshall was just over a year old when I realised I hadn't heard from them. More than a year after that a freelance reporter came around asking questions about the team's apparent disappearance. I don't think the guy was playing with a full deck though.'

Henri shook his head. 'How so?'

'His "information" took him to the States. He'd heard the medical team had been abducted by the American military. He was e-mailing me stuff for six or eight months, saying the womb-tank was being used to produce soldier mutants. The last thing he sent me said he'd seen the remains of a creature that was basically human, but with four arms, for extra weapons capacity, and eyes in the back of its head. Freaky.'

'Interesting,' said Henri. He paused a moment before asking his next question. 'Did the doctors ever speak to you of genetically modifying Marshall in any way?'

'They were prepared to alright. They pushed it pretty hard at one point. But I just asked them to spare him the eyes.'

Henri laughed. 'What sort of things did they suggest they could do?'

Jack shrugged. 'I can't remember many of them. Dr Lilly was keen on longevity though. I look at Marshall sometimes, he looks so young, and wonder if they went ahead despite me.'

Henri was silent then for a minute. He took deep breaths through his nose, as quietly as he could, to still the hammering in his breast. He felt it best to drop the matter. There would be other conversations.

The two men nipped at their drinks and discussed the menu and the wine list until Marshall arrived about twenty minutes later. He flopped into his chair as if exhausted beyond belief. At that point a call came in on his cell. He excused himself soundlessly and moved away from the table. A minute or so later he was back.

'Sorry I'm late,' he said. Then, looking sideways at McCambridge-LeMans, 'Something came up at very short notice.'

The Frenchman nudged Jack. 'I think you may have been

remiss in your parental duties, Jacques, in not signing Marshall up for the Boy Scouts. He seemed ill-prepared for my modest request this morning.' McCambridge-LeMans winked at Marshall who reddened a little, remembering who answered the call.

Jack laughed, oblivious to the covert exchange. 'We can but try.'

Marshall gave the pair of them a withering look. 'Don't start, lads.' He fished a disk out of his shirt pocket and placed it on the table in front of Henri.

'Thank you,' said the Frenchman. 'I'll review it later.'

'You ready to order?' Jack asked Marshall.

'I don't feel that hungry,' he said, 'though I can't remember the last time I ate.'

'Excellent,' said McCambridge-LeMans, sitting up in his chair to look for a waiter. 'Aperitifs it is then.'

(v)

'How long have we been here, Frank?' Mick gasped, rolling onto his back and mopping sweat from his brow with a forearm. He could only manage to squeeze out three or four press-ups at a time now, but over the last hour his total was close on two hundred.

'It's — what is it? — the end of our second day.' Frank was taking a brisk stroll on a treadmill, blindfolded. In front of him as he walked, on a tray suspended between the two handrails, lay the pieces of the pistol he had just disassembled and was shortly about to reassemble. 'We arrived early yesterday morning.'

'Is that all?'

'That's all.'

'Jesus.' Mick mulled it over for a few seconds. 'These fuckers here really have our number, don't they?'

'They sure as shit do, Mick. Could be the best thing ever happened to us.' Frank reached down to his right and pulled a grape and original malt *Moose* out of the bottle-holder. He drank half the contents and replaced the bottle in one fluid unseeing movement. He ran his tongue around the inside of his mouth. 'Are they trying to be funny with the *Moose*, d'you think?'

Mick shrugged. 'We were told the diet's mandatory. Doesn't bother me, I like the stuff.' He looked towards the small window near the ceiling trying to remember where he'd heard the word 'mandatory' before. 'It was incredible seeing Colonel Jim Thorpe in person,' he said then. 'I must've seen him interviewed a hundred times on ImprovB. Never thought for a minute I'd actually meet him.'

'You *and* me,' said Frank. 'He's some cool fucker alright.'

'Yeah. Christ, two days. I feel totally different. Like I've been taken apart and put back together again, only better. I swear, man, I actually *feel* thinner, I seem to be thinking clearer and I can't imagine why it hasn't always been this way.'

'I know what you mean, man. Sectioned out; psychologically and emotionally. I . . .' Frank surprised himself with the term 'sectioned out' and lost his train of thought.

'It was necessary,' Mick said, remembering his 'programming' that first day. 'But it's probably not time to talk about it yet.'

'All the graduates underwent the same thing.'

'Yeah. It gives us all a thing in common.'

'You're right though,' Frank said distantly, as if thinking aloud. 'I feel more focused or something. Like they were saying to do, I've "surrendered to the function".'

'Amazing.' Mick rolled back onto his front. 'Two days. And to think we're only a fraction along the first of seven possible paths.'

'One day at a time, sweet Jesus.'

Mick laughed, shaking his head. It *was* amazing, it really was. He grunted through three more press-ups, being careful not to jerk, but to keep the effort measured and smooth.

'C'mon, man, give me two more,' Frank encouraged, slowly and deliberately reassembling his pistol as his feet sped along beneath him, 'then we'll call it a night.'

Inspired by his friend's confidence in him and the fact that it was his last effort of the evening, Mick dug deep and found four more before rolling on his back again and taking a number of slow deep breaths. He got up and stood on his exercise mat, shaking out his hands at his sides to relieve his fatigued biceps.

Frank clicked the safety on his pistol and blindly tossed it into the centre of the bunk two metres to his right. He stopped the treadmill and removed his blindfold, then stepped off the machine, retrieved his bottle of *Moose* from the bottle-holder and walked to the bunk, where he sat down.

Two nights back Frank had felt it was touch and go whether they'd live this long or not. When McCambridge-LeMans' doctor friend approached him with the hypo he only gave himself evens on waking up, despite what the Frenchman had been telling them. Now he felt like a positive asset. They'd been greeted by Colonel Jim Thorpe, a regular contributor to a number of military-culture shows he and Mick had enjoyed watching on ImprovB. Colonel Thorpe shared a *Moose* with them and explained that to initiate their training, they'd be going into something called 'programming' first. Frank had a feeling it'd be a while before he could think hard about what had happened there, but when they came out seven hours later, Colonel Thorpe had been gushing with praise, explaining that they'd been the fastest ever through the process. It made a guy feel good to be appreciated like that, to know that you'd done something well enough to impress a real pro.

'Where do we go from here, Frank?'

Brought out of his reverie, it was a second or so before Frank answered. 'We do what the boss tells us.'

'What about Freeway and J.P.?'

'Forget about them. We're working for the Frenchman now. To be honest I'm happier. McCambridge-LeMans makes sense when he says Freeway and J.P. were playing us for saps; paying us buttons while foisting a huge responsibility on us, without us fully realising it, and allowing us to take the whole rap when the shit finally hit the fan.'

'But he's taken my plot in town, and our club.'

'Forget about it, Mick. We were directly responsible for the deaths of five people. They could've been worth more than the land and the club to the Frenchman for all we know. Let's get past it, move on. We're mixing with the real quality here, getting trained by the very best, and we'll be at the right hand of the chairman of WentWest. In time that'll be worth a lot more, I guarantee it.'

Mick nodded. He couldn't help thinking that the discussion was academic. He'd been extremely accepting of everything that was said to him these last two days.

(vi)

Jack Jones' was an eatery which stood directly across the road from the entrance to the WentWest Archive. Bluey had heard Marshall mention it often, usually in disparaging terms, and it was a reputation which was supported in Bluey's opinion by the weakness of the coffee – which probably wasn't a bad thing as he'd drunk five cups so far – and the strange aftertaste left by the few bites he'd taken from a turkey sandwich about an hour back. He took out his cell, spoke Marshall's name and sat waiting with the machine to his head for fifteen or twenty seconds. Marshall picked up.

'Hi, Bluey?'

'Yeah, man, it's me. You at work?'

'No, I'm at Le Manducat with Jack and McCambridge-LeMans.'

'Jesus. Henri's tab, I hope.'

'No doubt.'

'I thought I might come out and see you, if you were working late – poke around in the Archive. I'm looking for a particular book on a crowd called Steely Dan. Slide was on about them. Can't remember the publisher's name.'

'If you're quick you might still catch Charlie. I know for a fact he's got some stuff on them earmarked.'

'Nah, I wanted to look around anyway, for tunes and stuff.'

'I think you've exhausted our stocks on elementary clarinet.'

'Fuck you. But seriously, we should get lunch, chew the rag, man.'

'I'll be too busy for lunch next week. How about a few beers Tuesday evening?'

'Yeah. Anyway, I'll see you at the Pig tomorrow.'

Bluey hung up and leaned forward to get his coffee. The once white plastic chairs were screwed into the floor around the once white plastic tables. Everything was designed for people larger than Bluey, which meant that if he had wanted to put his elbows on the table, which he didn't, he would have had to put his ass on the very edge of the chair. Every surface was scratched and grimy and Bluey sat right back in his chair with his cup and saucer in his lap, trusting his clothes to insulate him from the filth on his seat and hoping distance would protect him from the table top. The walls looked as if they might be tacky to the touch, save where dust took from the sheen. It made Bluey wish he was wearing the gloves he had in his pockets, but he figured this would have looked a little ridiculous given that he was indoors and it was a mild evening. No more foolish he supposed than the black woollen hat he was wearing to hide the tell-tale red Afro, but then lots of people wore hats without reference to the weather, especially musicians.

'Nice timing, old-timer,' Bluey muttered to himself as Papa Charlie emerged from the doorway across the road a minute or so later. Like Marshall an hour before, the old man didn't so much as glance at the front of Jack Jones', which made Bluey scratch irritably at his scalp, itchy because of the hat, figuring he could have dispensed with it *and* have worn a pink T-shirt with his name emblazoned across the front for all the difference it made. Still it was best to keep a low profile all round, in case of mishaps. He checked his watch and decided to give Papa Charlie five minutes to get clear of the area. Then he finished his coffee and sauntered up to the register to pay the tab.

'Stood up?' the man behind the register asked.

'Yeah,' said Bluey, 'something like that.' He threw cash on the counter and looked around at Jack Jones' clientele. To a body they looked like they hadn't worked in years, but had avoided the shelters because some relative had been forced to give them their basement, attic or spare room out of some sense of duty. God only knew where they'd get money. It was clear to Bluey at any rate that no one had met a date in Jack Jones' in nigh on thirty years, if ever.

'Not that I want to be running my own place down, son,' said the man as he gave Bluey his change. 'But you might want to pick somewhere a bit ritzier next time.'

'Thanks. I'll keep it in mind.'

Bluey went out the door and turned left. He ambled a hundred metres to a crossing, pulling on his gloves. He crossed the road and doubled back towards the Archive at an equally leisurely pace. He turned quickly into the doorway when he reached it, briskly noting that the pavement behind remained deserted. He punched in the entry code J.P. had given him. The shutter pulled itself up slowly and Bluey punched a second code for the door. He pushed the door in only enough to allow his thin body through. He turned in the dark hallway and looked out to see if anyone, especially the man he now assumed to be Mr Jones, had noted his entry. Satisfied that he was thus far undetected, he closed the outside shutter again and took the elevator down to Marshall and Papa Charlie's office, where he was dismayed to discover he had to find a light switch.

Some minutes later he sat in Marshall's chair with a long narrow black box open on the desk at his right. He prised the logo from the bottom of Marshall's screen with a Swiss Army knife, having satisfied himself first that it was in no way individual. He replaced it with an identical logo he took from a selection in the long box, all of which were fitted with a broadcast microphone. It had been expensive, but it was beautifully direct, and Bluey would see to it J.P. picked up the tab.

He did the same thing at Papa Charlie's desk before bringing out the prize of his collection, a monstrous plastic logo equipped with two fish-eye lenses, which he fitted to the large wall screen at the head of the room. The tricky part was the receive and record unit, which, since the Archive was deep underground, would have to be left in the room. A miniscule vibrational sensor/trigger he'd pinned into the frame of the swinging doors activated the equipment once someone entered the room. Five minutes of relative quietude, like someone shuffling around the room on his own, would send it to standby mode, after which any sound the decibel equivalent of human speech, or the opening of the door, would start it up again. Bluey anticipated getting a lot of useless noise, and making frequent night-time returns to the Archive. He found a place for the unit under a collection of ancient and apparently never used electronic equipment in the bottom of a stack of shelves tucked into the far corner of the room. After a brief test he placed it there, leaving room enough to get a hand in and out quickly and being careful not to disturb the accumulated dust.

(vii)

When it had come down to it and the food was on the table in front of him, Marshall found that his appetite returned in an automatic, mechanical way, without relish. He employed it in the same obsessive fashion he had carried out all of his actions that day, and not a scrap was left on his plate uneaten nor a drop undrunk in his glass. He sat stuffed and slouched in his chair, a cup of steaming coffee in front of him and a warm bubble of drowsy well-being around him. He could hear his father and Henri murmur to each other and laugh softly, and he was aware of the waiter melting in and out of the candlelight to clear the table.

McCambridge-LeMans had provided them with the tale, as far as he knew it, of his lineage. Lucien LeMoine, some years prior to his arrival in Berlin (and masquerading as one Yves LeMans), had impregnated the young daughter of a Scottish officer in the French army, by the name of McCambridge, who resided at the time in Paris. Henri could find no further clues to the girl's identity and no record of an officer bearing that name in Paris at the time. He was given to think that the family had been wiped out in a cholera epidemic. Other anecdotal evidence indicated that some twenty years after these events a doctor bearing the name Jules McCambridge-LeMans came to prominence in the capital. He had been, it was said, a great campaigner for public health, his passion for his work inflamed by the memory of a family he had lost to disease. Henri's voice had dropped low as he stared at the tablecloth and told how other stories relating to Dr Jules suggested appetites of Roman proportions. To Henri's mind this pointed up the high possibility of a direct connection to Lucien. A grunt from Jack attested to his solemn agreement with this hypothesis. It was said the doctor's unsavoury proclivities had alienated the mother of his twin boys, and that she had left him and moved across town with their sons, denying him all access. The classifieds in a periodical issued thirty-odd years from when Henri supposed these events to have taken place had one Antoine McCambridge-LeMans seeking home help at an address some two or three kilometres from where Henri knew his grandfather had grown up.

251

Jack had then opened a portable to run Henri (exhaustively to Marshall's mind) through his years of scholarship and the results they had yielded him. Marshall, who knew the tale, pursued his own wanderings until Henri had asked his questions, the table was finally clear and a comfortable silence had fallen. At length Henri suggested they make for the piano lounge between the bar and the main door. Marshall stuck to sipping beer while the other two worked down the bottle of whiskey Henri instructed the lounge boy to leave. Talk continued to focus on the past. Marshall listened for the next hour, during which there was steady drinking and idle banter before they fell to silence again. Jack emptied his glass, placed it on the table and pushed it away from him. Henri relit the end of a cheroot that had been lying cold in the ashtray.

'All this talk of names, Jacques,' the Frenchman said, 'still leaves me with one question.' He was hunched over the table, looking sidelong at Jack and rolling his glass between his palms, the stub of the cheroot pinched between his index and middle fingers.

Jack raised his eyebrows and leaned into the table to hear.

'Marshall,' said the Frenchman.

'You mean why I called him that?' asked Jack.

McCambridge-LeMans nodded.

'Well mostly because his mother's name was Marsha, but also –' Jack stopped abruptly, looked at the table top and rubbed his chin. 'D'you remember Jimi Hendrix?'

'I do,' said Henri.

'Well there was a time I was enthusiastic about his work, so –' He waved a hand in the air as if it explained.

'I see,' the Frenchman said, nodding. 'You named him after the musician's amplifier.'

Jack shot a quick look of disbelief at Marshall before

addressing Henri in an almost patronisingly level tone. 'No, the guy's middle name was Marshall.'

With his cigar in the corner of his mouth Henri winked at Jack by way of saying *gotcha*. At the same time he made a burlesque gesture of clicking his fingers and pointing that left Marshall with the impression a drummer had just punctuated a punchline. The two men went into that soft, shoulder-rolling chuckle that Marshall was beginning to think of as more similar than the eyes. When they stopped they both yawned.

After a few moments Jack looked at his old wind-up wrist-watch and said that it was late. Henri put his hand on Jack's forearm to stall him a moment and called a waiter, into whose ear he spoke briefly.

'I have something for you, Jacques,' he said. 'I was afraid to give this to you earlier as I thought you might have been tempted to desert us directly after dinner.'

For a horrible moment Marshall entertained the notion that Henri had rented his father a prostitute, but he had already dismissed the idea by the time the waiter arrived back with a gift-wrapped package about fifteen by twenty centimetres and six or seven deep. Henri tipped the waiter and handed the package to Jack, who, turning it in his hands once, seemed surprised at its weight. He forwent the *what is it? – open it!* routine and began carefully tearing off the wrapping to reveal a gleaming perspex case, inside of which rested an old leather-bound book. As soon as he identified the object as a book, even before his father's exclamation, Marshall knew what it would be.

'Lord God almighty,' said Jack.

'Far out,' said Marshall.

'Can I assume you're pleased?' McCambridge-LeMans asked.

'Jesus, yes!' said Jack. 'There can't be many of these.'

'It was, as you know, a vanity piece,' said Henri. 'The dealer who found this for me says that Lucien had only fifty copies printed. The books were left with his solicitor with instructions that forty of them be distributed to assorted libraries upon the occasion of his death. The other ten were never accounted for. At some point a publisher of erotica reprinted the text from the original, but it did not prove popular and even those reprints are difficult to come by. But this is the genuine article.'

'I've never even seen the full text,' said Jack. 'Only snatches I picked up.'

'That reminds me,' said Henri, pulling a disk from his pocket. 'I had someone run up a disk copy so you wouldn't have to handle the original too much.' He handed the disk to Jack.

'This is fabulous,' said Jack, finally looking up from the book's cover. 'I don't know what to say.'

Henri waved it off. 'It's nothing.'

Jack smiled. 'I'd be lying if I said I was still tired, but I'm leaving you boys to it none the less.' He stood up and tucked the perspex case tightly under his left oxter, offering his right hand to Henri. 'Will you be in the country much longer?'

'Difficult to say at this point,' said Henri. 'But we will get together again before I leave, and Paris is less than an hour away, so you will visit soon, I hope.'

Jack nodded. 'I will.' He tapped Marshall on the shoulder as he passed. 'Talk to you later.'

Marshall and Henri watched Jack make his way towards the door of the restaurant, retrieve his coat and leave with a driver. Henri uncorked the whiskey and poured himself a thimbleful. Marshall stretched his legs out under the table and extended the muscles in his neck by inclining his head alternately towards each of his shoulders.

'Don't even think about going home yet, Marshall,' said the Frenchman. 'You have worked hard today. Balance in everything is important.'

Marshall put a hand to his forehead in mock despair. 'Where are you thinking of going?'

McCambridge-LeMans smiled. 'I'm going home to review your presentation against my meeting with Mr Lyons-Howard tomorrow.'

Before he had a chance to question the Chairman further Marshall was aware of a familiar scent and a hand caressing the back of his neck.

'Hello, Marshall,' said Mandy, taking the seat beside Henri. 'You remember Ingrid, don't you?' The blonde girl who had been with them at the Oubliette greeted him with a breathy 'hi' as she took the seat where Jack had been. Marshall's throat went dry and he was finding it difficult to swallow.

'Henri has asked me to manage a club he's recently acquired near Maymon Glades,' Mandy said to Marshall. 'We're going out to look it over. I have some small business with the present manager, then it's fun, fun, fun. We'd love it if you could come.'

Ingrid didn't actually speak, but she gave Marshall a look that said she was of much the same mind. Marshall's heart raced in his breast.

McCambridge-LeMans got up from his chair. 'I must go,' he said. 'I will contact you tomorrow, Marshall, about the Exhibit. I will see you ladies soon.' The girls waved coyly. Henri turned as he moved away from them. 'Indulge yourselves. It will do wonders for your confidence,' he said.

Word Made Flesh

PROGRAMME: Staines at 7.
DATE: Friday, 20th October.

STEVE: [time nearest minute], Friday the twen-
           tieth of October. You're tuned to TuMur
           Lite R.N. We're up to twelve and thir-
           teen degrees today, people, and it's
           going to be dry for the whole weekend.
           [CUE: it's too darn hot FX741. 1½"] Happy
           days. [pause]
               You all know about the big soccer match
           tonight. [CUE: roar of the crowd FX654.
           1"] You'd have to be on Mars not to.
           You may not know there's an even bigger
           showdown behind the scenes, as WentWest
           bring in the big guns and try to rumble
           Mantra. [CUE: spy music 10 FX159. 3"]
           Let's keep them fingers crossed.
CUE: Track 1. 3'15" crossfade with Steve
STEVE: [In a nagging manner] On the subject of
           evictions - now there's a tenuous link
           to give a man! - does the editor of the
           Chronicle own a home removals firm? Or
           what's up with him? His entire editor-
           ial today croaks out that old chestnut
           about how moving house is the most
           stressful thing anyone can do, [FULL FADE
           UP: Track 1. STEVE: out before 'Dave']
           and he advises us all to spend as much
           as we can afford on the removal firm.
           Get a real job, Dave! Honest to God!

The broad back of General Keane Somerville, Controller-in-Chief of the Transient Shelter Project, had been turned to the face of Steven Fox, MD of Hither Twice Toys, for some fifteen minutes now. Relations between them had chilled considerably since he, Fox, had attempted to jolly along the proceedings by asking if the present exercise contained an example of 'the classic pincer movement'. The General had ruffled his moustache and looked at the Hither Twice executive closely, then turned away to gaze out of the window. Where before Somerville had been relatively cheery and moderately communicative, now he communed, matter-of-factly and only, with his two aides-de-camp. Fox had not been introduced to these. They had been in the room before he and General Somerville had arrived and a casual salute had passed for greeting and introduction. Since his outburst the aides seemed inclined to take a leaf out of the General's book and hadn't been particularly outgoing towards him either.

It was turning out to be a really exciting evening, Fox thought bitterly. No one was talking to him and both windows were occupied, on the one hand by the thin, squinting figures of the aides with their nifty tripod-mounted night vision apparatus, and on the other by the huge figure of the General, which from Fox's present vantage resembled a section of mature oak more than it did a man. He wasn't even allowed to watch the start of the match while they waited, all outside broadcasts being forbidden from the outset. He dragged a map over from a pile on the table in front of him and looked at it absently.

'Up here now, Fox,' the General said then, holding a smaller set of the nifty glasses out behind him. 'Not too close to the window.'

Fox advanced brightly and took the glasses. Stepping into the space the General had made for him he looked through them into what would soon be his carport. The only thing standing between him and the commencement of building was one hundred shipping containers full of who knew what; and who knew what no longer had the owner's permission to stay.

The General grunted and a flabby arm darted towards the window pane and back, indicating the scene below. 'Airtight, m'boy. None of your nutcracker nonsense here.'

Fox didn't know exactly what the General was on about. Two possibilities occurred to him but both pointed up an element of gross misinterpretation on the part of the General. Rather than mention either, he opted for an intelligent 'ah-hah'.

Below him, in the green of the glasses, he could see eight stacks of twelve containers, each stack three containers high, and the four so-called 'bathrooms' near the entrance. The very idea made him want to laugh. Armed Transient Project Police waited around each stack to escort the inhabitants to buses waiting outside. Some of the TPPs would carry tasers with which to quell any initial panic in less than lethal fashion. He was told it had a wonderfully sobering effect on the onlookers to zap one of their number with a taser. Since most people couldn't tell a nightstick from a sub-machine gun they tended to assume the worst when they saw the guy go down – cooled them right out. Fox had to sympathise with them. With the exception of the stuff for making the tea, everything around him, down to the graphite pointing sticks, looked lethal.

The TPPs were expecting most people to be home, or indoors at any rate, on account of the big soccer match. They wanted quiet in the streets. Four buses carrying forty-eight passengers each stood by to escort what intelligence told them might be between one hundred and fifty and one hundred and eighty people. Thirty flatbed trailers taking one container each on an estimated two-hour round trip had until four the following morning, a little less than seven and a half hours, to get the one hundred containers off the lot.

Fox had been anticipating flying rifle butts and maybe even a couple of taser discharges when the crunch came, but it didn't happen that way. They were a shabby dispirited lot he saw shuffling towards the buses, mostly men. The few women there were each one half of a couple, probably, he reasoned, for protection. For thirty or so seconds he marvelled at how jungle-like that arrangement was, then he began to grow bored. He counted fourteen individuals who had to be carried to a bus, dead-drunk or stoned. That was particularly pathetic. If he ever got that way he had the decency to stay indoors. He took the glasses from his face and yawned. The General looked around at him and for a moment he felt sure of a verbal reprimand.

'Not an ounce of spirit among the bloody lot of them!' The General seemed even more put out than Fox that there hadn't been any action. 'This isn't what my boys are trained for! We could have used schoolteachers for this.' He lifted his cap and scratched at the back of his head, wiping spittle from his moustache before replacing the cap. 'Nearly done here, Fox,' he said, a hint of cruelty in his smile. 'Why don't you make us all a cup of tea,' the General pointed to the things Fox would need, 'there's a good man.' This was just getting better and better as far as Fox was concerned.

The aides had their tea at the far window while continuing to monitor the situation outside. Fox and the General sat at the table, but the General remained taciturn. Even apart from the silence, Fox wasn't enjoying his tea much. He had to drink it from an enamelled mug which looked much the same as the vessel his father had used for a shaving mug all his life. He kept checking it for bristles and dried soap. Eventually the General got up, opened an extending screen on a small portable unit and placed it at the far end of the table from them.

'Since the crisis moment has passed we might still enjoy most of the first half.' The General flipped over to the soccer and after a few minutes it seemed they did have things to talk about.

'Exquisite left foot − and a good brain,' said the General, pointing at the young midfielder.

'A bargain too,' said Fox.

Just as they began revelling in their mutual enjoyment of the game the screen went blank for a second. As three words flashed on the screen, a huge treated voice made the unit's small but powerful speakers fizz and rattle.

'Welcome to Coolsville . . .' it said.

'Christ!' said General Somerville, flipping off the unit in disgust. 'I always forget about that lot.'

Fox scratched his head. 'Some, me included, didn't reckon they'd show tonight − with the Cypol crack squad on their tail.'

This appeared to be news to the General. 'Cypol, you say?'

'The Latvians that saved Wells's ass last year.'

'Ahh,' said Somerville, lapsing into silence again. After a bit he took up his glasses and walked to the window. 'Do you have someone to take those containers,' he asked Fox, 'or what do you want us to do with them?'

'Hadn't thought about it,' said Fox. 'Wouldn't know anyone who had a use for them.'

'The Project can always find a use for something like that.' The General seemed pleased then regretful. 'With our meagre resources, however, it would need to be a keen price.'

'Listen!' Fox chopped a hand decisively in the air. 'They're yours, take them!'

'That is very good of you, Mr Fox, very good indeed.' Smiling broadly General Somerville looked towards his aides. 'Did you hear that, McGrory? Fox here is donating the containers.'

Fox looked around at the man the General had addressed. 'Trent McGrory?' he said, surprised.

'Do you know each other?' the General asked.

'We have –' Fox halted abruptly; his smug smile dropped. His eagerness to be liked had been suddenly and unexpectedly sated and he'd opened his mouth without kick-starting his brain. J.P. Gillespie had negotiated the sale to him of Mr Michael Cooper's vacant lot, that most elusive of prizes, on condition that he saw to it that one of his own employees, a Mr James Clarke, for reasons Fox did not know or care about, was tucked away incommunicado for the foreseeable future. To that particular end Gillespie had given him McGrory's number and he had arranged a meeting with his secretary. Obviously, it wasn't something that could be casually discussed. It had already cost him his highest offer to Cooper plus a twenty per cent finder's fee for J.P., and he wasn't finished paying yet. That was unless he'd just blown everything by letting it be known there was a connection between himself and McGrory. Fox wasn't sure if McGrory would want his boss in on whatever their deal might be, considering he hadn't bothered to introduce himself earlier. He desperately scrambled around in his head for a viable conclusion to the sentence he'd begun.

General Somerville looked over at the other aide, who had remained glued to the action outside, seemingly oblivious to the exchange. 'White, would you mind excusing us for a few moments?'

White saluted the General and left the room. McGrory walked forward impassively and stood in front of the General and the now highly embarrassed figure of Fox.

'Trent and I keep no secrets,' the General said to Fox quietly. 'Any arrangement you might have made concerning the Shelter Project, regardless of how seemingly personal or confidential, would have needed my sanction in any case. Is this not so, Trent?'

'Yes, sir.'

'So you needn't worry, Steven, about having spilled the beans.' Somerville twirled the left side of his moustache and turned back to McGrory. 'I'm not jumping the gun in my supposition that this does concern the Project, Trent?'

'I don't believe so, sir. I made the same assumption myself. Though I'd have had little more to report than that a meeting had been arranged.'

'So you've discussed no preliminaries?' the General asked.

'No, sir. Nothing.'

'Fine,' Somerville smiled. 'Why don't you take White down to the lot and give him his instructions while I take the details from Steven here.'

'Very good, sir.' McGrory saluted and left the room.

Fox sighed, quietly and evenly, and settled back into his chair.

He was glad it seemed to have worked out, and that he was, as he was used to, working with the organ grinder as opposed to the monkey.

Fox would have been less happy to have known that Somerville had intuited this snobbish propensity in him, and had resolved to multiply the normal fee for detainment by a factor of four.

(ii)

After repairing a frayed piece of cable, Marshall McLemon emerged from under the sound desk in the Blind Pig and was amazed to see Sister Jasmine Ylang-Ylang chatting amiably with a coterie of musicians at the bar. As a rule the musicians would freeze out any effort to engage with them by an audience member, or, as in this case, a stranger. The freezing-out routine involved nodding slowly and knowingly at the punter's opening gambit and responding to it with an appropriate monosyllable. Concerned with retaining an artistic mystique, they preferred to keep a discreet distance from their audience; it was considered Slide's job as bandleader to interface with the rubes.

Marshall watched for a minute as Sister Jasmine rounded up her exchange and moved to one of the tables to the left of the stage. Seated at the table was a well-groomed man in a reddish brown tweed jacket, narrow black trousers and black suede pointy-toed ankle boots. As he approached the table Marshall thought there was a familiarity about the man, but was nevertheless utterly gobsmacked to discover that it was his friend Papa Charlie McCormack, with a freshly cropped head and sharp new wardrobe.

'Jesus! Charlie!' he said, taking a seat. 'Or should I call you "Charles"?'

The old man looked at him with mock dismissal. 'Ah, sit down and give me a break.'

Sister Jasmine smiled at them. 'I think he looks very distinguished.' Papa Charlie made a 'so there' face at Marshall, who sat looking at his friend in silent disbelief. The scraggy grey hair and baggy, ill-fitting casuals abandoned, Charlie looked thinner, younger, and not unlike (to Marshall's somewhat inaccurate memory) one of Charlie's favourite screen actors, Steve McQueen.

Lucy, the co-owner of the Blind Pig and Slide's girlfriend, sauntered over and took an order for drinks. While she didn't know Charlie well enough to give him a ribbing about his fresh new look, she did flatter him with a double take. Marshall thought he saw Sister Jasmine move closer to Charlie as a result of this modest admiration, and a strange sensation, an amalgam of pride, nostalgia and melancholy, welled in his breast.

The three of them chatted for an hour. Musicians and the two technicians Slide could afford pottered about on the stage. The venue gradually filled. Charlie told them with a certain glee that Mantra's disruption of the big soccer match had apparently gone off without a hitch, and though the news reports doggedly insisted on talking up the probability of Cypol's countermeasures team finally rumbling the organisation, Papa Charlie seemed to think not. The head of the team had been interviewed on camera, and while he'd attempted to be upbeat, Charlie thought he hadn't concealed his disappointment well; which seemed to please the old man no end. The day before, Marshall had asked how long Jasmine would be staying. Charlie said he didn't know, but thought she might be here as long as Mantra remained a mystery. This undoubtedly accounted for his uncommon delight in Mantra's success.

Slide Benson came by after a while and flopped into a chair. Tapping the roach end of a spliff on his thumbnail he took a brief introduction to Sister Jasmine from Marshall then immediately turned to Papa Charlie. 'So, Charlie, long time no see. You should come down more often. You love this stuff. Anyway, you're lookin' good, man.' He leaned over sideways in his chair so that he could look Charlie up and down. 'That French guy givin' everyone promotions?'

'No,' said Papa Charlie, betraying faint embarrassment. 'Just a . . . y'know – a new look is all.'

Slide nodded and put the joint in his mouth. He stole a look at Jasmine, one at Charlie and cocked an enquiring eyebrow at Marshall, who shrugged. Slide bowed his head, ostensibly to light the joint, but in reality to hide a smile and cover their exchange.

'Everything ready to go?' he said to Marshall, continuing his deception.

'Yeah,' said Marshall. 'Just have to press the button.'

'Oh listen,' said Slide, banging his forehead with the heel of his hand, 'I left it at home, but I have a book Bluey thinks your da might be interested in. A songbook by some German bloke.'

'Günter Lehmann?' Marshall ventured.

'The very one.'

'Jesus!' said Marshall, wide-eyed, 'that's unbelievable. Jack's luck is really in this weather.'

'I'll drop it in to you before I go. I've got other stuff for you too.'

'Bring it down to the Archive, will you?' asked Marshall.

'Any time that suits you, I won't be going out for lunch next week.'

'Sure.'

Papa Charlie groaned. 'We'll be buried there.'

'It won't be so bad,' said Marshall. 'Our new man is starting.'

Papa Charlie looked singularly unimpressed and mumbled something under his breath. Marshall wasn't interested in getting into this topic on any level and turned to Slide again to arrest any darkening of atmosphere.

'So what do you have for us tonight, Slide?'

Slide, as cagey as ever about his playlists, stuck out his lower lip as he exhaled the last of the smoke from his lungs. 'Somethin' old, somethin' new, lots of borrowed and *lots* of blues.'

Papa Charlie brightened at the prospect. '"Milk and Alcohol",' he suggested.

'I'll do somethin' special for you, don't worry.'

' "Pistol Packin' Papa"?'

'Now that's not a bad idea,' Slide laughed. He got up from his chair and, walking around Marshall, patted Papa Charlie on the shoulder as he headed towards the stage. He stopped for a second, leaving his hand on Papa Charlie's shoulder a tad too long. 'Nice fuckin' threads, man!'

Slide gained the stage and retrieved his guitar from a roadie just as Bluey Gillespie sauntered into the venue unpacking his clarinet. Bluey collected a bottle of beer from the bar which he waved over at Marshall and company, stopping briefly at their table as he made his way to the stage. Marshall noticed Papa Charlie's eyes narrow as he nodded a curt greeting towards Bluey and introduced Jasmine. A Gillespie is a Gillespie is a Gillespie, he was given to telling Marshall; he would undoubtedly tell the Sister the same later.

'So,' Bluey said to Marshall, 'you ready to roll?'

'Yeah, yeah, everything's ready.'

Bluey looked at one of Marshall's cameras, fixed to the pillar near their table. 'That new equipment?' he asked.

'It's the Stripp 502. Most compact yet. I can now get all my equipment into one case. Still too big for any stealth work, though. Gretta Donald would have no problem spotting something like that.'

Bluey smiled, but there was a coldness in it that gave Marshall to think that he'd gone too far. Bluey didn't even meet the quip with his customary 'fuck you'.

Slide Benson's voice came over the PA asking if Mr Gillespie would please man his station. Bluey headed off. Marshall flipped open his portable and initiated his recording just as each musician began to execute a few short arpeggios, runs, shuffles and rolls by way of final checks. This conglomeration of disparate and unsympathetic riffs and phraseology was, to Marshall, the very essence of authenticity in musical performance, and for that reason he liked always to capture it in order to play it behind the opening titles. Slide referred to the same conglomeration of noises as 'spoo'.

The gig got going and rolled on in three forty-minute sets. Marshall watched as Papa Charlie shuffled in his chair like a schoolboy and tapped Sister Jasmine's arm to draw her attention to his favourite songs, often to expound briefly on some item of interest. Marshall, Charlie and Jasmine didn't see much of Slide during the breaks, as he was called upon to schmooze with the paying guests. He played the crowd as well as he played. In an open and honest way he could make each one of them feel, briefly, like part of the inner sanctum. That they imagined such a thing existed helped. Charlie opined that Slide was well liked because he had too much taste to be flashy with people. Marshall didn't think it made much sense, but Jasmine seemed to him to be quite impressed.

Ten minutes into the last set the stage lights dimmed. Slide Benson moved to a stool placed at the front of the stage. He carried a steel guitar. Teetering on the pinky of his left hand was the bottleneck that had earned him his name. Laughing into his sleeve and licking his lips like a vaudeville smut merchant, Slide advised his audience that the upcoming medley was dedicated to his good friend Papa Charlie McCormack. He hunched over his instrument and started into a slow funky blues riff.

Papa Charlie endeavoured to prevent any indication of smugness entering into his expression or demeanour by determinedly clamping a hand over his mouth and stroking his chin. As he readily intuited so soon as Slide started into the lyric, he needn't have bothered. Before Marshall and Jasmine realised anything ironic was occurring, it was necessary for Slide to sing the line, 'Every girl crazy 'bout a sharp dressed man.' Slide, to Papa Charlie's further dismay, decided to segue directly into Charlie's earlier request, 'Pistol Packin' Papa', which, following the tone set by 'Sharp Dressed Man', caused the old man to reach into the front of his collar and drag it away from the neck, in the classical manner, as if to release heat; in particular when, despite the fact that the rest of the lyric was in the first person, Slide looked directly at Jasmine and sang: 'If you don't want to smell *his* smoke, don't monkey with *his* gun.' Sister Jasmine seemed not to be bothered on her own account. Indeed she appeared to derive guilty pleasure from Charlie's discomfiture. Marshall watched her deliberately take the sting out of it for him during the worst excesses of the lyric, by affectionately rubbing his forearm and laughing gently at him with her eyelids fluttering. As he watched Charlie glow under the attention, Marshall had the sense that she employed the whole gesture as a tool, but with so much of her own honesty and confidence that he felt he knew her motivation to be eminently appropriate, positively warm. And still, he was aware at the same time that he was ignoring a part of himself: a shrill, resentful and indignant teenager yelping, *He didn't use to want help. He didn't use to need friends.*

The musical accompaniment to Marshall's selfish melancholy was the sound of Slide Benson laughing through the final verse of 'Pistol Packin' Papa', then abruptly dropping into, and conducting with tight staccato movements of his right hand, an orchestrated fanfare based on the opening line of 'Dedicated Follower Of Fashion'. He signalled the band into a holding pattern on the last note while he subdued his good humour and informed his audience that the evening was to finish with two new instrumentals of the band's own composition, short, everyone understood, of the encore. The band segued into the first of two pieces that would have been better suited to the middle of a set. Slide recognised this and encored with 'Johnny One Note', a suitably reliable mood lightener, yet even-tempered enough so as not to greatly contrast with what had gone before. Saved as part of his feature on Benson's career, Marshall had twenty-four separate instances of Slide saying: 'It's important always to try and get out on the right note, and consistency is always the right note.'

(iii)

Everyone was busy after the gig, the musicians and roadies with their equipment and Marshall with his, so Papa Charlie and Jasmine said their goodbyes and headed out onto the street. They steered left out of the Pig and left again at the top of the road, back towards the Mall.

'Where are we going?' Jasmine asked.

'To the Archive,' Charlie told her. 'I've arranged it so you can make contact with Vervain Prime and check the serial numbers on those caps you found at the accident site. I realise it's an academic exercise at this stage since I found the analogous bullet shells, but it'll help to reinforce our position.' Her expression gave him to understand she didn't agree, and he held up a hand to ward off any protest. 'I've arranged for the highest grade in civilian encryption, in addition to which you'll be making the call from within the WentWest block, which will serve to allay any suspicion. Anybody conducting surveillance on the net tonight is interested in Mantra and Cypol, not in anything coming out of a WentWest holding.'

Jasmine still didn't look convinced. She took her cell from her belt and punched a few keys on the pad. 'Very well,' she said. 'I've notified them I'll be calling shortly. If I can get the right person at the other end we may be able to augment your security measures.'

They arrived at the Archive and Papa Charlie waved a pass key over the panel to the left of the door, releasing the shutter. They went downstairs into the office, where he sat behind his terminal for a couple of minutes organising the link-up while she wandered about looking at the stuff on the walls.

'Now,' he said finally, 'you're free to call.'

He vacated his chair and went to the drinks dispenser. Sister Jasmine punched in her number and waited. He caught her eye and pointed at the drinks machine. She shook her head and smiled. As he turned to punch in his choice he could hear her greet someone in an Oriental language. They spoke for a minute or two before Sister Jasmine fell into silence. She turned towards Charlie and held his gaze without embarrassment. Charlie noticed his heartbeat picking up. Before either of them could say anything she was drawn away again by activity on the screen. She spoke with her colleague for a few minutes while Charlie finished his drink in the corner.

'Was that Chinese?' Charlie asked, after she had disconnected.

'It is a localised version of the Chinese dialect "kejia", which ceased to be an ongoing linguistic concern about thirty or forty years ago. Being unique it provides an extra level of security in sensitive matters. I called ahead earlier to avail of someone who could speak it.'

'Not taking any chances,' Papa Charlie smiled.

'Why should we?'

Charlie was gratified to be reminded he was part of a team. 'What did you find out?' he asked.

Her features darkened. 'The numbers correspond to a device produced by Leyner Defense, a shady subsidiary of Festung N.A., the company which heads the military wing of the Crackston, Britteridge and Thompson conglomerate. It is a device for destroying bodies beyond recognition, popular with government security agencies. A friend of the Society claims to have overheard a discussion in which it was described by a representative of the manufacturer as being "useful in the control of sensitive material".

'Our information says that the active element is a metre-long magnesium alloy, which is shot into the cadaver through the top of the skull, like a harpoon. At the bottom of the shaft the payload is more concentrated, to ensure the destruction of skull and dental evidence. Complete envelopment of the element in the *corpus delicti* necessitates the use of a mallet. When properly in place it is ignited with a radio trigger and burns at tremendous heat over a sustained period. It is rumoured that the manufacturer recommends removal of the undesired's legs so that they can be strapped to the torso to effect total peace of mind.'

'Nice,' said Charlie.

'My colleague was not pleased to have been exposed to this information. She said that her optimism for the future is diminished knowing that someone has produced a weapon for use on the dead.'

'It's grim, certainly,' Papa Charlie said, looking at her expectantly and hoping her mood would lighten. 'At least we can prove there was a crime.'

She looked at him and shrugged, a gesture that did not sit well with her. 'It's not proof of anything, Charlie. We have what should be compelling circumstantial evidence, and a theory to support it.'

'What now?' he wanted to know, worried at how the atmosphere seemed to be darkening.

'Perhaps we can find someone to take the investigation further, or who can put pressure on the police to take it further,' she said. 'I think we've done as much as we can.'

Papa Charlie started to feel a little panicky. He could sense an end coming that he did not want. He couldn't disagree with her that it was wiser for them not to pursue this present matter further, since desperate characters were now clearly implicated. At the same time he was not happy to arrive at the end of what he regarded as a promising start. The start of what, he had still not properly acknowledged to himself, because each time his thoughts went off in that direction he began to see himself as something of an old fool. He took a deep breath before voicing his next question, so as to lessen any trembling in his voice.

'What will you do now?'

She heard the hesitation in his voice, sensed the regret in his question. She had been expecting this exchange. Charlie hoped her sad expression was an outgrowth of her sombre mood following the conversation with her colleague. He dreaded the idea she might be feeling sorry for him.

'I'll wait a day or so and see if anything develops with the Mantra thing. If nothing does I must return home.'

'If something did though?' he asked.

'I don't hold out much hope, Charlie.'

'But if something did, you'd have to stay, right?'

She considered it a moment. 'If it was significant, yes.'

He tossed the plastic cup he'd been holding into the waste-paper basket and walked to the corner of the desk where she was sitting. He couldn't stop a smile, and put a hand to his jaw in an effort to drag his expression into a more serious shape.

'It's me,' he said, looking down at her.

She cocked her head to one side. 'What's you, Charlie?'

'Mantra,' he said. 'I'm Mantra.'

She did something then that he couldn't ever have imagined her doing: she laughed scornfully. One high-pitched yelp that a moment later he recognised as manufactured.

'Wouldn't that be marvellous?' she said, standing up suddenly and gripping him by the left elbow so hard that he knew she felt something very serious was up. She pushed him towards the door. 'Let's go outside,' she said, a little too loud. 'I need some air.'

When they got out into the street again she released his elbow. They walked for a hundred metres without speaking. He began to think that she didn't believe him, that she might think he'd only said it to encourage her to stay.

'I was serious,' he said finally. 'About Mantra,' he added, as if it needed clarification.

She stopped and looked him in the eye, concern wrinkling her brow. 'Yes,' she said, 'I was afraid you were.'

Serious Ground

PROGRAMME: Staines at 7.

DATE: Monday, 23rd October.

STEVE: It's - wait for it - [time nearest minute], twenty-third of October. You're tuned to TuMur. Monday again, [CUE: funeral march 7 FX473. 1½"] oh, boy. It could be worse I suppose. Like we talked about last week, it could be Tuesday. [CUE: funeral march FX473. 1½"] Anyway, we're back down to nine degrees after that very mild weekend, but at least the rain's holding off.

CUE: Can't . . . hold . . . on . . . much . . . longer . . . FX033. 3"

STEVE: I see the Congress of Employers commissioned a report released today which recommends among other things that in order to improve employee satisfaction and efficiency they make themselves more approachable. Seems we're all afraid to ask our bosses for stuff, or to air grievances. There's something you can all do today, since we all know you won't be working.

CUE: Track 1. 3'15" slow fade up behind Steve

STEVE: Get in there and tell your bosses what you want. Get yourselves a raise. It'll make Tuesday easier to deal with.

FULL FADE UP

(i)

James Clarke senior remained oblivious to the death of his son, James Clarke junior, in the ambulance crash outside Maymon Glades a week before, and was still in shock from his and his wife's forcible removal from their apartment the previous Friday. He stood in the office of Trent McGrory, Administrator of the Transient Shelter designated S17, watching the sharp creases in McGrory's green uniform trousers quiver under the desk each time the Administrator drummed his fingers on the keyboard in front of him. By the clock behind the Administrator's head Clarke had been kept waiting for seven minutes; it seemed longer. Each time he shuffled his feet or moved to relieve any accumulating discomfort, the Administrator peered imperiously over the wafer-thin screen in front of him by way of admonition.

Out of the long narrow window to the Administrator's left, through a gap in two prefabs, Clarke could see the tall coniferous trees that formed what was in all probability the outermost perimeter of the camp. In front of the trees he knew there to be a fence, taller than the one he came through to see the Administrator. Beyond the trees, the best he could figure, it was about a hundred metres to the road. No one who'd whispered any of these things to him seemed to know which road.

A lot of people here didn't have much interest in where they were. Most of them grimaced and groaned when he asked questions. When he had persisted, a few of them told him, in quiet but none the less certain terms, to stay away. The ones who did talk tended not to be the brightest stars in the firmament. No one, dull or sharp alike, travelled out here past the dwellings – there was no reason to. Where they were put to live was comfortable enough, a tree-studded tarmac grid laid over grass. The accommodation was prefabricated, but in a less bleakly functional fashion than the buildings the administration had out here. The 'client' accommodations were detached, softly if cheaply furnished, and they were really warm. The only public buildings were the market where you could get various food items and cigarettes, and the mess, where you went if you didn't want to cook. In contrast to the dwellings, both buildings were never as warm as you'd like. The market, which the 'staff' po-facedly referred to as 'the mall', closed at six, the mess at eight sharp. The mess was like a hangar, but individual booths and waiter service couldn't be sniffed at in a place like this. There was enough variety in both the market and the mess that you couldn't complain. Alcohol and drugs were officially outlawed but the guards would sell cheap booze in the market after four. Sale was on the understanding that you took it home and drank it quietly. You got credits every week to spend – discretionary income. As far as Clarke could see nearly all of this went into cigarettes and booze. The guards exchanged the credits they collected on the booze for cigarettes in the market and sold the smokes for cash on the outside. As part of a generous food allowance, the clientele could eat at the mess fourteen times a week maximum. That would still leave you a sizeable allowance at the market. Most people ate two squares daily at the mess and blew their remaining credit on tea, coffee, savoury snack food, assorted sugar products and booze. If you worked at laundry, sanitation or in the mess you got a supplement. Traditionally the jobs were filled by short-timers. The others, a hard core of the troubled, the hopeless and the impossibly lazy, which Clarke estimated to be seventy-odd per cent of the camp's population, emerged rarely except for food and supplies, content otherwise to watch the tube and await their fortnightly visit from the doctor.

Clarke and his wife had not received a response to their application for work. He saw to it they applied immediately upon their arrival on Friday night. As terrified as they had been, he had remembered to try and make the best possible impression. Of course their employment situation was of less concern to them than why it was they were here in the first place; a direct answer to which had not been forthcoming in previous visits to the Administrator on Saturday and then first thing this morning. He thought the Administrator was not a man gifted with great patience and worried that he was running out of good excuses to come here. He wanted to get shot of this place as soon as possible. He wanted out of the clutches of this private military. They were a different breed, strange and frightening to him. Mostly he wanted to hear as soon as possible that this was all a mistake, to receive some communication from Hither Twice to say, sorry, *big* mistake, sit tight, we're on our way.

The Administrator finally sat back, bestowing upon the screen in front of him a look of great satisfaction. He told the machine to save and close the file he'd been working on before turning his attention to Clarke.

'Now then, Mr Clarke,' the Administrator smiled, 'hotel tango tango zero one five, isn't it?'

'Eh, yessir.'

'How could I forget?'

The Administrator punched the registration code into his machine and briefly scanned the details that popped up onto his screen. 'Now. In response to your earlier query I see here, Mr Clarke, that your contract specified no onus upon the employer to divulge the rationale behind any correction of a workforce imbalance.'

'I realise that, sir, but in light of the unusual circumstances of our removal I thought –'

'Unusual?'

Mr Clarke, worried that he seemed to have caused offence, wondered what the most delicate way of phrasing his idea might be – it had, after all, been a highly unusual experience for him and his wife. 'It just didn't seem to me to adhere to the normal procedure for these things.'

'*Normal* procedure!' McGrory looked as if he could hardly believe his ears. 'There is only *proper* procedure, Mr Clarke, which I assure you we abide by.'

'We were taken out of our apartment . . .' Clarke coughed, 'I don't want to say "forcibly", but –'

'And I don't want to *hear* you say such a thing, Mr Clarke,' the Administrator cut across him with an indignation equal to his incredulity. 'I will not tolerate such a slur against any member of my staff!'

'I'm sorry, sir, I didn't mean that; but without warning, in the middle of the night? I've seen a good deal of surplus reduction over the years at Hither Twice and there was always notice given, a chance to arrange for another employer to pick up the contract, transfer of the deeds to the home. I never heard of anything like this.'

The Administrator squinted suspiciously at Clarke. 'Are you dissatisfied with your lodgings?'

'No, sir, they're fine, they're just not mine.'

'They are yours, Mr Clarke. Provided for you by the state via the Project free of charge. "Your" apartment, as you seem to think of it, was the property of Hither Twice Toys. They have reclaimed it as is their right and they have, without question, elected to refund your credits against another apartment once your contract is picked up.' The Administrator peered at the screen again a moment. 'I see they've also transferred your pension and holiday entitlements – with bonuses. You haven't *lost* anything, and as far as I can see, outside of some small inconvenience, you have very little to complain about. Need I remind you, Mr Clarke, that there are people in this world a lot worse off?'

'I know, sir, I know. But as well as that, the wife's worried about our boy. We haven't seen him for some months and she's concerned that he won't know where we are.'

'We are aware, Mr Clarke, who your son is, and why he's where he is. In any case, even if your employment situation had not changed, I'm advised he's involved in trials which are conducted in strict seclusion, meaning you wouldn't have seen him for another nine weeks anyway. This you are aware of, Mr Clarke. Your wife, it would seem, is unnecessarily agitated. You should make some attempt to explain this to her and not exacerbate any anxiety she's experiencing by coming down here on fruitless errands and needlessly bothering me.'

'Yes, sir, but –'

'But nothing, Mr Clarke. There are recruitment officers arriving this day next week. One whole week away. According to your permanent record you have been a loyal and diligent employee at Hither Twice. You should have no problem securing a placement. You will then be free to leave here, your new employer will help you locate accommodation and when your next visit to WentWest Correctional is due you can advise your son of the change of address.' The Administrator gestured expansively with his hands. 'Now what is the problem?'

Clarke shuffled his feet a bit, looked at his shoes a moment, then timidly back at the Administrator. 'Granted, sir, when you put it like that we do seem to be well taken care of, but we don't know where we are, we can't contact anyone we know, we can't leave.'

The Administrator inhaled deeply. 'Mr Clarke, are you suggesting that impecunious, jobless and homeless people should be allowed to trot about willy-nilly? What sort of a society would that be?' Clarke was silent and McGrory went on in a softer tone. 'You are here so that it is ensured you have a roof over your head, sufficient nourishment and the opportunity to avail yourself of gainful employment elsewhere. To that end, as I have already mentioned, companies are sending recruitment agents –'

'But Mr McGrory, I still don't know why I lost *my* job. There wasn't so much as a rumour at Hither Twice about lay-offs and –'

'Only agitators and deviants deal in rumours and hearsay!' The Administrator was out of his chair and leaning across the desk towards Clarke. 'Are you an agitator, Mr Clarke?'

Clarke looked startled, as if a gun had just gone off over his head. 'No, sir!' At that same moment McGrory admitted two uniformed and armed men to the office who took positions on either side of the door behind Clarke.

'That will be all, Mr Clarke, for now,' the Administrator said. 'Thank you.'

Clarke couldn't have got out of the room much quicker if it had been full of vipers. He paused only for a split second to nod deferentially at the two armed men. The door closed quietly and the Administrator sat down again. He scrolled through the display on his screen before addressing the man to his left. 'Mr Clarke resides in Block Seven, Sergeant. Have you briefed many in that block?'

The Sergeant nodded curtly. 'Yes, sir, we processed fifty-eight yesterday. No one knew Mr Clarke on Saturday morning, everyone knew him by teatime yesterday. I believe him to be gathering information in a less than covert manner.'

'That's a bit quick off the mark for someone with malignant intentions. You'd think he'd check out the layout, or whatever they do.'

'Depending on the circumstances, sir, his behaviour could be seen as justifiable curiosity.' The Sergeant said it, but he didn't believe it.

'Don't do anything for the moment. I'll need to check this first, but we may require, at the very least, heavier surveillance on Clarke.'

The Sergeant's face reflected the fact that this didn't surprise him one bit.

'Thank you, gentlemen,' said the Administrator. 'That will be all.'

The Administrator waited until his aides had left the room before patching himself through, on a private direct line, to the Controller-in-Chief of the Transient Shelter Project, General Keane Somerville.

Somerville, when he picked up, was seen to be busy brushing crumbs out of the enormous moustache that spanned the red face of obesity. 'Ah, Trent. 'Fraid you've caught me at my elevenses.' He raised, by way of a toast, a coffee mug that must have held, to the Administrator's mind, half a litre. The General's appetite was legendary and the bulk which filled the Administrator's screen was testimony to the fact that the man broke fast in a heart-stopping manner at eight, had elevenses, a very modest meal by his standards, at ten, then a three-course lunch at twelve, a snack around two followed by the alarmingly misleading 'tea' at four, and dinner at eight. Often there was supper. If the Administrator had felt there was anything ridiculous in this, or in the General's appearance, he would not have betrayed it. Somerville made a formidable enemy or ally and McGrory chose to go the latter route. In addition to being the sole owner of all the Project's assets, Somerville commanded unwavering support in the legislature by virtue of his politician father's dying bequest, reputed to be an assortment of skeletons that would have been the envy of J. Edgar Hoover.

'Shall I call back in a while, General?'

'Not at all, Trent, not at all. What can I do for you?'

'It's Mr Clarke, sir, late of Hither Twice Toys. As you predicted he seems edgy, and inordinately concerned with the reasons behind his expulsion and,' the Administrator paused and raised his eyebrows as if he could scarcely believe what he was about to say, 'with getting out of here. He's been to see me three times already, and I have the sense that he'll be requesting an advocate soon.'

The General was surprised and a little irritated at this. His eyes drifted to the surface of his desk as he considered it, and his tongue drifted slowly across his upper lip. 'Haven't you made it clear to this character, McGrory,' he said, having jumped onto a parallel train of thought with McGrory's enunciation of the word *advocate*, 'that alcohol, regardless of how seemingly innocuous, is not permitted in any of the shelters.'

It took the Administrator a few moments to work out that the General was in viscerotonic rather than intellectual mode, being as he was at his brunch. 'No, no, General,' McGrory smiled. 'I mean to say he'll be seeking representation, legal advice.'

'Ah!' The General nodded regretfully, unable to hide the fact that he was disappointed to be moving away from the subject of food and drink and a cosy Christmas reverie he'd fallen into. He paused for a moment, then knitted his brows and cleared his throat.

'Is that allowed?'

'Is what allowed, General?'

'Representation.'

'Well . . . yes. Can take a while though.'

This seemed to provide the General with a morsel of satisfaction. He moved his jaw up and down, staring past the screen into the distance. When he turned back to McGrory the eyes were pinpoints of light, whose focus occurred seven centimetres in from McGrory's forehead.

'You're secure, of course, McGrory,' he said, extracting a long black cigarette from a silver case, which he lit with an oddly slim lighter held delicately in his fleshy fingers.

McGrory looked into the bottom right of his screen to see a red panel flashing. He quickly performed three more checks at his board.

'Full spread.'

'Classification A1, Trent. This is not to be recorded. Its full range is me, you and two operatives, your very best men.'

The Administrator nodded. 'Of course, General.'

The General exhaled smoke and shook his head in a gesture of distilled avuncularity. 'Steven Fox, that ridiculous little man from Hither Twice Toys we met last Friday, was anxious to get rid of Mr Clarke because he was stirring up trouble on the shop floor. He wasn't, however, in on the full picture regarding this reprobate. Clarke has been under suspicion for some time now as the prime mover in an armed and dangerous workers' solidarity movement,' he said. 'He's even been tied to that damned Mantra organisation. We felt that his sudden disappearance might serve to flush out a number of his accomplices. Unfortunately, it's thought that we may not have been decisive enough, and that some atrocity long in planning will be pushed ahead of schedule. We'll do all we can, of course, to contain a possible outrage, but we cannot allow society to be held to ransom by these animals. Clarke is particularly deadly – squeaky clean. He's never been caught at anything – absolute master of duplicity. We know their own people furtively refer to him and the wife as Mr & Mrs Macbeth, so she must be even worse. Clarke is a likely object of pity to woo the public in some anachronistic campaign, a campaign solely designed to boost the public image of his organisation while masking a trade-off that has the threat of mass mayhem behind it. With Mrs Macbeth coordinating the production from the wings they'll be quick and deadly. If the campaign gets going and we're holding Clarke, there's a danger that the authorities will be drawn into bargaining with the organisation for his release. If he's out of the picture before he builds himself a profile, that's not a problem.'

'And the wife, General?'

The General nodded solemnly. It was all a terrible shame. 'Nevertheless,' he said.

The Administrator nodded with equal solemnity. *Nevertheless what?*

'You have a cover story, should there be enquiries.'

'Naturally.'

'Well then,' said the General, pressing his lips together. 'Sooner rather than later, I think.'

(ii)

Marshall McLemon sat deep in the bowels of WentWest Archive and Record Management uploading a clutch of documentaries on John Ford. It was late on Monday evening and he was dog-tired, having worked most of the weekend. In contrast with the week before, Marshall was in love with his job and with his life. On Saturday afternoon McCambridge-LeMans had called him out to a meeting with John Lyons-Howard. Marshall had been impressed, mostly, with the producer. It had been easy to see why he'd been successful. He appeared to have a great deal of energy. At times almost too much.

Lyons-Howard breathlessly told Marshall that he thought the stuff he and Charlie had written was terrific and felt the Exhibit should comprise as much of their work as possible. He suggested, however, that the material for inclusion that Marshall and Charlie might be less keen on should perhaps be presented by people for whom it was more important. People with personal fan sites, who had been making do for years with degraded sounds and images. People with good technical ability who would jump at the chance to work with grade A material and who might do the work for the pleasure of it, or little more. Lyons-Howard felt he could have this running in three months, before freeing himself up for other tasks. If they wanted to outsource half of this work, they would more than halve the time for completion of the project. Marshall got excited about it and agreed immediately. McCambridge-LeMans told him he should ship out all of the non-entertainment Archive material as soon as possible. On Sunday, yesterday, he had supervised, back to back, two eight-hour shifts of ten men, all on time and a quarter, who had cleared the

Archive completely of this. First thing this morning the call went out to WentWest offices worldwide, that any entertainment-related Archive material was to be sent to Marshall, not, as was normal, through Head Office in Dublin, but directly to a new address on the WentWest e-map: COOLSVILLE.

As happy as he was, Marshall felt he'd done enough for the evening. He pushed through the swing doors of the basement storeroom and walked to the elevator. He walked inside and selected the floor above. It was late, probably eight o'clock or more, and he was surprised to hear a booming mechanical backbeat emanating from the direction of the office. He walked through the door to find John Lyons-Howard slouched in a chair in front of the big screen, a remote hanging limply in his right hand and ancient synthesised music blaring from the speakers.

'Hey!' Marshall shouted over the noise.

Lyons-Howard turned his head, his mouth set in a skewed smile. He closed his eyes a moment and opened them again slowly as if having difficulty with it. 'Hello back, young feller,' he shouted, making an oblique reference to a movie he knew to be one of Marshall's favourites.

'Didn't expect to find anyone here,' Marshall roared, smiling at him. 'Papa Charlie long gone?'

In an effort to shrug and shut off the music at the same time, Lyons-Howard dropped the remote. He leaned unsteadily out of his chair to retrieve it. 'Two hours,' he said, a tad too loud in the now quiet room. 'Somethin' like that.'

'Right,' said Marshall, aware all of a sudden that Lyons-Howard was out of his gourd. 'So what are you doing?' he asked.

Lyons-Howard waved the remote at the screen in front of him. 'Watching, listening and thinking,' he said pointedly.

'Good,' the young man nodded enthusiastically. 'Any more ideas for us?'

Lyons–Howard shook his head. 'Different type of thinking.'

Marshall squinted at him and dropped his nod rate by half. Lyons–Howard smiled indulgently and held up the remote by way of explanation, before cueing something up on the large screen. A picture of a man on water in a makeshift raft appeared with a list of songs down the right-hand side, cover art from some long-forgotten recording.

'You know these guys?'

Marshall shook his head and answered matter-of-factly, trying to hide the fact that he'd noticed the trouble Lyons–Howard was having focusing on him. 'I've seen this before alright. It's one of Papa Charlie's. Is that what was playing when I came in?'

Lyons–Howard nodded.

'Sounded like a lot of machinery in the production.' Marshall curled his lip ever so slightly to convey distaste.

'Fuck the machinery,' Lyons–Howard said quietly and evenly. 'Listen to the words.' He skipped down the track list and hit play, too quickly for Marshall to read the title. The same mechanical sounds that had greeted Marshall's arrival jerked out of the room's speakers at a rigid and unflinching one hundred and sixty beats per minute. After a brief synthetic intro it was a relief to the young purist to hear a nasal, reedy tenor pick up the tune. There was no visual to accompany the sounds, and under the watchful if inaccurate eye of Lyons–Howard he tried his best to concentrate on the lyric, but it seemed little more than gibberish to him. The nearest equivalent he knew would have been 'The Akond of Swat' or 'Calico Pie'. Such stuff as his father had a tragic weakness for, and with which he vainly tried to infect his young son. A mercifully brief time later the song finished.

Lyons–Howard pointed the remote over his shoulder and

stopped the playback. He pulled a silver hip flask from his jacket pocket and took a swig. 'What did you make of it?' he wanted to know.

Marshall waved away the offer of a drink and smiled apologetically. 'The composition is surprisingly, eh, *complete*, given the period, but I maintain they should have used real musicians. The lyric sounded, I'm afraid, like a lot of nonsense to me.'

Lyons-Howard rolled his eyes towards the ceiling, swaying ever so slightly in his seat. 'It's my take on it,' he said, 'that the protagonist of the song –'

'Mr Horrible,' Marshall cut in, to show he had indeed been listening.

'Yes,' said Lyons-Howard patiently. 'The protagonist is representative of us all. He's constantly put upon by tormentors hell-bent on denying him the smallest shred of dignity; who taunt and jeer him mercilessly about the death of a friend, who treat him as if he were an inanimate object, who have exposed him to toxic waste, who have caused him brain damage. I don't know if the tormentors represent his environment in general, or if they're meant to be something more specific; it's probably not important. The point is that faced with such intense vexation all this sad fucker can complain about are inconsequential irritations, in this case the position of his chair.'

Marshall was wondering what the point was, while Lyons-Howard looked at him expectantly, as if he had made some startling revelation. 'Kind of like Mantra,' Marshall ventured. 'Making reference to what they believe to be some intolerable status quo, while the people the message is aimed at can only complain about the fact that their sporting fixtures – which I suppose are relatively inconsequential events – have been interrupted.'

'Yes!' Lyons-Howard, in a rather uncharacteristically macho display, punched the air in triumph, and for the second time nearly sent himself to the floor. 'We live in a world of shit!' he declared when steady again. Marshall noted another possible movie reference and wondered if Lyons-Howard thought this was the only way to communicate with him. 'Our environment is fucked,' Lyons-Howard continued, 'our offspring are cold, uncultured, homicidal maniacs, our lives a meaningless back and forth from the isolation of our dog boxes to jobs that hold no interest for most of us. The only relief from this monotony is endless sport and tacky voyeur TV and,' he pulled a joint out of his jacket pocket and held it up as an exhibit, 'whatever drugs you can score to numb yourself. We do anything but face the reality, 'cause that might demand action.' He took a long draught from the flask, which emptied it, then, tossing the vessel on a desk top, he reached into another pocket and extracted a yellow capsule which he broke under his nose, inhaling deeply. He threw the spent capsule at the waste-paper basket and the joint towards Marshall. 'Get with the programme,' he said.

Marshall sparked up, partly to placate the possibly volatile figure in front of him and partly because the diatribe had begun to sound so much like Papa Charlie that he was becoming intrigued. He wanted to be closer to the place Lyons-Howard was coming from. He drew the heavy smoke deep into his lungs and felt a familiar tingling sensation wash into his legs.

'This low-grade shit most of us are happy enough to deal with,' Lyons-Howard went on. 'Because somewhere in the backs of our minds we know that we're pretty well off, that someone somewhere is a lot worse off, that the real power to do anything about anything lies elsewhere, that individual endeavour isn't worth squat, and that our collective personal contributions to energy conservation and garbage compartmentalisation and amnesty and peace and homey-fucking-opathy don't count for shit beside the organised life-wrecking savagery of the smallest military industrial complex.' He stopped for a breath and reached towards the joint, which Marshall passed to him. After a couple of quick pulls he resumed. 'Occasionally though, one of us gets inadvertently dragged up to the mother lode – has his face pushed into the humongous faecal saveloy of true corruption, so's he can't do anything but gag in disbelief and acknowledge the unique bouquet as the foetid air of hell itself.' He looked fixedly at the floor between his feet, heavy smoke billowing from his mouth and nose. 'What the fuck's anyone supposed to do then?'

Marshall pushed out his lower lip. 'It's one of those things, I suppose. You don't know until you're there. Assuming there is a *there.*'

'Oh, it's there alright.' Lyons-Howard's head and body came up and around like a marionette's to face Marshall. 'And not in Africa or South America or the Middle East, but closer to home than you think.' He tried to stare hard at McLemon for a moment, but his eyes kept rolling up into his head. 'If it's possible to expose a part of it, should I do it to get even?'

Marshall just looked at him, suddenly without anything to say for himself. So sure had he been that Lyons-Howard, fuelled by drugs and alcohol, had been rambling on in the abstract, that he was taken by complete surprise to discover the man was talking about himself, about something deeply personal. Marshall watched him for a minute, slumped in his chair, gazing at the floor, blinking like a petrified rodent and nipping at the barely burning joint without any real purpose. Finally the young man thought of something he felt might be useful.

'Papa Charlie always says that when your back's to the wall you're freer in many respects to do whatever you want.'

Lyons-Howard laughed half-heartedly. 'To do whatever's right,' he corrected. 'I was put in mind of that too.' He picked the remote off the arm of his chair and flicked the cold butt of the joint back to Marshall. 'I watched this after Charlie left. Have you seen it?' A trailer for some old movie that was unfamiliar to Marshall played on the screen in front of them.

'No,' said Marshall. 'Must be another of his hidden treasures.'

With one eye closed, Lyons-Howard pointed to a small, dark, intense-looking young man on screen. 'This guy's brother is run off the road and killed by the mad sheriff of a one-horse desert town. The sheriff has a thing for speeding motorists 'cause his kid was killed by one years back, but we don't find out about that immediately. The guy – the hero – comes into town, cool as you like, in this outrageous car, to bait the sheriff and beat him at his own game. There's never a question in his mind about whether what he's doing is right or wrong, no procrastination, only the calm, single-minded knowledge that what the sheriff did, regardless of what scars he carries, was wrong. Slowly he reveals his identity to the sheriff, goading him all the time. And when everyone's sure who everyone else is, he calmly calls the sheriff out to the dead man's curve where his brother bought it.

'Before the final showdown, the two guys are face to face in a barber's shop or something.' Lyons-Howard seemed to think this was funny and chuckled to himself. 'They both know that they have to do this thing, that they have no other option. Even the sheriff regains some dignity. On the one hand by not taking an easy way out, like shooting the hero or something, and on the other by the fact that he's made to realise he's caused someone else the same pain he was put through years before. When they get to the field of battle they're equals, without blemish, allowing fate, through their individual skill, to determine right and wrong. It's fantastic.'

Marshall tried to look convinced of this, but the production values apparent to him weren't encouraging. Besides he was keener on discovering what was up with their new colleague than he was on discussing the merits of B-movies.

They sat in silence for a few moments, Lyons-Howard continuing to watch the trailer, grunting every time he saw something he had especially enjoyed earlier, and Marshall wondering how he might phrase a question asking what kind of trouble Lyons-Howard was in exactly. In the end he opted for the direct approach.

'What kind of trouble are you in exactly?'

'Me!' Lyons-Howard's surprise was bitterly ironic. 'I don't have troubles, I have crises of conscience.'

He seemed disinclined to speak again, so Marshall went to the drinks dispenser and got two hot chocolates, the only selection to contain actual caffeine. He gave one to Lyons-Howard and went to fish some cigarettes out of a pack on his desk. He put two in his mouth and lit them, passing one along to his seated companion.

It occurred to him how outrageous these gestures would have seemed two weeks before, so rich were they in sure patience and mature understanding. Maybe this was what happened when someone put a little faith in you, as Henri had with him. He sat down and stretched his legs out in front of him towards the forlorn figure of Lyons-Howard. He sucked audibly on his smoke to let the man know he was still there, with all the time in the world.

'Didn't use these until the night I got offered this job.' Lyons-Howard looked at his cigarette and laughed up some smoke, remembering his first meeting with McCambridge-LeMans the previous Tuesday and comparing it to every other job offer he'd had.

'It's hardly the up-and-at-'em, cut-throat world of investigative journalism,' said Marshall, looking around the office.

Lyons-Howard followed his gaze for a moment. 'It's more like the dreamtime of an amok psychotic ogre.'

Marshall leaned forward to use the ashtray on the edge of his desk. He stayed there with his elbows on his knees. 'What are you getting at?'

Lyons-Howard sighed. The inebriety seemed to fall away from him suddenly, until he just looked tired and beaten. 'Someone close was killed recently. She died on account of her involvement in experiments which I gather are designed to make a certain class of human being docile . . . manageable, but productive at the same time. I suppose she died really because she wanted to expose this to the public.' He paused to give this further thought. 'Naturally there was a small consideration involved,' he said. He uncrossed his legs and pushed himself up straight in his chair.

'How did she die?' Marshall asked.

'I hope the impact killed her. The bodies were burned beyond recognition.'

Marshall's heart leapt in his chest and he swallowed carefully before speaking. 'A motor accident?' Lyons-Howard nodded at him grimly and seemed not to notice the tremor in his voice. Marshall leaned in closer. 'You said bodies. There were others?'

'Another doctor, three "patients". Happened in a small ambulance a couple of kilometres away,' he jerked his thumb towards the front entrance, and beyond it the West Road and Papa Charlie's place. 'She tried to break three of the subjects out of the research facility so I could put them on TV. A security unit followed them, there was a chase and a crash.'

'And the people running the experiments, do they know you were involved?'

'Yeah. They caught up with me already. Nice people. I was told the two security guys who initiated the chase had been overzealous in their attempt to contain the breach. They apologised.'

'The security team?'

Lyons-Howard laughed bitterly. 'You won't get an apology out of that pair without a Ouija board.'

'They're dead?' Marshall was incredulous.

Lyons-Howard put his index finger to his temple and made a shooting mime. Marshall's attitude remained one of disbelief.

'I saw the fucking bodies, kid,' he said scornfully. 'And they didn't get those holes in the head picking at scabs.'

'So how come they didn't take care of you? Aren't they afraid you'll go to the police?'

'They don't believe I have anything that can hurt them, and they probably feel I'm sufficiently scared. That's of course outside of the fact that they probably own half the cops in town.'

Marshall shook his head. Papa Charlie was going to freak when he heard this. 'Who are these people?' he asked.

Lyons-Howard laughed and threw his spent cigarette into the ashtray. He looked at Marshall and smiled cruelly. 'Would you believe me if I told you it was J.P. Gillespie, under the watchful eye of your particular friend at court, Henri McCambridge-LeMans?'

Marshall gave him a level stare, hoping to see the lie.

'Think about it. Who else has the captive workforce – WentWest Correctional – the money for R&D, not to mention the fucking gall?'

Marshall's mouth was open a couple of seconds before the words came out. 'J.P. maybe, but Henri?'

'Don't kid yourself, McLemon, he didn't get to be chairman of the board because of his patronage of the arts and his fine table manners.' Lyons–Howard got out of his chair and took another cigarette from the pack on the desk. 'Anyway,' he said, 'that's my crisis of conscience. Do I attempt to expose them, thereby avenging the woman I had half a mind to marry, or do I sit tight and hope one day they'll trust me enough to allow me to retire alive?'

Marshall was asking himself how Henri might have got mixed up in something like this, wondering if he should tell Papa Charlie at all now, thinking about how work on the Exhibit might be affected if it got out, half hoping that Lyons–Howard would take the easy way out and keep quiet, and trying to convince himself that he himself could find a way to deal with this knowledge, should it be true and should they opt for silence, so that he or his work would not be sullied by the iniquities of his benefactor. He looked at Lyons–Howard, who was smoking peacefully.

'You said yourself you didn't have anything to hurt them with.'

'I never said that.' Lyons–Howard smiled. He got up out of his chair and buttoned his jacket. He began walking out and stopped at the door. 'Anyway, I was thinking that since you're the new decision–maker on the block, maybe it's your call.'

(iii)

Steven Fox, MD of Hither Twice Toys, sat in his booth in the Westpark, looking across the room at J.P. Gillespie, who hadn't as yet seen him. Never the best at bearing bad tidings, Fox was debating how he might approach J.P. with the news of his former employee, the unfortunate Mr Clarke.

All of a sudden it was too late. J.P. had caught sight of him. The fat man waved across the room, excused himself from the people he was with and bounded enthusiastically towards Fox. 'Steven! How the hell are you?' he bellowed from about fifteen feet. The greeting made heads turn and Fox attempted to retract his head into his shirt collar.

'How are you, J.P.?' Fox smiled unconvincingly. 'Sit down. Can I get you something?'

J.P. stuck his hand in the air and clicked his fat fingers. A waiter arrived almost immediately and J.P. ordered without looking at him. 'Cognac.'

'Yes sir, Mr Gillespie.' It was as if his day had been made.

'So Steven, how's your carport coming along? Pleased?'

'Oh yeah, J.P. Great.'

'You don't seem overjoyed.'

'Oh, it's not that, J.P., the carport's fine, it's, eh, Mr Clarke.'

'Clarke?' J.P. squinted at him. 'I thought we had Mr Clarke taken care of.'

'Well, yes. More so in fact than we may have wished.' J.P.'s drink arrived and there were a few moments' silence before the waiter left them again.

J.P. took a sip from the glass and leaned forward across the table, dropping his voice to a confidential baritone. 'What exactly are you getting at, Steven? You contacted McGrory like I told you, didn't you? Mr Clarke should be neatly tucked away for the foreseeable.'

'Right. Well, as it happens, I didn't make the arrangements with McGrory himself.'

J.P. looked at Fox, afraid to ask the question. 'What did you do?'

'I met his boss, General Somerville, at the clear-out a day or so after we spoke. We got to talking, and he offered to handle the problem directly. McGrory was there. He seemed happy enough about it.'

'Oh sweet Jesus Christ.'

'I figured it was okay – he's the boss after all. I've always found it better to deal higher up.'

'Oh yeah, sure,' said J.P. contemptuously. 'Except when the "higher up" in question is a fucking lunatic who treats murder like it was a fetish.'

Fox made a how-was-I-to-know gesture. 'He *seemed* fine.'

J.P. glared at him and Fox shrank back in his seat. 'Of course he fucking *seems* fine! It's just that he gets a fucking hard-on writing death warrants.' He put a hand to his forehead. 'Oh Christ.'

J.P. was breathing slow and deep, thinking hard. He took another swig from his cognac and looked at Fox wearily. 'They're the military, Steven, they're all mad. They're only separated by degrees of madness. The maddest get to give orders to the slightly less mad, but where you and me think an order is a request for a pizza, they think it's something that has to be obeyed on pain of court martial, which to them is the only thing worse than death.'

Fox was fiddling with the plastic wrapping on a pack of smokes. 'I didn't think you could get people killed so cheap.'

'What's cheap to you is serious bananas to these people. What did you spend, fifty, seventy-five grand?'

Fox swallowed hard. ''Round about.'

'You could've had a small village eradicated for that, depending where it was, but Somerville would have had this done for a square meal, if it had come to it.' J.P. finished his drink and called for another. 'What about Mrs Clarke? Is she raising a stink?'

301

Fox nervously lit a cigarette. 'I daresay, but not in the way you're thinking.'

'They did the wife too?' J.P. thought his head was going to explode. Fox remained silent. 'You hear the cover story?'

'Yeah.' Fox coughed up a lungful of smoke. 'They poisoned themselves with illegally distilled booze smuggled into the shelter.'

J.P.'s drink arrived and he drained it in one draught. 'Oh well. Did Somerville get a whiff of my involvement?'

Fox shook his head.

'Just you, me and McGrory?'

'Yes, J.P.'

'Right, this conversation never took place, got it?'

'Sure, but what should I do?'

'I don't give a shit, to be perfectly honest. You're in hostile territory with your boats and bridges burning behind you. If I were you I'd sit tight and hope I never hear anything about this again.' J.P. got out of the booth to leave when something else occurred to him. 'And I sure as fuck wouldn't talk about it to anyone else, Stevie.'

Adios Coolsville

PROGRAMME: Staines at 7.
DATE: Tuesday, 24th October.

STEVE: It's just gone [time nearest
              minute], Tuesday the twenty-fourth
              and you're tuned to TuMur. It's not
              only the lousiest day of the week,
              folks, it's also the coldest in a
              week - six degrees. [CUE: arctic wind
              8 FX538. 1"] No rain though. [CUE:
              hallelujah 4 FX869. 1½"] Dry must
              be the new wet.

CUE: Groovy riff 14 FX777. 5"

STEVE: I see this morning that three high-
              ranking investment bankers in Athens
              are answering embezzlement charges.
              Now get this, these guys are telling
              the police that they met a nice-
              looking redhead at lunchtime yesterday
              who bought them a couple of drinks
              and talked them into giving her half
              a million in cash. Just like that!

CUE: Track 1. 3'15" slow fade behind Steve

STEVE: The men can't explain their actions
              and the extent of their defence so
              far is to say that it all seemed
              perfectly reasonable at the time.
              The Federation Police say they're
              treating the matter with an open
              mind for the moment and have issued
              all agencies in the area with a
              description of the woman in ques-
              tion. Do these guys think we came
              down with the last shower, or what?

FULL FADE UP

(i)

Bluey Gillespie pushed through the heavy glass doors into the foyer of WentWest Head Office and sauntered up to the reception desk. Three uniformed men sat behind it. The nearest to the door smiled as he came in.

'Morning, Sam,' said Bluey. 'On my way up to see the old man, okay?'

'Sure,' said Sam, 'but if you hang on a second, J.P. left a pass for you.' Sam reached under the counter without looking and groped around. 'This must mean you've signed up then,' he ventured.

Bluey waved his head from side to side as if unsure. 'On a sort of part-time basis.'

Sam handed him a flat black card about five centimetres by three, which Bluey studied briefly before pocketing it. 'Everyone knows you by sight,' Sam said, eyeing the young man's red Afro, 'but this might get you out of a spot if there's a new man on.'

'Yeah,' said Bluey, 'or if I get a haircut.'

Sam laughed. 'God forbid.'

'You never know, Sam, it might just be time for a change.'

Bluey walked to the elevators, jumped into an empty one and called for the penthouse. On the way up he tapped his jacket pocket to make sure he'd brought the disk. It was the fourth time he'd checked that morning. He'd been back to the Archive last night to recover his recording and replace it with a fresh disk. He had then been up all night, trawling through hour upon hour of Marshall, Papa Charlie and a new guy at the Archive, John Lyons-Howard, as they bullshitted each other about the value of various pieces of ancient crap they might or might not wish to include in their Exhibit, which as far as he was concerned was ninety per cent worthless.

Watching the playback Bluey found it was easy to despise people you normally liked. When you got to step back and view them dispassionately they were different. It was Papa Charlie, who he was normally wary of, that had appealed to him most in playback, with his dry designation of spades as spades and his habit of cutting through the bullshit which the other two seemed capable of producing as easily as they did carbon dioxide. Despite the occasional blast of fresh air blown in by the old man the recording had been an unmitigated bore, and it wasn't until near the end, when his eyes had been closing on him despite the coffee and cigarettes, that anything vaguely worthwhile had happened.

He stepped out of the elevator into the relative quiet of the penthouse and padded across the deep Persian blue carpet to the exterior of his father's office where Josephine was scrolling through one of the dailies.

'Morning, Jo!'

Josephine, J.P.'s secretary, looked around slowly, warily. She hadn't been aware of his approach. She looked at him in silence for a couple of seconds. 'Everything okay, Bluey?'

'Yeah, why?'

'Just never figured you for an early riser.'

'Haven't been to bed yet.'

'Ah.' This seemed to put her more at her ease.

'Can I go in?' Bluey asked, heading towards the door of his father's office.

Josephine waved him away. 'He's on the line with the Chairman – another barney. Better give him a few minutes.'

Bluey rolled his eyes to heaven. He sat in one of the big leather armchairs outside the door and lit a cigarette. He could hear the muffled sounds of his father's raised voice from behind the door, but couldn't make out what he was saying. He gave up listening, and pointed at the screen Josephine was engrossed in. 'Anything new this morning?'

She looked over the top of the screen and scrunched up her nose. 'Nothin' much. Cypol's final report is in. They've struck out completely on the Mantra thing; which might explain why the Chairman's so crusty this morning.'

'They don't like each other anyway,' said Bluey, hooking a thumb over his shoulder towards the door, 'and Mantra, I'm inclined to think, has perpetrated one of *the* great illusions.'

Josephine smiled. 'Yeah, lots of people are saying that now.'

Bluey wasn't happy being told he was repeating the commonest of ideas and shot her a look that said 'no shit'. He finished his cigarette in silence. After another minute Josephine told him he could go in.

Bluey walked into the office to find his father staring into space. It occurred to him how often this job seemed to get the old man down and wondered why, with the long hours and everything, he put up with it. Were money and power *that* addictive? He briefly considered the thrill he'd got as a result of his own covert meddling and felt the power trip might be worthy of further investigation.

'Morning, Coleman,' J.P. said to him dolorously.

'Morning, Dad,' he replied quietly. He said 'Dad' as a calculated, but sincere, effort to cheer the old man up. He knew J.P. liked it, which was why he'd stopped calling him 'Dad' at fourteen and started calling him 'J.P.'.

'Want a coffee or anything?'

'I want a break, Coleman. A bit of luck. I'm long overdue.'

'Would fair warning do you?'

J.P. looked up, his eyes slits. 'What are you talking about?'

'I organised an eavesdrop at the Archive, to keep tabs on . . . McLemon.' It was easier if he distanced himself that little bit; Marshall was a friend he'd once had, McLemon was a shitwit he'd seen in a recording.

J.P.'s eyes widened. 'And?'

'The new guy, Lyons-Howard,' said Bluey, 'mentioned something about a car wreck and a connection with you and the Frenchman.'

It took a second for J.P. to realise what his son was talking about. 'That fucking moron! I can't fucking believe he's talking about that fucking shit! He must have a fucking death wish!'

Bluey pressed his lips together to stop himself from laughing and looked directly at J.P. until the old man realised what he sounded like. Bluey pulled the disk out of his pocket and dropped it on the desk in front of J.P.

'It's one of two interesting things I got off the recording. You want to fill me in on the background or would you rather watch it?'

J.P. looked as if he had only half heard him. It took him a second again to get up to speed. 'No, we'll look at it first. I'll tell you the rest over brunch.'

Bluey was impressed. 'I deserve brunch?'

'Maybe,' J.P. wrinkled his lip, 'let's see what you've got first.'

Bluey handed the disk to J.P., who plugged it in and ran it. From the control panel in the arm of his chair, J.P. locked the office door, closed the blinds and activated the big screen.

'This is edited from an original image shot with a motionless and, therefore, very wide angle lens,' Bluey began explaining, 'to capture as much of the periphery as possible –'

'Blah, blah, blah, the picture'll be crappy sometimes.' J.P. was carefully studying the image of John Lyons-Howard. 'Is he drunk?' he asked.

'And the rest,' said Bluey, reaching towards the keyboard on the desk. 'The sound quality, you'll be glad to know, is second to none. I'll move past this, there's a lot of old nonsense before he gets to the nitty-gritty.' He shifted to the correct index and they watched. J.P. went back over parts of it again and again for a couple more minutes.

'So, what?' J.P. looked at his son. 'The producer prick has something, evidence of some description, which he's going to give McLemon in the hope he'll do the decent thing with it. Is that what you get?'

'Sure, or he wanted Marshall to think he had something on you and the Frenchman.'

'He was out of his box. It might have been an empty boast.'

'Possible,' said Bluey, 'but he's still yapping about something sensitive, which McLemon now knows about. And it won't be long before McLemon's talking to his good friend and colleague Papa Charlie, who'll be very interested on account of the fact that, in the middle of the night last week, he called the emergency services to a crashed and burning vehicle on the road outside of where he lives.'

J.P. blanched. 'It can't be the same thing. He'd have been mentioned in the police report.' He tapped at his console a second and pulled the document up, then scrolled through it and read intently for a number of seconds. 'Philip McCormack! Shit! No one saw the connection.'

'Marshall mentioned it the day after it happened,' said Bluey. 'I'd forgotten about it until I saw a recording from the Archive on Friday night with Papa Charlie and his Chinese girlfriend sending covert communications concerning cremation munitions. My best guess is that this pair are conducting their own private investigation into your crash, and they seem to be making some serious allegations. There's an interesting curiosity right at the end too.' Bluey reached towards J.P.'s console again. 'Wanna see?'

'Hang on, hang on,' J.P. was trying to organise his thoughts and brushed Bluey's hand away irritably. 'Did you say Chinese girlfriend?'

Bluey nodded.

'Henri's going to go fucking bananas.' J.P. sat frozen for a moment, barely breathing, a loosely crooked index finger poised an inch in front of his lips. He dropped the hand as he exhaled and spoke Freeway McCann's name at the machine in front of him. As he waited for a pick-up at the other end he settled himself back in his chair.

The burly figure of Freeway McCann popped onto the screen.

'Freeway!' J.P. began, in a level but urgent tone which precluded any greeting. 'Drop what you're doing and find John Lyons-Howard. Keep him on ice at his own place until I get back to you. He looked like he was headed on a bender last night, so he may be sleeping it off. He's to talk to no one. I'm sending you a recording from the Archive which should explain.' McCann assented silently and J.P. disconnected and called McCambridge-LeMans immediately. The cool single-mindedness of these actions left Bluey in the highly unusual position of being impressed with the old man, though he hadn't quite figured out yet what he was doing.

The Chairman appeared on the screen.

'Henri,' J.P. said, sighing before he continued, as if to say that if he'd had wits he'd be at their ends. 'We might have some trouble with Marshall.'

The look that came across the old Frenchman's face as the words were uttered prompted Bluey to drop his eyes.

J.P. was shocked to see Henri give away so much, but kept his own composure. Marshall's importance to Henri was clearly considerable. It would have to be weighed carefully.

'You may know my son Coleman and he are friends,' J.P. said to him.

'Yes, J.P.' The Frenchman had recovered his cool.

'Coleman,' J.P. indicated the young man across the desk, 'spoke to him late last night. Seems he's a little upset.'

Bluey nodded at the Chairman gravely to say it was true.

'Lyons-Howard was drunk and maudlin at the Archive,' J.P. continued. 'He said some things to Marshall about that unfortunate incident with the ambulance. I thought you'd like to explain the situation to him personally.' J.P.'s eyes flicked towards his own son, as if to say, *I'll do the same here.* While he was talking he had pulled up a list of active workstations and noted that Papa Charlie was at work but Marshall hadn't logged on. 'Marshall isn't at his desk yet, I don't think. If you could get to him before he has a chance to discuss it with his colleague . . . they're quite close.'

'Yes,' McCambridge-LeMans said impassively, 'I'll call him now. And thank you, J.P.' He disconnected without further ado.

'"Mystify your enemy by false reports and appearances",' J.P. said to Bluey, clearly pleased with himself. 'Now, let's see what you've got here.' He cued the second recording and let it roll.

Bluey reminded him that it was recorded on Friday night. Two people appeared on screen, Papa Charlie McCormack and a young Oriental woman. J.P. yawned through the first few minutes and said, 'They've got nothin'', about five times before Sister Jasmine said pretty much the same thing to Papa Charlie onscreen. J.P. was about to speak before it ended, but Coleman stabbed his finger twice at the screen to get his attention back there. When J.P. found his bearings in the picture again, McCormack had walked into centre frame in front of the girl. As he'd drifted away J.P. had been left with the impression she was leaving the country, which he was pleased about, and so the first thing he heard properly when he got his attention refocused was Papa Charlie say, 'It's me.'

J.P.'s heart fluttered in his breast and a lump rose in his throat. He heard the girl on screen ask Papa Charlie what he thought was him, but a twitching in his jaw that J.P. considered his 'critical success indicator' was reading off the scale, and he already knew what Papa Charlie would say.

'Mantra,' said the voice in the box, 'I'm Mantra.'

'Ha! Wouldn't that be marvellous,' its companion replied.

J.P. agreed with the girl's image. It would indeed be marvellous. His head fizzed with the excitement of it. He looked at his son as if he were the very personification of the impenetrable enigma. 'Why in God's name didn't you tell me this last night? We could have taken him then!'

Bluey was incredulous. 'You don't actually believe that!' he said. When his father didn't respond he went on. 'He's trying to impress that skirt, J.P. He's silly about her. She's obviously interested in Mantra, so he says he *is* Mantra to keep her in town a few more days. Weren't you listening?' J.P. maintained his pensive silence another second then started working his computer again.

'I've listened to Marshall complain for years about Papa Charlie's inadequacies with systems, J.P. He's from back in the Stone Age, there's no way he could do the work. He wants her to believe it's one person doing this. He has no idea of the volume of work involved. You must know that yourself.'

'I know he spoke the truth,' said J.P. calmly, tapping at the keyboard.

'Jesus, J.P., you can't *know* that. His fucking girlfriend didn't believe him and she was looking into his eyes. She laughed, for chrissakes!'

'She was making smoke.'

'Why in hell did she think she had to? Up until then they'd been freely discussing the destruction of evidence connected to what they feel is a serious crime. Why's she suddenly so careful?'

'Because what went out on the web about the crash was unintelligible to all but a few people. What was said about the crash and the munitions might or might not be picked up on in the event the room was being monitored – probably not. But she knows, *if* the room was bugged, that any references to Mantra would light an indicator somewhere and require – unequivocally – a second look and some order of evaluation. She reacted the way she did to diffuse the suspicion of a possible evaluator, because she also knew the truth of his claim. She was trying to make it seem as if this is the sort of thing that McCormack is always saying.

'She's trained in stuff like this, highly trained. A contact on the force alerted me to the fact that she'd been snooping around the scene of our accident. I got a small amount of background from him on the secret society she works for, some bleeding-heart kung-fu convent for anarcho-feminists.'

Bluey was becoming exasperated. He'd had the girl's story

from McLemon already. He was losing his train of thought. 'Okay, J.P., say you're right and Papa Charlie McCormack is single-handedly responsible for the Mantra phenomenon. If that's the case, then the whole thing's an illusion and the program doesn't do what it appears to do. If he's bamboozled every systems expert from here to Silicon Valley, it's because of trickery and deception, not because of his tech skills.' Bluey sat back with his arms folded. He was taking this personally. He wasn't prepared to accept that he could have missed such an opportunity, and sat on it overnight. He had disbelieved the old fool's claim as immediately and completely as his father was now believing it, and his father's overwhelming confidence made him doubt himself.

J.P. was silent another minute as he continued to work at his keyboard. Then finally he had what he wanted. 'Now look here,' he said to Bluey, pointing at a list on the screen. 'These are all the evenings that McCormack has worked late this year. I'm thinking that if he used WentWest as cover for a small secret message the other night, then he might also have used it in the past for a bigger movement of data.' J.P. hit a key and a second list popped up beside the first. It was titled 'Mantra Events'. Red lines began travelling from the items on the first list to items on the second list, which then lit up.

'There's a seventy per cent correlation with Mantra events and that fucker working late or on weekends. I'm not suggesting he's the sole responsible party. He's probably, as you say, exaggerating his involvement for the benefit of Hanoi Jane. I'm just saying that he's involved some way and that I saw the truth of it when —' J.P. stopped suddenly.

'What?' Bluey wanted to know.

J.P.'s right hand cupped his forehead. He grimaced. 'It's so obvious,' he said.

'What's obvious?'

'McLemon's involved too.'

Bluey shook his head sadly. 'This is getting ridiculous.'

'No,' said J.P. quietly, 'it makes perfect sense. Why else would the Chairman of the Board of WentWest Europe have any interest in a lowly clerk and his stupid idea for a virtual museum? I can't tell you how he found out, but he's trying to get the inside track on the Mantra device through Marshall.' J.P. ran his hands back across his head, still grimacing in disbelief. 'And for a while I actually thought that fucker was getting sentimental in his old age.'

Once again Bluey found himself swayed by his father's conviction, and once he began to entertain the possibility that J.P. was right, he found himself excited by the prospect. If the old man was on the money about McCormack and McLemon, and even if the device turned out to be nothing more than a clever illusion, it would at least be worth something to control the illusion for a while.

'I hate to tell you, Dad, but if you're right you've just sent McLemon into the arms of the Frenchman, at a crisis moment, when one might say anything to the other, and just when it might be advantageous to have a serious talk with him yourself.'

J.P. looked at his son and smiled, pleased he had moved to agree, pleased also that he seemed to be thinking ahead. 'I doubt we could have moved on him without going up against McCambridge-LeMans for real, and no one wants to do that unless they have to. This way we know they're busy, and we can travel for a while where there is no enemy.'

'Right,' said Bluey dryly, guessing the aphoristic ejaculation was one of those gems of wisdom from some 'Master' J.P. had been wittering on about for as long as he could remember. 'So what happens before we embark?'

J.P. treated his son's sarcasm to a cool sideways look before calling up another connection with Freeway McCann. He quickly checked that they had a secure link.

'Forget Lyons-Howard, Freeway, plans've changed.'

'Oh yeah?' Freeway seemed monumentally unconcerned with this turn of events.

'You know the old guy works in the Archive with McLemon?'

'Yeah, Papa Charlie McCormack, been there years.'

J.P. nodded at Freeway, as if prodding him forward. 'His given name is Philip. Philip McCormack.' McCann squinted as if he had a strong feeling about the name but couldn't recall why exactly.

'He lives just outside the Glades on the West Road,' J.P. announced.

'Fuck,' said Freeway, as the realisation came to him.

'It's not real important at the moment,' J.P. reassured him. 'I'm just telling you 'cause he's been spending time recently with Madame Butterfly, our Eastern crash fan, and you don't want any witnesses when you take him.'

'Take him, J.P.?'

'We've good reason to suspect that he may be involved with Mantra. He might even be able to lead us to the device.'

'Jesus!'

'Precisely.'

'Is he at work?'

'Yes, but stop by his house first. I want you to collect his hard drive and motherboard. Bring his personal computer equipment from the office too. We'll want to talk to him in depth, so try not to kill him.'

'Hey,' Freeway made a pleading gesture, 'easy with the sarcasm, J.P. This has been hard on both of us.'

J.P. acknowledged the point with a penitent nod. 'McLemon and the Frenchman are keeping each other busy for the time being, so you shouldn't be disturbed.'

'D'you want me to take him to the usual place?'

'No. Somewhere the Frenchman hasn't been.'

'That room in the car park above the Archive,' Freeway said. 'It's empty since we moved the canvases.'

'Yes,' said J.P., 'hold him there until we can organise a team to look at his machine. Call me when you're done.' He disconnected and turned to Bluey. 'D'you think we're on serious ground yet? The Master advises gathering in plunder on serious ground.'

Bluey smiled at his father. 'You could gather in Jack McLemon so. He doesn't leave the house sometimes for days at a time, no one would miss him. And he might prove a useful bargaining chip should we find ourselves on very serious ground.'

J.P. looked at his boy admiringly. 'You're making an old man very proud.'

(ii)

Freeway McCann had procured for the day's activities an almost silent black van with heavily smoked windows. It sat nice and low on the road and it had the big chunky tyres he liked, plus it had nifty automatic sliding doors in both sides. It was intimidating, as far as Freeway was concerned, because of a government/military police vibe it gave off. Either way, between a bad case of stomach acid and a sadistic headache, both brought on by anxiety about Mick and Frank Cooper, the vehicle was the only thing today to give him any pleasure. He'd already had it parked outside Papa Charlie McCormack's house for twenty minutes, while he disabled the alarm system, broke in and removed Charlie's hard drive and board. In his mind's eye he could still see how well the van looked through Papa Charlie's living-room window.

He pulled up outside the entrance to the underground car park above the WentWest Archive. He activated the car park gate with his ID badge and drove down the ramp into the darkness, the van's lights throwing shadows about before the overheads kicked in. He turned at the foot of the ramp and all but circled the floor, before pulling left out of the travel lane through a line of concrete pillars. He drew the vehicle to a halt between two doors in the wall about five metres beyond.

He got out of the van, opened the driver's side sliding door and extracted a refrigerated picnic basket containing provisions and water. With his other hand, and more gingerly, he took out a small chemical toilet. He brought these as far as the door in the wall to the rear of the jeep and pulled an old-style latchkey out of his pocket. The room was one of those areas that had remained unchanged since the building was erected. Freeway believed he held the only remaining key. He pushed the door and flipped the light switch to find that this wasn't, in fact, the case. Rather than being empty, for use in an emergency stash situation, it was almost two-thirds full of green storage boxes. He lifted his two parcels inside and shut the door behind him. He revised his earlier estimate to three-quarters full. To augment his headache a vessel began throbbing in his left temple. He rubbed his affliction gently and took a slow, deep breath.

A brief inspection revealed the boxes to have accumulated

over the weekend. They were full of papers from the Archive which appeared to be destined for foreign climes. He presumed McCormack and McLemon were using the room as a halfway house. The collection date stamped on the boxes was two days away, so his plans today weren't going to be disturbed.

The room had had a storage function once upon a time, but he imagined no one had much liked coming down to the car park, so a new home had been found for whatever was to be kept here in the first place and the room had eventually been forgotten about. It made sense that McCormack might have a key. He'd probably been here since the building went up. He might have been using the room a lot longer than Freeway had. McCann had found his key about three or four years before, when it fell out of an old pair of overalls wrapped around a piece of faulty plumbing in the bowels of Head Office. It had taken better than a year to find out what the key was for, and even then he'd only used the room on four occasions. He wondered if McCormack had ever seen any of the stuff he'd brought and left here. The throbbing at his temple grew worse.

He tried to make himself think positively.

He positioned a heavy iron garden chair in the middle of the empty section of floor space and walked around it once, looking at the small room carefully. He stopped, facing the door. There was plenty of room for his guest. One of his legs could be secured to the chair, which in turn could be secured to the radiator. He reminded himself he'd have to check McCormack for the other key to the room before double-locking the latch, to be sure.

He decided he'd give himself a couple of minutes. There was no real hurry at this stage. This would be nothing. Most men had no fight in them; old men were even less exceptional. He would get McCormack in here under some pretence, slap him hard to make a believer out of him and ankle-cuff him to the chair while whispering sweet nothings about how everything'd be okay as long as he played ball. Ten minutes' work. Ten minutes' easy, well-paid work.

Freeway sat in the chair and lit a cigarette. He inhaled deeply and exhaled in a slow, controlled manner, like a singer exercising with plumes of blue tobacco smoke. It wasn't normal for him to have to steel himself against a small matter like this, but the abduction of the Coopers by McCambridge-LeMans and their continued absence had him spooked more than he ever would have credited. They were his men, after all. If they'd been killed outright on account of their fuck-up he was sure he'd have been affected less. What did it say about the esteem he was held in, that his enquiries were brushed aside, let alone that his say in the fate of *his* employees was left unconsidered? He had always cherished the notion that he commanded at least professional respect from his employers. If not even that, what then about *his* expendability? He didn't worry that J.P. himself would do anything to bring him to harm, but he was aware that, depending upon the circumstances, J.P. might do nothing to help him either.

McCann stood up and went out to the van and got two pairs of handcuffs, the kind with long chains between the ratcheted hoops. He cuffed the top of the chair to the radiator and attached one end of the second pair to a feature in the right front leg, leaving the other end open on the ground. He then placed the picnic basket and toilet on either side of the chair, within arm's reach of his prospective sitter.

He stepped out of the room and pulled the door shut behind him. He stood for a few moments, staring out into the car park. He finished his cigarette with what could only be described as grim determination. Flicking the butt towards a gutter, he walked around the front of the van to the elevator doors which would take him back up to the ground floor or down to the Archive. He buzzed the Archive from a panel to the right of the door and waited.

'Yes?' The tone of voice at the other end didn't strike Freeway as inviting, exactly.

'You McLemon?' said Freeway as dully insolent as he could manage convincingly.

'He's not here. Can't say when he'll be back.'

'I've got some boxes for him.'

'Good for you. Do you know what to do with them?'

'Deliver them.'

Down in the Archive Papa Charlie sighed. It came through the speaker at Freeway's end like an unhealthy, malignant crackle. 'You didn't get more detailed instructions?'

''Fraid not.'

'Alright, there's a door about three, four metres to your left. Leave them outside it and I'll get them later. 'Bye.'

The intercom in the wall clicked and went dead. This wasn't working out as Freeway had hoped at all. The way this scene had played out in his mind, Papa Charlie had been good-natured and helpful. This guy's mother must have mated with a rattler. He pressed the intercom button again.

'Yes!' So venomous was this acknowledgement that Freeway nearly took half a step backward.

'Listen,' said Freeway, trying to sound conciliatory, 'eh, Charlie, is it?'

'*Mister* McCormack to you, Curly.'

'Yeah, can you come up and unlock the door? I can't leave these boxes out here.'

'If you're that worried, put them in the lift and leave them down here in the corridor.'

321

'Don't suppose you'd be willing to come up and give me a hand? My trolley's bust. Two of us would make it one trip.'

A short, scornful laugh sieved through the speaker grating. 'I'm not sure you're in the right career, son. You don't appear to have the mindset for deliveries. You care too much.' Papa Charlie laughed again. 'My lifting days are twenty years behind me. Although, I have to say, I'm right behind that nifty initiative of yours to get the client to do the work for you – that's right out of the top drawer.'

Freeway hit the button for the elevator and nodded grimly at the speaker panel. 'A million laughs, granddad. I'll be down to you. Somebody's got to sign for this.'

(iii)

Lucy was sure it was the same girl. Slide wasn't, initially, but he was coming around to the same way of thinking. They were only getting intermittent glances at her, now that they were nearer the centre of town and the crowds were thickening. She appeared to be about the right height, and dressed in the same black clothing they'd seen her in at the Blind Pig. Lucy thought the walk was exactly the same too. Slide figured whoever it turned out to be she didn't walk like any nun he'd ever seen. She seemed to be heading for the Archive. It had to be her.

If only Slide had called to her when he'd had the chance, he'd be rid of McLemon's book and on his way to the airport, with an extra ten or fifteen – dear God, maybe even twenty – minutes to spend in the first-class lounge. He could afford to travel first class once a year and he always reserved this luxury for his long holiday. If he had to travel for work, he travelled with the band. He really liked the first-class lounge, but his old habit of spending three or four hours in there before his flight had been forbidden by Lucy in recent years. Now he was allocated one hour, so every extra minute he could get in there was to be savoured.

'Stop walking on people's heels,' Lucy said. 'We'll be there in plenty of time.'

Slide had no intention of slowing down. 'Have you got the tickets?' he asked, to throw her off.

'You know I have the tickets. You made a point of watching me put them in my bag. Do you have the passports?'

Slide slapped at the inside pocket of his jacket as he dragged Lucy through a quickly diminishing gap between two groups of converging pedestrians. The pocket was reassuringly weighty. 'Still there,' he said. Up ahead he caught a glimpse of Sister Jasmine turning the corner. That would bring her to within a hundred metres of the door of the Archive. It was looking less and less likely that he'd catch her, unless she was a minute waiting to get buzzed through, or the lift had to come from the top floor. He grabbed Lucy's wrist and took advantage of a gap in the traffic to get onto the road and past a large mass of lumbering humanity which clearly was not on its way to a private yacht in the Mediterranean via the first-class lounge at the airport.

'Jesus, Slide! You're like a fucking madman! Will you relax? It'd be reasonable to expect that at your age your enthusiasm for booze and bars would have waned.'

They were nearly at the corner, and in no time flat.

'Sorry, chicken,' he said, 'it hasn't.'

They'd been so fast that when he got around the corner he

fully expected to see Jasmine up ahead waiting for Charlie or
Marshall to release the door. By the time he got a line of sight,
however, she was already through. One of the boys must have
given her the door code. The next decent view he got was
from about twenty metres out. Slide could see that the door
hadn't fully closed yet. He remembered it was one of those
old glass doors that took ages to swing shut, especially at the
end of its arc. Charlie and Marshall would tell you to leave it
if you went to pull it closed behind you. Slide thought if he
could get to it before it closed he might save something; and
every moment counted. It might bring them a little luck with
a cab, which might convert into entire minutes, depending on
how smoothly things went at the check-in. He lunged forward
to deter a mousy suit from occupying a position of advantage.
The mouse demurred and Slide went through. A reluctant clat-
tering of heels followed each of his purposeful surges.

'Slide! Cool it!'

'Okay, chicken. Nearly there.'

(iv)

Jasmine was aware of activity to her left, at the street entrance,
just as the elevator doors came together in front of her. Her
right hand shot forward and hit the minus two button. The
elevator dropped immediately. Whoever it was, it was unlikely
that they were going down. Besides, she wasn't in the mood
to share such a small space.

She had received a communication from Sister Suki de
Chardin that morning, summoning her back to Vervain Prime.

There was a seat available on a flight to Singapore that night. With the passing of Mantra's first anniversary and the apparent failure of Cypol's best to garner one iota of useful information on the perpetrators or their device, Suki felt that Jasmine should return to undertake the conclusion of her work from a removed perspective, yet while the experience was still fresh.

Jasmine, when she thought about the news she had to bring home, fantasised briefly of a glorious return. Then she remembered Charlie talking about how pride goeth before a fall, and she was properly ashamed. It would be sad to leave.

Still, there it was. Her maiden assignment and look what had happened. Her superiors would take the news calmly, of course. Jasmine would deliver it calmly, with measured scepticism. But the fact would remain. The Vervain Society had been offered exclusive use of a tool which, on the face of it, had an awesome potential. She had earlier persuaded Papa Charlie not to use his device again until she received a response to his offer. He realised that she would have to travel home to receive instructions, but she had indicated that her leaving might be as much as a few days hence. He would be upset at the news of her sudden departure. She would tell him that the sooner she left the sooner they might meet again.

The elevator came to rest and the doors opened. Jasmine adjusted the bag on her shoulder, walked out of the elevator and turned left for the office. As she pushed the office door open she saw that one of the desks had been pushed towards the right-hand wall and that there were some books strewn on the floor. The door swung behind her and her attention was immediately drawn to Papa Charlie in the far left corner of the room. He was tousled, out of breath and apparently terrified, shielding himself with an office chair. Standing in front and to the right of her, near the wall screen, was a big, suited man, wrapping a handkerchief around a laceration on his left hand. He was red in the face and appeared extremely angry. Assuming the big man was the aggressor in whatever had transpired here, Jasmine moved very slowly to her left so as to free up the door should he wish to make good his escape.

He didn't.

She had made about two metres when he noticed she was moving. He stepped back to come between her and Charlie. They stood still for a couple of moments, listening to Charlie suck in lungfuls of air. Jasmine gauged the man to be within her striking range, but he was side-on to her, presenting few targets, and he was very big. It might prove difficult to incapacitate him quickly.

'He's trying to abduct me,' Charlie said to her, still gasping.

'Shut up!' the big man warned.

'He knows about Mantra,' Charlie added.

The big man rolled his eyes sadly and reached inside his jacket, smoothly drawing an automatic pistol which he levelled at Jasmine. Just as Jasmine was rueing her decision not to attack when she'd had the opportunity, another one presented itself.

Slide Benson and Lucy barged through the door on Jasmine's right, Benson producing a painful cacophony of mock anguish on his way over the threshold, pleading for someone to relieve him of a certain book. As the big man swung around to cover the new arrivals, Jasmine sprang forward sideways. She drove the blade of her right foot into the fleshy part between the big man's hipbone and ribs, at the same time grabbing the sleeve of his gun arm and pushing it upward. Two shots were discharged into the ceiling. She had hurt him with the kick and wanted to capitalise on it quickly. She attempted to knock him off balance by pushing her foot into the back of his knee joint, but he was immensely strong and caught himself less than halfway down. She was beginning to worry about her grip on his gun arm, when out of the corner of her eye she saw Lucy perform a short skip-step towards him. Lucy swung her slightly bent right leg from the hip. Her timing was immaculate. Her small shod foot connected with the assailant's undercarriage to such devastating effect that all three men in the room crumpled in the middle. The big man meekly relinquished his hold on the weapon and Jasmine quickly and expertly ensured the chamber was empty and the safety was on, then ejected the clip. In mid groan, Papa Charlie pushed his chair forward so that it rolled up behind the big man's knees. Jasmine pushed him back into the chair and dug three fingers of her right hand into a pressure point between his neck and shoulder, rendering him unconscious.

There was a moment's silence as everyone caught breath and gathered their thoughts. Slide Benson was looking sidelong at his girlfriend, as if Lucy were a she-wolf who had just dropped a rubber ewe's head to the ground with a flourish.

'Jesus!' Papa Charlie gasped, echoing the gist of Slide's ruminations, 'that was some blow to the stones.'

Lucy shrugged. 'He had a gun! No one else was doing anything to help!'

Jasmine turned to Lucy and nodded her approval and thanks.

'Who the fuck is he? What did he want?' Slide demanded.

Lucy looked over at Jasmine who shook her head. 'Maybe we'd better leave well enough alone, Slide,' she said.

Slide looked from Papa Charlie to Jasmine and back. 'You want us to split?'

'Probably be best,' Charlie said. 'Thanks for showing up, though.'

'Any time,' said Slide, holding out a book to Papa Charlie. 'Will you see Marshall gets this? It's for his old man.'

'Sure.' Charlie took the book. 'Where are you headed?'

'The Mediterranean,' Slide said. He looked meaningfully at Charlie. 'We can catch a later flight if you need a dig-out here.'

'No.' Charlie shook his head. 'I'll, eh, probably call the police. You don't want to spend the first day of your holiday doing this shit.' He shooed them towards the door. 'Go on, beat it.'

Slide didn't require further encouragement. He still had his original hour.

(v)

Marshall sat in the back of the limo Henri had sent for him, brushing Danish crumbs off his trousers onto the floor of the car. He drained his coffee mug and wiped the back of his hand across his mouth. He figured to be about ten minutes or less away from the Frenchman's hotel. He wanted to play the recording again before he got there. He said the word and it started.

My name is Kiely Elizabeth Flanagan. Up until three years ago I was a registered medical doctor . . .

The front desk in his building had given him a small parcel with a disk in it when he got home the night before. He now understood what Lyons-Howard had meant by that 'new decision-maker on the block' crack. There were other files with the recording, copies of all of the records from Dr Kiely Flanagan's workstation and some encrypted material. Dr Flanagan said in her statement that the encrypted files represented all of the information on the experiment kept by J.P. Gillespie's associate, a man she only knew as 'Freeway' McCann. Marshall didn't want to touch any of these files more than he already had. His initial intrusions had revealed the encryption to be military-ware, and that, as Papa Charlie would be sure to tell him, was bad juju.

Marshall noted that Dr Flanagan didn't implicate Henri in any of her accusations. She did, however, cite a French doctor, Julie Bertillion, as the head of the project, which might be significant. Lyons-Howard had implicated the Chairman in no uncertain terms, placing him at the aftermath of two apparent murders. Dr Flanagan seemed only to be aware of J.P. as the party responsible for bankrolling what she clearly wanted you to think was an unspeakable outrage. He looked at her face and wondered if she was convincing him.

The limo turned into the hotel car park. Marshall retrieved his disk from the car's console and pushed it back into his cell. A man opened the car door for him. He got out and walked into the hotel foyer. He enquired at Reception and was told that Henri was expecting him. The man behind the desk found another flunkey to escort Marshall to the Presidential Suite.

Henri was at the top of the main room, in front of a floor-to-ceiling plate-glass window looking out over the city. He turned as he heard Marshall enter.

'Good morning, Marshall.'

'Morning, Henri.'

'You neglected the "good". Is that significant?'

Marshall eyed the Frenchman searchingly. Had he heard something? Did Lyons-Howard get even more out of his box and call Henri to give him a piece of his warped mind? And if so what had happened to him?

'I don't know, Henri,' Marshall kept his tone cool yet friendly, 'what've you heard?'

'Have you seen John Lyons-Howard today?' Henri asked him.

Marshall shook his head. 'Not since yesterday evening.' He decided he would proceed on the assumption that Henri was curious about Lyons-Howard's whereabouts. 'Have you tried calling him?'

Henri ignored the question. 'I understand he's briefed you regarding a project J.P. is heading up.'

Marshall met Henri's eyes. There was no threat in them, no anger. The Frenchman appeared honestly curious. He must have spoken to Lyons-Howard after all.

'He said you were involved too,' Marshall said.

'The project was conceived by my close friend and personal physician, Dr Julie Bertillion. I suggested she bring it here and I arranged for J.P. to facilitate her. I persuaded the WentWest board to throw some capital at it, but I have no hands-on involvement. I did take it upon myself to oversee the damage limitations following last week's crash, but that was to make Gillespie appear foolish and ineffectual more than anything else.'

'Seven people are dead,' Marshall said evenly.

'Five,' Henri said. 'John Lyons-Howard saw what he *thought* were the bodies of the operatives responsible for security at the research facility. I allowed him to believe they had been executed for failing in their duties. A little baroque, I'll grant you, but I wanted to scare him into silence. I made him accept the job with you hoping he would presume himself to be under constant surveillance. It was, and is, very important to keep the project secret.' McCambridge-LeMans unhooked his cell from his belt. 'Both of you, in here now,' he said into it, before turning back to Marshall. 'I'm just protecting an investment. As I see it, Dr Kiely Flanagan is responsible for her own and four other deaths. She attempted to remove those people from that facility without any authority, in order to sell the details of their treatment for profit. If she had been truly concerned about any perceived wrongdoing she would have gone directly to the police.'

There was a businesslike rap at the door and two large, suited men walked in and approached Henri deferentially.

'This is Michael and Frank Cooper, Marshall. They are not related, but they are quite alive. Feel free to ask them any questions you wish.'

Marshall looked at the two men standing there impassively. It was an easy thing for Henri to make the offer. They might say anything Henri had instructed them to say. Marshall shook his head and Henri dismissed the men.

'Did Lyons-Howard give you anything purporting to relate to the experiment?' Henri asked when they had gone.

'A disk with a statement from Dr Flanagan and some encrypted files. I assume that's where Lyons-Howard and herself figured they'd find the big names.'

Henri nodded. 'Probably.'

'Yours?' Marshall asked.

'No. As I've said, I have no hands-on involvement. Gillespie would undoubtedly have featured large, as might Dr Bertillion. Do you have it with you?'

'No,' Marshall lied, 'it's at home.' He moved to the window to take the view. Stretched out beneath him the city looked like a huge, grimy circuit board.

Yesterday he had everything he wanted, or at least the promise of everything. It saddened him that now it seemed to be slipping away from him, or him from it. All that had been on offer yesterday was there still. It was only necessary for him to disregard certain matters. Matters, it occurred to him, that would never impinge upon his working or other life. How difficult could that be?

Marshall heard McCambridge-LeMans move towards him. He turned from the window to face him. 'Dr Flanagan said that the subjects of the experiments believe themselves to be participating in a study investigating how nutrition and environment affect productivity.'

Henri had come to a halt at the steps. 'That's true,' he nodded.

'But you're giving them drugs to make them perform better and they don't know it.'

'Yes,' Henri said, squinting and moving his head from side to side as if it were a very difficult concept. 'Marshall, these aren't normal people. I know it's not fashionable to admit it, but some of them have more in common with chimpanzees than rational beings. Everyone we worked with was a long-term inmate. Long-term means perpetrators of rape, murder and serious assault. Some people consider that convicted criminals abdicate their right to liberty only. Others might consider it fair, in the case of serious offenders, that they lose other of their rights also. Certainly the idea of rehabilitation for these people was never before honestly considered. They were to be locked up and forgotten about. No one said it in quite that way, but that was it.

'These creatures were useless, a drain on resources, but we have found a role for them. With the drug they are manageable and productive, and happy. Does the fact that there is a chemical agent involved in their rehabilitation render it worthless? Or render the fact – *the fact* – of the prisoners' happiness void?'

Marshall began to feel this was the sort of stuff he could work with here. It would be more of a problem convincing Papa Charlie, however, were he to know about any of it. Not telling him had its advantages. He only wondered if it were a gift he could afford.

(vi)

Papa Charlie and Sister Jasmine had duct-taped the big man to the office chair and wheeled him into the elevator. Charlie didn't think the tape would hold him permanently, but hoped it would keep him in the chair should he come to, long enough for them to lock him into the storeroom in the car park. Sister Jasmine removed the man's cell from his breast pocket and scrutinised it briefly.

'His name is Vivian McCann,' she said.

Papa Charlie thought for a moment. 'There was a guy known as "Freeway" McCann that Gillespie brought with him when he took over WentWest operations here. He used to be around and about quite a bit, but I haven't heard anything of him in years.'

Jasmine punched at the portable console some more. 'His occupation is listed as "consultant".'

'That's a help.' Papa Charlie walked around in front of the big man and pulled his head up off his chest by the hair. He took a good long look at the face. 'I'm sure it's the same guy,' he said.

'You think?'

Papa Charlie mulled it over for a second. 'This "Freeway" had a reputation as something of a thug. This one certainly fits the bill. I didn't pay much attention, but I seem to remember the talk was that he did J.P.'s dirty work.'

'Perhaps he still does.'

'Yeah, I guess J.P. bugs the office then sends him.' Papa Charlie looked up from McCann's face and back at Jasmine: 'Why bug the office in the first place though?'

Jasmine shook her head. 'You realise you can't stay here now. You may have to leave the country.'

'It might not be possible to leave. Gillespie has considerable influence.'

'We'll see,' she said.

McCann started to exhibit signs of life as they wheeled him out of the elevator, around the van and over to the door of the storeroom. Papa Charlie quickly unlocked the door, pushed it open and rolled McCann into the room as far as he could without actually crossing the threshold himself. He pulled the door to and locked it. When he turned around again Jasmine was looking through the open driver's window of McCann's vehicle.

'Do you want to go back in and get his keys?' she asked, not altogether seriously to Charlie's mind. 'We could borrow this for our getaway.'

Papa Charlie didn't need to think twice about it. 'No,' he said.

Jasmine smiled and tossed McCann's cell onto the driver's seat. She tried the side door of the vehicle and found it unlocked. She reached in and pulled out a motherboard.

'That's mine,' said Charlie, taking it from her.

'He thought he would find the Mantra program on it.'

'He'd've been wrong,' Charlie said, turning the board over in his hand and smiling grimly. He threw it into the vehicle.

'What now?'

'We should get out of here in case someone comes looking for him.'

Charlie moved to the elevator and hit the button to open the door. They got in and went up to ground level.

'You can access the Mantra device?' Jasmine asked him as they hit the street.

'Yeah, I just need to connect to the web.'

'We need to get somewhere we can set up a secure line of communication, so I can make some arrangements to get us out of here,' she said. 'For the time being I think we can count on the fact that Mr Gillespie will not wish to share his discovery with anyone else, unless he is a fool.'

'He is,' said Charlie. 'We should get into the city, use one of the libraries. They'll be quiet at this hour.' He began scanning the street for a cab. It wasn't long before one picked them up. 'I should talk to Marshall too,' he said when they were underway.

'You shouldn't make any unnecessary calls,' she advised, flipping to a news channel on the cab's TV and turning up the volume to cover their conversation.

Charlie looked at her worriedly. 'He was summoned to McCambridge-LeMans' hotel this morning. I want to make sure he's okay, on the off chance that Gillespie thinks me and him are in this together.'

They moved along in silence, both of them staring blankly at the TV as the headlines were declaimed, until a shot of John Lyons-Howard appeared behind the anchorman, causing Papa Charlie to sit bolt upright in his seat.

'The body of John Lyons-Howard – up until recently the producer of Channel Ten's hit show *Expo-Zayet* – was taken out of Dublin Bay early this morning, having been spotted by the skipper of a Greek cargo vessel. Initial reports suggest the police are keeping an open mind as to the cause of death.'

Charlie fumbled his cell out of his jacket pocket and opened it on his knees. He put in his earpiece and attached his throat mike for a quiet exchange.

'What are you doing?' Jasmine asked.

'I'm calling Marshall now,' he said. He wasn't about to get into a discussion about it.

(vii)

The ring tone was ultra-urgent. It was Papa Charlie. Marshall stood up and asked Henri to excuse him so he could take the call. Henri said he had some business at the front desk. Marshall watched him leave the room. He opened his cell on the coffee table and picked up. Papa Charlie's head was filling the screen. It was clear he wasn't at the Archive.

'Charlie, where are you?'

'Never mind about that, are you okay?'

The tone of the old man's voice lacked that hostile apathy Marshall was used to. 'I'm fine, Charlie,' he said earnestly. 'What the hell's going on?' It was then that Marshall noticed the encryption icon winking in the bottom right of the screen. Something about it made him think of the icon beside the files Lyons-Howard had given him. He knew he didn't like it. 'Jesus, Charlie, what the fuck have you got me hooked up to?'

'Don't worry, that's working for me. It's necessary. What did McCambridge-LeMans want with you?'

Marshall didn't know whether to get into it. He hadn't decided what to tell the old man about Lyons-Howard's revelations. Papa Charlie would want to do the decent, moral thing, he knew that. 'It's a long story, to do with Lyons-Howard,' he said finally. 'Henri will be back here in a minute. Tell me what's going on.'

'So you know Lyons-Howard is dead,' Charlie said.

'What?'

'They fished his body out of the Bay this morning. I got panicked. I wanted to make sure you were okay.'

'Dead?'

'Yeah, dead,' Charlie said. 'The news said the cops might be treating it as suspicious.'

Marshall felt butterflies in his gut. Could McCambridge-LeMans be that cold-blooded? He couldn't believe it. 'I saw John last night, Charlie. He was really fucked up. Sad about something too. It could have been suicide.'

'If you say so.'

'Come clean with me here, Charlie. Why did you think that might have had something to do with me? Why are you calling me using what seems to be military encryption, and where did you get that bruise on your head?'

Papa Charlie sighed deeply. 'I had a visit from a gentleman name of Freeway McCann,' he said.

'The bogeyman?'

'No,' Papa Charlie widened his eyes and said it again slower, 'Freeway McCann.'

'I heard you the first time, I just wasn't aware he actually existed. I thought he was a scare story.'

'He's real enough. And pretty fucking scary. I assume he was there at J.P.'s behest.'

'What did he want?'

'J.P. seems to have the idea that I'm involved with this Mantra business.'

Marshall's eyes flicked to the encryption icon again, then

back to Charlie's face. Instantly he knew the truth of it. 'Jesus, Charlie,' he said breathlessly.

Papa Charlie pressed his lips together in a thin effort at an apologetic smile.

'How did you get mixed up with that?' Marshall asked him.

'I didn't get mixed up with it,' Charlie paused, 'I am it.'

Marshall was puzzled. 'But you're no good with systems.'

'I'm a little better than I used to be, you've admitted that yourself. As to the rest,' he shrugged, 'it is, as you say, a long story.'

Marshall could hardly believe it. He groped around for something to say. 'How did J.P. find out?'

'We were down in the Archive on Friday night after we left the Pig. I mentioned it to Sister Jasmine. J.P. must have us under surveillance. It's no wonder he doesn't like us.'

Marshall's face blanched. He remembered Bluey's reaction to his jibe about Gretta Donald on Friday night, just before he took the stage. It had to be more than a coincidence. Marshall felt like a fool. A Gillespie is a Gillespie is a Gillespie. How many times had he heard that?

'Did you find the bug?'

'No, why?'

Marshall didn't want to tell him. He was embarrassed, betrayed. He didn't want to hear *I told you so* from Charlie. Finally he spat it out. 'I think it was Bluey. No, I'm sure it was. He told J.P.'

Papa Charlie was silent a moment. 'I'm sorry, son.'

Marshall was grateful for the fact that Charlie didn't want to gloat, but this was quickly replaced with a silent rage. His head buzzed with it.

'You weren't to know,' Charlie said to try and snap him out of it.

'It was said to me often enough.'

'Fuck them. There's nothing to be done about it now. I'm going to have to split, for a while at least. I just wanted to make sure you were alright. I take it the Frenchman doesn't know anything about this.'

'No, I don't think so. Listen, Charlie . . .' And then it all came out. Marshall told him as quickly as he could about his conversation with John Lyons–Howard, about the disk that Lyons–Howard sent to his apartment and about his meeting this morning with McCambridge–LeMans.

'Those sons of bitches,' Charlie said.

'I'm sending you the contents of the disk now,' said Marshall, tapping at the console in front of him. 'Can your device crack these?'

'So far I haven't encountered anything it can't crack.'

'Good. Then you'll have no problem generating media interest with it. They'll be all over J.P. within the hour. This'll keep him busy for months. It'll give you some breathing space to consider your position.'

'There's nothing to consider. Either way I've got to go. If J.P. knows he can't get to me himself, he's sure to expose me or put out a contract. Anyway, if you allow this to be released it'll put you in hot water with the Frenchman *and* with J.P.'

Marshall had made up his mind. He had a few ideas about spite himself. 'I think I'll be okay with Henri. And I feel I owe the Gillespies one. Maybe it's time I got out of Coolsville for a bit.' There was no sense from Marshall's delivery or expression that he was a young man embarking on a new adventure. There was only bitterness and the desire for revenge.

'Marshall, you don't have to do this.'

'Where are you organising your travel arrangements? I'll meet you there.'

Papa Charlie didn't feel he could dissuade him, and a good part of him didn't want to try. 'The Robinson Library,' he said. 'We'll be there in fifteen minutes.'

'I better get Jack. Wait for me.'

Marshall called his father's place but got no answer. He was in two minds whether or not to leave a message. He didn't know what to say. If J.P. was as ruthless as it appeared, there was a chance he might do anything. If someone happened to visit his father and saw the message he'd left, and heard him mention the library, then Papa Charlie would be exposed. He would have to travel out to Jack's house. There was no other way.

Marshall closed his unit and pulled a cigarette from a box on the table. He flopped into the sofa and brought his lighter towards the tip of the smoke.

'So, you're going away,' said Henri's voice behind him.

Marshall froze with the burning lighter in front of his face. After a moment he lit the smoke, inhaled and exhaled. 'How long have you been there?' he asked the Frenchman.

Henri took the chair opposite Marshall. 'Long enough.'

'Look, Henri, it's not personal –'

'There is no need to explain,' the Frenchman smiled. 'Everything J.P. touches eventually turns to shit. This may work to my advantage in the long run.' He sat silently for a moment, then smiled again. 'And rest assured, you *are* okay with me.' He patted at his pockets until he located a box of cheroots, and borrowed Marshall's lighter. 'The device you referred to – I assume it is the Mantra device.'

Marshall nodded.

'Were you involved in that?'

Marshall shook his head. 'No, that took me completely by surprise.'

'Good. I cannot protect your friend.'

'He wouldn't expect it.'

'J.P. will be uncontrollable for some time. Short of equipping you with an armed escort, I'm not sure I can protect you either. Perhaps it is better that you are going away.'

Marshall nodded. 'Something different, at least.'

Henri laughed softly. 'We should not lose contact, you, I, or Jacques. That would be a great sadness to me.' Henri extended a card to Marshall, which he took. 'This is a private and secure address. Either of you can contact me there any time. Leave a message if I'm not available. Any help, money, anything I can give you I will. In time, J.P. will be no threat to you, I guarantee that. But you must promise that we don't lose contact.'

Marshall nodded again. He didn't want to speak, didn't know if he could. The back of his throat was hot and thick with mucus.

'Say it,' Henri encouraged.

'I promise.' The words were barely recognisable.

'Take the car and driver. My plane is in Hangar 18, South Coast. You'll need it to get to Europe. I will tell Sylvie to take your instructions. Her number is also on the card if you need to contact her ahead of time.'

'Thanks, Henri.'

'You had better get moving.'

Marshall left without looking back. As soon as he had gone through the door, Henri picked up his mobile and called Mick and Frank Cooper back into the room. 'My young friend is on his way to the Robinson Library. Do you know it?'

'Yes, sir,' Frank answered.

'He is travelling in my car. Go after him, discreetly,' said Henri. 'See he gets there safely. Make sure no one follows him, and above all make sure no one,' Henri eyeballed both of them, 'and I mean no one, interferes with him. Clear?'

'Are we thinking of anyone specifically?' Mick asked.

'Any of Gillespie's people. Don't take any chances. Call me again when he reaches the library. Hurry.'

(viii)

J.P. and Bluey Gillespie were enjoying their coffees in their booth at the Westpark when the maître d' approached them wringing his hands. To be truthful J.P. was enjoying his coffee more than his son, for he had the floor, and had done for the past twenty minutes. Bluey was supremely bored. J.P. was expounding upon some financial mumbo-jumbo. The doings at the research facility had been far more interesting, but the story had wound up during the main course. Bluey wanted to hear more about the seamy underbelly of the business world. He could imagine himself as a character in this landscape, skirting the bounds of criminality, rubbing shoulders with vice, to gain the all-important edge. If enduring a lecture from J.P. was the price of entry, it was perhaps a small price to pay, and the coffee *was* good.

Just as the head waiter arrived at their table Bluey was aware of a commotion at the entrance to the dining area. A number of men, poorly attired to his mind for the Westpark, were being ushered, pushed actually, back into the bar area by the concerted efforts of three of the restaurant staff. The head waiter made two short but unmistakably obsequious bows before addressing his father.

'I am sorry to disturb you, Mr Gillespie. However, quite a number of reporters have gathered in the bar asking if you are here. They're not taking no for an answer.'

J.P.'s breath grew suddenly shallow. He put his coffee cup in its saucer. He looked at the waiter as if he couldn't in the world imagine what was going on, which for the moment was actually true.

'Did they say what they wanted?'

The waiter smiled and bowed again. 'They wouldn't discuss it, although Marie says she heard two of them talking about a motor accident as they came in.'

J.P. nodded sagely. 'Carl, I need a quiet place to make some calls.'

'Of course, sir.' Carl took two steps back and bowed while extending his left arm in the direction he wished them to walk.

'Let's go,' J.P. said to Bluey. As they climbed out of the booth and headed towards the back of the restaurant they became visible to the reporters at the entrance, who began clamouring for J.P.'s attention. The only clear sound J.P. heard as he moved away from them was the voice of Ethan Collins, that prick from the *Chronicle*, reedy but strong, carrying above the rest of the crowd.

'J.P.! Do you have any comment on the allegation that you're conducting secret drug experiments on the inmates at WentWest Correctional?' When it was clear he wasn't getting a response, Collins became even louder. 'What about the suggestion that the death of John Lyons-Howard is in some way connected? Any comment? J.P.?'

J.P. levelled a lethal gaze at Bluey, almost as if this were all his fault. 'McLemon is a fucking dead man,' he said. 'And if Lyons-Howard weren't already dead, he'd . . . he'd –' J.P. shook his head disgustedly. 'I can only hope it wasn't quick.'

Bluey looked at the floor and covered his mouth with his hand to hide a spreading grin. He could hardly contain his excitement. 'Does "the Master" recognise such a thing as "desperate ground", J.P.?'

'Yes,' J.P. said grimly.

'What do we do there?'

'We fight.'

As they slipped behind a curtain at the back of the room, into a short corridor with six doors leading off it, J.P. heard Marie, the restaurant manager, address the assembled reporters.

'Ladies and gentlemen, please! Mr Gillespie has left the building.'

(ix)

Freeway McCann stood in the men's toilet on the ground floor. He had done quite a good job wiping the vomit from his jacket, trousers and shirt. You could see dark patches only if you were up close. They'd be dry soon enough. The effort of breaking his duct-tape bonds following that kick in the 'nads, and whatever that Chinese bitch had done to him afterward to put him out, had brought the nausea on. He'd been too weak to get himself into optimum puking position. The last time he'd been into one of the cubicles he was still pissing blood, but he was beginning to feel better. The blood would pass in time. It wasn't the worst going-over he'd ever had, but it had to rank among the most unexpected – chicks, for Christ's sake.

He came out of the men's and took the elevator back down

to the car park. He climbed into his vehicle, started the engine and drove back up the ramp out onto the street. Gradually he recognised the fact that he was sitting on something, and extracted his cell from under his left buttock. He glanced at it to see that J.P. had called about five minutes back. Still unsure in his abilities, he pulled over to the side of the road to return the call.

When J.P. picked up, Freeway thought for a minute that the colour balance had gone on his monitor. He realised very soon that the beetroot hue was an expression of J.P.'s mood.

'Where the fuck have you been?' J.P. roared at McCann. 'I've been trapped in the Westpark for the past twenty minutes by a gang of marauding reporters. McLemon fucked us over and broadcast everything Lyons–Howard gave him. I had to send Coleman to McCambridge-LeMans' hotel to see if Marshall's still there. I don't know what the fuck he thinks he's going to do when he finds him. I want that fucker dead. Did you get McCormack?'

'No, J.P.'

'No! Why the fuck not?'

'He had company. I was taken unawares.'

'Did you get his hardware?'

Freeway looked into the back of the vehicle. 'I've got the one from his house, but I forgot his work computer.'

'Leave it, I'll have someone collect it.' J.P. was silent at the other end, thinking. 'Are you still in Maymon Glades?'

'Yeah, I just left the Archive.'

'Good. Go around to Jack McLemon's place and collect him. We can use him. Take him over to Coleman's apartment for the time being. I'll have him meet you there. And try not to get taken unawares this time. I'm going to get some computer people to look at McCormack's machines, so be back at my office as soon as possible.'

(x)

Mick and Frank Cooper had been waiting fifteen minutes for the re-emergence of Marshall McLemon. They pulled into the kerb a discreet distance behind the limo which was stopped outside Marshall's father's house. They took the opportunity to drink their *Moose*, two bottles a day, all part of the new regimen.

Minimal orchestral music, which one of their instructors had introduced them to, flowed softly from the car's speakers. Frank cracked the passenger door window to allow his cigarette smoke out. His eyes never left the front of Jack McLemon's house for more than a split second. Mick monitored the rear-view mirror. Except for the music, all was silence. They were content to wait, it seemed.

'What's this?' Mick said, after a few more minutes had passed. He noted a black vehicle with smoked windows approaching from behind.

Frank turned in his seat to take a look. 'Even if he's not behind the wheel, I'll bet Freeway picked out that van.'

Mick nodded in agreement, smiling. 'How do we play this?'

'We don't take any chances,' said Frank, attaching a silencer to his pistol. 'See if you can wave him down.'

Mick rolled down his window and leaned out as far as he could, smiling at the oncoming vehicle and indicating that it should pull up at the opposite kerb. Frank opened the glove compartment and extracted a hypo which he put in his jacket pocket. He got out and walked across the road as the black vehicle came to a halt, smiling and holding a hand up in greeting. The passenger window rolled down and Frank found himself face to face with Freeway McCann, who looked surprised to see him.

'Where the fuck did you guys come from?' Freeway wanted to know. 'Why didn't you call me?'

Frank turned up both of his palms and shrugged apologetically. 'We're only back; early too, 'cause our progress is good. We haven't been allowed to contact anyone yet. We're still in training – on the job. We're with the Frenchman,' Frank pointed to the limo further up the road, 'he's visiting a gentleman here.'

Freeway thought the word 'gentleman' didn't exactly trip off Frank's tongue. He looked out of the window past Frank. 'Is Mick coming over?'

'No,' Frank said without turning. 'We can't both be away from our posts at the same time.'

Freeway laughed. 'If you guys had been this conscientious to start out with, we wouldn't be in the situation we're in now.'

Frank looked puzzled. 'What situation?'

Freeway had been sloppy letting that slip. He had a niggling feeling in the back of his mind that since the boys had been under McCambridge-LeMans' influence the past week, he really ought to be careful what he said until he knew better what had happened with them, and how much they were now expected to report back.

'Well, y'know,' he attempted to cover himself, 'you working for the Frenchman and me left doing all of J.P.'s running for him.'

Frank nodded and smiled indulgently. 'So,' he said, as if skirting around some embarrassment, 'what has you out this direction, Freeway? It's a bit off the beaten track.'

Freeway turned his head and looked up the street past the limo. 'I'm picking up something for J.P. from a guy . . . I think actually on the next street over —'

A click sounded in Freeway's left ear and he turned to find himself staring down the barrel of Frank's silenced weapon.

'Jesus, Frank!'

'I know, man, I'm sorry.' Frank reached into his jacket pocket and pulled out the hypo, which he tossed into Freeway's lap. 'Do you know how to use that?'

'Yeah. What the fuck's in it?'

'It won't do you any harm. Jab yourself with it. I need to keep you on ice for a bit.' Frank glanced briefly at the pistol in his hand. 'It's a lot better than the alternative.'

Freeway sighed and began rolling up his sleeve. 'People complain about Mondays, but it's fuckin' Tuesdays get me. This has been a poxy day.'

(xi)

As quietly as she could, Dr Julie Bertillion came down the steps into the lounge area of the suite she shared with Henri McCambridge-LeMans. Henri sat in the apex of the wrap-around sofa, staring blankly into the space in front of him. Julie settled into the chair opposite and took a cigarette from the wooden box on the coffee table. He watched as she lit the cigarette, but said nothing.

'How are you?' she said finally.

Henri smiled wearily. 'I'm fine,' he said.

'You spoke to him?'

'Yes.'

'Where is he now?'

'He's with his father and his colleague, airborne, *en route* to Paris. From there I don't know.'

Julie nodded. 'Out of danger at least.'

'Out of danger from Gillespie, certainly. I'd be happier to see him distant from McCormack.'

Julie wasn't worried about McCormack, Mantra, or Marshall, except inasmuch as the boy's continued existence affected Henri. She was concerned, however, that Henri's resolve with regard to their ultimate goal might have softened. 'I don't want to seem overly mercenary,' she said. 'But he may value your aid in saving his friend more than the salvation of his own hide. It's not a bad thing to have him beholden to you in this way. He'll remember it before he'd remember a promotion.'

Henri laughed bitterly. 'Overly mercenary? Let's not delude ourselves, Julie. In our quest to block the exits from life, we have in the past been bloodthirsty. Do you imagine that in this we mellow with age, of all things?'

Julie shrugged insolently. 'Mellow if you like, just as long as I know you're properly motivated.' She was happy enough with that morsel of reassurance, and saw no need to discuss the matter further.

Henri sat up straight, recognising that she had whatever it was she had wanted from the exchange and was finished with him now. He pulled his shoulders forward, stretching the dorsal muscles, then flopped back into the sofa, extending his arms across the top. He watched Julie, who appeared to be absorbed in extinguishing her cigarette. He smiled and shook his head. 'Who was it, Julie, who said that the dream of immortality propped up all human existence?'

She eyed him balefully; he was aware of her distaste for

philosophical discourse. 'I work for a living, Henri. I don't get so much time as you for reading.'

He picked up a small cushion and lobbed it at her. She batted it aside easily and smiled back at him. She feared for a moment that he was again about to give vent to something weighty, but then he seemed to change his mind.

'Don't worry,' he said to her at last. 'I'm not giving up anything.' He took a cheroot from his shirt pocket, unwrapped and lit it. Julie pushed the ashtray across the table to him. 'I was sure you'd feel we'd lost time,' he said.

She pouted. 'Do you think we have?'

'I don't know.' He waved his hand back and forth through the smoke in front of his face. 'You said yourself nothing would happen in the short term, but you must have had some time frame in mind.'

'I imagined we might have him on the table by April or May.'

Henri thought for a second. 'I've no reason to think that won't happen still.'

'I suppose if we needed,' she ventured, hesitantly, 'we could always tell him you were terminal, that we wanted to test his suitability as a donor, to see if a gene graft might save you.'

'Really, Julie!' Henri admonished, smiling. 'Let's hope it doesn't come to that.'

(xii)

Shortly after their train got under way for Marseilles, TuMur TV News gleefully reported that 'a source close to WentWest' had provided them with a startling exclusive, the upshot of which was that the Federation Police in Dublin were engaged in a citywide hunt for one Philip McCormack, believed to be a key figure in the organisation responsible for the events attributable to Mantra over the past year. Papa Charlie figured Gillespie must have let it slip when it became clear that the disclosures about WentWest Correctional and the drug trials looked like they might be turning into real news.

There was no going back for him now, that was clear. Being already long in the tooth and time at a premium for him, it was a fact he decided to quickly accept. The rest of his life, whatever it might turn out to be, was in front of him, with Jasmine. He was beyond wondering if there was something between them; there was, and that was his future. They'd taken dinner together in the buffet car, just the two of them, and after some beating around the bush on his part she'd explained clearly and concisely her feelings. He had relaxed a little then, and they continued to talk through a meal he was still too nervous to really enjoy. The two proved a wonder to each other, which was more of a surprise to him than to her. He'd been amazed to discover that the scuffle they'd experienced in the Archive hadn't been overly vexatious to a woman who'd once killed an army regular in hand-to-hand combat. For her part, she marvelled at the privileged, cosseted existence that had produced his practically useless – but to her, increasingly fascinating – cultural specialty. Before they returned to their compartment, and to Jack and Marshall, he considered briefly, if regretfully, all that he'd left behind him, then forgot about it. It hadn't in reality been all that terrific. That had been that; no agonising over it and no talking it to death. Jasmine reminded him that he could open up to her if he needed. He assured her he wouldn't need to.

351

'Yes, I forgot,' she'd said to him. 'You Tarzan.'

Marshall and Jack, to their great relief, never got a mention in the news, though Gillespie, if he didn't know for sure, must have guessed that they'd disappeared in company with Papa Charlie. It was assumed that McCambridge-LeMans' influence had thus far kept their media anonymity intact. Marshall had been pretty quiet on the flight to Orly, sullen almost. This mood had perpetuated through the train trip. He had perked up a little when he learned that on arrival in Marseilles Jasmine was to organise passage aboard a Korean freighter to the South China Sea, and from there to Vervain Prime, but he wasn't what you'd call his old self. Charlie had to commiserate with him; a few days ago he appeared to have the world at his feet, today he was little more than a fugitive.

The most dismaying thing for Papa Charlie was that J.P. looked to have escaped from all of this unscathed. More than that, Charlie's own activities as Mantra, once exposed, served to divert media attention from the so-called Environment and Nutrition Initiative. Charlie began to rue his promise to Jasmine not to use the Mantra program again until such time as its future could be discussed with the elders on Vervain Prime. He felt that in all probability the Society would elect to decommission the device, deeming it too dangerous to use or to keep. Privately, Charlie wondered if there would be any harm in taking a last swipe at J.P., something that would unsettle the fat, smug bastard, even just for a while.

About twenty minutes outside of Marseilles, as Jasmine and Marshall slept in their seats, Papa Charlie gave up trying to read and stared out the window. Jack McLemon tapped away at the keypad on his cell.

'Isn't it strange to be here at our age?' Jack said, when he saw Papa Charlie had put down his book. 'On the lam.'

Charlie smiled at the expression. 'I suppose so,' he said.

'You even have a moll,' Jack said, looking at Jasmine.

Charlie laughed and nodded towards the cell in Jack's hand. 'How's your identity crisis shaping up?'

'Can't seem to settle on one name.'

Jack had been working on a change of identity for himself and Marshall, to help protect them in the future from Gillespie or anyone who might link them to Mantra. He had asked Papa Charlie if the Mantra device could be utilised in the procurement of passports and other papers they would need. Following his promise to her, Charlie had mentioned it to Jasmine, and she had acceded to the suggestion with an ease which, for reasons of his own, Charlie chose to consider significant.

'Why stick with just one, Jack? Multiple identities could be useful. It'd give the character a roguish quality too. You'd have your own moll in no time.'

Jack laughed. The idea thrilled him. It had, surprisingly, taken him a little while to recognise what was happening to him, but his arrival in Paris brought the realisation that, in keeping with a long-standing family tradition, he was in the process of *shifting*. Since then he'd been having the time of his life.

Epilogue

Having ingloriously lifted his leg against the trunk of society, Philip 'Mantra' McCormack, his year-long reign of terror at an apparent end, has gone to ground. I use the word 'terror' advisedly, for those of us who extrapolated the vile potential of his technology from the ongoing success of his irksome ventures were indeed terrified. Even as I write, corporate, military and political leaders remain on tenterhooks, uncertain whether he will again deploy, or, indeed, whether he has already deployed, his appalling device, perhaps with more sinister intent. It is precisely because of the possibility of such invisible atrocities that this agitator must be brought to account, not, as has been suggested, because of any overreaction by the establishment to a mischievous prank. If we consider the probabilities of funds reallocated or disappeared, undetected because the books have been made to balance; of records erased or created in order to enrich, hide or disguise who knows what number of criminal elements; of arms diverted to rogue states or to extremist factions; or of time-bomb viruses ticking away in the heart of civilisation's engine, then we can only add our voices to the clamour for his arrest, and with that demand the extraction from him of the identities of his accomplices and the keys to his evil weaponry.

'Off,' she instructed the screen, languidly. She recalled that John Lyons-Howard had always regarded *Timesene* as a fascist rag. Its editor, out of necessity, would be an unreconstructed Nazi, and unlikely to see eye to eye with Philip 'Mantra' McCormack on matters of protest. She was sure John would have bemoaned the fact that nowhere in the mainstream media had anyone attempted an understanding of McCormack's position, nor afforded him recognition for dislodging a few of the more inert media elements from their normal routines.

Mantra's epiphany had brought the immovable TuMur news anchor, Tom Richard, out on location to Maymon Glades, and had lured the gargantuan American, Zeke Ather – the proto-type for Tom Richard and a thousand like him – out of LA and into Dublin to broadcast a series of pieces from the Mantra living room. The two of them raked over McCormack's stunningly dull biography, marvelled at how he had covered his tracks, and speculated ad nauseam upon the myriad of barbarities he might yet achieve with the Mantra device. Tom blathered on about 'the cross of terror' and Zeke about 'hidden, anonymous, silent menace'. The surveillance footage that had allegedly tipped off WentWest in the first place was alluded to but never aired. The Federation Police were endlessly interviewed about the absolute absence of leads. Systems experts and reformed hackers lined up around the proverbial block to confess that they too were baffled. Cultural commissars and celebrity rent-a-shrinks mercilessly overanalysed McCormack's reading, watching and listening preferences to no end other than to fill air time. TuMur had come up with a new slogan for the winter season: 'All day, all night, all news'. John might have observed that two out of three wasn't bad.

It would have appealed to John's sense of the bizarre that a nun-like organisation called the Vervain Society was implicated in the Mantra affair. He'd have been most impressed with its handling of the matter. Tackling these ladies looked to be like mauling an urbane skunk. One of their spokeswomen glibly pointed out to Tom Richard on prime time TuMur that not only had no actual evidence been produced of McCormack's culpability – let alone the alleged alliance with a Vervain sister – but that no one at WentWest, the source of the slander, seemed inclined to take responsibility for either allegation. These, she felt, were elementary issues to which 'media meat-heads' seemed wilfully oblivious. The spokeswoman freely admitted that one of their number had been in the locality investigating the Mantra phenomenon, as had many other inter-ested parties. She told Tom that their representative had approached WentWest for comment but had been treated to a hostile reception, most probably on account of the Society's continued opposition to that organisation's penchant for African child labour, its use of improperly tested ingredients in many of the economy food products it sold in the developing world, and its open contempt for all things environmental. At that point Tom Richard felt it was in his best interests to quickly end the interview. If it hadn't been for her wounds and her grief she'd have laughed.

A waiter arrived and set her coffee on the table.

'Thank you, David. Charge it to my room, would you?'

'Of course, Ms Vaughan.'

The upstairs lounge of the Victoria Hotel looked out onto the harbour, across which she could see Kowloon, its neon halo pulsing and shimmering against the night sky. Hong Kong's opulence was trimmed with a fast, edgy quality that appealed to her. She'd been right in thinking that this was the place to convert her Athens score into nice clean, official credit. They'd taken twenty per cent in commission from her, but she'd heard that if you wanted a cheaper cash conversion you had to deal with the triads. She'd had enough excitement for the time being, she decided, and once she'd completed her transaction with the shady but cutting-edge pharmaceutical operation from the New Territories, extravagance would never again be a problem.

She moved around in her chair, the better to view the harbour, and winced. The abrasions on her back were healing well. Her ribs and her neck still ached a little, but only late in the evening when the painkillers began to wear off.

She figured she did the majority of the damage squeezing through what had been the passenger window. She couldn't remember a lot of it, but bits would come back to her every now and then. She recalled finding herself in a shallow ditch beneath the bushes at the side of the road. Staying in the ditch, she'd started to crawl away, but her pain had been everywhere and intense, and she'd whimpered involuntarily as she moved. She stopped to gag herself with a couple of handkerchiefs, muffling the sound in case the men on the road heard her. While rummaging through her pockets she'd discovered, still intact, three phials of the slave drug, Boxer. By the time she reached Maymon Glades she had a good idea what she was going to do with it. She cleaned herself up in the bathroom of a twenty-four-hour diner, then got back on the street to flag a cab. There had been a brief, nerve-racking stop at her apartment to collect a small travel bag and some painkillers, then on to the airport and her flight to Athens.

She put down her coffee cup, dropped her gaze from the harbour to the screen in front of her and reactivated it. For the third time that day, she cued the only news item she'd seen, since hearing of John Lyons-Howard's death, that had given her any satisfaction. J.P. Gillespie, fresh from having the government rubber-stamp his submission for a new environmental and nutritional project at WentWest Correctional, had received a prestigious invitation from a committee comprising corporate bigwigs, politicians and media luminaries. The committee had succeeded in bringing one of the quarter-finals of the *Timesene* Global Baseball Series to Dublin for the very first time and had requested that Gillespie attend as the guest of honour. The Kyoto Bobcats and the Havana Hackbolts had been introduced and Gillespie himself was set to throw in the first pitch when a familiar crackle sounded across the stadium sound system. There was a groan from the crowd, then a deafening voice began repeating a single phrase. It took most people a few seconds to realise that this wasn't the usual routine. J.P. was a little slower on the uptake. He was there on the big screen, puce with rage, straining to catch the words. Many in the audience began to laugh when finally his expression gave them to understand that he realised what was being said. He threw the ball into the dust in front of him and stormed off towards the tunnel.

'Louis,' the voice boomed, 'I think this is the beginning of a beautiful friendship.'